$8.95

ROPE OF GOLD

JOSEPHINE HERBST

With an Introduction by Alice Kessler-Harris and
Paul Lauter and an Afterword by Elinor Langer

ROPE OF GOLD

ROPE

OF

GOLD

A Novel of the Thirties

Josephine Herbst

With an Introduction by Alice Kessler-Harris and
Paul Lauter and an Afterword by Elinor Langer

THE FEMINIST
PRESS
Old Westbury
New York

Library of Congress Cataloging in Publication Data

Herbst, Josephine, 1892–1969.
    Rope of gold.

    (Novels of the thirties series)
    Reprint. Originally published: New York: Harcourt, Brace, c1939.
    I. Title. II. Series.
PS3515.E596R6 1984   813'.52   84-18793
ISBN 0-935312-33-1 (pbk.)

First Feminist Press edition

Cover design: Marta Ruliffson
Cover art: Isabel Bishop, "Blowing Smoke Rings." Reproduced courtesy of Midtown Galleries, New York City. We wish to thank art historians Thalia Gouma-Peterson and Linda Nochlin for their suggestions and assistance.
Back cover photo: Josephine Herbst, 1922. Courtesy of Betty Davis and Elinor Langer.
Manufacturing: BookCrafters, Inc., Chelsea, Mich.

CONTENTS

INTRODUCTION

Alice Kessler-Harris and Paul Lauter

The first phase of the women's movement, so the historical tradition goes, ended in the twenties. Its passion spent in the successful campaign for the vote, its remnants torn apart by divisions between those who wanted equality at once and those who insisted on retaining hard-won protections, the movement was stifled finally by a depression that mocked individual ambition. But if one kind of feminism ended in the twenties, another emerged in the thirties. Largely overlooked by historians, its existence is documented by the literature of the period.

The old movement that ended in the twenties declined in the affluence of that decade. After the vote was won, activist women set out to translate their political success into the economic equality it seemed to promise: Alice Paul's Women's Party pushed for an Equal Rights Amendment; coalitions of women's groups supported the Sheppard-Towner Act to provide maternal and well-baby care; the Women's Bureau successfully defended the rights of wage-earning women to minimum wages and shorter hours. The prosperity of the twenties made room for ambition, nurturing the talents of such writers as Edna St. Vincent Millay, Katherine Ann Porter, Zora Neale Hurston, and Anzia Yezierska. For a while it seemed as though the women who flooded into arts and letters as well as into banking and insurance were merely the vanguard of a new generation of self-confident and fulfilled womanhood.

Then came the depression, and widespread unemployment put an end to illusions of economic equality for women. The crisis of the thirties revealed the extent to which women's ambitions had relied on the opportunities offered by an expanding economy. With 25 percent of the work force unemployed by 1933, the picture changed dramatically. State and local governments tried to drive women, especially married women, out of the work force. Private industry took advantage of socially sanctioned discrimination against women to undercut the wages of poorly paid men. Opportunities for promotion and advancement shriveled.

To return to the home was no answer for most women. Families doubled up. Husbands and fathers lost their jobs. The home reflected the poverty and insecurity of unemployment as women and their children coped with the psychic tensions of maintaining family life and the economic pressures of insufficient incomes. Young women postponed marriage to help their parents survive, and they avoided pregnancy for fear of its economic consequences.

But women did not abandon the search for women's rights. Rather, as the crisis exposed their vulnerable positions, they began to question the degree to which the ambitions of the twenties were circumscribed by social reality. There would be no freedom for women at work while millions were unemployed; no genuine partnership in the home while clothing and food remained luxuries; no equality of opportunity for male or female children who grew up without medical attention or education. To women of the thirties, poverty and the social conditions that fostered it seemed as much women's issues as individual advancement had seemed in the twenties. To fulfill their own thwarted ambitions, women were required to connect themselves with the larger struggle for social justice. They would rise or fall with it. In this new generation, women who might earlier have been called feminists became social activists of a broader stamp.

As the old individualism gave way to concern for eliminating unemployment, preserving home life, and collective survival, women began to turn to available political movements for answers. Some moved into New Deal agencies, hoping to find a cure for despair in government social programs. Others chose to organize workers into the newly militant trade union movement. Many turned to the socialist and communist parties of the Left. Here, in an atmosphere of revolutionary possibility, they introduced questions of equality between the sexes, of women's education, and of reproductive and sexual freedom.

Left-wing groups like the Communist Party, USA, welcomed women into their ranks. They provided increased opportunities for women to act in the political arena, but they remained ambivalent about specifically women's issues. Though leftist ideology in the 1930s recognized the "special oppression" of women and formally espoused sexual equality, in practice, the Left tended to subordinate problems of gender to the overwhelming tasks of organizing the working class and fighting fascism. Both ideology and practice opposed feminism, fundamentally on the ground that it drew working-class women away from their male working-class allies and into the orbit of bourgeois women. Women constituted a formidable proportion of most left-wing groups, and Unemployment Councils, neighborhood groups, and even the emerging CIO relied heavily on them for leadership and support. By the end of the decade perhaps 40 percent of the membership of the Communist Party, USA, was female.[1] If the Communist Party did not provide a comfortable haven for women, if it subordinated women's questions and often refused to challenge sexual segregation on the job or rigid gender roles at home, its language of equality provided women with opportunities for debate, and its political programs opportunities for organizing and leadership experiences. The Left offered a forum and more serious attention to women's questions than any other group of the decade. It also provided women with a community of shared experience.

Female voices, primed by the rhetoric of equality, resonated on the printed page. A remarkable number of politically active women wrote. Their poems, stories, and songs, as well as their novels and essays, give us access to some of the issues seldom addressed in political practice, even on the Left. If the nature of women's participation in political action limited the issues about which they wrote, it also provided depth and insight into the critical social and personal conflicts that underlay activism. Their political views help clarify why most of the women writers of the thirties and in this series worked in a variety of forms: each form had both an artistic and political motivation as well as a particular audience. Fielding Burke, for example, had published many volumes of verse under her real name, Olive Tilford Dargan; Josephine Herbst was an active reporter throughout the thirties, as well as a critic; Mary Heaton Vorse, whose novel about Gastonia was a rather crude and obvious effort, wrote some of the decade's best books and articles about the developing labor movement. These writers strove not only to perfect the forms in which they wrote but to choose the forms most appropriate for the various political tasks in which they engaged.

We have chosen in this series to begin with fiction because it seems to reflect most closely the unfettered consciousness of women in the decade. The books in this series are part of a long tradition of literature about working-class life. Because they are written by women, these novels do not sit comfortably inside most accounts of that tradition, nor do they conform precisely to theories of "proletarian fiction" produced in the thirties. Yet the ways in which this women's fiction differs from that of men alert us to the particular qualities of some of the best female writers of this century, including Agnes Smedley and Meridel Le Sueur, and provide the most important reason for The Feminist Press to undertake this series.

In the 1920s, literary rebellion, in the words of Jack Conroy, "was directed principally against the fetters of form and language taboos."[2] By the thirties, literary theory had provided a systematic alternative to the modernist emphasis on formal experimentation, ironic distance, and linguistic complexity. Its major breakthrough, particularly for the work of left-wing and working-class writers, was to validate the experiences of working people. In her speech to the 1935 American Writers' Congress, Meridel Le Sueur made the point this way:

> It is from the working class that the use and function of native language is slowly being built. . . . This is the slow beginning of a culture, the slow and wonderful accumulation of an experience that has hitherto been unspoken, that has been a gigantic movement of labor, the swingdown of the pick, the ax that has hitherto made no sound but is now being heard.[3]

"Proletarian Realism," Mike Gold's widely adopted phrase, would thus deal in plain, crisp language with the lives and especially the work of the proletariat, optimistically urging them on "through the maze of history toward Socialism and the classless society."[4]

Though this is in fact a rich and complex aesthetic, it presented immediate problems for women who took their own experiences seriously. Less than a quarter of all women and fewer than 15 percent of married women worked outside the home during most of the

1930s. If the workplace was to be a major focus for art, as it was for Communist Party organizing, then, as "workplace" did not include work done in the home for the support of the family, only small fractions of women's lives would find their way into art. The rest would be ignored, subordinated once again to the demands of male politics. More important, since proletarian fiction, by the definition of the times, rested upon the central distinction between the experiences of the working class and those of the bourgeoisie, it would underplay, even deny, the relevance of other distinctive group experiences. Blacks, Hispanics, women—as groups suffering their own persecution—would have no place in it. In denying the commonalities of female experience, the vision of the proletarian aesthetic undermined such crucial issues for women as the uneven division of household labor, the sexual double standard, and male chauvinism within the working class or the Party itself.

Women writers who perceived such problems were placed in a certain dilemma: theory maintained that their work should be based upon the experiences of the working class; yet the experiences of one half of the working class—males—were clearly of more significance than the experiences of the other half of the working class. Where did that leave distinctly female experiences, like childbearing, or those, like the nurturance of children, which continued to be primarily women's tasks? And where in that theoretical framework could one find a place for the strengths and ambiguities of love, of rearing children, of family life, of the problems of control over one's body, the struggle to find emotional and sexual fulfillment?

Women writers of the Left chose to flout male convention and to write about themes that fell outside the frameworks of their male peers. But so strongly masculinist was the cultural theory and practice of the Left that it remained virtually immune to the feminist implications of their themes. The cultural apparatus of the Left in the thirties was, if anything, more firmly masculinist than its political institutions. It is not that women writers were ignored. Josephine Herbst was a "guest delegate" to the Kharkov conference of the International Union of Revolutionary Writers in 1930. Tillie Olsen and Meridel Le Sueur were among the (few) invited women speakers at the American Writers' Congress in 1935. The Communist Party's book club, the Book Union, selected as its representative "proletarian novels" Fielding Burke's *A Stone Came Rolling,* Clara Weatherwax's *Marching! Marching!*, and Leane Zugsmith's *A Time to Remember*. Herbst, Le Sueur, Zugsmith, and Grace Lumpkin, among others, were active reviewers for *The New Masses* and certain other Left journals.

But women were often, in fact, tokens at major conferences. Accounts of the John Reed clubs (the Communist Party's cultural associations), of the editorial boards of magazines like *The Anvil, Blast,* or *The Partisan Review,* and of other Communist Party and Left cultural organizations hardly acknowledge the existence of women—though many did, in fact, work in such groups. The hitch-hiking Wobbly style of life extolled by writers like Jack Conroy left room only for the rare Boxcar Bertha, while the hairy-chested polemics of left-wing critics like Mike Gold placed women's issues squarely in a male context. The worker-poet was inevitably male, his sexuality "evidence of healthy vigor"; his comrades, cigar-smoking talkers, in from the wheat fields or the Willys-Overland plant. In a *New Masses* editorial announcing the advent of "Proletarian Realism," Gold pictures the new writer as "a wild youth of about twenty-two, the son of working-class parents, who himself works in the lumber camps, coal mines, and steel mills, harvest fields and mountain camps of America. . . . He writes in jets of exasperated feeling. . . ."[5] Women writers were recognized on the Left, indeed occasionally puffed, just as women's issues were recognized. But the values and outlooks *institutionalized* in magazines, editorial boards, conferences, and theories of the Left were decidedly masculinist.

At the same time, there appear to have been few distinctly female cultural groups or networks of support among women writers on the Left. Meridel Le Sueur mentions in her American Writers' Congress speech a group of "a hundred and fifty women from factory and farm" who "wrote down their great proletarian experience." Myra Page, novelist and reporter, recalls the way experienced women took newcomers under their wings, but notes that women "felt that the general issue was the most important thing: depression and unemployment."[6] Support among women was directed at achieving the larger goals. Women intellectuals in books like Tess Slesinger's *The Unpossessed* and Josephine Herbst's *Rope of Gold* seem, from the perspective of the 1980s, strikingly isolated from one another. While there were female-centered cultural institutions during the 1930s—the YWCA, for example, supported a Women's Press—they were not of the Left. In fact, they were likely to be noted by the Communist Party, if at all, with suspicion. In short, there was little institutional support on the Left that might have validated any distinctly female culture, and much that discouraged it. Not perhaps by design, but effectively for all that, any female—much less feminist—tradition was submerged.

Within a few years, the entire world of left-wing culture was ploughed under by the attacks of McCarthyism. It is not always easy now, thirty years later, to perceive how successful the campaign was in silencing and burying writers on the Left. One good indicator is that copies of books by the writers with whom we are concerned are absent from libraries and used book shops. After the thirties, some of the women turned away from "political" subjects; some fell into silences; others continued to write but could find no publisher; many, like Tillie Olsen, were subjected to public attack. That happened, of course, to men as well as to women. But, in addition, women were confronted with that hostile ideology we have come to call "the feminine mystique." More profoundly, perhaps, the concern for working-class life and for understanding the relationship between gender and politics was suppressed in the fifties as anti-communism, suburbanization, and consumerism controlled the environment. As the cultural soil dried up, writers lost their audience. The run of stories, novels, poems, and songs that had established for an audience certain expectations, artistic conventions, and ideological perspectives, came to an end.

When the writing of the thirties began to be re-discovered twenty-five years ago, critics persisted in denying its feminist proclivities. In his comprehensive book, *The Radical Novel in the United States,* for example, Walter Rideout suggests that "the explicit linking of political revolution and sexual freedom rarely appears" in left-wing novels of the thirties "as it did in *Daughter of Earth.* "[7] In fact, however, sexuality, personal liberation, and radical politics are closely intertwined in Fielding Burke's *Call Home the Heart;* sexual politics are at the center of conflicts described in Tess Slesinger's *The Unpossessed;* personal and sexual relations provide the critical counterpoint to emerging political differences in Josephine Herbst's *Rope of Gold.*

Female writers who accepted the central class division of socialist realism nevertheless paid attention to women-centered issues. In Tillie Olsen's *Yonnondio,* as Deborah Rosenfelt argues, "the major transformation is based on human love, on the capacity to respond to beauty, and on the premise of a regenerative life cycle of which mother and daughter are a part." For feminist proletarian writers, these issues are not separable from the capacity to effect a successful political transformation. As Rosenfelt tells us, "Women's work in preserving and nurturing that creative capacity in the young is shown in *Yonnondio* to be an essential precondition to social change."[8] Such themes, ignored by male critics, are not peculiar to Olsen. Both in her story "Annunciation" and in her novella *The Girl,* Meridel Le Sueur focuses on the regenerative power of pregnancy and birth. The action in Leane Zugsmith's *A Time to Remember* concerns a department store strike, but the emotional conflict that constitutes the dynamic tension of the novel comes from the attempts of strikers and their families to cope with the social reality of women's subordinate positions.

The books in this series demonstrate the substantial and vigorous tradition of women-centered literature. We find in these books women of intellect and strength—like Victoria in Herbst's *Rope of Gold*—seeking work that is politically meaningful and yet consonant with their need for personal independence. We encounter in Slesinger's *The Unpossessed* many of the same conflicts between ostensibly progressive politics and real chauvinist behavior that helped generate the women's liberation movement of the late 1960s. With Ishma in Fielding Burke's *Call Home the Heart* we experience the contrary appeals of full-time, heroic but often grubby, work in a movement for social change and of the rich, green pastures of the hill country. These books present women (and men) in varieties of workplaces—including the home—participants in strikes and demonstrations, observers and reporters of what seemed a growing, international revolutionary movement. Their steady grasp of sexual politics illuminates the inner contradictions and struggles of movements for change. These writers are the sisters and comrades of Agnes Smedley, Meridel Le Sueur, and Tillie Olsen: their work asserts the richness, as well as the continuity, of the traditions of left-wing feminism in the United States.

Certainly all the female authors of the thirties did not write in ways that distinguished them from men. But some of the best works written by women addressed the distinctive experience of both working-class and female lives. Women in that decade produced a body of writing with qualities that overlap but are not identical with those of the male writers of the period. This literature—we might now call it "socialist feminist"—is only beginning to be explored by scholars with an eye to what it tells us about the complex factors that encouraged women to write both as activists and as critics. In presenting these books as part of a series, The Feminist Press hopes to underline the need to reconstruct the cultural context that helped shape them.

That process will require us to re-examine questions around which debate swirled in the thirties. What is the function of art in a revolutionary movement? Do we cast aside as merely absurd the notions of some socialist critics, who suggested that art was a "weapon" in the class struggle, that writers must under all circumstances convey a sense of "proletarian optimism," and that they must write only in language plain enough for plain people? Or are we to understand the criticism of the Left in that period as a creative effort to confront issues with which the artists themselves were struggling? Are there ways to resolve the tensions between the slow, sustained discipline which the artful rendering of experience demands and the more immediate requirements of writing hitched to the needs of a political movement? How can a writer bring alive the vision of a triumphant socialist future, which no one has seen or fully imagined, with anything like the power to evoke the struggles and devastation of capitalism in decline? Just who is one's audience? And if the audience for socialist art should, at least in part, be working-class people, what functions does art serve in their lives, and are these different from its functions in the lives of the traditional audience for writers?

The writers in this series largely avoided the more formulaic demands of thirties criticism. Their endings are not always unambiguous and hopeful as "socialist realism" theoretically required. Their heroines, like Ishma in *Call Home the Heart,* share both the virtues and the profound limitations of their class origins. They portray retreat as well as triumph; confusion and ambiguity as well as possibility. But struggle was never simple. Together these books provide another piece of the puzzle that illustrates how women have come to consciousness over the years. In publishing this series, The Feminist Press calls attention to the varieties of feminism and its expressions. The fiction of the thirties is part of our common heritage. We hope it will be useful in conceiving of our future lives.

Alice Kessler-Harris
Hofstra University

Paul Lauter
State University of New York,
College at Old Westbury

Notes

1. See Robert Shaffer, "Women and the Communist Party, USA, 1930–1940," *Socialist Review* #45 (May–June 1979): 90 for this and for additional information on women and the Communist Party.

2. Jack Conroy, "Introduction," *Writers in Revolt: The Anvil Anthology* (New York, Westport: Lawrence Hill, 1973), p. ix.

3. From "Proceedings of the American Writers' Congress," New York, 1935, reprinted by West End Press, Minneapolis, 1981.

4. Edward Seaver, "Socialist Realism," *The New Masses* 17 (23 October, 1935): 24.

5. "Go Left, Young Writers," *Mike Gold: A Literary Anthology,* ed. Michael Folsom (New York: International Publishers, 1972), p. 188.

6. Interview with Alice Kessler-Harris, December 1, 1982.

7. Walter Rideout, *The Radical Novel in the United States* (New York: Hill and Wang, 1956), p. 219.

8. Deborah Rosenfelt, "From the Thirties: Tillie Olsen and the Radical Tradition," *Feminist Studies* 7 (Fall 1981): 398.

ROPE OF GOLD

I. DIVIDED HEART

November, 1933

FOR THE first time, the living room of his father's house
seemed to Jonathan Chance small and stuffy. He remembered it as a sumptuous room with heavy bro-
caded curtains and chairs that stood in their places, year
after year, waiting for company far more elegant than
had yet appeared. Only a year and a half ago his mother's
coffin had stood in front of the fireplace with the little ala-
baster urns on the mantel. Shoals of relatives had turned
up, uncles and aunts unreconciled for years wept on each
other's necks, and Jonathan had stood erect and unbend-
ing trying to erase the disapproval from his last memory
of his mother's living face.

The traditional expression now sat glumly on his
father's otherwise serene face. It was the same expression
and the identical features that used to bend over him
when, as a little boy, he had been led to the woodshed for
a dressing down. His yelps of "help, murder, fire, he's
killing me" had defeated his father then. The neighbors'
complaints had stopped the punishment but the disapproval had lingered on. Even his sister Margaret and his
brother Tom preferred to look out the window rather
than meet his eye. Only his wife, Victoria, standing uneasily near the radiator, gave him a quick look of reassurance. Her face, pinched from the cold after a long
drive from Chicago, was half turned from the room as if
reluctant to look at his judges.

Mr. Chance was at work at an absurd occupation. He
was actually darning his own socks with woolen thread
raveled from the pieces left over from his expensive
tailored suits. His busy hands gave him an advantage over
his son. The orderly process of the darning completely
concealed the bleak jumble of his thoughts that shuttled

fearfully between the present and the past. Jonathan's
brother Tom, lolling in the best chair, was the more at
ease. A born compromiser, he was relishing the opportunity to act as mediator in what appeared to be the start
of a first-class row.

The family had just come from the dining room. Mr.
Chance upon leaving the room had ostentatiously switched
off the lights. The gesture, extinguishing the bright table
with its Sunday night lace cover and fine silver, was intended as a reminder that the acquisitions of prosperous
years were in peril. Accustomed as his children were to
the habitual belittling of his fortunes, this precaution
against waste did not impress them. Rents had fallen,
Rhino Auto stock was a batch of paper, the luxury business of fine leather goods was no doubt running in the
red, but Mr. Chance was far from bankrupt. He was, however, a widower, alone.

Ill at ease as Jonathan felt in the hostile room, he was
no longer unnerved as in the old days. While his mother
had lived, "changing the will" had been a favorite pastime. He believed he no longer cared for the will and he
had learned to live without the benefits of property. An
old sympathy for his father troubled him more. What he
had to say would add to the old man's isolation. It was
painful to conclude that the big dramatic moments of his
father's life had no doubt centered around property. Yet
when Jonathan's mother died, it was the love letters the
two had written in their youth that had concerned his
father first. He had hurried to the top shelf of the wardrobe and had wrapped the neat bundle in one of his wife's
black silk slips, hiding it from his children's eyes.

There was the time Jonathan's grandfather had died
and the sizeable estate had broken the family into camps.
One said Uncle Edward was cheating; the other, that he
was the soul of generosity and sacrificing time and money
for the common good. The two camps had met in this
very room for the last time. Uncle Richard had put Jonathan, then a little boy, out of the room, closing the var-
nished double doors, now a thing of the past. Jonathan,

squeezing one eye to the crack, had watched Aunt Hettie hissing away.

Her little black veil had whistled out over her teeth as she gesticulated in her black kid gloves. White wrists, bleached as bone, had shown from between glove and cuff with a morbid threat of the grave. She had begun to cough with a kind of fury, calling names and yelling something about stacked cards and Uncle Ed holding all the aces and their poor father turning in his newmade grave. Jonathan's father had shriveled with the disgrace of the quarrel that threatened to rupture the family forever. He, of all the connection, had acted a noble part. He had resigned his share to be reallotted as thought fit. Aunt Hettie had thereupon grabbed the bank corner and for thanks never spoke to him again.

No piece of property was at stake tonight. Mr. Chance was shrewd enough to see that actually the future of every scrap he owned, might inherit or hoped to bequeath, was involved. Jonathan had almost concluded to answer questions baldly, so that no misunderstanding might arise in the future, when he caught his wife trying to signal him. Her look confused him; he brought out a package of cigarettes, there was one left.

"Come on, big boy," said Tom lightly. "Give us the redhot lowdown. When you planning to bomb the country?"

Jonathan said, "If you want to hear about it, O.K. But don't talk nonsense. Don't you ever grow up?"

Tom sobered, a little ashamed of himself. "I was kidding, can't you take it anymore, big chief?"

"You said something about farmers. You call yourself a farmer?" said Mr. Chance, not deigning to look up from his work.

"Farmer Chance of Skunk Gulch," crowed Tom.

"I was made a delegate from our section," said Jonathan. "We're living among farmers. But a lot of real farmers came from our part of the country, a truckload of them." He looked around at the big room, at the table with his mother's picture, the shaded lamps giving off a discreet and pleasant glow, heard the burr of the new oil-burning furnace. How could he make the Chicago event seem real? If he were alone with his father it would be easier. His father must have had generous impulses, even dreams in his youth. He had convictions now that had solidified into church-going and an almost violent respect for legality.

His father, now old, had at least taken his life with seriousness. His brother and sister baffled him. For what were they living? Most people envied Tom. He was handsome, had a young furniture business that would soon be backed by the prestige of a rich wife. He would have a big sailboat on the lakes, a couple of cars, several homes. It seemed to Jonathan, in his present state of mind, a flabby, even boring existence. It would take a new language to convey anything at all to the people in this room. He could see from Victoria's expression, the way she bit her lips, frowned and attempted suddenly to smile, that she thought the talk would lead to nothing and would be wiser to avoid. He fumbled for his words, said slowly, "The farmers were having a conference in Chicago. Not so different from the Elks or Chambers of Commerce as you would think. I mean, they were meeting from all over the country and talking over their affairs, just like anybody else."

"Talking what over," said Mr. Chance, tugging at his needle.

"Their troubles," said Jonathan, looking at Victoria who looked back with an expression that plainly said, go on, you've begun, now finish it but I wash my hands of the business.

"Theirs troubles," snorted Mr. Chance. "You have to run to Chicago to hunt trouble. There's plenty right here in Michigan. Haven't you any back there in Pennsylvania that you have to run to Chicago hunting trouble. Mr. Henderson lost his business. He clerks in Harmon's store, a pretty comedown. Mrs. Peabody is out of her mind; her son shot himself. The Erskines don't know where they are at. Tom here goes along humming as if he thought prosperity were around the corner."

"No use gumming up everything with a glum face," said Tom testily. "There are plenty who can do that better than I can. I'm not going to compete there. Well, so you had a conference."

"Yes," said Margaret nervously. "Let Jonathan talk. I want him to get it off his chest before Ed gets here. Ed is rabid these days. Whatever you do, don't pick an argument with him."

"I never did," said Jonathan. "He's the one who always picked on me."

"Oh, forget it," said Tom. "Go on, wise guy, give us the lowdown." He looked at his brother as if he expected something in the nature of an oracle. He had not forgotten that it was Jonathan who had warned their father not to buy bank stocks six months before the bank closed its doors. The skies had been blue, stocks were soaring. How had Jonathan known? He had sneaking respect for his brother, for all his crazy ideas. The lifelong habit of looking to his older brother as the whiteheaded boy of the Chance family, certain to bring home the bacon, held even now, when Jonathan's latest developments had become practically an enigma. Give the boy a break, was Tom's motto, he might pull the rabbit out of the hat yet.

"Well," said Jonathan, a little mollified by Tom's interest. "About seven hundred farmers came from all over the country to talk over the situation. It's a very difficult thing to explain in a few words and involves more than the eye sees. Not just prices or mortgages. Vicky's doing a piece about it. You can read her piece for the details," he ended weakly, suddenly concluding from the cold antagonistic eyes that it was hopeless to talk.

"What's the matter with you doing it?" said Tom. Jonathan flushed painfully and looking straight at his brother said, "As a matter of fact, she does that kind of thing better than I do."

Mr. Chance sniffed and in sudden revenge for Tom's

remark, intended to be cutting, Jonathan pulled a mimeographed sheet from his pocket. It gave him the illusion
that he no longer cared one way or another what his family thought of him. But as he began reading in the hostile
atmosphere, the fine words sounded wooden, even to
him. The feeling that had taken possession of him at
Chicago, solving, as he thought, his very life, could never
be explained here. He would not even try.

His voice shook a little as he tackled the farmers' program that sounded in this room almost preposterously
audacious. He cleared his throat and was surprised to hear
the words pop out with force, compelling the reluctant,
antagonistic family to listen. Margaret turned to look
her brother full in the face. She was struggling, not to
understand, but to control the rising terror at what she
considered his betrayal. He was as unreal as a Judas and
the violence of her anger put bright spots in her cheeks
and made her eyes shine as if with tears.

As if stimulated by the opposition, Jonathan's voice
grew strong and calm. He had been one of the com-
mittee to draft the program and, as he read, he was impressed by the language, identifying his own contribution
to the total with pride. As he came to the meat of the
document, he took a deep breath, fumbled for the last
cigarette in the package, lighted it, took a single puff, and
holding it in his hand, picked up the paper again. He
spoke slowly, looking first at Victoria.

She was trying to measure her husband's relatives. She
could see only resentment in their faces; they would not
forgive Jonathan for not running with the pack. Jonathan's voice, touching in its cadence and pure almost
childlike conviction, had no power over them. It was years
now since they had read aloud together. Then it was
Dr. Faustus and *The Waste Land,* read on winter nights
in the country beside the potbellied stove. The scene
was as clear and whole as if it had flashed upon a screen,
Jonathan's long legs, his hands propping up the book, the
oil lamp with the brown shade, and the words, that had
sent a chill down her spine as if a window had suddenly

opened on a black and rainy night, echoed again, "I, that was near your heart, was removed therefrom. To lose beauty in terror, terror in inquisition, I have lost my passion. . . ." With an effort she switched off the scene and heard Jonathan come triumphantly to the finish.

"Last year we demanded a moratorium of debts." He let the words sink in, one by one. His father bit off the thread with a vicious click of the teeth. His sister sat with downcast eyes as if something indecent were about to happen. Only Tom looked straight at his brother with good-humored tolerance.

"This year we demand cancellation." He waited, suddenly involved with the subject matter. Was it too extreme? Would it only isolate the morsel of farmers who dared to stand up and snap back at last; they were not, after all, the great mass of men stuck on the land. The hesitation he felt had slowed his voice. The family looked at him curiously. He plunged into the final sentence feeling relief at its extreme view as a good swimmer takes to deep and icy water. "Possibly next year we shall demand confiscation."

The easy assured voice was too much for the father. He could not even snort. He was shocked in the deepest sense and his cheeks burned as if scraped raw by a clumsy razor. Picking up the daily paper he pretended to scan the headlines. Tom lit a cigarette and politely passed the case to Victoria. Mr. Chance having turned several pages of the paper turned toward Jonathan.

"A man's first duty is to pay his debts. No one can get out of that and remain a Christian. If the bankers can't trust the farmers, they won't give any more loans. You can't do business without the banks."

He could not look his son in the eye. He did not pretend to understand that rigamarole. Jumbled indignant phrases danced in his head. His eyes hurt as if he had been crying. He turned hastily aside and began fiddling with the radio dials. It was too late for Amos and Andy but a little music would be soothing. Nothing but bawls rushed into the room, tightening his head like a drum.

He twirled the dial angrily. It was this stuff that had poisoned the young people and softened their brains. At last, faintly, he could make out *The Thousand and One Nights* and he held the dial steady, balancing it, bringing gradually clearer the soothing gracious waltz that poured its balm on his wounds. He stood with his back to the room, lonely for the support of his wife.

Tom looked at his father's back and cleared his throat. "Don't you think that's going a little far, Jonathan? How can anyone do business if that happens? Lots of old people hold mortgages. Mrs. Sloan, for instance. What would she do if her mortgage was declared worthless?"

"I should say so," said Margaret, articulate at last. She glared at her brother for the first time in her life. Her desertion came as a surprise to him and seemed to cut the final cord with the family. So much the better. "It's putting a premium on shiftlessness, that's all it is doing. People who have worked hard all their lives and made investments must be sacrificed to clumsy louts. An ignorant farmer can destroy their lives. Look at Ed. His family have to stand up and take it, they can't tear up their debts. His father has lost everything. Everything."

Jonathan winced at her expression but forced himself to answer. "He could afford to lose. You aren't out on the street are you? You're even driving the same big car."

"Don't talk like that," said Mr. Chance. "I don't see why you couldn't stick with your own people. We've got troubles. Why run after farmers? Why track all the way to Chicago? It beats me."

"Yes, Jonathan," soothed Tom. "After all, they don't suffer the way people like the Hendersons do. If you want to get worked up, why not pick on people like yourself, sensitive educated people who got somewhere by their own brains and now have lost out?"

Victoria laughed rudely. It startled everyone. The laugh ended abruptly but she continued to smile, a curious innocent mocking smile that said nothing and put the idea into Mr. Chance's head that she might be going crazy. No wonder.

"All you are doing," he said to his son, "is giving a premium to incompetents."

"Leveling everybody," said Margaret, moving restlessly as if the carpet beneath her feet were burning hot. "What's the use of being smarter and getting somewhere if it's all to be taken away? Think what you are saying, Jonathan. You just penalize the worthwhile people for a lot of feebs. You talk about Morgan. It's just jealousy, that's all, he's smarter than the rest or he wouldn't have it." Her voice shook. Catching a glimpse of herself in the mirror, she was startled at her own face, a mottled and distorted version of her idea of herself. Jonathan was her favorite brother and at one time she had hoped her sons would be like him rather than like their father. She had even allowed her mind to dream of her boys turning into writers or musicians, men who understood the art of life. Hard times had changed that. She seldom had a maid; rarely went out, knitting was her pastime. If this kept up her whole life would be slowly knit into endless chain stitches that might unravel at the jerk of a hand. With dismay, she saw Jonathan start out of the room away from her, very stiff, as if his knees had a rod in them. Old Mr. Chance was fussily calling for the spaniel, and Victoria had flounced upstairs with a last angry speechless look. Just as Margaret hoped the argument had ended, Tom began all over again.

"You see, Jonathan"—in a tone calculated to soothe— "if you cut at the heart of private initiative, where are you? I admit things are bad. But will you right them by making a privileged class out of farmers? Class against class. Is that American?"

Old Mr. Chance snorted. He was completely befuddled. To hide his panic, he folded newspapers angrily as if to restore order to some small part of a mad world. "Anyone who won't pay his debts is no good. A loose wild way of talking. The farmers have always complained, always will. You'll have to explain better than that to get me to understand." Jonathan started to explain. Patient explanation; this was the era of patient explanation. Even as the thought came to him, something in himself gave it the lie. There would be some people who would never listen.

He knew who those people were; he believed he knew their faces. Jim Barclay, the union organizer, who had come up from Harlan with his young hair streaked with white, knew them. All he could think of was guns. "We don't need literature down there," he had said. "Guns and gas. That's what you want for skunks. They're using them, so must we." Barclay was all wrong of course. He had lost his sense of direction and a good man had for a time become rabid and useless. They had taken him down to the country, to feed him up and get his mind off the Kentucky mine war. In the daytime he would sit around in the sun. Sometimes they would hear him whistle to stray dogs trotting along the road. At night they could hear him thrashing around in his sleep. From their room, they heard the headboard of his bed crack as his arm hit it. Sharp cries, ominous as yelps of an animal in pain, turned their bones to pulp. They would cling to one another in a kind of agony, listening to the tossing, the moan that was like a telegraph code of trouble. Barclay was in Harlan in his dreams. A bomb had dropped through the window where the miners sat. He was young Harry Simms, coming over the mountain toward Pineville with a bunch of miners for something to eat. Then the man in his bed gave a deep groan and the two in the next room could feel the shot in the dark; the thugs had got the boy in the belly and with that sigh Harry Simm's blood once more soaked into the earth at Brush Creek.

They heard these sounds, the two in their bed, huddling together in the dark, trying to make their love extend beyond the room and not become just a shelter, but morning came with a chill through the window.

Anger suddenly focused sharp against his father. Before his own father, in his old family home, the words of Jim Barclay glared before his mind's eye as if scrawled in chalk on the living-room wall. He looked with hopeless antagonism at his father. His father looked back with a steady indignant betrayed expression. Then Jonathan bit his lip. He began slowly, "Well, father, the farmers have had the cards stacked against them for a long time."

From the upstairs hallway Victoria could hear the voices. She pulled two long plushy towels from the linen closet stuffed like a granary after full harvest and sank into the warm water of the tub. The voices moved to the dining room; new hearty tones from the hall joined them. Margaret's husband, Ed Thompson, had come. Someone laughed nervously; Margaret's voice, a high pretty note rose above the rest. Now they were moving to the kitchen. They would lean against the shiny enameled equipment, perch on the edge of the table. The big refrigerator, the electric range, the electric dishwasher would be clean and sharp as surgical instruments. They would stand looking at one another politely as if they were in an impersonal operating room, thinking bitter thoughts, feeling cheated and betrayed. They would all be tall, handsome people, and Jonathan, a little apart, would be different not only by his less elegant clothes but by the expression of his face. The kitchen walls would gleam with new wall coverings; from the plugs, electric coffee grinders, orange reamers, egg beaters and cake mixers could be instantaneously set in motion.

The equipment had been refurbished and installed the summer before Jonathan's mother died when Jonathan had asked for a small loan to tide over Victoria's illness. Jonathan had been told to mend his ways, as if writing were one of the major crimes. It was that summer that he had practically ceased to go upstairs to the typewriter and the familiar sound of the keys tapping away dwindled. She had nearly died that summer and she wondered now what might have happened. His family would, no doubt, have swallowed their sermons on wastefulness and he would have been tenderly welcomed to his old home, where he might if he wished stand every day in the kitchen and watch the shiny machinery whirl. She had not died; instead, Jonathan's mother had dropped

dead after a shopping trip. In spite of the photograph
on the living-room table, the dead woman seemed to have
completely vanished. Had she lived, she would be one
more figure to stare at the offender.

Victoria remembered the dead woman now, as she seldom was, lighthearted and laughing like a child. The
mood had been becoming to a woman who often seemed
ill at ease with life. No one around her, least of all herself, had ever questioned the appropriateness of the world
she lived in except her son. Her son had been a riddle;
his choice in life a betrayal. In all his adult life, he had
done little to please his father or mother.

Lying in the big bed that had been the parents', Victoria blamed them bitterly for their lack of faith. There
were times when she wished Jonathan had qualities he
had not but the next moment she was mortified at herself; who could ask for everything in this world? A better
nature could not be imagined; with her fiery temper she
often felt a shrew in comparison. If she wished he had
stood up more firmly against his parents it was with a
kind of jealousy of them and their strange hold that nothing seemed to rupture completely.

In the big bed she could hear the nervous tremor of
voices in the kitchen. The walls tightened with human
speech. She listened for Jonathan's voice and, in the dark,
childish phantasies about their future distracted her. She
dwelt with pride on his virtues; his nature was without
guile but seemed to abandon him to a stern and ribald
world even as it protected him with the trust people instinctively gave him. She had turned out the light and
the big mute objects in the room were obscured now in
shadow. Darkness was calm and refreshing and she could
leave this tortured house. But her father rose before her,
standing in his soiled workclothes on the street corner,
waiting forlornly and with terrible patience for the street
car. She had been in high school on her way home, and
from the window had deliberately turned away her head.
The remembrance was shameful, rousing her to wakefulness just as she was dropping into a faint doze. What a

fool she had been! While she had been in tragic suspense over *The Brothers Karamazov* her father's life had been fraying to pieces and she had been so cut off from the living world as to feel only irritated as he sat silent at the evening meal, his eyes struggling to meet his wife's, grateful for the bread passed him as if he had not earned it. Shut in within her little world, she had not seen her father and his comments on the weather had been only boring and inane. "If this keeps up the crops are ruined," might have been an empty phrase.

Jonathan came into the room softly. "Hello," she said in a low voice.

"Hello, aren't you asleep yet?"

"I couldn't. What happened?"

"It's a good thing you left, you would have lost your temper. You never saw anything like it. It's got them all right; they are bitter as gall. Tom is mildest, perhaps because he's going to marry a rich girl. They won't listen to reason, their minds are shut as clams." He was taking off his clothes, moving lightly around the room.

"Better close the window, you'll catch cold."

"I'm all right," said Jonathan, but the tense voice sounded as if he were trying to keep his teeth from chattering with excitement. "They are hard as nails. It's almost funny. Do you want to hear?"

"I'm listening," she said, propping herself up. "We might have known."

"Ed is taking a law course at night. He thinks he is going to be fired and says the only jobs worth an ambitious man's attention soon will be with the government so he is going into politics. Closing the Detroit banks scared them all right and they think Roosevelt is running the country to ruin. No one should be helped but the rich. To hear them you would think they are the only ones worth saving. Ed talks about how he rose by his brains but forgets he wouldn't have got where he is without his old man. He finally said he believed a smashup was coming. He said he had read Henry Adams and Marx. Even Adams prophesied chaos and Ed thinks it is coming

around 1940. He wanted to know where he would stand.
'After all,' Ed said, 'I'm an expert technical man. Even
Russia is after guys like me now.' Then he began to argue.
He said the technical men ought to get the breaks because
so much rested on them. What he was after was my assurance that his kids would get a better education than
other kids. Not as good, mind you, better. I burst out
laughing. It was funny. You had to laugh at him, he was
really in earnest. He said he knew better than to oppose
the march of history, he got oratorical and Margaret
looked at him as if she'd never realized what she had
drawn before. He thinks I'm just being smart to get in
on the ground floor. That's absolutely all it means to any
of them. They all listened to Ed and after while Tom
began to think I might not be a fool and, in fact, might
just be feathering my nest. But Papa was disgusted. In
his mind farmers meeting like we did in Chicago is a
denial of God. He said you can't live without God. Then
he got me aside and told me his worries. It's kind of
pitiful. The housekeeper doesn't clean the silver as often
as she should and Tom complains about her cooking
every time he comes to the house. Papa says her cooking
is all right for him and Tom just wants to put on the
dog. He's given Tom five thousand to put in his business.
Tom showed me the check."

"You might know it," said Vicky bitterly, shrinking
down in the bed. "He can help Tom but when did he
ever help you? Are you going to ask him about the well
money? After all, if he helped Tom . . ."

"I hate to ask for anything but I will about the well.
It was his idea, not mine. When Mother died he felt sentimental and told me to get the well drilled so you
wouldn't have to pump water. Of course we never got it
piped to the house, there it is, almost as useless as a diamond mine and what's more the fellow who drilled it
won't wait forever for his money. I don't blame him. Besides, the place is Papa's, not ours. It's in his name."

"That's another thing, after all the promises."

"Let it alone, Vicky, you don't understand Father. He'll give us the house some day."

"When we're dead, no doubt," she said, soberly. "He'll see us both under the sod. He's got no worries."

"He's still downstairs, just wandering around looking at things," said Jonathan. He walked to the window and pulled up the curtain. A fine snow was sifting over the empty street. "It's going to be a bad night. Pity the sailors at sea," he said.

"All the fellows driving home from Chicago with their rotten tires. I hope the Alabama boys don't get pinched."

"We got them new tires, they won't have to limp home the way they limped out there." He came away from the window, the rough sore feeling aroused by the talk smoothing out with the mention of the boys from Alabama. "How you fixed, Jackson?" he had asked. "Got a two room cabin, one cow, four hogs, one heifer, twenty bushels corn, fifty gallon syrup, mother, father, wife and child," Jackson had summed up briefly. Jonathan envied him; Jackson's way seemed so much more inevitable than his own. This particular moment in history fitted Jackson like a glove, whereas Jonathan felt he would need trimming to fit anywhere. He did not want to be on the sidelines, good only to raise money or be a front. He wanted to belong, as he had never belonged to anyone or anything, not even to his wife.

He forgot that at this moment a cop might be ordering the Alabama boys to pull over to the side of the road with, "Where you think you going, you bums?" He even forgot the chain gang and remembered only that they were traveling without baggage in a light car with a sure notion of their journey. The well-to-do had been able to purchase speed but not flight. He wondered what the family would have said if he had told them of the three rich men's sons who had come to the conference or had backed it. The son of the Chicago grain king, Silas Greenough, would have floored them. Young Si would be driving toward Montana now in a Ford car in a blue serge suit and a plain dark overcoat. The cars and trucks would be radiating out from Chicago across the country, over mountains and rivers, through falling snow to distant places.

He felt suddenly lonely, conscious that in his father's house he was forever an outsider. This had been his parents' room and as he turned toward the bed covered with the pink satin eiderdown quilt that had been selected by his mother, he could see her dead face as he had looked upon it for the last time. With an artlessness she had never had in life, her dead body had been laid upon a simple couch with draperies flowing from it as from a barge. One of her arms had rested lightly across her body, the other was at her side as if about to trail the hand in water. Suddenly she had seemed to him like Elaine, the lily maid of Astalot, in his first boyish impression of death. Tears had gushed from his eyes; he had been grateful for his sudden bitter feeling of loss that allowed him at last to pity his mother. All her coldness to him, the expression of a proud, forbidding love, had at that moment been absolved as he saw her as a young girl slipping downstream from one dream to another.

Victoria was watching him with a curious expression that seemed a transition for his thoughts. He envied and resented the way she seemed pulled together within herself, looking out at him now with the detachment of some little squirrel. He was reminded again of his loneliness and his longing was reflected in his face. They looked at one another, terribly conscious of their early reckless love. A look of guilt and. supplication softened her eyes; framed in her loosened hair she was childlike and touching. He wondered at the complexity of existence that held so much in a split second and for almost the first time was not terrified at the vision. Standing in his bare feet, he felt as if he were on earth cracking into a thousand prisms. His father's life, his brother's activities, and his own life with Victoria might be like so many pressed ferns in wet unformed rock waiting their final construction, but man was not altogether helpless in a world of men.

"Don't stand there," Victoria said in a pleading voice. "What's wrong?"

"Nothing," he said, getting into bed and touching her body with the old gay assurance that had made him certain in his ways before their baby had been born, too soon, dead.

Footfalls sounded lightly in the hall. A door slammed. Someone was letting water into the bathtub. The oil burner started a protest against the invasion of cold from opened windows. Jonathan tossed and dozed. The conversation was like a toxin in his blood. He reached out for his trousers hung carefully over a chair, fumbled and found a package of cigarettes, lit one. The small red end burned steadily in the cold air. He lay on his back holding the cigarette stiffly so as not to wake Victoria. She was curled in the middle of the bed and did not move.

A beam of light fell on the hammered brass frame of a photograph of his mother, sister and himself as a baby. He could see the shine of the frame and remembered how he had made it in school for a Christmas present for his mother. She had displayed it to the family connections with pride, later the picture had been installed on the wall and never taken down. No one looking at the chubby face of the youngster could have foretold the evening that had just been concluded. Not in this bedroom, but in one like it, he had been wakeful as a young boy, reading forbidden books until the chilled house put him shivering beneath the covers. Here he had planned to run away with Mildred Benson in his uncle's Oldsmobile when he was seventeen; when he was nineteen, a sophomore at college, he had imagined himself bowing to thunderous applause from a great New York audience on a clue no bigger than a hit he had made in the college production of Shaw's *Pygmalion*. In imagination he had run through a fortune and he was puzzled now that the actual events of his life had sneaked up on him, like the headlights of a speeding car overtaking his own slower machine.

The only period that had been lived serenely in the present had been as a boy when on summer vacations in northern Michigan he spent days in a sailboat knowing sun and air, wind drift and cloud formation, the shine of fish as they were lifted from the lake, the clear red eye of a fire burning on sand, the flash of a jackknife and the smell of resin as it hit the flame. One did not need to conquer or impress a world like that; it had only to be lived in. The lungs, stomach, and muscles were its instruments.

He squeezed the butt of the cigarette carefully and, from old cautious habit, dropped it on a space on the bare floor outside the rug where he could pick it up in the morning and throw it in the wastebasket. His mother's voice, "Jonathan, you've been smoking again," was suddenly as clear as if spoken in the next room. He felt a nervous urge to laugh. His parents would have barred all roads except the one to money if they could. Marriage was admitted because it was respectable; it was no fault of theirs that his own happened to include love. Love was proscribed as a household regularity and yet how forlorn his father had seemed the day he had gathered up the old love letters. The early transactions of Jonathan's life that in daylight had grown remote were incredibly near as if he had suddenly chosen to examine detail for detail old photographs in an album, of which each separate page has the power to wring the heart.

He did not want to remember himself; he wanted to see himself in his new role. For the first time in his life he felt that he had deliberately chosen. Even his marriage had not been so emphatic a choice. He and Victoria had been living together; it was his parents who had insisted on the ceremony that had put the compulsory edge to his romance. Resistance to all his parents thought fit had been for years his expression of freedom. It had become a habit dangerous as a drug.

He remembered now with pain Victoria's face when he

had said brutally he would run away if she had a child. She had been standing at the window in the farmhouse in the country. Her head had turned slowly to look at him; her eyes had rounded, wide and brilliant, like a cat's when it prepares to pounce. Not a word had been spoken but now he knew that her long slow withdrawal from him had really begun at that moment. Later he had taken back his words; his own deep sense of guilt that the child had finally come, years later, only to be born dead, found hurried alibis. Why had she made such a mad trip three miles to town that day? He hadn't ordered the weather. Who could have foretold that her father would fall ill and the telegram find her alone? She had run to town to send the sick man a telegram to get well, to say that she loved him as if his death would somehow be blood upon her head. If Jonathan had been present then, he could not have seen her more clearly than he did now, in the coat that would not button, slipping and sliding over the icy snow. Too late, the wire had gone to a dead man and Victoria had lost her baby.

A half-articulate groan could not stifle his thoughts. Memory could become a chain as well as poverty; one had to cut it sometime or become a cripple.

Suddenly the bed was intolerable. He got up and went into the bathroom. It was comfortably warm with thick rugs on the chilly tiles. He rummaged through the cabinet on the hunt for something to put him to sleep. An assortment of nostrums choked the shelves and he thought contemptuously of American well-to-do homes ridden with plumbing and laxatives. He finally unearthed some small yellow pills; swallowing two he went back to bed.

A wind was stirring through the rigging and if he did not lash down the foresail she would rip in two; he clambered over the deckhouse, the slippery canvas throwing him off balance. He caught at one of the spars but it was slick as grease; falling, he grabbed for the mainsail that tore under his hand. He was surprised that it had rotted and reproached himself for not having treated it with red tar. The shock of icy water shot his hands in a reflex upwards, he caught at the rail, it slid under and the boat tipped, exposing its decks with ropes and anchor sliding, compass slipping with slosh of bilgewater and he was astonished to see Victoria sitting calmly at the tiller. He clambered to the deckhouse as she brought the tiller down hard and came about, without a glance at him. Her expression was pleasant and he was hurt that she did not notice the high seas or appear to be upset that he had nearly drowned. He yelled to her but a big wind flung his voice back; he heard its echo, and gripped hard, crouching to keep his place. Salt spray got in his eyes and hair, he felt the boat tear along and rejoiced that he could swim like a fish. Suddenly remembering that Victoria could not swim, he looked back in concern. She had vanished. He went below and a hand pushed him into a child's school-seat before a tiny desk. He fumbled for a pencil and tried to read the long examination paper. An unseen clock ticked loudly and he began to sweat for fear he could not get the answers down in time. Reading the questions he was pleased that he knew the answers but his pencil point was broken, he sharpened it and looked up at Miss Barnes, the buyer in the bookstore at Cleveland. She grinned at him and said she could not possibly order more than two books and, unless he wanted to let her have them on consignment, the deal was off. He began a long argument to show her that lack of faith was the only thing that was keeping prosperity from coming around the corner and, unless she ordered, the wife and kiddies couldn't have shoes. She smiled broader and broader; the smile seemed to radiate heat like the sun. He jerked away violently.

He woke drenched with sweat. A dim gray light was coming in the window above the soft furred edge of snow. He had a wild scrambling for place; thought he was back in the little hotel at Louisville on his last trip on the road selling books for a New York publisher. His mouth felt furry as it had then after a bender he and another salesman had taken over the weekend. He raised his head, the picture in the brass frame was there; turning, he saw Victoria with one hand under her cheek, peacefully sleeping. He felt so relieved that he lay for a second enjoying his position in bed, the warmth of the covers, the frosty air, and throwing an arm around his wife, he went to sleep.

The family assembled the next morning for breakfast with the outward appearance of harmony. Mr. Chance rose politely as Victoria and Jonathan came into the room; pulling out her chair with a smile, he sat down and went on busily. On the other side of the glass doors, crumbs were freezing on the wide step. The bird house was empty now, a few wisps of straw dangling from the miniature door. Even this structure had been erected on an ambitious scale, with tiny shutters and towers.

"You ought to ask Ella not to cut the bread for toast so thick, Father," Tom said.

"I like it that way," Mr. Chance said briefly and firmly. His hands were very white and inclined to be puffy around the joints. They did not look like hands that were so expert at judging leather. Seeing him in his reserved expensive suit, his children completely forgot his boyhood and his apprenticeship to his own father who had been a stern taskmaster. The grandfather had not emigrated to America for nothing; even in the land of opportunity he needed hands, especially if they belonged to his children who were after all brought into the world to be of some use to their parents. The young Abel Chance had been at the bench at thirteen. The children of Abel Chance never thought of their father as once a boy. He seemed always to have been a parent, somewhat stern, rather remote. They had no way of knowing how much more generous he was to them than his father had been to him.

Mr. Chance hurried with his breakfast. He would feel

more at home in the shop than in his own home today. It was a tacit agreement that no word of the evening's discussion should be brought up, but Mr. Chance was no booby to be put to sleep on peppermints. He knew what he knew. The hope that Jonathan might repeat his grandfather's spectacular success was finally doomed and he felt as if he had looked into his boy's coffin.

He ate with small rapid bites, his eyes down, and now and then sought the headlines of the paper that lay beside Tom. What had been wrong with his upbringing of the boy? His children had never known want, had gone to the best schools and to Sunday School. In the summer, their mother and the children cooled themselves in the lake breezes up north while he sweated away at the shop. His own boyhood in the old country was stark as a picture from the Old Testament in comparison. What would his children have thought of the cold rooms, of the little ones huddling under the red featherbed for warmth? Even now he could see, through a rain-soaked pane, two old blackclothed women rush out with little pans after a horse had passed. Even offal had been a treasure to be placed like a jewel among the vegetables. If they went for a walk, didn't they have satchels slung around their waists to fill with every little twig that God placed in the path?

His hands shook a little; he reached for the paper and read, "Farmers Arming, Roosevelt is Told." He pushed the paper away violently, looking at his son with blazing eyes. "That's what such foolishness will come to. Bloodshed." He smacked the paper down and stalked from the room. Jonathan made no attempt to answer. He went on with his conversation with Tom. He finished his sentence. The front door closed gently and a few seconds later they saw the top of their father's hard hat pass the front window swiftly. Jonathan pushed aside his napkin uneasily. The sting of his father's last words hung like the bitter smoke of an explosive in the room. The two sons looked at one another warily as if suddenly sizing up an enemy. Then Tom laughed, "Don't take it so serious. Dad will get over it. You're his favorite, you know that."

"I'd rather have got his help a few years ago as you have, in that case," Jonathan said drily.

"Stick around a couple of days. Dad's lonely."

"We can't," Victoria said in a positive voice.

Jonathan laughed. "Got to be on our way, Tom. Thanks a lot."

"Anyhow, you ought to come to the luncheon at the Rhino Hotel—I promised Ed I'd bring you. You'll get the lowdown on insurance. A big shot from Philadelphia is going to tell the boys all about it. They're in a panic in this town and lots of fellows are dropping their insurance. The insurance company is sending this guy, if you ask me."

"I don't carry insurance," said Jonathan. "Can't do it, Tom, we have to be on our way." He stood up firmly trying not to show how upset he was at the premonition that he might never be in this home again. He wanted to strike at some central spot that would be clear of dissension now they were parting, thought incongruously of the time he had tied his little brother up with clothesline when he wanted to play with his gang. Remembered how they had got drunk together one weekend in Detroit, and how Tom had reproved him for not sending their mother a dutiful telegram on Mother's Day. Tom was on his feet looking soberly at his brother. The two stared at one another but could find no words.

"Well, I got to be running along," Tom said weakly. "Try to stick around but if you go, don't do anything I wouldn't do. Don't take any wooden nickels." All three laughed and Tom put his arm around Victoria. "Make him be a good boy," he said. "I'll try," Victoria said. The maid stuck her head in the door, then withdrew hurriedly like a scared rabbit.

"What's the matter with her?" Jonathan said.

"Oh, she's afraid of me," Tom said airily. "I told Dad to fire her but he's soft and doesn't mind her terrible cooking. She's got kids in high school and her old man can't get a job. She nags the life out of him, you should hear her jawing him over the phone."

There seemed to be nothing else to say. Tom put on an elegant muffler, a fine topcoat, and a hat that sat jauntily on his fair hair. He waved good-by again, and turning slowly, went out of the house with his chin down as if he were brooding.

Jonathan turned toward Victoria. She took hold of his hand and he squeezed it, remembering how she had held his hand the day of his mother's funeral when he began crying in the rain at the cemetery. They walked slowly up the stairs side by side, still holding hands. "You pack up the things," he said in an uneven voice. "I'm just going up to the attic to take a look around. Some of my old things are up there and I may not be here again." He paused a moment and added, "For a long time."

There was not much to pack, their nightclothes, toilet articles, a couple of dirty shirts, and a big towel Jonathan had been tempted to add to their luggage. After all, no one would miss it. Victoria packed it, then looking sharply towards the stairs, went to the hall and opening the linen closet took two more towels from the high stack. With an innocent look she tiptoed back and closed the bag.

Jonathan was sitting on the floor of the front room in the attic. The rooms were finished and plastered, as this had been the maids' quarters when the children were small. Trunks and expensive bags stood neatly. An out-of-fashion dresser was stacked with books. A China cupboard all the rage in the early nineteen hundreds now held schoolbooks that had belonged to the Chance children. Jonathan had opened a bureau drawer and was examining photographs. "Here's Mildred Benson," he said, turning towards Victoria. He held up with some pride the photograph of a young woman in a black lace gown. "She looks like an actress," said Vicky in a critical voice.

"She wanted to be one bad enough," said Jonathan.

"Are all these your girls?" Vicky said, pouncing on the stack of photos and running her hands through them. Jonathan tried to look modest. He was actually looking at the pictures with wonder. What had become of these expectant girls in low-neck dresses who had been so ardent? "That's Lurinda Field," he said, holding up a picture of a plump girl in a lace collar, with round china eyes. "She's married and has four children. And this is Betty Deacon, she married a big shot who afterwards embezzled and got into a lot of trouble. Here's Laura Martin." Victoria took the picture of Laura Martin and looked at it steadily. Large serious eyes, enormously alive, looked out of a small intent face. Furs and a mane of dark hair gave the impression of a little wild animal peering from some ambush. "She's a lovely creature," Victoria said soberly. "I wonder you didn't marry her."

"She wanted to," said Jonathan, sliding nearer his wife and resting his chin on her shoulder so that they could both look together.

"What happened? Really, I mean. I have a feeling you did some wrong."

"Wrong, I did nothing. Why do you say that? You're always trying to make me out worse than I am," he said, not unpleased.

"You know what I mean."

"I don't know what happened. That's the funny thing. It just stopped. We were crazy kids, I suppose, and suddenly it was over. I was out there one weekend. Her mother liked me a lot too. I had to leave to go to Detroit and that was the last I saw of her."

"Never saw or wrote her?" said Victoria in a horrified voice. She held the picture closer as if to discover the secret of misfortune.

"I couldn't. I went on the road then, it was a long time ago, we were kids. She wrote a couple of times and then stopped."

"Did she marry?"

"Yes, I heard she did and then I heard she was divorced and living with her folks again." In spite of his discomfort and guilt at the cross-examination, he relished the memory. It was in his voice. Victoria looked at him sharply. "You can never fool me," she said. "You know you hope she loves you still."

"I love only you," said Jonathan. "Only you."

"Only me," said Victoria, putting the picture down with a shiver as if she had seen a ghost. "I guess you wonder why you didn't take one of them instead of me. I guess I'm not much good, if I ever was." She looked at the picture, at the eyes, the thick hair, the mouth. Why had such ill luck fallen upon someone really lovely? True, it had brought her good fortune but it did not console her. The inexplicable in life brought her up sharply as if confronted with her own body laid out and covered with a sheet on its last bed. The unanswerable questions had a strange comfort all their own, steeling the nerves as if to dwarf small misfortunes to their proper stature. She leaned against Jonathan, holding his hand and turning it over curiously as if she had never seen it before.

"Hey, hey, what's the matter," he said. "Come out of it," and he shook her, kissing her and almost at once getting to his feet. Who could help loving him, she thought. He's so kind of innocent and truly good, and yet every now and then I feel terrified as if I didn't know him at all. He had already begun digging in the drawer again and had dumped more treasures on the floor; Indian arrowheads, a slingshot, an Indian headdress with molting feathers, a string of wampum and a fisherman's bonehook for mending nets.

"What's this?" asked Victoria, pulling out a map of the world with childish lettering an inch high and a bright blue card cut in the shape of a star. Inside the star was the outline of a child's palm stitched in red thread. "That's little Jonathan's hand," said Jonathan tenderly as if of his own child rather than himself.

"Oh, Jonathan," said Victoria. She turned it over. In Mrs. Chance's bold writing she read, "Jonathan Chance's hand, aged six years." She stared at the small empty palm and pitied the mother whose anguish of expectation had separated her from her child. "She loved you, Jonathan," she said. "She loved you more than all the others."

Jonathan felt overshadowed with the oppressive love of women whose expectations had seemed to threaten his early life. The photographs and their reproaches, Victoria herself, sitting pensively with her head bowed over the little hand, the final token of his mother's curious unexpressed love, crushed the air from the room. There was no answer to such love; never had been. Even as he felt joy at the thought of being loved, his eye searched for the door. The sun came obliquely from a high window under the roof and he followed the slanting beam to the dark branches of the maple tree upon which new fallen snow rested lightly as cotton.

The Alabama boys would be heading into Talapoosa county now. He picked up the packages, tying them together with quick resolute fingers. "Let's get started," he said in a voice that seemed, in its finality, to have called the last train from a station about to be abandoned.

In half an hour they had left the house and stopped at the shop to say good-by to Mr. Chance. The old man came out bareheaded; with eyes averted, he lifted his cheek to be kissed. "You'll catch cold," called Jonathan from the driver's seat.

"Take care of yourself and come to see us," Victoria called earnestly. Mr. Chance nodded nervously and stood looking after them as they pulled away. They drove in silence. "I suppose there was no chance to speak of the well," Victoria said.

"I asked him," said Jonathan. "He said to send the bill and he'd take care of it. It's Saturday and he didn't have any cash on hand."

"He might have given a check. It's very decent of him," said Victoria.

"Damned decent," said Jonathan. "One thing you can count on with Father is a sense of honor."

They drove on. "I wonder he didn't look me in the eyes," said Victoria. "I'd feel easier if he had written out a check."

"He'll take care of it," said Jonathan. "He promised."

Ed Thompson waited impatiently at the door of the dining room in the Hotel Rhino for his brother-in-law. He wondered if Tom would bring Jonathan. He was mentally rehearsing a little speech that he intended to get off that night at the public-speaking class. With a politician's contempt for people, he considered that a glib tongue was all that was needed to swing the mob. Although his family had come of humble origin, his father's success had long obliterated early days in the minds of his children.

Ed Thompson thought of the men who worked for him at the plant and the people in this room as two different species, as far apart as the pushcart and a custom-built car. But the men at the plant were too many to ignore, one had to learn to handle them. It was being done. Huey Long and Father Coughlin understood the trick, why not Ed Thompson? That morning he had been studying the face of a bigtime banker who had piled up millions. The mild gentle face had impressed him.

In his spare time he had studied the lives of the really shrewd politicians. It was his conviction that they were invariably charming, gentle, lovable creatures. Their power lay in their disarming personalities. Ed Thompson had inherited none of his own father's gentleness and he had grown up in the rapid advance of the automobile industry that bred men ruthless enough to get results. Until that year he had patterned himself along arrogant lines, but he saw clearly that he needed overhauling, as an automobile needs a new model to survive.

He did not have any too much respect for the men and their wives who were lined up at the tables chewing celery and talking in subdued tones to one another. As they struck up with "Put on your old gray bonnet," Ed realized that the tune sounded silly and weak and wished they had instead some spirited marching tune. Most of the men were on the shady side of fifty and they were not the brisk noisy crowd that had assembled here years ago when the hotel was first opened to the swing of bands and a cabaret from Detroit. He had half a mind to start eating when Tom came in looking conspicuously tall and handsome. Ed moved up to him and said, "Jonathan not coming?"

"They left," said Tom, still subdued after his farewell to his brother.

Ed shrugged his shoulders and as the two tall young men moved toward their table, the song leader swung his arm and started in with "I want a girl just like the girl who married dear old dad." They sat down next to Al Bender, the realtor, who was crouching glumly with his turtle's head withdrawn between two hostile shoulders.

"Cousin Fred Krieger was in to see Dad the other day," Tom said, eating olives and ignoring the fruit cup with its insipid cherry. "Even he is shaking his head and drinking like a fish. Guess he wishes he had taken up that offer he got from Russia five years ago. They wouldn't let him take the money out of the country then, was the only thing, but later, they changed it. Now he's stuck with United Farm Machines and they are taking even old buggies as initial payments, in order to get farmers hooked up to buying, he said."

"I'd like to see Fred," Ed said. "Let me know when he comes around again." He wasn't sorry to hear that even Fred Krieger was getting it in the neck. Fred was selfmade and had been held up as model long enough. At the same time this was only one more crushing indication of the trend, and it had a curious effect, like a piece of cold ice suddenly slipping down one's spine. He thought the sensible thing would be to provide a few cocktails on an occasion like this but none of the men would want to put up the cash now. His attention was unnaturally sharpened to stray conversation as if he were pinned beneath a wrecked car waiting for help. He heard Mr. Applebee argue that Harding was to blame for their troubles. "A weak man is worse than a fool. When he appointed a personal friend, Christiensen, head of Federal Reserve, my heart sank. I knew then we were in for it," he said triumphantly trying to glean some comfort from his proph-

ecy. But the fat man next to Applebee was not going to
stand for that.

"What about that crackpot Wilson involving us in war?"
The chairman was rapping for order and necks craned
to see the savior. He was a tall thin stooping man with
the patient expression of a bewildered stork. In spite of
the rapping, Al Bender was hissing his final verdict,
"Woman suffrage was a big mistake, just increased the
ignorant vote." Everyone at that table frowned at Al who
sizzled back between his shoulders, glaring ferociously at
the speaker.

Tom looked at the speaker critically feeling himself
something of an authority on public speaking and ready
for any pointers. The speaker settled his tie as the chairman rapped a glass again and, in the silence following,
the word "Friends" dropped with the alarming quiet of
a physician's voice about to reassure the family of a desperately sick patient against the evidence of their own
eyes.

"Friends, I am not here to buoy you with false optimism. We have had enough prophesying. No serious student of affairs can fail to understand that this is no ordinary crisis. Something more than a typical financial
depression has fastened upon our national life." Ed swallowed a glass of water hastily. He felt suddenly clammy
and acknowledged that his wife had probably been right
when she had opposed throwing good money away on
any more insurance. Hell, if the bottom dropped out of
insurance, the jig was up.

"An honest plumber will not put his finger over a leak
and smilingly assure you the pipe is mended. Yet, let us
not forget, that the pipe, though broken, is still there and
the water supply in unabated. Our resources are still here,
factories, farms, consumers and producers. Lack of faith
has frozen the pipes and the break cannot be fixed without recognizing that fact. Men do not know where to turn
and an honest man cannot guarantee an investment without grave risk anymore. Yet even during this depression
certain stocks have yielded profits. The truly seeing eye

could discover opportunity today, perhaps as never before. Is a man to invest in railroads? In oil? In automobiles? If I believed in the expansion of the railroads I would advise you to invest in Timken Roller Bearings. I do not have any conviction about railroads."

Tom nudged Ed who was listening with strained attention. "The old duffer isn't exactly hopeful," he whispered. Applebee turned a look of annoyance. In the old days no one cared if a speech was interrupted; today every man was sitting on the anxious seat. Insurance was the bedrock of their lives; if insurance went, what was left? The speaker conscious of the dying spirit of his audience now began his buildup. He described the farmlands that formed the basis of insurance, bought at less than fifty per cent of their assessed value, and drew a picture of a nation still hungry and bound to eat as long as it survived at all. A few near Tom and Ed began relaxing. Mr. Applebee even ate an olive.

"I do not guarantee the future at this moment. I am talking to you confidentially, as friends, but I want you to bear in mind that as long as *this government exists,* insurance is the one basic reliable investment."

It was none too consoling. Insurance is good if we eat, and we eat to live and live to pay insurance, and then our widows and children get the benefits. So long as the government holds the jackpot, thought Ed with a sudden savage resolve to break out of the vicious mediocre circle. Was man to have no higher status than a dung beetle rolling up pellets for its offspring only to lie down and die at the end of its toil? The impulse to embark on some spectacular career, by hook or by crook, had never been so powerful as at that moment, when, with his eyes slightly bloodshot from strain, he turned his solid face with the carefully shaved cheeks from side to side searching for a possible able confederate.

His eye circled the room, came back, rested promisingly on the arrowcollar profile of Spencer Gibbons, son-in-law of Rhinegold. Benton was still Rhinegold's town, though his days were no doubt numbered. Jonathan was right when he had said Rhinegold would be brought to his knees by the big bankers. Were the banks to have the whip hand? An ambitious man, he thought proudly, is not stopped by an obstacle anymore than Napoleon had been thwarted by the Alps. Even the threat of some final Waterloo could not retard the resolute.

Ed Thompson was a student of certain periods in history that fed his own design of life and he thought now, with some complacency, that he knew his Machiavelli.

THE FORSAKEN WELL

WHEN Jonathan and Victoria Chance got back to their house in Pennsylvania they found an illiterate note from the welldriller under the door. "I nede monie bad now plese," he had scrawled on the border of a newspaper. They enclosed it with an itemized statement showing that they had already paid the welldriller forty dollars and sent it to Jonathan's father.

The house needed cleaning, a mouse had already found its way to the pantry; the question of getting some cash stared them in the face. Each year the sources of revenue seemed to dwindle. They had sold their first editions and had even pawned Jonathan's old fraternity pin and a pair of opera glasses that had belonged to his mother. The road trips for publishers had been canceled "until things picked up," and they, like nearly everyone else they knew, waited for that wind that would bring health to the country.

"We're better off than Nancy," said Victoria, reading a letter from her sister. "Nancy and Clifford are stuck in a rooming house in Des Moines with the two children. He's peddling shaving cream. If something doesn't turn up Nancy will have to go to Boone and live with his parents."

"Tough luck," said Jonathan, picking up the letter. He had never known a time when Victoria's relatives were not more or less in hot water. Her sister Nancy talked in a dolorous way of the "cursed Wendel luck" that irritated Victoria beyond endurance. "Luck, Wendel luck," she would say. "What's the matter with my luck? I've had fine luck. Didn't I marry you, haven't we had a fine time? We're alive, aren't we, we have our health." She hated to feel one of those not blessed. She could even remember her sister Nancy's early married life, when the couple owned a car, bought victrola records, entertained their friends. True, it was a long time before the children came and that shadow had almost crippled Clifford Radford's life. But when, after ten years, a boy came and, two years later, another boy, Clifford had been a man reborn. He had quit trying to help his own relatives, who shiftless and helpless drifted from farm to town, from town to farm out in Iowa; he even finished helping his wife's relatives. His wife's mother, Mrs. Wendel, died and when Mr. Wendel followed in a few years, his life insurance providentially stalled off the first years of the depression. Through no fault of Clifford's, that he could humanly see, he was almost at once on the skids. The mill folded up and his life completely changed from that model of steady, virtuous living that had been his aspiration.

To her sisters, Victoria and Jonathan had always seemed a couple somehow apart. Nancy Radford and Clara Monroe were separated from Victoria not only by space but by an entire generation. They had married before the War and in the early days of her first flight from home, had half envied, half despised her wayward disposition. They now thought of her as the wife of a handsome interesting young man whose wealthy father either helped him or was bound to help some day. They were incredulous of Victoria's accounts of her primitive country home. "It's just like Vicky," they told one another. "She always exaggerates." And they had the conviction that she was merely belittling her position in order to defend herself from poorer relatives who might be tempted to ask for a loan.

Only their father's reports of his last visit to his daughter shortly before his death opened their eyes a little. It was true, Vicky did not have a bathroom. The country was grand though; there was a real little mountain across the road. There was a brook and electricity had lately been installed. The two sisters wondered a little at the compensations of such a life, so far from a movie or neighbors, but they continued to envy her a little and each in turn imagined the peculiar blessings of her existence. They told friends who inquired that Victoria, who had "gone east" years before, lived right near New York City and met the most interesting people, and both sisters were convinced that whatever else Victoria missed, she had had her share of romantic love. All that she seemed to lack was children.

The core of the family was certainly gone. The parents were dead. Rich Uncle David Trexler was no more. Only Aunt Hortense Ripley kept alive, holding her head proudly erect as if she still practiced with a beanbag. Since she had quarreled with their mother, the sisters did not write the old aunt, but on Christmas mysterious boxes of dried fruit arrived from Oregon and were traced to Aunt Hortense who wished, thus late, to oil her conscience.

Clara Monroe and Nancy Radford brought up their offspring with a true respect for their forebears. "Never forget," Clara Monroe cried to her children, "that your grandfather went to the legislature and our people were in this country, living civilized lives, a hundred years before the Revolution." These dark words, conferring heaven only knows what gifts, merely gave the impression to the young Monroes that the ancient family had somehow lived in a fort, alone and in solitary splendor, while the country seethed with wild Indians. Nancy was more specific and fondly sentimental, continued the saga of Uncle Joe who had gone to the Black Hills and had died, tragically, insane.

And although Victoria had no chick or child to impart family lore to, she too dwelt in some penumbra of family feelings that sometimes fascinated her husband, sometimes disturbed him darkly as if, lost in so many tangled roots, he could never truly find her.

As he read Nancy's note he wondered at Clifford who, in spite of his sufferings, had calmly voted for Hoover in the last election. There were times when the habits and superstitions of men seemed so tenacious that to hope for true progress appeared a weakness. True, Clifford had voted for Hoover on the grounds of prohibition, and he had read his sons a little sermon on the nasty stuff Roosevelt was allowing people to pour down their throats. Jonathan felt irritated now at the man for his worthiness and stubborn hold on some plan of life. In Jonathan's mind, it had no more reason for being than Nancy's belief in numerology. "Cliff is a Capricorn subject," she wrote in the same breath that she cheerfully admitted she seemed always on the move, packing suitcases in her very dreams. "He is due for a change. Success comes late in life to them it seems and all I can say is that any change is welcome and success has waited late enough for me."

He had to admire her buoyancy and, shaking his head and smiling, said, "When that check for the well comes, we can shave off a little for your sister." Victoria looked at him with touching approval so that he had the sensation that he owned a bank account, could write out checks, give donations to causes, and send a hundred dollars to needy friends as if it were a box of candy. He had all the good intentions of a man who has never suffered from actual want and has not struggled very much for money and is not even much interested in the things it can buy.

When they were almost stony broke, he still did not worry, not so long as Victoria knew so well how to manage and their life together had a way of glossing over poverty. He never did know how they had managed three months one winter in Florida after he came back from a selling trip in the middlewest practically shot. She had taken it upon her shoulders and they had packed one morning in February and the same day were floating in their old car down the valley, past Washington, into Richmond where the daffodils were in bloom.

They had a whole house in Key West, a crazy rowboat with a real sail, and they drank Cuban liquor in a dump owned by a one-eyed Cuban who cooked marvelous dishes and talked hoarsely about terrors under Machado, emphasizing his words with a silent gesture of the finger slitting the throat, his eyes squeezed shut as if his life's blood had begun to flow. In the afternoons they fished with a line on the bridge or went down to the wharf where those wellheeled sportsmen in white with rods and reels running into the hundreds set forth on trips to the Gulf Stream and came back, burned red and beaming, with a huge sailfish cluttering the decks.

Sometimes at night they sat for hours looking across that dark expanse of water toward Cuba, watching the tiny lights of ships passing at sea, and coming back through the silent moonlit streets when all the dogs would start up out of the glistening white coral dust to bark, and the moonflowers would give forth such an overpowering fragrance, they could not go to bed, but sat on the front porch watching the sky lighten, smelling the lime tree by their gate, and hearing the rustling of the palm as a breeze began to stir.

Jonathan had scraped up an acquaintance with some bigshot doctor from Johns Hopkins who took him off on a fishing cruise to the Dry Tortugas. A northern kicked up and they were marooned for a week. When a huge yacht anchored near, Doc and Jonathan eyed her and talked over the chance of getting some grub. It was too stormy to fish. When they boarded the big yacht, Doc yelled out, "How's the market?" and the owner, a big fat septuagenarian, recognized him for a brother under the skin. The two had come aboard in old blue dungarees and beards like Jesus H. Christ, but the stockmarket inquiry fixed them up to a six-course dinner on what was practically gold plate with two kinds of wine and liquors.

They stayed all evening smoking Corona Coronas and listening to the life story of the old pirate who had cleaned up a fortune in washing machines and who presented each of them with a handtooled leather edition of a work by himself on the beauties of marlin fishing as compared to deer hunting.

When they left, the steward loaded them down with enough imported scotch oatmeal and de luxe bacon, cognac, and French wine to last a month. Most of it was still left when Doc and Jonathan docked at Key West, and Victoria salvaged it from their boat. The Negroes were standing around, with their empty hands hanging down, watching them unload the catch and waiting for someone to throw them a barracuda or a yellowtail. Victoria cooked the scotch oatmeal and rationed the brandy. "I wasn't poor for nothing," she used to say, making her plans and managing to make it seem free and easy when there wasn't much more than a nickel in the house.

Money had never been Jonathan's aim. He would never have to accuse himself of going after money and gypping people. Although his early years had been crammed with people who thought passionately about money, not only as money, but as moral good, he had somehow not taken the virus. When he was sixteen he had his first job and it had paid well. He went on taking jobs in college vacations when he might have loafed around, because he wanted to be free. He and other young men talked about literature and life and about being free and all the time he made money that was no earthly use to him. He drank a great deal and shone as a social light and thought fondly of that day when he would begin to write a novel and then he met Victoria. They had met, providentially for both of them, and started at once keeping house in a very methodical way. Before he knew it, he was in his own home at his own typewriter and turning out books that were actually published. Not many. He had to admit that it was a battle to live, but still they did it without congealing. His parents had interfered with them and an honest marriage had come out of it.

His father's scoffing at his written words had at first no
outer effect, as a tree does not at once show when the
vital bark has been damaged. He only knew that it became harder to say what he had intended when, fresh
and enthusiastic, he quietly shut himself up expecting an
easy burst of language to flow at once from that impulse
that seemed to take so complete a form as he put the car
away. It was as if a righteous parent was always standing
at his elbow, as indeed both parents had stood there, at
his marriage. His father, leaving the Municipal Building,
had been the flippant one, able to joke with "Might as
well get a license to hunt and fish while you are here."

What he wanted was to move from the road, where he
had talked easily to Mr. Schieber about hunting in the
swamp, to his typewriter without that cold mist inter-
vening somewhere on the way, drenching his words with
an acid bitterness that seemed to betray him. And although
he had no such illusion as spouted too easily from many
of his New York friends, who, after the crash of 1929,
began to say that only factory workers were worth writing
about and he must go to a factory if he were to find anything to say, these current ideas added to his troubles. A
frenzy shook well-intentioned young men like the palsy.
Some pushed frantically into picketing, rode cars to
hunger marches, sweated at the midnight lamp of Marxist
discussion.

Jonathan had always believed that literature was not
argument but the history of men's feelings, the search for
the hidden springs of men's actions, and if he turned to
farmers now, it was not as a substitute for a job undone.

What he wanted was to touch actual people, find work
bordering on that mythical "revolution" that had begun
to seem a reality, not only to a little group who studied
the course of history, but to innocent men who had
dreamed only of living a full life and of dying honorably in their beds. He wanted to push across some border,
as yet unseen, and harder to find than the Black Hills
into which Victoria's Uncle Joe had plunged recklessly
with a little band of outlaws, hunting gold.

He did not expect any sudden millennium. He remembered Lester Tolman arguing in the Coolidge era that any revolution would be purely a mechanical one. Some of his friends had changed violently. One, Ward Bacon, who in 1931 had written to a magazine of left tendencies edited by Jonathan and a few cronies, saying that workers were only to be spit upon and that their lousy sheet was an orgy of sentimental notions and wallowings in inferiority complexes, had lately completely forgotten this outburst and had written Jonathan advising him to shake out of the idiocy of rural life and come to the city where the real struggle of the proletariat would begin.

Jonathan had thrown the letter away, laughing a little, and had gone gladly to meet Jake Tentman and James Honeywell in the latter's barn, where the little awkward leaflet James had scrawled for the approval of the others was as sound as a good cedarboard made with the intention of serving some structure and not empty air. Life was certainly not to be lived as if revolution were just around the corner. Or a world war. He was already trying to build some kind of protection so that these perhaps far-off events might not shatter years of living. Earlier he and Victoria had puzzled what to do when war broke out. They had talked of getting to Mexico. Now he thought he should get into the war, when it came. This war would certainly turn into a class war. It would be the one decisive war of history; it was the kind of talk in circulation. It gave Victoria cold chills to hear him. For a second everything in her trembled, then she threw her arms around him. "I'll go too," she said. "You can't make me stay home knitting. I'll put on pants and go with you. I won't stay home if they take you." He would hold her away from him, chuckling a little. Probably his happiest moments, his most certain, were then, when her fierce little face looking up at him convinced him completely of her love.

"We'll be the Rover boys together, on land, on sea," he had said, and then they could not speak, held each

other grimly, their throats bursting, the black war as near
as if a giant dirigible had just passed between them and
the sun.

Victoria could remember the World War and how some
people then also talked of the class war that would end
the war between nations. She had been a student at the
University of California, proud of herself for not having
knitted one sock for one soldier. There hadn't been a
half dozen people she could talk to; she wondered now
what had become of them.

Barney Blum had left the San Francisco paper to risk
his hide with the crew of a salmon fleet to Alaska. He
had come back with a story that shook up the industry.
The North was a region of frozen hands and feet, stinking holds and the fish running like a bright and terrible
spring only to pollute and cripple the men who took a
last chance with them. Gold had petered out, had been
tamed in the Klondike, but the salmon pay-streak was
running strong.

Barney had jumped into headlines, then he had gone
to South America, had for some unknown and mysterious
reason sold out Sandino. Sandino's men were only ragged
bandits to him now and what he had understood in the
salmon belt, he missed in the new region. He was not
good at the pick and shovel anymore but he rose in the
estimation of his paper and sailed firstclass for Europe.

The last Victoria had heard, he was foreign correspond-
ent in Rome, not exactly taking a shine to Mussolini but
uncertain, full of ontheonehand This and ontheotherhand
That. He sent long dispatches about the havenot nations
struggling for a place in the sun that gave one the cold
chills with their reminder that the hemlock cup brewed
during the World War had never been emptied. But the
castor oil joke must have stuck a little in his throat. He
must have remembered sometime his old Socialist father
with his fine eyes blazing against injustice; his dispatches

often zigzagged as if he were trying to get his bearings. Victoria and Jonathan sometimes debated what would become of Barney when war finally broke out in Europe because everyone said war would come, in a month, in a year, in five years, but certainly.

The fate of her other old friends was obscure. There was the radical Caseman who had played a part in the Seattle general strike years before. He had virtually disappeared. Even latter-day friends, made in New York, might as well be buried in Cambrian rock. One of the girls had become a concert singer and sometimes in the pages of literary reviews she came across the puzzling tragic face of Cora Constance.

Once she heard about George Gates and remembered how he had hid in her apartment in St. Luke's Place. He was wearing a checked cap and carried a *Saturday Evening Post* the last time she had seen him in the hallway at night when he snatched a kiss and had run off in what he fondly thought a disguise. The police had hunted for him on Mulberry street along with the rest of the I.W.W.s who were jumping bail after the Chicago trial. Her informant had told a garbled tale about George rising high in the new regime in Russia; he had become an official in a bank then he had mysteriously disappeared, a part, so it was said, of some rumored opposition. George had always been a poet-agitator; he was doubtless one now, in some part of the world. Yet it did seem true that the I.W.W. had gone down as Bill Haywood had stepped aboard the ship at Montreal, a big confident man hiding his broken hulk under an overcoat that might have been a banker's, his hat off and hair blowing defiantly, the black patch over his blind eye blazing forth his identity as he stood in full view with jaw set, his one eye fixed on America for the last time. The law had not dared lay hands on him then but it had smashed right and left at his fellowworkers who remained.

Some of Jonathan's friends who liked to dabble in social ideas had a way of dismissing the I.W.W. as if it had disappeared from American life like the woodpigeon. "You

can't argue with a certain kind of mind," Jonathan would
say, when they were finally alone and Victoria was empty-
ing the ashtrays. "You can't kill man's revolt. It's like the
bird in the fable, bound to rise from the ashes."

As Jonathan left the house, he called to Victoria he
would be back soon. He already regretted that he had
promised to help Nancy. Tim Robb with a family of
seven was the one who needed help. Helping Robb was
helping the whole farm movement; there wasn't a farmer
in the county needed more.

She heard the door shut. The house felt hollow without him. Through an open window, the air cleaned the
rooms like a new broom. There would not be many days
like this, a rare flower, thrown down at the beginning
of a hard winter. Chicago conference, or no Chicago conference, life must be lived, wood brought in, food found
somewhere. An easy life was not in her blood but she
sometimes thought that the rifts that came between her
and Jonathan came from their opposing pasts. Whatever
happened, the farmers would help them out with eggs,
with an occasional chicken. There were odd jobs she
could do. The Hollywood writer owed her for typing his
proletarian play about the Kentucky mine war. It was
Nancy who was in trouble and Victoria thought of the
little family in the room in Des Moines as if they were
shipwrecked on some island.

Not that she and Jonathan always seemed on a sound
and rocky coast. She had only to turn on the radio to
feel a trembling in the very air. It was not like the home
of her childhood when she and her sister used to sit tranquilly on the front porch at evening time, breathing up
the scents from the newly watered grass and listening to
the singsong of the katydid that seemed to promise some
dazzling happy future. If she so much as sat down with
folded hands, she was likely as not to hear an echo of the
voice of the farm boy from South Dakota or the Negro

from South Carolina who, swaying at the edge of the platform, had repeated like a chant, "We on the brink, we on the brink, one step more and we lost forever." Steve Carson's voice had come like a chorus, denying the forever. He too had stood at the very edge of the platform as if to warm the chilled hopes of the timid. "We young folks don't want to wait and wait. I've seen my father and mother wait and do without and get worn down with waiting. We want a good life now." Every kid in the audience had stomped and yelled. The older ones had even applauded but the boy had been taken aside; told it was dangerous to be too hasty. He had to learn, they said, and he had agreed a little sullenly, saying he saw the point but he didn't want just a good farm. It wasn't even going to be enough to pay off the mortgage. He had tugged at the neck of his sweater as if it choked him. He had gone on recklessly. What he wanted was a new kind of world. And he wanted it NOW.

She sat down on the bed. The memory of his voice saying "Now," put gooseflesh on her arms. She made quick work of the rooms, went downstairs, swept off the front porch. Now it was in order, ready for anything. Looking through the front windows, she saw with satisfaction the table and corner cupboard Jonathan had made after old models, the birth certificate of her grandmother, Mary Trexler, with the blue angels and their red, red crowns hanging on the wall, the dishes on the welsh dresser that came from way back and had held pies for men and women who had moved away, had children, built new homes and turned to dust.

There was greatuncle Jacob's sugarbowl, and she thought of him as he had appeared to her as a child in her mother's stories, the handsome, thoughtless, reckless bad man who for some undefined reason she had pitied most and loved best. There was the blue plate that her mother let them handle on Sunday afternoons when they were also allowed to take down the big old Bible and look at the colored illustrations, reserving the head of John the Baptist with its deathly pallor and deep dark blood for the last when, shivering and shrieking, they shut the book. Her mother had carefully cherished these things as if they were seeds of some rare plant to be shared by her children and carried to new parts of the earth. The kitchen clock was wagging its pendulum; the little house looked like a stageset in its order and emptiness— as if, at any moment, the back door to the left would swing open, and the hero would enter.

She sat down on the topstep, looking out at the little valley, saying over and over, what a day. The sun poured into the very stones, into the naked twigs of the trees, into her own bones. High in the blue sky great white clouds lumbered slowly by. The great white whales, she and Jonathan called them, and she remembered the day when they had gone bathing in the brook with the stones slippery with violent green moss and trees dripping like ferns into the water. They had looked up at the big swollen clouds. "There go the white whales," she had called. And Jonathan had said, "There goes old Moby Dick," as the last of the fleet shoved across the patch of sky.

She had never been one of those who sighed to be placid like an animal munching its cud. There were enough moments in life when the blessed feeling of being alive made one conscious only of the sun and the way it fell on one's skin, of the blood running through one's veins and the food one ate and of love. Each of those things was a revelation in its turn; as for love, it was still unwinding and would until the grave. Men often enough thought that they alone were human, that little girls were quiet eggs waiting for the great moment. Most of her early heartaches had come from not being a quiet little egg. There was the party long ago with everyone in fancy clothes and she had danced with the best-looking boy out into the courtyard. They had stood close together and she had pressed up to him, shamelessly, murmuring, "Kiss me, kiss me," and he had kissed her, too ardently, never to speak to her again except in an angry confused way as if she had betrayed him. When she was older, if she too could not adore, it had only seemed embarrassing to be dogged and followed by some abject adorer.

She was a lucky woman to have Jonathan and she could have wished nothing better for her baby boy than that he had grown up the spit and image of him. She bowed her head on her knees; the light wiped out of the skies. Lord, how it sent a knife to her very spine; he would be almost as old as that picture of Jonathan as a baby on the dresser upstairs, sitting in the sand with his eyes all squinted up from the sun. A woman with her life before her and the world full of troubles and work to do has no business thinking of what's over and done with, but the past had a way of tolling, like some bell. It could bring you to a dead stop in the middle of the day. Jonathan was a wonderful man with a nature that would stop your heart. She had washed his socks, mended his clothes, read, walked, rode with him; they had talked to all hours of the night. There were times she did not know where she ended and Jonathan began.

It did seem, though, that losing her baby was a sign she should have something of her very own to do and be. Her grandmother had clamored for education as a young girl and had been bound out to work for others; her own mother had to quit school at eleven and pedal a sewing machine until her legs ached. No wonder she had been so eager to get her own daughters to college. She had put ideas into Victoria's head; having no boys, she had picked on Victoria.

"Maybe you'll go the legislature someday, like your grandfather," she had said. "You might be a lawyer," look- ing at her with her head on one side. And she had never breathed such foolishness as that she must choose between a "career" and marriage. It would have been the last thing on earth for Anne Wendel to suppose that a child of hers should forfeit love and children. Her girl was merely to have everything the world holds.

The words her mother had used, the idea of being a lawyer, or a member of the legislature, had never taken

hold of Victoria's mind; the terms had, in fact, meant
little to Mrs. Wendel. They were symbols of some bursting kind of life she had wanted for her daughter. When
her rich Uncle David Trexler came on his rare visits, it
was as plain as could be that he fondly imagined his life
was a beacon and an inspiration to his sister's children,
even though they were, poor unfortunates, a lot of girls.

Victoria could say honestly she had not so much as
dreamed of being the wife of a rich man or of anyone
who went after money. Her first thoughts of marrying had
come when she was a child in highschool sitting up late
reading *Plutarch's Lives* and she had wanted to be like
the wife of Panteus, a beautiful and noble-looking woman,
who had been but lately married, and suffered disasters
in the height of her love. Victoria could slip back into
that dim past with the familiarity of a relative, and she
went in search of Panteus's wife now, where she was standing ready for the execution. Her parents had tried hard
to keep her safe at home but she had escaped, found a
horse and a little money, and at night made speed to
Taenarus, where she embarked for Egypt, came to her
husband, and cheerfully endured to live in a foreign
country.

Some of the language, the very words, still stuck to her
mind, as the germ of life continues to survive in ancient
seeds found in tombs. And when Ptolemy gave order that
the body of Cleomenes, king of Sparta, should be flayed
and hung up, and that his children, mother and women
that were with her, should be killed, Panteus's wife had
been among that number. It was she who gave her hand
to Cratesicla, as she was going to execution, held up her
robe and begged her to be courageous. When they came
to the place, the children were first killed before their
eyes and afterwards Cratesicla herself, with only these
words in her mouth, "Oh children, whither are you
gone?" But Panteus's wife, fastening her dress close to
her, and being a strong woman, in silence and perfect
composure, looked after everyone that was slain and laid
them decently out; and after all were killed, drawing her

clothes about her, she courageously submitted to the stroke
and wanted nobody to wind her up after she was dead.

The whales had passed from the sky and the Tesh
boy was rattling by in his broken-down car that looked as
if it would fly apart. He waved a hand like a disjointed
wing at her and she got to her feet, watching him bounce
over the ruts. He would be going home to the craziest
farm in the countryside where buildings were swaybacked
and chickens wall-eyed. His old man never bought an
animal that wasn't halt or lame or blind. Yet you never
saw such energy for passing out papers, collecting pennies, standing shivering in the snow to stuff mailboxes
with news of meetings. His rasping nervous highpitched
voice drove the men in Willy Blaine's store crazy. A
politician who wanted to win would do well to bribe
the Tesh boy to back the other fellow. A cause he espoused
was certain to lose. Yet finally some of the things he had
been repeating were coming true; the mills along the
river were throwing more and more men out of work.
The idle men sat in the store and the remarks of the
Tesh boy stuck in their skin. They itched and scratched
to get rid of his barbs but their flesh was no longer
whole.

He had a clear strong voice and one night sailed by
singing, "There'll be pie in the sky bye and bye." They
woke up and talked for hours about what might happen
that winter. Would a world war break out; and if so
where; who would fight whom and why; how had that
little wart Hitler managed to get his paws on a whole
German people;—and talking, time slipped by, the moon
went down, and they wondered what had happened to
Jonathan's old Detroit friend, Lester Tolman, who used
to write long letters about parties in Germany. Was he
still collecting the curious work of Hans Arp, the trap
drummer, or had he finally shot himself as he used to
threaten? So talking, they heard the cocks crow on Yaeger's
farm and the first rumbling of the milk cars going down
the road to the milk station where the big trucks snapped
the cans up for the city.

Timothy Robb listened to Jonathan Chance. His thin
shoulders showed sharp beneath the old bathrobe that
was fastened roughly at the neck with a big safety pin.
He played with a child's shoe, absently turning it over
and thrusting a finger through a hole in the sole. Under
his tan, the pallor of his face made him seem a man within
a man. Jonathan had the uneasy feeling that if he spoke
to the man with the tan, the man with the white face
might answer.

"Your health comes first," Jonathan said, trying to
sound casual and at the same time firm. "I don't count
on that doctor the way you do. I don't know as he has
ever found out what is wrong." He did not know how
to make Tim properly careful and at the same time not
frighten him. He was a hard man to frighten.

Tim said, "I got to get my strength back." His voice
sounded hollow and unconvincing and he felt that he
was only echoing the hopes of everyone ill. He had tried
many remedies. Mrs. Honeywell had told him to sip
hot water between meals. Mrs. Bacon said there was nothing like bathing the feet in hot water and sticking to a
milk diet. Her brother had been saved from the grave
by that little device.

Almost everything had been suggested, except perhaps killing a frog in the light of the moon and tying
its heart with two horsehairs and then burying it under
a large flat stone. There were some in that neighborhood who might have suggested even that final resort
against death. Witch signs still flourished on some barns
and many homes kept little books with such recipes against
ill fortune. Farmers who did not believe in witches, half
believed in some ill-assorted destiny against which any
device was worth the trying. The old ways died out hard.
The land had shriveled from its early bloom, did not
yield the big crops that once sprung naturally from the
soil. New people came in, the old ones perished or moved
away.

The waves of misfortunes in the city refurnished the
farms with a new breed. With each new depression, the

old line of farmers moved further west, moved off, went to cities. A new class came in, leaving some of the old fellows stranded, feeling almost homeless in their homes. The new faces came from factories, from New York, from Philadelphia. Many were men who had been born in the old country, had worked in cities, saving all they could lay aside. Tim knew these men well; he spoke their language.

Tim Robb himself was no doubt not meant for the land. He had been a machinist in the days before the World War, a young fellow, muscular, healthy, and without envy. The War sucked him in and when he came home his lungs were jammed with gas, he breathed hard and was winded easily. His young wife, Emily Robb, took everything on her shoulders. She was a bright plucky girl from the mills who got patterns for her clothes and made them herself, could stand before a store window, go home and make a fair copy of the fashionable dress the wax figure had worn. When they started life on the farm she had planned to sew curtains, make quilts, hem towels, have crocheted rag rugs on all the floors. Nothing of the kind had happened.

Tim Robb drew a poor piece of land at a fancy price. It was early in 1921 when he bought his land, and the mortgage scarcely lightened around his neck with the years. The bright posters luring returned soldiers to the land had said nothing about interest. They had pictured grassy pastures and well-fed cows. They did not show the bank.

They never gave a recipe against a cow dying. They didn't tell you what to do when tuberculosis hit the herd and the government men took away the cows leaving you with a sprinkling of cash that never again would buy back a proper base. Children were the one sure crop.

Tim Robb never had laid hands on the deed to his farm. The bank kept that, too. Tim and his wife talked about the time when they would own the deed, when the mortgage would be paid off, and meanwhile they paid interest. They paid taxes. The wind blew the gutter pipes down. It ripped off the shutters. The well went dry. The government came along and said they had to have a cement floor in the barn. They had to keep the cows clean. They had to keep the milk cool, a certain precise temperature.

Now and then they paid off something at the bank, going together triumphantly.

It was a great day to march in the bank, hear from all sides, "Good morning, Mr. Robb. Good morning, Mrs. Robb." It took several days after each triumph to feel blank dismay, to see the flushed exalted moment when they had marched in the bank as a vain show that had given them no shoes, no new dishes, no screens for the windows, no blankets for the bed. The Bank became a maw to be filled. It was like a bull critter that hasn't got what it takes, but eats his head off just the same, terrifies the herd and lives for himself, strictly speaking, with nothing to offer. The Bank got snacks and it growled. It got a full meal and it purred.

The Bank was always in their thoughts. "Sonny, you can't have that, we got to pay the interest this month," Emily would have to tell her boy. "Put that penny in the Bank, that's a good boy," Tim told little Robbie. "If you're a good girl you can go with Papa to the Bank," Emily would console little Grace. The Bank had its hand on their shoulders, stood beside their bed, pulled the shoelaces from their shoes.

The Bank. Nice Mr. Mullins with his cream-pie face and nice ways, purring, "Good work, Mr. Robb," and "Nice day, Mrs. Robb" and when the Day came, the Interest Day, sending a curt little note, "Interest due," until their spines froze and they looked at one another. They couldn't dig interest from the ground, peal it from the hides of their cows, squeeze it from the milk, like butterfat. Interest was a bogey, chewing them alive. It waited outside in the cold night air ready to nip their ears. The children suddenly chilled when their parents spoke of "interest." Little Robbie began sniveling. "Never mind, darling," Emily would say, snatching up her little man, her pride and joy. "Never mind, mamma's own lamb," looking over the child's head with furious burning eyes at Tim, as if he were to blame.

Doubtless he was to blame, he often thought, standing in the barnyard with his feet in the ooze and the milk pails full of the creamy foam that should at least keep them from dreading the wolf at the door. What was the matter with the milk, all good stuff, that went off each morning in the big cans to the city? His mind juggled with the regulations of the big city dairies, with their bewildering language, with their butterfats, and their surplus quotas, with their This and their That.

A man did not know if he was living or dying. He had milk and then he didn't have milk. The city had milk, it had, moreover, everything that milk could make. Tim did not know why it especially enraged him to learn that the milk companies even used the whey and made comb-sets. He found himself looking at the pink and blue combs in drugstore windows with peculiar rage, as if they had been robbed from his home. Who paid him to give up comb-sets? Where did they come from? His cows that stood patient as death each morning, that never said boo—who could blame them for misfortune? Who could blame the clover, or the corn, or the wheat? It grew well enough. If he filled his barns, the milk still did not overtake the mortgage. It might inch up a little, as if the two were running a race and the milk was riding an ox cart and the mortgage, driven by the crafty Mr. Cream-pie Mullins, was speeding ever ahead in a fine eight-cylinder car.

Maybe he was to blame for being born. But he did not intend that his Aunt Hazel should have spent her life in vain. She had not fed her dead sister's brats, paddling from table to stove in her bare feet, heaping up their insatiable plates, spreading corn syrup on their bread and coaxing them with promises of butter some day, to hurry, to wash their faces, to comb their hair, to go to school, to have him blame himself for being born or to go back on his life. Not he. "You'd appreciate an eddication if you'd never had it, like me," he could hear her say, shooing them out the door, getting rid of them and like as not sitting down for a minute, exhausted in the litter of their nothingness.

There's no litter in the world like not enough to do with, not enough dishes, not enough food, not enough clothes. Thank God for it, Aunt Hazel had pieced old underwear into quilts, she had found a use for newspapers. Take a few old newspapers and put them between the mattress and the springs and you got warmth. You got a resistance to cold that is heartening. You can stuff sacks and tuck them around a child to warm his little bones.

Timothy Robb had never expected to use his Aunt Hazel's ingenious resourcefulness against nothingness. He had fancied himself as somewhat smarter, better equipped, and even a little sly. He had been commended in the army, had been gassed, and in the hospital had been encouraged to think that he had done well for his country. There had even been times when he thought of his country as an expansive and multiplied Aunt Hazel, welcoming him home. He had been welcomed home with a band and the music over, the jobs were hard to find as hen's teeth. He had snatched at the first thing he could, then had used his bit of savings and Emily's savings to get started on the farm.

The house had looked solid enough. It had been built more than a hundred years before by a race of men not afraid to use their muscles. It was good to inherit not only land but a house that had been lived in, born in, struggled with for generations. He had to live in it almost a year before he got the hang of the place and could feel the house taunt him for taking it on.

Some men can't stand a taunt. They shrivel and are licked, but once Timothy got the prick beneath his skin he was ready to scrap. When the milk co-operative sold them all down the river to the big milk companies in the city, it had taken only himself, Tentman, and the two Honeywells to put a crimp in their highhanded plans.

The fake co-operative that had been a shame to its name thought farmers didn't have gumption enough to stand up and yell for their rights. They were supposed to be natural-born suckers so busy milking they couldn't think.

The farmers had shown them they had something beside skimmed milk in their veins. It had looked like a strike through the whole Philadelphia milk shed. Tim still had at his fingertips the plans for a strike that would tie up the whole works overnight and paralyze the city. Those plans were not in any bank vault.

He had gotten out on a limb with the strike talk, though; if it hadn't been for Si Greenough coming along, they would have sniped him. When he said "they," he couldn't have named names or identified faces. He wished he knew who the buzzards were who had left a note scrawled on a dirty piece of wrapping paper stuck like chicken manure to his front door. "Keep your nose out of what ain't your business or get ready to ride."

"The Devil never walks," Aunt Hazel said.

If they had said, "Come on out and fight," he would have given them a run for their money. The note had no arms, no legs, no voice. It hid Its cowardly face and at night, in the crumple of pebbles under the dog's feet, in the grinding of a broken hinge on a shutter or the slamming of a door in the wind, the Robb family dreaded Its coming.

Emily got so she could not eat, fearing It. The children began to cry, smelling Its breath. Timothy had stuck it out and gradually they ceased talking about Who could be behind it. Was the Klan getting ready to ride again? They had puzzled over it, in Arty Sturmer's kitchen, in Jake Tentman's barn, in Jonathan's home. But it was Timothy who had been obliged to take Its marks upon himself. He began complaining he couldn't eat. His food shoved up on him, he swayed dizzily as he milked the cows. A faint nausea tinged his thoughts as if always waiting, behind him, was Something ready to get him down.

When he had turned a pale putty color under the tan, his friends, the farmers, had scurried around for miles

taking a collection. They had found a doctor, who had
treated him for nothing. One fine morning he woke up
in a nursing home; they fed him oranges, milk, but the
firm flesh melted like wax from his bones. He missed his
family and the true nourishment of his life was too remote from him. He puzzled, as he lay in the clean bed,
about the organization that had sprung up like a new crop
out of virgin land. His mind dwelt with pride on the
Delter sale. Five hundred farmers had blocked the sheriff's
sale four times. He would go over it, detail for detail,
remembering the words spoken, the sheriff bawling out,
"I'm the law," and Tentman coming up, his head thrust
forward out of his blue workshirt, moving up on the
sheriff, saying, "You ain't the law. We are the law. We
put you in the job. You do what we want or, by god,
you're out." The fellow's face turning to putty, backing
away and feeling for his gun; Honeywell, the Quaker,
leaping for it and wrestling with him on the ground. The
shot that sent a bullet into the shed back of Tim's head.
The capture of the gun. A great moment.

He sighed in his bed, sinking back luxuriously, smiling
and cherishing the picture—as he used to think of Emily
in the days of the War when he lay with his belly braced
against the sandbags, aching in every bone, just waiting. He would go over in his thoughts every feature in
her face, her funny turned-up nose, the tears in her eyes
as he said good-by, picturing her again as she would be
when he came home. Then he would look up at the innocent blue sky, the puffs from the guns coming idly
like peaceful clouds. The deceptiveness gave him the feeling of nightmare and he would hold to Emily as if she
alone were real; the little mole on her right lip, the feel
of her hand behind his head. His stomach would contract with a kind of painful joy that a second later, when
the guns began or the rain washed down in torrents,
seemed as hauntingly unreal as the song of birds that
sometimes soared unbelievably in the early dawn from
the crushed fields.

Tim fretted so in the nursing home, they were glad

to get rid of him. "You're an awfully bad patient, Mr. Robb," the nurse had said reprovingly as she had buttoned him into his shirt. All the way home he was worrying about the farmers who had already begun to shy away from the stiff fighting. They had rallied around the foreclosure sales, but a strike was another matter. He couldn't get it into his head. Perhaps he didn't understand farmers. After all, he was fairly new to the land.

Tim worried over the farmers as if they were lost lambs. He didn't know just what step to take next. All around the causes of their troubles were open and plain to the eye. They should fight for better milk prices, even if it came to a strike. They should pick holes in the government programs and get more relief. And even more than that, they should try to gimlet a little light into men's minds so that they could see they would either lick or get licked, in the long run.

He had been listening to Jonathan's voice for some time without taking in the words. He had said something about Tim taking care of himself, about a doctor in New York who knew his stuff, about the Tesh boy who would actually be more of an asset to them if he belonged to another crowd. Now he was talking about that cancellation business they had threshed out in Chicago.

"It's too hot for them, they won't grab it," he said flatly. He hated to admit it. "Listen, Jonathan, the farmers are sewed up to the banks. The minute they come out with that kind of a slogan, the banks will step on them. Those guys at Chicago are too far ahead. It won't work here, all it will do is bring the buzzards down on us again." He opened the lid of the coffeepot on the stove and sniffed. Grinning, he looked at Jonathan. "Nothing here but a little hot water and a few coffee beans she's been holding out on me, but let's have some." He poured two cups, angry at his hand that shook. Jonathan took the pale brew and, without looking at it, began sipping. He wasn't sure that Tim was not dead right. Admitting it made the darned business seem unearthly slow, as if he were pushing a truck uphill by hand. If you got a crowd too fast for the main mass of farmers it just cut itself off and became a debating team, smug but getting nowhere. Tim began, "There's many that haven't enough to eat. They'll fight for relief this winter." Then he winced, turned deathly white and sat down suddenly.

Jonathan rose and patted his shoulder. "Can I get you something?"

"There ain't nothing to take," said Tim. "Grin and bear it." But he wasn't grinning. He felt as if he were slowly sinking and he looked at Jonathan with the frantic helplessness of a child. Jonathan got up and began putting on his overcoat. He opened the door to the other room from which the noise of the kids playing had come in steady thuds upon their talk. "Hey, Emily," he called, "get your old man's overcoat. We're going to a doctor in New York."

When his car came out of the Dark Hollow road the house loomed up across the creek and he was surprised to see a light in their bedroom window. Ever since he had dropped Tim at his house, he had uncomfortably wondered if Victoria had worried when he did not come home. He hurried the car in the barn, and crossed the porch loudly. Opening the front door he called out cheerfully, "Hello. Here's your poor boy."

He could hear her feet thump the floor and come running. Her face, tearstained and swollen was a dreadful reproach. He began to defend himself, "You didn't worry, did you?"

"Worry? What do you think I am, a stick of wood?"

"I thought you trusted me more than that. You know I'd let you know if I could. I took Tim to New York and it's good news we've got about him."

"I'm no mind reader. How did I know? I sit here imagining things. The car might have run over a cliff. You might have got killed." She began to cry, not softly but in sharp angry gulps, moving away from him as swiftly as she had come. He followed her up, trying to get his arms around her. She squirmed away from him, blazing out at him, "You might have been drunk, run off with someone else."

He began to laugh and, at his almost pleased laughter, she shoved at him again. "Laugh. You can laugh. I have to stick here. I haven't a car to drive around in. I have to stay here and read your father's letters. Read that if you want to read something." She had walked toward the table and grabbed up a letter and thrust it at him. He looked at her soberly, wondering how much of her rage was against him, how much against his father. He read the letter, feeling her anger still sizzling around him in the room.

"So," he said. "Damn him." He crumpled the letter angrily and at his anger, hers melted. She came up to him and put her arms around him. "I felt so awful all alone getting that. I thought you'd never come." They stood close together, holding each other tight, not mentioning the letter, not speaking. Something unspeakably mean seemed to have entered the room, to have shamed them. She did not want to remind him of his father again. Better to forget that he had a parent so heartless. Such calculation, such pride was beyond her.

She had it on the tip of her tongue to say that she could not understand such a man, that her parents, though poor, would have bitten out their tongues rather than hurt their children in so cruel a way but she stopped herself. She could feel Jonathan's shame, it seemed to have penetrated his bones and to be standing limp and weary in her arms. She tightened her arms, said breathlessly, "Never mind, darling, never mind. We don't care. We don't need even to answer it. I wrote him a hot answer this afternoon but perhaps it's better not to send it."

"Let's see it," Jonathan said tonelessly.

"No, not tonight. I'm going to make you some nice hot tea. You're tired out. We won't think about it tonight, but to write like that. He promised. He was the one who told us to dig the well. Then to rub it in about the interest, when he knows we are broke."

"It's not the well. He just uses the well. He gave Tom five thousand. And never has helped us. Unless you can call this house helping, and the house is in his name until we pay for it."

"All I care about is the well man. What will he do?"

Jonathan did not answer. He was folding the letter smooth again and reading it once more. The even characters of his father's handwriting seemed full of deliberate malice. He had made a mistake, no doubt, to tell his father about the farmers in Chicago. He said, "I shouldn't have told Father about Chicago."

"No, you shouldn't. You have always been too nice to your family. Look what happens. He thinks you are trying to get out of your debts and that's all he thinks the farmer is doing. It's all snarled up in his head. Maybe he'll go crazy."

"Not Father," said Jonathan, reading, *"and while I would like to see my children with all the comforts, I do not see myself paying for them. If you saved your money and quit traveling around you could pay your debts and I propose that you get a steady job and begin sending the interest on the house which is long past due. I could use the money right now."*

"He proposes," said Jonathan, shrugging his shoulder, "that I get a steady job. If I only could." He suddenly wadded up the letter and threw it viciously on the floor. Vicky came in from the kitchen with the tea. Her eyes were still swollen and he thought of her wrestling with her resentment the long day. "Jesus, I'm sorry I wasn't here."

She had a swift feeling that he had often not been there when she was in deepest trouble; he had been somewhere else when her father died, but she didn't intend to rake over the ashes. He looked beaten; it wasn't the well, it was the walls of the house that were theirs and yet not theirs. They had scrubbed and scraped, they had made gardens and planted trees, painted and puttied, filled in holes in the plaster and holes in the cement, built walls and cleaned corners and attics. A job that rushed back on them dozens of times overwhelming them with plaster and wood and mud and stones. It was like building a new house to patch up an old one, and after it was over, the house was still insecure. They had no stake in it; the solid walls mocked them. Though they paid taxes and repairs, they had the feeling that it could be snatched out from under them as if it were a raft and the earth were a moving river.

Jonathan was sipping his tea. "I almost forgot," he said. "The most important news of all. Tim is going to be all right."

"Not really?"

"You had the right hunch when you said our doctor should look at him. Today when I got there he was so sick I was scared. I bundled him up and we drove right in, that's why I didn't come home. Dr. Parks gave him the works, X-ray and all. He says it isn't ulcers at all. Tim could hardly believe it. He kept staring as if in a daze. Then Parks says, Eat meat. Three times a day. Round steak ground up, a pound of it. Eat potatoes or rice, lots of rye bread. Canned fruit. All the time Tim was staring. He said, All that? Parks says, every bite. Then he says, And clean out your barn, for an hour every day. Tim says, I'm too weak, I'll fall down. Parks says, Did you ever fall down in front of an automobile? No, says Tim. Ever fall down in front of a street car? No. Well then, says Parks, fall down. But clean out the barn. Parks told me he would be all right, says it's nerves and a pronounced allergy. He's trying him out on this diet; if it doesn't work, he'll try something else, but he figures it will work."

"Oh, isn't that swell," and Victoria sat down on the chair near her husband. Her hand rested on his knee as he swallowed his tea; she patted him softly, hoping he would forget her silly anger. He surely knew she didn't mean anything. Tim was all right; they must forget the letter. How many times had they not nailed Mr. Chance

down in his box, only to have him pop up again? He
was a strong old man, and she thought of him surrounded,
cushioned, barricaded with multiple towels, chandeliers
with crystal drops, dozens of lampshades, and his body
pinned in a tiny cubbyhole in the midst of these objects
with one arm out vaguely waving for help. This vision
came suddenly as from a grotesque movie and cheered
her. She began to laugh. She remembered the time they
had torn up their marriage license and had thrown it
down the toilet in resentment of him, then they had taken
a walk and Jonathan had bought *Armance* by Stendhal
for her.

"Now we have to find money to buy meat for Tim,"
said Jonathan.

"We'll ask the city people," said Victoria. They sat
quietly checking over the list of city people who had
moved into that neighborhood. Newspapermen, Hollywood writers had moved into old farmhouses and installed
improvements that were an eyeopener to natives who had
struggled along with the old pump and an outdoor back-
house for generations. When they finally went to bed,
the letter lay crumpled in a ball on the floor.

GIT ALONG, LITTLE DOGIES

NANCY RADFORD believed that every day might be
the turning point in their lives. Every morning
she ran down the three flights when the mailman
came to see if there were any letters. On her way upstairs
she could feel the mysterious occupants of the boarding
house waiting behind their doors to spring out and go
downstairs for their chance at life. She did not know who
might write a letter but Victoria was almost certain to
scrape up a few dollars to help them with the rent.
When the rent was paid, she and Clifford could feel

safe for another week; she felt as if they were holding back some dreadful event with their naked hands.

They knew only too exactly the nature of their fear. If they left Des Moines there would be nothing for them except to stay with Clifford's old father at Boone, Iowa. His income was tiny enough but there were times when Nancy almost wished Cliff had managed to get into "the war to end wars"; being a war vet seemed the only way to secure anyone a decent old age.

Paw Radford had fought in the Civil War, and although for the last twenty years he had carved the Thanksgiving turkey with the pious remark, "Well, guess this is the last bird I'll carve on earth," he was still going strong. Now nearly ninety, he used his little one hundred dollars a month as a rod over his middle-aged sons. He had tyrannized over them in their youth; he tyrannized even more now, loquacious with advice as to how he had weathered through the depressions of 1873, '83, and so on.

The couple dreaded to put themselves into his well-meant clutches but at least the children would have a big yard to play in, they could eat without wondering where the next meal was coming from, and Clifford would be free to be on his own, making his way in little towns through the state where there was a better sale for his shaving-cream special than in the bigger cities. He had to congratulate himself on a naturally fine skin that showed off well as an advertisement for his product and he even had a joke with Nancy about it, to the effect that it was because he had never touched a drop of liquor.

Practically everything that Clifford had once considered a rock of ages had been chiseled away. When he first met Nancy he had been a church member, believed dancing and card-playing were of the devil, gave one-tenth of everything he made to the church. While he had never regretted what he had given to God, still he could plainly see that he had not been repaid tenfold as the Rev. Kremer used to insist on those Sunday mornings when he shook the little boxes labeled "Help Our Missions" under everyone's nose. Clifford occasionally wondered how the heathen Chinese had made out with the money that had been sent them, and certain it is that they had had to get along without his help for some time. He had broken down first when he had to help his family, then he had come to the rescue of Nancy's family, and finally, when it came to boosting himself, it was 1929 and his chance seemed over.

It was then that he had finally listened to Nancy who for years had been prevailing on him to go out West. She had made a trip there as a child and from her reports one would think that the climate was free. When they finally made the break, expecting help from her Uncle David, it was too late. David Trexler was on his last legs and was soon to die.

Clifford Radford remembered with a curious bitter pang, as if another door had slammed in his face, the Christmas eve they had walked in the rain to the Trexler home at Roseland, Oregon. The little family had only arrived from the middlewest two days before and Nancy had waited for all their trunks so they might dress in their best clothes. Uncle David had written them months before that the West always had room for more, but that had been before several crashes bumped the market ever lower. The two children had run over the big lawn at Uncle David's place like little goats, to look at the brilliant display, all electrically lighted, that was to give David Trexler first prize for the best-decorated home on his last Christmas.

A real honest-to-goodness manger, with a Child and Mother and somewhat decrepit Joseph, stood near trees dazzling with little stars. Two sheep, life-sized, and a lamb grazed tranquilly in brilliant pinpoints of light on the lawn nearby. It was an impressive outlay, and Clifford, seeing the sheep, the Child, the Parents, defying the weather, felt a quick rush of confident happiness, as if the Star of Bethlehem were shining upon his neglected fortunes. Uncle David, miracle maker, would help him, but when they were escorted into the big room, Uncle David was already sick and haggard, himself forsaken.

Staring out the window at his little show, he had turned his head to greet them absentmindedly, shuffling his shaking hands into his pockets. His mustache looked weedy as if he had been chewing it in his sleep, he hardly noticed the two little boys who gaped at the big room, the rugs, the chandeliers with bright drops and plates piled with expensive fruits. They had just begun to veer from the weather as a subject when the lights went out and, while electricians ran around, Uncle David had fumed nervously, repeating over and over, "If I was myself I could fix those blamed lights in a jiffy," speaking in the lost voice of someone who mourns a strong man, now no more.

Later, Clifford took the remark as a sort of omen, and he, like Nancy, chose to believe that if her uncle had lived he would have helped them get on their feet. As it was, Uncle David's life simply petered out a few months later; he was borne magnificently along a floral display arched like a rainbow on each side of the path from the street to the grave. An oration was said over him, columns of the paper were devoted to him, but Clifford and Nancy could not find any of David Trexler's influential friends who were able to help them. It was "when spring comes" or "don't think of leaving, something will turn up," until the insurance money was almost exhausted and acquaintances pretended to look in store windows when they passed. They had stored their goods and had gone to Portland, from Portland to Chehalis, from Chehalis to Seattle, from Seattle to Spokane, and in Spokane the event they dreaded, as they dreaded going back to Paw Radford's now, loomed finally and irrevocably upon them. The middlewest with its flat gray face was the only possible friend.

They would go home. Home was the last place they wanted to be but home they would go. Home where Clifford had worked for years, where lodge brothers knew him, where relatives of Clifford's still held jobs, where

Paw had a pension. Sometimes in the night, they woke now, both of them suddenly, hearing rain coming down on the roof with a soft patter. Nancy would sigh, "Oh, I had such a nice dream. I thought we were in Seattle and had gone to Cowan park on a picnic."

Clifford did not tell his dreams. They were confused and from them he woke violently, wondering if it were night or early morning, what city he was in, if he had missed an appointment that might mean a job at last. He would try to pray, concentrating in the dark, folding his hands as he used to when a boy. The image of the old church, with the green carpet bought from the receipts of many icecream socials and chicken suppers, the stained-glass windows—to Brother Small and Brother and Sister Edgelow and Sister Means—with their bright blue and green and yellow lilies and angels and open Bibles and clasped hands, soothed him. He could almost hear the Doxology and was again that young man in his best black Sunday suit marching up the aisle with three other upright young men. They would pass the collection boxes, they would again assemble at the altar for the blessing. The happy assured brisk life of those days soothed him in his bed; for a little he felt steadied again as he had in the days when his job was certain and nothing except lack of ambition could hold him from a successful life.

In the night he would sometimes hear the two little boys hoarsely breathing and, before Nancy heard them, would leap out of bed to hurry to their side, feeling their heads for fever. If they were moist and had only tossed or been too closely covered, he stood in his oldfashioned nightshirt looking down at them, grateful for their lives, his insides hardening as if he had swallowed steel. He would stand in his bare feet, shaking with more than cold, gripping his hands, seeing again the children they had met in their wanderings who were running half wild, turning to little savages as if pursued by a plague.

If he could not protect his children now, his life was indeed worthless, and when such thoughts came, he swore softly, as if making a vow, as if he had held up his hand and taken an oath on the holy book.

His old father had urged his son to "come on back home" with the optimistic conviction that, where he was known, something was bound to turn up. The entire Radford clan had scurried around trying to dig up some piddling job for him. When he picked up the papers, the glittering efforts of the government seemed destined to help everyone except men like himself. In Oregon and Washington he had been shuffled from one spot to another. Relatives in Roseland had been anxious to get rid of Clifford and Nancy and their children. They had talked glowingly of the better opportunities further North, and only Aunt Ella, Uncle David Trexler's wife, through fierce loyalty to the state her husband had helped build, urged that they stay in Roseland and see it through.

"Seeing it through" was one thing, but eating was another. The long lines at employment offices, the blind ads that led finally to tempting proposals to sell stockings, razor blades, soap and toilet lotions, sparkplugs and electric gadgets, always turned out to be chiseling efforts to dig off another little piece of his flesh. The Ranol outfits, the Queen stocking line, the Brisk and Ready blades all had proved investments rather than jobs. The little shiny outfits, put up in cheap suitcases of leather, the folders lined with fake silk, all cost money, and the would-be peddler found that, before he started his rounds, he had stripped his pockets of his last bit of capital.

Even then, he must take a chance. Clifford had plunged up to two dollars, three dollars, two seventy-five in one line after another and sometimes, after days of pounding the pavement, managed to clear expenses and a dollar or so. In the case of the sparkplug, he had actually been tipped off to a good market in the Transfer Company in Portland where he was once employed on one of those brief temporary jobs; for a few months he had gone to work early, stayed late in order to make good. Nancy decided to send for their furniture in Roseland; they had rented a house. "God's gift to the antiques," she called it

in letters to her sisters, but who cared if you had practically to get a ladder to crawl into the bathtub, if the
toilet must be handled with care. It was a real house
with two apple trees and a rose vine. At night, with the
children asleep, they took turns at their one recreation, walking. Nancy would come back, her eyes shining.

"Oh, I just love a city like this. I stood on the hill
and looked at all the lights. This is better than Roseland
where you couldn't take a walk without breaking a leg
in a ditch." They had begun to plan on the day when
they could buy a few clothes and make some friends
when the son-in-law of the owner of the company decided
to save money and handle Clifford's job himself.

After he was fired, he kept in touch with the men in the
Transfer Company. Now and then he had a coca-cola
with one of the drivers who told him how to sell his
line to other fellows. He began to sell them sparkplugs
and then the driver demanded his divvy. It had been a
blow and in the end the sparkplug was no good and his
feeble earnings never paid for the price of the outfit.
He had been almost glad to turn his face toward the middlewest. If the retreads had blown out in the desert, it
was at least in the past now and only came to haunt him
in his dreams.

Sometimes as he walked from door to door he would
pass a little park and sit down to rest. His hands would
spasmodically reach for his vest pocket. He would find
himself checking up on his prospects, figuring how long
this could go on, what to expect next. On other benches
figures of men sitting stupefied goaded him off the bench.
He would not become one of them, to get groggy with
failure. Once he sat next to an old man who was reading a little New Testament; he had looked idly over his
shoulder to see the chapter. Without being able to make
out the text, he recalled his youth when for months at
a time he was tortured by thoughts that he had committed
the Unforgivable Sin.

He remembered the nightmare of waking at dawn with

thoughts of Judgment Day. He and several other boys had discussed the nature of the crime. Fatty Winslow said it meant playing with yourself. Clarence Gates said it meant having ideas about teacher and Walter Chase, who afterwards got thrown off a train when he tried to hook a ride, said it meant denying your God. They said, "How d'ya come to think that, Walt," and Fatty said, nuts, but in the end Walt talked them around. They began to think that denying your God was the most unforgivable sin because you could do it without knowing it. It could happen, it could steal up on you, life a thief, robbing you of eternal life.

Clifford Radford had seriously worried in those days about the unforgivable sin for which there was no re-demption. He kept himself pure and paid his tenth to the church and did unto his neighbor as he would like his neighbor to do unto him. He tried literally to be his brother's keeper. Not that he went out of his way grab-bing buttonholes and asking fellows to give their lives to Christ, but he helped when anyone asked him. He was bled white by his family. His church was using him up fast when he married Nancy and her ideas began clashing with his own. Card-playing was no sin, dancing was a pleasure. He wasn't going to be an old stick-in-the-mud, was he?

The church itself gradually relented. Confusion some-times added to his miseries. Wrong in one decade became right in the next. The stern face of God changed to a smiling Father; the theatre, no longer a spot to be washed off with the blood of the Lamb. He was troubled and not altogether assured by the transformation but he wanted to rise in his business. He did not want to stay a book-keeper; he wanted to be a salesman, one of those brisk, busy, dynamic men who put things over and helped keep affairs in the world tingling. He even began to take up Sunday golf. He might have got a leg up in the sales-men's world if the crash had not put a stop to dream-ing.

In the morning when he bustled out into the raw air,

he began to look forward to crossing paths with several men like himself who took the same route. "Well, what luck," they would begin, and the sight of one another would be bracing. Once in Oregon he had met a man who was something to remember. It was the week he went on road relief. For weeks he had waited for the chance as if it were a coveted prize. Finally, he had set out, with two sweaters, a pair of rubbers, an old raincoat he used to wear when cleaning the furnace. Working on the icy road, they could see the long low red buildings of the penitentiary. At noon they heard the whistle and, sitting on the damp ground against a car, the fellows cracked about wishing they were those guys behind the bars who had nothing to worry about and plenty of grub to eat. If it hadn't been for the architect, he would have felt like crawling into a hole. But the fellow knew everything. All that week he had pumped his ideas into Clifford. To Clifford his notions would have sounded nutty in former days; now he listened with respect.

Clifford had come home and stood like a draggled wet dog on the porch, looking at his filthy feet. Nancy opened the door, tried to be funny as she called out, "You look like a drowned rat," and then her face had lighted as he had marched in grinning.

"Say, we got college men on that team," he said. "Fellow there who was an architect in Chicago." She had brought a hot bowl of soup for him, got him warm socks, even warmed his nightshirt before he crawled into bed. But when the lights were out and they were lying in the dark, it was all he could do to keep from sobbing like a child. He felt somehow humiliated, as if he could never lift his head again. He started shaking as if he had chills, and tried to stop it, gritting his teeth. He knew Nancy was awake, he could feel her sudden stiffened awareness, just as clearly as if he had seen her eyes staring wide open into the dark. He wanted to touch her, she wanted to touch him, to put her arms around him, to console him, but neither dared. They felt that one touch would break down the dam, that they would crumble and collapse and in the ruins would be forever lost. They lay each alone, apart, trying not to think of this disaster for the sake of the boys, for the sake of themselves and the dignity they hoped to regain in life.

Morning came at last. Nancy borrowed a pair of hip-boots from a neighbor. He put them on, joking about them, and went forth again.

In the back of Clifford's mind was one last resort, even beyond the necessity of going to Paw Radford's. He had a ranch. He had a piece of land north of Pierre, South Dakota, left over from the days when he first fell in love with Nancy and had been impelled to "invest." Land was to be had cheap then. It was all good land, home-steaded painfully by schoolteachers, clerks, and broken-down little businessmen who took a last chance on the prairies. They had stuck it out in sodhouses and most of them finally sold to the landsharks for small sums. Clifford had never had much luck with his investment that lay, like a disgorged hunk of earth, out of the path of richer farms. He had rented it for sums small enough to pay taxes; when prices had gone leaping during the War, he had actually cleared a little something. The grass had been ripped off, it was no longer grazing but good deep soil, they said, fine corn land, fine hog land, and he had kept it in reserve in his mind until his old age, when he would sell it for a fat sum, and he and his little family could take a trip to the East, see New York City, and maybe go to California.

He did not know what blight could have spoiled this dream but he knew that mysteriously prices dropped, crops failed, land became a pain not a profit. He had tried to sell. No one wanted to buy. When he had driven East with his little family, Nancy had especially asked to route the car through the Black Hills. She wanted to see Deadwood where her Uncle Joe had lived in the days of the gold rush. But Clifford had wanted to take a look at his Land.

Nancy had pointed out the Homestake Mine to the boys, telling them how rich they all might have been if

only poor Uncle Joe had dug there instead of in the
Escondida a few miles further away. The boys had stared
obediently but were more impressed with the bad lands
that were tinted like bright ore, were scarred and dented
and bleak as a desert, with not a soul in sight, with no
birds except vultures in the midday sky and small piping
dull birds in the brambles at dusk.

The land further east had not looked much better to
Nancy. She had shuddered, saying, "Let's get out of this,
there aren't any trees," and it was all Clifford could do
to get her to stop at his place. The tarpaper shack was
not imposing, the buildings were gray as a wasp's paper
nest. An oldish man in a ragged sweater treated Clifford
as if he were a city dude. Last year when he had a part
crop, corn was selling next to nothing, you might as well
throw a match in the wheat. This year the grasshoppers
got the crop but prices were a little better. He didn't
know how he was going to pay back his seed and feed
loans. He didn't know how he could afford to pay any
rent. He figured he'd be moving.

He stood with his face like a slab, chewing tobacco,
his tiny gray eyes never budging from Clifford's face. He
looked at Clifford as if he was someway responsible for
his failure. Clifford had been appalled at the shiftlessness, at the kids with molasses on their faces who poked
their heads out of the door like little gophers. In the dim
kitchen he could make out the shapeless form of a woman
in an old dress with an uneven hem, who kept edging
nearer the door only to dart away when anyone looked
toward her. A smell of burning fat came unpleasantly.
Nancy had tried to hide her feelings, had even scolded
as they drove away over bumpy roads, "Whatever makes
them keep so many dogs? Did you see? Why, the place
was overrun with them, and they can't feed their children."

"They weren't feeding the dogs, by the looks of them,"
Cliff had said. They had not wanted to discuss the family
that somehow seemed to threaten their existence, to haunt
them as a warning. The old colored cards Clifford used

to get in Sunday School, showing the dreadful perils of the Drunkard's Home, did not have the fascinating Ominousness of the remembrance of the farm home, with the children peering out the door and the man with the bristles on his face swallowing his Adam's apple and barely opening his mouth to say finally, "We figger we better be gitting."

Clifford thought of him oftener than he would dare admit. Sometimes when he met one of his fellow canvassers and they stopped to chew the fat, assuming for a second a briskness neither felt, cold chills ran up and down his spine as he detected a look in the other man's eye, a suggestion around the mouth that suddenly reminded him of that gray face, staring at him grimly, and he could hear again, plaintively, as if it were his own conscience, as if it were the voice that he used to dread accusing him of the Unforgivable Sin, "We figger we better be gitting."

It was then that he wished, many a day, that he was a smoking man and he looked with envy at the other man, perhaps cherishing a precious cigarette, burning it clear down to the last ash and sometimes standing, meditatively, holding the last ash in his hand, feeling it absent-mindedly in his fingers, laughing a little as he tossed it out on the dead grass as if he had hopes it would seed itself and grow some kind of a crop for him.

Clifford would look at the fellow, his own fingers moving as if to crunch the butt of a cigarette, and there were days when he actually looked in the windows of bars, at the men standing in groups together, and he caught himself guiltily wishing that he could drop in and rest his feet.

GOLD IS MUSIC

ED THOMPSON was stunned by his own success. He hardly heard a word of his wife's speech as he rehearsed his own argument that had won for him a place in the new organization. The memory of his voice startled him with its persuasiveness, its logic, and he thought a little contemptuously even of Marvin, who had gravely inclined his impressive head at the evidence assembled.

He put his paper down as his wife playfully stepped on his toe, and looked at her with a bland and shining face. "What's pleasing you so much?" she said. "You haven't heard a word I said. I was trying to tell you that Father is angrier than I've ever seen him at Jonathan. He thinks it was a deliberate insult for Jonathan to bring up the well after what had gone on here. It's only flaunting him, he thinks. I don't believe that. Jonathan hasn't any malice and after all Papa did promise them the well. What do you think?"

Ed looked at her indulgently. Margaret Thompson was a handsome woman and, once automobiles started selling again, stocks would go up. They could get a really good car and she could have all the clothes she liked. He did not want her to be a plush horse; his mother was still his ideal. He wanted quiet and the kind of luxury that you read about, not the showy ostentatious stuff of the get-rich-quick crowd that had infested Detroit since the days of the industry. "You look pretty nice," he said.

"In this old dress? Poof, if I could ever have a decent rag again," she said.

"We'll get you some clothes soon."

"With Rhino stock backed off the map? I don't see how."

"The industry will pick up. It's bound to. I was telling them today; the used car market is about exhausted.

It's time for a pickup. We are beginning to tighten up the organization to get ready for it. I'll tell you now I've been pretty nervous about it. Glen got the gate day before yesterday. I didn't want to tell you but I will now."

"Then all your brothers are out except you. And your father is out. How does it happen they keep you?" She looked at him suspiciously, her features sharpening, and he drew his feet back from contact with her skirts.

"Your boy is a smart boy," he said, trying to look pleasant but unaccountably irritated.

"Wait a minute," she said. "Don't begin hiding behind your paper again. Tell me what you think about Father getting so mad at Jonathan."

"What's the use? Your father knows his business, I suppose. Jonathan is a fool to talk so much if he wants money." He thought of his own canny maneuvers that had secured him a firm place in the organization at the very moment when he was popularly supposed to be on the way out. The speech he had made was a composite of gleanings from Jonathan's informative conversation, data from the R.O.T.C., wide reading on the world economic situation, and inside dope from Glen, whose connection with Liberty Laboratories at Cadillac had proved invaluable. He also gave full credit to his public-speaking class. His delivery that afternoon had been a model of restraint and force, spoken with emphasis and no wavering. The sum-total had silenced the babble in the long room which the eccentric taste of a former president had endowed with the mixed character of a highclass club and the parlor of a tony callhouse.

"Strikes, imminent labor trouble" had an ominous sound. Markham had at first smiled contemptuously, as if hearing "wolf, wolf" too often. Ed had not taken his eyes from his face thereafter, but had stared him down, needling him with evidence and fear. So far, their plant had appeared foolproof. Benton had always had the advantage of being a non-union town. The men had worked at the same job or the same plant for years. A nice family had grown up. They had a clubroom, pool tables, and lectures, free. Unfortunately, the depression had chiseled away at goodwill, as well as at profit. The necessary wage-cuts, the tightening up all along the line, the superior methods of production that in the end would reap benefits, had for the moment antagonized the men. They did not fully realize that the interests of employer and employee were one; that the suffering was general. You couldn't expect too much of an ordinary workman. Actually, fellows were trying to organize their own plant right now.

Marvin had knocked on the table. "Facts, Thompson. Proof. Naturally, a few bellyachers are always on the job. But how serious is this? The unions have tried to do the job before. They failed and every strike they tried to pull in autos has proved you can't organize the auto-workers. They aren't craftsmen, they are strictly production men. We don't need to know one cog from another. With the woods so full of unemployed, we can always get new men."

Ed could feel dismissal like icewater creep along his spine. Dismissal wasn't a word; it was a state, a nervous tremor beginning nowhere, ending everywhere. The Thompson clan had been scheduled to go. His father, of the old school, had been too austere for the new jobs. He abandoned his father, his brothers, in his mind. Stick to Ed Thompson, he counseled himself, conscious that his hands were long, tanned, and powerful. He put them conspicuously before him now, holding his notes steadily to show that he was in perfect control of the mechanism of his life. Marvin's eyes had fallen on Ed's hands; his own hands shook occasionally as he tried to light a cigar. He stared fascinated at the able hands as Ed Thompson continued.

"I never make a statement I am not in a position to prove," he said in a carefully modulated voice, controlling the impulse to arrogance with difficulty. He had pressed the buzzer, sent for Mac Tyler and Jim Ferguson. The two fellows slouched in; Ferguson made the better showing but even Mac's halting remarks had weight.

Sure there was trouble. The boys had troublemakers spotted. Talking union stuff. They meant to pull something as soon as pickup began. Not only for wages, but against the speedup and especially to get the union as sole bargaining agent for the men.

Marvin turned slightly purple and the others, with the exception of Reynolds, who leaned forward with an empty smile, tightened in their chairs.

"That stuff has been nipped in the bud in Detroit, in Toledo, in Flint before and will no doubt be nipped again," said Ed as the two men were shown out. "But you gentlemen should be aware that the situation is sharpening under our noses. This last year some serious signs have arisen. When farmers try to lynch officers of the law as they did in LeMars and dozens of other places, the whole setup has begun to melt down. We're like ostriches if we don't see it. We're underestimating everything. The White House, for one thing. Hoover isn't there now. Money is pouring out all the time to oil the palms and build up a machine. Don't forget everybody has a vote. They are all yelling for soup and Roosevelt has to give it to them. The stronger he gets the more he will begin training on us. Why? He'll have to. We tried to put him in our pockets and so far haven't done much. I have a list here of firms, confidential, I may say, who are using their brains faster than we are. The R.O.T.C. gets out stuff to show you how strong the reds are. This information proves that the bigshot industrialists are taking the situation seriously. They aren't just talking. They are organizing secret police squads, laying in guns and gas. I don't mean our normal protection; I mean an added organization trained to break strikes. Moreover, we've got to make contacts with other plants. Competitor is just a word in a case like this. We're all in the same boat. Don't overlook anything, legislative pressure, publicity, constant vigilance is needed."

There had been a long silence. Someone struck a match. Foster spoke up nervously and asked to see the list of companies who were making the purchases referred to. Ed

handed it over gravely. He began again, referring to labor
troubles abroad, in Cuba, in Australia, in England. His
use of world terms held their attention. Marvin even
smiled. "Our little braintruster," he said and caught himself, as if indulging in an indiscretion. His cheeks folded
on each side of the wide mouth, his eyes gleamed as he
retrieved leadership. Clearing his throat, he said Washington would without doubt put over something fast on
business. Its damned Mediation Boards had been helpless
in the face of labor trouble. While they talked it over,
strikers quit work and held up production all over the
country. Thompson was right when he said we had ignored
too much the political angle. It would inevitably take
that form, just as it had in European countries. Business
was going to be up against it in the next years—*perhaps*.
Teddy Roosevelt had swung the big stick but in the end
he proved a friend. This man might change his coat. Don't
take the mob too seriously. Wasn't it Gerard who said the
country was ruled by about sixty men? They weren't
farmers, or politicians either. He sucked in his lips, looked
at Thompson with a flattering smile.

It had ended neatly for Ed Thompson. He thought over
his triumph now, savoring it, enjoying it and almost forgetting, as a convalescent does his pains, the dark days
when he had sweated about his insecurity. He had at once
made a lesson of the men who were known to be union.
They got their slips, turned in their tools, and that was
that. He had, moreover, worked on a method to further
scare any more guys who had union ideas. He wished he
could get hold of Jerry Stauffer to handle the secret police
detail. Jerry's distant relationship, the husband of Victoria
Chance's dead sister, had been embarrassing when the
fellow first asked for a job. He had had him out to the
house where Stauffer's familiarity with the books in their
library had upset him a little, implying as it did, that
Stauffer was a man out of his class. But Stauffer had melted
into his job at the plant and had never bothered them
again. He had become a firstrate trimmer, then he had
disappeared. No one knew what had become of him. If

he had stayed he would be ideal, keeping the setup in the family, as it were.

The other fellows were going to find out it wasn't going to be any fun to be blacklisted. He had sent out the list at once, the word co-operate churning pleasantly in his mind. He wondered if Stauffer had married again. He couldn't remember; a married man is steady and, once the wife gets the idea of the value of buying on the installment plan, you have a situation that makes for reliability that can't be beat. Ford had a good one, hooking them up to his own cars, but Ed had never figured that was strictly necessary. Their market anyhow went to the higher brackets. It was a steady labor market that was now his concern.

He lit a cigar and tried to settle himself, but a vague uneasiness had lodged under his vest. Was he smoking too much, or had she put too much garlic in the lamb? What he needed was diversion. He almost resented his own contentment with home life. It was an actual weakness. Alexander Hamilton had been a ladies' man and even George Washington had been a great wencher. He could remember Rhinegold's advice to one of his vice-presidents who had lost an only son. He had told him to travel, to go to Paris, London, Rome, the Riviera. "Women," Rhinegold had remarked, in words tinged with superior suavity, wisdom that was more desirable than virtue. "Take them for medicine. Don't fall in love. Use them, my boy. A different one every night. Then you'll forget. Go to it." Edgewater had not looked the part. A professorial face, a rather timid body, he had launched bravely on his career. He had come back from abroad with many stories, a few wise leers, and the same empty stare in his eyes. His hand, partly covering his mouth, could express hints of international intrigues; bigshots seen at certain hotels, a mixed assortment of dopes, diddlers, and playboys crossed and recrossed the pattern of his talk with men, in hints and fits and starts. His own fitful mind had been wrenched from its moorings, thenceforth to drift.

Ed did not think of Edgewater as a warning. He knew

his own solid worth, looking at himself in the glass to measure his build, bold eye, roving expression when in a room with women, as against the more timid man who had fallen from grace. The process of contemplating, not a flight of the Edgewater brand, but new excitement, in which nothing detrimental to his home would be involved, soothed him. A man owed it to himself to keep alert, his nerves would be his fortune, they occasionally needed toning, and he should take life as he saw fit.

Thinking of Jonathan Chance raised his self-esteem. There was a man whose worldly ideas on some questions were canceled by a simple-mindedness that was alarming. When had frankness ever won a battle? Did you broadcast to the enemy? He sank back in his favorite chair, listening. His wife was playing the piano, tenderly if not expertly, and he smiled at the idea of buying her a new instrument for her birthday. A new piano. His earlier concern for his life insurance seemed trivial and he thought of himself in the still recent past indulgently, as one thinks of early youth.

He wanted to put his hands on new things, be surrounded with them, to remake his life and do it while there was time. Talks with Spencer Gibbon had first shaken, then excited him. He felt as if he had looked at lantern slides of the viscera of other men, at spotted liver, decaying kidneys, overbright heart. Spencer had a muddled but uncannily receptive head. Like an old wardrobe, it held damned near everything and Ed congratulated himself on having a mind shrewd enough to sort the treasure from the rubbish. Once Ed felt the pulse of the nervous undercurrent of the industry, he could concoct his own remedy that would let him, like the doctor, straight in the front door. A new piano. A new car. New people. Good old world.

In Abraham's Bosom: Washington, D. C., 1932

*H*ow *lovely the lights shine on the water and light old Abe, of Springfield. You going to let us down, Father Abe? We're still here, another batch of men, wearing different skins, different clothes. We never forgot what you said. We're making the same old fight, property versus human rights.*

It hasn't changed much since your day. There are more of us now. We're running into millions fast. We're spilling over from the mountains and the prairies. The sodhouses burst with us, long past, and the mills burst with us today. Walls, you aren't strong enough for this army. We are looking for the new camping ground, we are hunting for our country. You told us, Father Abraham, that this country was dedicated to the proposition that all men are created free and equal. Some babies are puny, some strong, some mothers haven't milk, some too much. Some get a big chance from the drop of the hat, some are shot down the chute and never get finished around the edges. But what you meant was some kind of equal chance to live. Every man knows what that is in his bones. We're still waiting for the amen to that dedication.

Here we are, in Washington, the fair city. Look at us. There must be some hundred of us here. We came here like our forebears went to the great prairies. Like they went with shovels and picks and made the roads and built the bridges. We got nothing in our hands. We got memories for shovels and promises, long overdue, for picks, and the future is on our heels.

You got some follower up in that White House, Father Abraham. The Great Engineer can only say No. He is the Great No-man of the Age. He has iron chains before his door. He has himself hemmed in with dusty lawbooks, ledgers, blueprints of a future that will back us down the hill. He calls it American Initiative. A word. Is there initiative to be found in the chinks of a slammed door?

They needed us in factories so we left the farms. They called for more wheat so we plowed up the prairies. We cut the big trees that they sold. We built the roads they ride upon. Our father's bones enriched the great plains and lie among the foundations of the cities.

We are the forerunners of many men. We don't look like much. No silk hats here. No canes. Eloquence is not our hobby; it is the buried treasure of our hearts. Here we are, at midnight, Father Abraham, at the hour you used to walk the floor at Springfield, pondering the future. We came to this magic city from a dozen cities, ingenious as of old, riding, walking, hitch-hiking our way. Not the lazy-bones they make songs about. We didn't play crap in a back alley or lose our shoes to the ponies. In 1929, when the rich were losing their shirts, we already had no shirts to lose.

We came for an answer. But the Great Engineer is a sphinx with one answer. No. Charity begins at home. Neighbors love one another. Home is a job; where is home? Cattle get fed; what man lets a calf walk a naked road? Charity has bottom; comes to a dead-end. Business washed its hands; No Help Wanted.

Father Abraham, where is the promise? Should life, liberty, and the pursuit of happiness be buried in the safe-deposit vaults. We got hands, we got heads. We know a hundred skills. Are the roads perfect? Have we all got shoes?

Tonight at midnight we have no place to lay ourselves down. No room, shuffle along. There is a big wide space right here at your feet; it's late, we're tired. We can lay ourselves down. We can lie on the stones. When morning comes we shall begin again. We shall keep on asking the question.

II. NOW, NOT TOMORROW

TIMOTHY ROBB was surprised to find that he could clean out his barn without falling down. Dizzy spells unbalanced his hand and through a dim film he saw the broad flanks of his cows waver in the halflight, but he did not relinquish the pitchfork. Sweating under his heavy coat, he stood up and, wiping his forehead, gulped the cold air. The cows righted, the big heavy beams of the barn were as immovable as ever.

With every bite of the good red meat, his strength came back. He hardened himself to eat, sitting alone in the kitchen with the children shut off in the other room where their round staring eyes would not stop his hunger. He would groan as his wife filled his plate, "I can't eat it when they're looking." She had to shoo them away, giving them later the soppings of gravy over pieces of bread and watching their little faces brighten as they sucked the crusts as if they were juicy bones.

The city people had dipped into their pockets. Their contributions would ration Tim for weeks. Their hands had come up with bills; some sent clothing, too, and one woman sent a basket of delicate dresses, barely worn, for the little girl, that made poor Emily Robb burst into tears.

She did not know why she should cry at such a wonderful gift, tiny underslips for a three-year-old, little nightgowns with real lace, dresses with cross-stitch and even bright, different-colored socks and little shoes. Little Grace Robb looked like a changeling dressed in her new finery. The other children stood off from her, shyly, sucking their fingers as she preened herself in her soft pink sweater and pale challis dress.

Tim was not certain he wanted her to dress like that.

His face got red, he burst out with, "It's one thing having
to take money for meat so I can get my strength, but I
ain't aiming for charity." Charity that was dressed up in
such finery, seemed to mock him. He felt soiled by these
well-meant offerings and, after several stormy scenes, Mrs.
Robb put the little clothes away. Even Gracie did not miss
them too much. She liked playing with her brothers and
sisters better than standing aloof like a little goddess.

The little clothes seemed to Timothy like a bribe. He
could not account for his unreasonable anger that smol-
dered while he was at work on his barn, while he was
walking to Arty Sturmer's, while the two men stood talking about the farm-meeting that had been dismally a failure. The farmers around them were a house divided,
they had too thorough a sprinkling of newer farmers
called "foreigners," the land was slipping from under
them, and the city people seemed to be coming in, standing around, waiting for that moment when the farms
would be put up for sale and they could establish themselves in the deserted houses. They would come in with
vans of furniture, with truckloads of plumbing equipment
and bathtubs in green and rose colors. Lawns would grow
where once were fields, fields would turn to weeds, ancient trees would be lopped down, and the departing family, at the last solemn occasion vouchsafed them, the Sale,
would watch Grandma's old chest sold for a song.

Even the chamber pot would be raised on high while
the irrepressible Matthias auctioneered as if he were mowing, moving through kitchen equipment, nutmeg graters,
potato mashers, up to the bedroom sets with the big flow-
ered pitcher and washbowl that had belonged to Great
Aunt Minnie. "Who's bidding, who's bidding, come now,
come get, who wants, who'll get this handsome useful
household article that I would have give five dollars for
many a time in my life," raising high the chamber pot
with the red crocheted silencer on the lid. Everyone tittered, enjoying it, applauding when young Newlywed Mr.
Buckthorn boldly bid "five cents." "She's going, she's
going, she's going, a sound proof, absolutely indispensable

household article, she's going, going, going, gone to Mr. Buckthorn. Here you are, Buck, a bargain, and in the nick of time."

The city people stood around, some shyly, some boldly. A few determined souls uncovered old mirrors, red ware, handmade chests, and rusty ancient rifles that had killed pheasant and rabbit for many a household in their day. In the noise and confusion, the more predatory bid loudly and firmly, and drove off at last with flushed cheeks, their loot bristling from the cars and tied to running boards. The country people stood in their old clothes waiting for a chance to bid on the farm tools, on the cracked dishes, egg beaters, and potato mashers, that had served a lifetime. After a few years, they woke up to the value of Grandpa's armchair. Doubt unhinged the old sales. People spied on one another, snatched bargains from under other people's noses. The city people had gradually altered the ways of the land.

Timothy Robb and Arty Sturmer, though as different as could be, seemed in the same boat. If Robb was not a Grade A farmer, Arty was as good and faithful a man on the land as you could find.

Arty was no newcomer. He could tell about his family in the days of William Penn, when the Greatgranddaddy of his tribe had come from the Palatinate at the urging of the old Quaker. He had immediately applied thrift to the land that for generations seemed to be curried with a comb. Thrift had built fences and barns, raised crops and cattle. Arty had grown up as a child in the house that sheltered his children. The big barn had been an impressive monument in his earliest recollection. The barn was almost a wing of his Mennonite church. It held the store of the Lord himself. Cattle were a sacred obligation. One's children, one's wife served.

Arty Sturmer was not a man who rebelled at service. Long before the Rotarians of the land had made their slogans, Arty Sturmer's people had patiently served their land and their Lord. The bones of Arty's body, thigh bone, leg bone, hip bone, ankle bone, served. Arty's children, by all rights in the world, should have followed in their father's footsteps. It had never occurred to Arty, when as a young man he brought home his bride, that any strange hand might play a part in the destiny of his house.

He had calculated his children long before they entered the world and it had been a matter of guilt that his whim had unshakenly fixed on a slim tiny creature who might not bear him as many children as he wished. His gratification when children came had aroused his belief in his chosen state. The Lord would honor his good works just as the Lord had made his wife fruitful.

The land too had yielded. He had not been one of your loose-mouthed, loose-pocket men to invest thoughtlessly, but when the bank itself suggested that now was the time to take advantage of a loan, Arty had considered it nothing short of a duty to enlarge his operations. Profits were no shame to a man of Arty's thinking. *Increase ye the talents I have given ye.* Arty worked industriously in the vineyard of the Lord and increased. He put up a new silo and bought new machinery, installed a new cement floor in the barn, and built a new spring house. Nothing fancy; that would be a vain show to a man of Arty's persuasion. Hard work and sweat supplied their portion as always. His sons went to their chores naturally; the girls to the kitchen. Each to his appointed place, like a hymn.

It took Arty several years to catch up with events. Then he had dipped too far into the future; the future had betrayed him. He stood, a man betrayed, reading his Bible, then had rushed out as if to inquire of the winds, where are my talents?

Arty was no wooden head. He read the papers, he began to search for the truth, began talking with his neighbors. At first, he had sunk his hope in the Tri-state co-operative that thrust its fingers into Delaware, Maryland, and up into the rich land of Lancaster. He had expected a rebirth but nothing of the kind happened. Milk prices continued to drop.

Co-operate had been a sacred word to Arty. He was a man who had a natural liking for fellow-beings; was it not an injunction of the Lord? He liked to stand around talking about the price of cockerels that chewed up more than they were worth. But the farmers were one thing, it appears, and this Big Man, this Head Man, this King Pin, Bachman, what of him, where did he come in? He rode around in a big car, did no work, sat at a desk, sucked up their good milk, shook their hands, said, "Boys, I'm taking care of you," and all the time he was riding around, shaking hands with the Big City Fellers who ran the milk business, saying, "Boys, leave it to me. I'm taking care of things."

He was taking care, was Mister Bachman, the big Care-taker, who was slipping the profits into his pants until the seams cracked. He was taking care of Number One while the farmers sweated and milked. "You take a farmer," Arty said. "He's got his hands full milking and feeding, sowing and reaping. He's got milk on his mind and feed on his mind and he's dogtired with the feeding and milking and trying to make out what to do with that corner patch and when does the critter go bulling and what will he get out of that sow. He's a singleminded feller, not always too bright. Is the world to belong only to smartalecks?"

Arty's first idea had been to start a real co-operative, true to its name, but things were going too fast. Men were shoved off farms, and one day he found himself at a penny sale, bent on saving the man's farm. Arty caught hold of a new line and forgot his church that turned its back on him. He was out for a fight at last. City boys like Tim Robb never did have a chance, but when the Lord began to play an unaccountable trick upon him, he was going to try to save his neck before he let himself be marked for lost. If his talents were to be sent drifting, they would perish, and he set up his voice like one proph-esying. His farm was slowly, inexorably mortgaged, until every twig, every stone, bore its trace.

Victoria was often lonely at a time when loneliness was a sin to confess. Jonathan seemed the only needed one and he was laboriously going ahead, as if he were eating his way through some vast mountain. Sorting clothes in the attic in the hope of finding something warm for the Robb children, she turned her back on the little trunk where fragments of her mother's wedding dress lay swathed in blue tissue paper and the dress her dead sister Rosamond had worn on the day she graduated from high school waited for some girl, yet unborn, to lift it up and marvel at the tucks and lace. Rosamond might have softly stepped from the stage of the Peavy Grand, where she had said her graduation piece with its fiery youthful remarks about slums and crime, and might have been moving behind trunks, secretly and endlessly packing for a journey Victoria herself must make.

And if she began singing "O dem golden slippers" in the same tone of voice her mother had once used as she sang to her children, she had the sense to stop suddenly, as the tune saddened her, to shake herself angrily and to scold for getting morbid with the world popping to hell around her and so much to be done. If she had been a farm wife taking lazily to her bed in the midst of a good harvest, with the kitchen full of threshers waiting to be fed, she could not have been more ashamed.

She washed the woolen dresses hurriedly, drying and ironing them and carefully cutting little shirts for the Robb boys out of the skirts, sewing with hard tiny stitches and trying not to stop and stare ahead. If she felt tears, she was furious, winking hard, wondering angrily if all her life she would be nailed to that cross. Must she be always looking, thinking, now he would be five, now he would be fifteen, and, when she was old, search crowds for a young man's face? That was no way to live. Suppose women on the early prairies, having babies in sodhouses, had stopped at one small death. Oh, but he had been a perfect little image of a child, with everything except nails and hair, a little bud that seemed in memory to be bound, hands and feet, in perpetual swaddling clothes.

She would get up suddenly, to walk the floor, angry at her sorrow, and with raging looks would whirl upon Jonathan, suddenly entering, fresh and rosy from cold, as if he had committed some unheard-of crime.

"You're getting awfully hard to live with. Whatever's the matter?" he said one day.

"What's the matter? Why, nothing's the matter. Everything's fine. We've got money in the bank, your father loves us and is always writing to ask how we are, I don't have to carry in wood when you forget, and what is best of all, I go where you go all the time."

He looked at her, turning a little pale. "You don't love me anymore," he said quietly. He sat down and began unbuckling his heavy overshoes.

"There you go, I can't make a word of complaint just to let off a little steam without hearing I don't love you. Is that all there is, love? Love makes the world go round. It leaves me sitting here, that's all I know, worried to death about what we're to eat. Maybe I should go to the city and see what I can do. Perhaps I could get a job. You get gas for the car but I'm still puzzled about what to eat."

He said cheerfully, "Something always turns up. When have we ever starved?"

"No, and when have I ever not had to worry?" As soon as the bitter words were said, she could have bit out her tongue. She would lose him, if she kept on like this with her fishwife scolding. She came up softly behind him and, leaning over him, held his head tight against her breast. He pulled her down into his lap. "I'm not good enough for you," he said humbly.

She pulled away from him and laughed. "You? You mean I'm not good enough for you. I see through you. You can't fool me," she said, pushing at him and pretending anger. Then she put her arms around his neck, holding tightly, as if she were a little girl saying good-by. He tried to see her face that was hidden in his neck. She's unhappy, he thought, over and over, as if it were a judgment chalked up against him. He had never had much

confidence in himself as if at some early point in life
he had been ruptured in his belief. Her unhappiness
seemed like a third person, standing in the room, waiting like the Grim Reaper with a scythe to part them. He
held her tightly, unable to bear the thought. His communicated fear tightened her hold upon his neck. They
held to one another, quietly and completely, hardly
breathing.

"Maybe Ted Watson will pay me for the typing today,"
she said softly, as if to convince him that nothing was
wrong that a little money would not heal.

"He'll pay you. Did he finish his play?"

"It's fishy. It stinks. I tried to tell him Jim Barclay
didn't talk like that. He makes him talk like an organ-
grinder."

"Jim went to highschool. And he's an educated man.
Does he think union organizers are wops?"

"I don't know what he thinks, and I don't want to. But
he's got two bathrooms."

They began to laugh, holding to one another and
laughing helplessly as if laughter were magic that might
save them. She ran upstairs for the pennies and nickels
she had been saving in an old cigar box and he went to
town to get a steak, as if they had something to celebrate.
They broiled the steak and got out a bottle of homemade
wine. They even made a fire in the fireplace and Victoria
tied a red ribbon in her hair.

"This wine looks nicer than it tastes," said Jonathan,
holding it up critically to the light.

"It's not the noblest work," said Victoria. "But it's fun
to drink it. The way I feel right now anything would
taste good. I keep looking at you, thinking, that's my
husband."

"And that's my wife," said Jonathan, bowing in imitation of her as if he were introducing her to someone.

"We ought to sing. Everyone sings when they feel good.
Let's sing 'Where's my wandering boy tonight.' " She
looked off meditating and then began alone slowly, "Oh,

where is my boy tonight, tonight." Jonathan joined in as they ended on an exaggerated tremulous note.

"I ought to put a light in the window for you when you're gone," she said. "You're my wandering boy. I know another song. How would you like to hear me sing 'Lead, Kindly Light.' I remember once when I was a little girl I sang that song for my mother and I didn't understand then why tears came to her eyes."

Her voice was clear and young and, looking at her now, he knew exactly how she had looked then. When she stopped, he said, "You'll have me crying, too, if you sing like that."

"Aren't we silly? I liked that song, *from out encircling gloom,* that's the way it seems some time."

"You should never feel like that. How you make me feel!"

"There you go. See, I can never talk. It's always as if I couldn't for fear you'd feel bad."

"But I never do unless you do. I'm happy when I've got you." She looked at him soberly and her eyes turned thoughtfully away from him. "You've got so many other things too," she said. "Not only me. How would you like it," she said, fixing him with a shrewd eye and bending toward him, her cheeks flushing and her face intent as if trying to see someone looking in the window. "How would it seem to you if your only line of communication with the living world was me. Just me. Think how'd you feel, rattling around with only me." She laughed, tapping his hand with her fingers, then taking hold of the wrist and holding it as if feeling for the pulse.

"I'd like it," he said stubbornly, "besides it isn't true. You've got everything I've got."

"You'd like it?" she said. "Don't tell me. A man like you? Why, I can just see you. The times you've gone off to New York, bent on heaven knows what hellish business. The times you've gone off with that souse Benton and disappeared all day. I could fiddle, for all the good it did me to wonder if you were coming home or staying. And what about that woman that came here one summer, sailing down the road every day for the mail like a white bitch poodle, ogling you?"

"Don't," said Jonathan. "Why do you drag up all that old stuff? That's past and done with."

"Why, if I did such things, what would you have done? You'd have kicked me out of the house."

"You're just talking. You could have done anything you liked, you know that."

"I know," she said soberly. "The trouble is, I didn't want to. I really was satisfied just to be here with you."

"But you're not now," he said. "I think you don't love me anymore."

She shook her head, slowly, from side to side. "It's no good if it always comes back to whether I love you or not. I love you, all right. You might as well ask me if I breathe. Or do I want to live without my liver or lights? The trouble is the earth's shaking and we stand here talking about love." She got up, standing erect with her face turned from him. He was afraid she was crying and his own eyes hurt; the words came slow and hard.

"Things may get very serious soon. No one knows what is going to happen. A bunch of farmers out in South Dakota just got arrested. One was Steve Carson—remember that young fellow who made the speech you liked at the conference?" As she turned towards him with a quick bright look, he went on, feeling suddenly cheerful. "And around here it isn't so hot. The mills are giving the men about a day's work a week. The farmers may call a strike. Look at the fool plan to cut down the herds. It only means farmers will be driven off the land, And you got city people trying to get the unemployed back on the soil. Two great streams passing each other. It's all crazy. I guess you should have married a man who could make money to make you happy," he finished.

"You know that's not true. You're trying to make me ashamed."

She had never asked to ride around in a hearse of a car like Jonathan's father. She didn't ask for a lot of money, although it was true you couldn't live on air. She wasn't bent on finding a gold mine or making a fortune like her Uncle Joe whose young boy's face, in the locket her mother had worn, showed wide eyes and a generous mouth. No miser there. He had been led forward, step by step, with his head in the clouds, to the deathtrap of his day, the hope of a great fortune. No one went prospecting anymore or talked hopefully of piling up family heirlooms. Among the younger people, the acid of their day had burned deep. The sun shone equally on all and she thought of Jonathan's father strolling in his box-edged garden looking at the roses his wife had once planted. Of young Steve Carson in jail. Of her sister Nancy tucking her boys in a broken-down bed.

THE BLACK SOIL

I'D BETTER take care of this business," Walt Carson said. "You leave it to me." He checked the list and turned to the wall-phone again, but he could feel her eyes boring into the back of his head. He turned around and looked at the woman sitting numbly with her hands on the table.

"I could take him a pie, maybe. Have they got covers in that jail?" she asked.

"Sure, make a couple of pies," Walt Carson said. He smiled at his wife's brightening face. "You go ahead and bake up some pies, Stella. Let me wrastle with the phone. Too many folks have been taking out their phones is the only trouble. I'll have to drive around some but the other boys are working on this, too, clear up into Minnesota. Lord, this is no disaster. It's no bad wind, whatever way you look at it. We'll get the boy out, don't you fret."

"Murder," Stella said slowly. "It's an awful thing."

"It's none of our murdering. They'll try to pin it on Luke Anderson and our crowd, like Steve. But they won't

get away with it. Everybody knows our boys were picketing the road with nothing to fire with. Our boys ain't
killers. They were fighting for their milk rights and now
the law tries to pickle them. The law," he snorted. "When
did the law ever help us?"

Stella knew the words by heart; they'd been bread on
her table for seventeen years. Law was for the rich. The
workingman never got the fruits of his labor. We got
free institutions but the Interests are gobbling us alive.
The only bogey man little Steve ever heard of was the
Interests. When she first married Walt Carson she had
The Appeal to Reason for breakfast. The tarpaper shack
had been papered with it, and for *God Bless Our Home*
there was "While there is a lower class, I am of it, while
there is a criminal class I am of it, while there is a soul
in prison I am not free."

Granpa Carson's picture was in the parlor and the little faded photograph of Walt Carson's family before the
cyclone was in the album, but the picture on the kitchen
wall hanging over the table, looking down to bless their
food, was of a big skinny man with a dome of a head
and a smile that was better for everyday consumption
than Granpa's grim look. "That's Debs," Walt had said,
and then, the day after they had all gone up to Lincoln
to the speaking, Walt had said, "That's Gene" as if he
had somehow been incorporated into the family just by
being listened to from a crowd. Stella had absorbed *The
Appeal to Reason* with her oatmeal and, after the boy had
gone to school and Walt was at his chores, she had lingered, with the kind of languid dreamy quality a young
bride has, to think about her new life and to let her eyes
run over the wall on which the little mirror and the picture and the motto hung. Before they left that home she
had grown fond of the words; she hated to admit that
she was almost lonesome for the papers on the walls in
their bright, new, gleaming home. Then the War had
come and there had been no more *Appeals*, and no more
papers. Patriots set fire to Walt's barn and he had moved

his little family off angrily, fearful lest some new disaster born of man might once more destroy his home.

The cyclone had wiped out his first family, all but Steve. Walt Carson had been a young man homesteading on the Nebraska prairies, and all five children from his first wife were born in a tarpaper shack. Cows got into the corn and died; lean years had followed lean. In spite of lean, he had read and studied; finally, he went to the Legislature, with hardly a change of underwear to his name. "You can't buy Carson," had been his friends' boast. "He don't want things. Give him linoleum on the floor and he thinks he's got something. Carson's for the people." But Walt Carson, for the people, found himself up against ambitious men, politicians, who knew the ropes, and in the mess of struggling for the people's rights he showed up as a backwoods idealist, dubbed a dreamer, to practical men a slow harmless fool. Men can be bought by other things than money, he found, and when a cyclone lifted his house from its new foundation, banging the timbers down upon the little family, the children bowed near their mother's skirts, he had given up the Legislature as a way to fight. He had come home broken, with only little Steve salvaged from the wreck.

The great slug of a storm had nipped his barn, torn a hole in the corn crib, snatched a limb from the big cottonwood tree, but upon his home it had wreaked its force. He could trace the march of the great beast as if it had dragged its slimy tail in a swishing circular moving path across his land, taunting him with what it did not take, mocking him with its spoils as if it had had a brain to choose and pick and knew how best to hurt him.

He had put up another tarpaper shack, had begun papering it with *Appeals to Reason*. He plowed with his head bowed as if to learn by contemplation of the earth itself. Perhaps his pride had misled him and under the banner of pride gone wrong he had thought to lead the people. The people had not even heard his voice, and among the little town merchants and the bigger town politicians, he had been a hayseed.

He studied at night after little Steve was in bed, pausing at the lonesome banging of the clock, looking around the little room, the stove, the pots, the empty walls, hearing the wind swoop like a pack of wild birds around the corners. She was gone, his helping hand, they were gone, the helpless children, but he must not grow weedy and lush, brooding over the fate that was foreclosed. Steve was alive and he was still a sharp tool to carve the world. Strong men had to crunch the very bones of those they loved; they had to bury their dead and let the earth lie. No digging up of sweet bones here, the earth was full of worms.

He tried to keep the wicks bright but lost the trick, read with a smudged chimney, sighed and burned the oatmeal. Little Steve grew thin, cried at night with whimpers like some little calf. Only teacher at school knew how to make him happy. Teacher gave him an apple out of her box. Teacher showed him how to make a valentine for Papa. Teacher sewed the button on his little shirt and teacher tied up his finger. Teacher, teacher, he sang at night, coloring pictures out of the paper from a box of crayons teacher had miraculously given him.

Walt Carson heard of Teacher for a whole seven months before he had a look at Teacher. Teacher was a tall thin girl with eager beseeching eyes and a blush that went straight up into the roots of her hair and vanished suddenly, leaving her skin pale and fresh and imploring pardon for her blushing. Teacher was a farm girl who had gone to highschool in the city, then to business school to learn shorthand and typewriting, thinking to become some bright city clerk, but something had gone wrong in town. Teacher had come back home. Teacher had taken the little school near home. Teacher teacher.

Teacher was Stella Regan. Teacher had been hard to court, as if she could not quite believe he had come courting. She had been slow to speak but great for listening, tilting her head as if to bring his words sharply to her. Teacher had never heard of social injustice or of the crimes of railroads or how the farmer was the least honored of the nation's toilers. She was hayseed, too, and when he popped the question, standing uncertainly in the Regans' parlor, feeling the roses in the carpet with their great flaming faces, as if they were his own face, gaping up at him, mocking him for daring to ask this girl to live with him and share his broken life, she had burst out crying. He had to take her hands down to look at her poor face all distorted, and it wasn't that night nor the next that he got the reason.

She wrote a letter, spilling out some of it in awkward phrases that left him puzzled and angry. She wasn't ever to marry she was afraid, and something awful had happened that she must tell him if he could forgive her. She'd never blame him if he couldn't but remember him with gratitude forever. It took a week to get the story out of her in little pieces. Some of it came hard, as if she had swallowed glass. He wanted all of it so that no shadow stood between them; he was even glad as if it brought them nearer to each other. Teacher teacher.

As a little girl, Stella Regan had been a gangling child, too tall for her years. "Well, Minnie, I'm afraid you'll have one old maid in the family," her aunt used to sigh in no private fashion to her mother, not naming names, simply sighing with a huge heaving gasp and making large expressive eyes toward little Stella. Or some relative would come after long absence and exclaim, "Mercy, child, when are you going to stop growing?" and she had the feeling she would never stop. At farmer gatherings she was the girl too tall for boys her age, too young and awkward for older boys.

I'm going to be an old maid, she mourned until resentment at her fate grew stubborn. She would be smart if not loved, and she would be loved. At night looking at the stars she wondered if at that moment some boy might be looking, too, the boy who was growing up to love her someday. Love had to be, she could not face her life without it; she would be smart and corner it, she would give herself away, she would lie down in the fields, she would give birth and have children. She would leave

the stupid country and go to cities and be Somebody and
find Someone. Mr. Regan thought it foolish to send her
to highschool and Mrs. Regan scraped the egg and butter
money to its limits for a purse to help her. Even then she
had to go as hired girl.

Mrs. Sharp was smart and homely and Mr. Sharp was
the town's big lawyer and their boy Tom went away to
school in another state as if Nebraska was none too good
for him. No, it hadn't been Tom who did it. No, it wasn't
Mr. Sharp with his toupee and his kindness to her. He
was always trying to make it up to her for Mrs. Sharp's
hard ways and keeping her at it until late at night washing up, so that she couldn't study and fell behind and got
up early at the harsh alarm, the attic floor icy under her
feet, to run down and put the kettle on, shake the furnace, put on coal, get the breakfast, and stack the dishes
in the sink, come home in the afternoon, and scrape the
cold egg off the plates, scrub the vegetables, put on the
meat, set out lard, the flour and the sliced apples, so Mrs.
Sharp could make a pie and hear her later say, "Oh, I've
been baking all day, if I only had a girl could bake."

Then the dishes stacked high, and the ironing to be
sandwiched in, and little Evelyn's dresses to rub out because they shouldn't go in the big wash, and Mrs. Sharp's,
"You're lucky to be in such a nice refined home." And
Mrs. Sharp's club meetings and the ladies reading papers
on "The Life and Times of William Shakespere" and
"The Peril of Alcohol" and "Chinese Art." Then the little trays with the whipped cream cake and the coffee
smelling marvelous and fresh, so that Mr. Sharp came
stealing in the kitchen to beg a cup and laugh with her.
"*We* never get such good coffee, only those old hens."
Her shoes were always too big because they were hand-
me-downs, or too small because Mrs. Sharp gave her old
ones of her own. Her dresses had been worn by someone
else.

But on Sunday she could go to the library and come
out on the steps in the late afternoon. The sky was opal-
colored and her feet in the hand-me-downs were wings;

there was a world outside of this small place, bursting like a bubble. She could not dance, always hugged the wall in corridors in highschool, was happy when it was over. Business school would be the road. The road would be slick and she could skate out of town to Omaha. But now there was no money at all. Pa Regan shut the purse. Ma sickened and almost died. Pa Regan couldn't pay the interest that year and the bank threatened to sheriff him off the land.

Stella stayed on at Mrs. Sharp's and, now that she had finished highschool, she did the washings, too, and hoped to save her $2.00 every week towards business school tuition. In July the heat beat down, the wash was heavy to lug into the yard; the clothes flapped in a high wind, bringing the line down in the dirt. She had to rinse them over. It was nearly lunch time. Mrs. Sharp was upstairs, telephoning the members of the Heart's Ease Club. The brand new aluminum saucepan that cost seven dollars burned a hole clear through, big enough to stick two fingers through. Stella stood looking at it in horror. Then she hid it, like a corpse.

She made lunch with shaking fingers, dreading the moment when Mrs. Sharp's voice would wail that her best pan, her pride and joy, had been ruined. Late in the afternoon she ironed, mopped the floor, got the dinner, and made cherry pie as if to propitiate Mrs. Sharp. She made a tall pitcher of iced lemonade and served the dinner, trembling with fatigue and fear. A cup broke in the kitchen, sending the blood into her temples. She stood strained, her hands wrenched together, hearing Mrs. Sharp's acid voice tell Mr. Sharp that she thought breakages were needless and the only way she knew to teach these stupid girls to be careful was to make them pay for what they broke. Stella felt the cold sweat on the back of her neck, her forehead beaded with it. She began to cry softly, as if her life were being robbed from her. The bright business school with its shiny typewriters, that she knew by heart from studying the picture in the catalogue, dimmed to the remoteness of the South Sea Isles.

Mrs. Sharp would find the pan; she would make her pay for it. She would be chained to debt and her little two dollars would be gobbled up, week by week, for accidents she could not seem to help. There was still washing to be ironed; her eyes ached, her back seemed about to break in two. While the Sharps sat on the front porch, she could wash the dishes and finish up the ironing. She had managed to save eight dollars but her mother had borrowed three dollars on her last visit home. She had spent fifty cents for some dress goods and every night she took it out and looked at it or draped it across her shoulder, looking at herself shyly in the glass.

Two days later Mrs. Sharp found the pan. She was above making scenes, she said coldly. "I paid a lot of money for that pan, Stella," she said in an even voice that was so much worse than shouting. "I know no other way to get you girls to appreciate the value of things except to make you pay for them. I'll have to hold back your wages until the pan is paid for." Then she had swept from the kitchen. Stella looked at the swinging door through which Mrs. Sharp had so lightly vanished as if into thin air. The ladies of the Crescent Club were coming that afternoon. She would have to make sandwiches, pitchers of lemonade, get the dishes out of the way. This was the day for cleaning the guestroom. Her head buzzed. She turned around and around, vaguely, as if she did not know where to begin. Her hands took charge of her; she looked at them scraping away at the dishes, obediently minding Mrs. Sharp. She stopped suddenly, humiliated at her own hands. She lifted her hands from the sudsy water; sobs were bolting up into her throat. Hands, hands, who do you belong to? Her eyes suddenly spouted with tears, frightening her. She looked out at the pretty green lawn where little chairs were placed for the ladies to sit and sew. She was lonesome for her mother. She rinsed her hands, suddenly. It wasn't fair; she wasn't a piece of dirt.

Upstairs she rolled her few clothes into a bundle, stole out the back door and across the corner lot. Good-by, Mr. Sharp, good-by, Tom. They were the only ones who ever talked to her as if she weren't some gangling giant with no feelings. Good-by, good-by. Stumbling, she hurried to the main road leading out to the farm. It was a good ten miles, but she got a lift part of the way.

It was good to sob on Ma's bed, feeling her mother's hands stroking her hair. "There, there," Ma said, choking too. Even Pa hadn't said a word except that maybe she would learn home was best. The Lord knew there was plenty to do around here. But together she and Ma plotted. Stella wasn't to give up her dream. And when Mrs. Sharp drove out to see whatever had happened to Stella, Mrs. Regan had made Stella go into another room. The farm woman sitting up in bed had faced the town woman in her cool summer dress.

"Mrs. Sharp," she said. "Stella wouldn't have burnt your dish if she hadn't too much to do. There was too much at your house. She's only a young girl, Stella's a good girl but she can't stand that. She can't pay for that dish and she ain't agoing to." Mrs. Sharp had been all twittering conciliation. Why, she had never really intended Stella should pay for it. The very idea. She only thought it might teach the girl but she never meant it to be taken seriously. A silvery laugh. Why, Stella must come back. She'd raise her wages, too. And Tom was coming home soon. Stella and Tom got on so well. She liked a girl around who was friendly but had her self-respect. Boys were boys and she always said that so much rested on girls. Mrs. Regan had not opened her mouth. Then she said it was up to Stella but, "If it was me," she said, "I'd never show my face again." Mrs. Sharp had sailed out of the house without seeing Stella.

Stella had gone to town and got a job washing dishes in the Cozy Eat-a-Bite restaurant. She learned to say "All Righty," and to yell orders in the lingo of the restaurant. Ma made her new dresses and she saved a dollar every week. Men looked her up and down, smiling at her blushes. It was nice to be noticed. It was nice to have Charley, the cook, sing out, "Say, watch out, you sure got that travelin' man goin' some." She could hardly be-

lieve that she had it in her power to make a man smitten
with her. She began to hold her shoulders back and her
head up. At night she rubbed lemon peel on her hands
and sat hunched, her shoulders aching, in the little smelly
room next door to the restaurant, counting over her little hoard, figuring that by summer she could go to business school.

The traveling man, Art Chessman, talked to her. He
said he liked to see a girl with ambition and spunk. When
he pulled up in his new model-T before the restaurant,
Stella's heart beat faster. She tried to keep her hands from
trembling when she stood next him, waiting for his expansive order. The other girls made fun of her; told her
she ought to learn how to kid or she'd be taken down the
river. Stella tried to laugh and joke lightly but her eyes
gave her away. Art Chessman smelled of shaving cream
and soap, he wore silk shirts and said pardon me. He
read books and could quote Elbert Hubbard by the yard.
Chessman sold pop; he believed in the soft drink and its
future. America was a dry country of sober folks and
the Anti-Saloon League would play its cards and turn
the land stony sooner or later.

Stella loved to hear him talk about Ideals and Living
Clean and having a home someday with a Nice Bright
Girl. Spring came and they went riding in Art's car. If
her aunt could only see her now. She wouldn't be an old
maid. She'd make something of herself, have a family, sons
and daughters, and love; she'd have love and wait on
someone, wash his shirts and socks, cook his meals, make
his bed, wait on him with her hands and feet. Oh, oh,
the days were wasting in the spring and she was wasting
with so much to give, her hands and feet wasting and
everything in her wanting to belong.

She stopped at that place in her narrative on the night
she tried to tell Walt Carson why she didn't think she
was one to marry. She put her hands over her face and
tears trickled down. . . . How could she ever tell him
how she had felt for so long after, and then when she

broke her arm and had to go back on the farm, the chance to teach the school had come.

They couldn't keep a teacher, the kids were so tough. She had gone to the little one-room school where some of the boys were bigger than she was. The floor was rough with dried mud, the desks dirty and nicked with knives, the blackboards scarred and broken, the walls gray and the windows half blind. She had stood, slight and frail, with big eyes, and her shoulders stooping with the burden of the sling in which her useless left arm hung. The kids had stared at her. She had laughed a little. She felt happy, sure of how to care for them; their defiant looks hadn't fooled her.

"I don't blame you," she said. "They told me you wouldn't mind. With such a looking school, no wonder. I can't whip anyone. See, my arm is broken. But order we're going to have. We're going to learn." They had spent the first day scrubbing the school, the windows, the floors, the desks. Everyone worked, laughing and shouting. Teacher-teacher.

Teacher-teacher forgot her troubles. Day by day, the little school lifted itself out of the mud. They learned songs, they wrote problems on the blackboard. Teacher-teacher forgot she was only a Thing, nothing to keep, nothing to cherish, to have and then to have not. She was teacher-teacher. Walt Carson did not even ask to know.

"Don't tell me, I don't care," he had muttered. She walked on air; it was a dream from which someday she must wake to hear her aunt's voice, "Well, Min, guess you got an old maid in the family." Steve she took as if she had made him. Man and boy, she married both. She even took the little family that was gone, looking at the picture of the luckless woman with her children wiped out forever. Her luck was built on another's bones. It frightened her; she was respectful of it as if she had touched a profound secret. On the dead woman's birthday she never failed to talk to little Steve about his real true Mamma who was gone and who had been so good to him.

Teacher-teacher fixed the house, raised chickens, gave up the business school forever. Teacher-teacher was Walt's pupil, listening with rapt face to him expound what was wrong with the world. Teacher-teacher wanted the kind of world he wanted; where thou goest, I shall go, thy people shall be my people, thy God, my God. When little Steve set traps for the muskrats, she had looked at the little animal's skin, drawn over a shingle, with troubled eyes.

"He never did any wrong," she said. "Seems a pity to kill him." But Walt had laughed her out of her pity. "He's a boy. Let him go. Do him good to hunt and trap. He's not doing it for sport." Little Steve pored over the mimeographed ads stuffed in the mailbox from the Hide and Fur house in Sioux City. "Sixteen million men fighting in Europe Need Shoes. Sell your hides now. Get top prices. Best yet for muskrats, wolf, and fox pelts."

War was in Europe. It came into the house with the ads and Steve went out for pelts, stripping the muskrat skins on shingles, handling them with small expert hands, washing himself briskly before supper and grinning at his father as he counted the change when the check from the fur company came. Not much, a little over a dollar for ten muskrat skins. No big money there. Only a boy could be so content.

The War inched up on them, it burst over Nebraska, it entered homes all around them. A good thing Steve was a little boy. It took neighbors' sons and Walt couldn't keep his mouth shut. He talked against the War and his barn was burned. Walt left his farm; he sold out at a loss and moved out. His farm had become a black blot. He would go to a new place, start all over. He had moved his family and stock to South Dakota in the Bijou Hills not far from the Missouri. The new soil looked deep and black and war silenced him. Men who had talked as he did split in pieces; some men went to jail and some went

up and down the land turning to minutemen and war's
expounders.

Walt hung Gene Debs's picture in plain sight in the
new kitchen. He kept his mouth shut and plowed, waiting for men to come to their senses. The workingman
wouldn't stand it forever; Walt's hopes banked on the
workingman. Farmers plowed up grassland when prices
topped; Walt went loco with the rest and plunged in
land. High prices spun like big goldpieces on a new table.
Stella's baby was twin girls and Steve, the only boy, lorded
over things. Stella talked of how they could educate him
and money was nothing to scorn. Money seemed in the
farmers' cards at last, and man and boy ripped off the
grass and plowed.

The more land they plowed, the harder they worked.
They got new machinery; the topheavy load staggered
them all. In all those years they had never let down;
Steve had gone to school in town, then he had come
home, to tinker with the tractors, never so happy as when
a tractor went wrong. In spite of their sweat, prices hit
bottom, the land frayed out; it dried like a cut apple and
shriveled up and they stared out on crops frizzling. The
grasshoppers came.

Stella thought of the last summer with grasshoppers
jumping into their very mouths, gumming up the radia-
tors of the cars, stripping the foliage of the trees and
vines, like hail. She tried to look back at the years, to
count the good years and the bad, the lean and the fat.
In the lean years when they had nothing to sell, then
you got dollar wheat. When you had a full granary it
went down to thirty cents. You couldn't hold on to wheat,
it might as well be water. You had to store it and the
Big Fellows owned the elevators. You had to get it to
the granary, then there was the banker and the machinery
people all nosing around, holding out their hands. Their
palms were always itching and you had to oil them. They
could clap a sheriff on your back; they could snake your
good tools and your farm away. Men in town got money

for what they sold. Looked like the farmer was the only
jackass, paying for the chance to get up early and work
in the muck.

Stella took food to the picketers. She and Walt sat up
one night with them on the road. Steve was here, he was
there, he was rousing up the clods who would snooze
through a tornado unless lightning struck. "All out, on
the road," he yelled, sending tingling shivers up and down
a man's spine.

Murder was a crime; Homer Morse had been murdered. He was a sniveling selfish cuss who had tried again
and again to bootleg milk past his neighbors. Useless to
come out and stand arguing, "We all got to hang together." He'd agree and the next time find a way to slink
past. But no farmer had killed him. The shot had come
from high up, where no farmer went. The farmers hugged
the road where the trucks passed close. Deputies had
swarmed over the place the second the shot whipped out.
Where had they come from? Had they some secret information from Godalmighty that the shot was going to
puncture that scab's spine?

Steve, Steve, was in Stella's thoughts more than her own
two twin girls, more than the third girl baby. The Lord
must have wanted her to have only girls so that she
would never do Steve a wrong. Steve was the coming
man and she baked pies for him now, holding herself and
her anxiety tight as if to stand ready for any blow.

AMERICAN MAGIC

WHEN her two boys were in bed, Nancy Radford shut the door and went into the other room. Would the day ever come when she could have a whole house to herself again, no matter how old or ramshackle it was? The little cardboard farm the boys had cut out and colored with crayons was scattered over the floor. She picked up the pieces, hung their clothes neatly over the backs of chairs. She was still humming the tune that seemed a part of the children's bedtime. "Hush, my dear, lie still and slumber, heavenly angels guard thy bed." The boys, going on seven and eight, were too big for such songs; she sang it mostly for herself.

The anxiety that had begun when the clock struck seven and Cliff had not yet come home, now kept her near the window looking down at the slippery street where the lights made the freshly fallen snow sparkle. No sense to worry. She would just dash off a few letters, because, say what you pleased, she seemed to suffer as much from social poverty as from the daily pinching of pennies.

There weren't any friends in Des Moines and no way to make new ones with the clothes just hanging on her and nothing but her old coat to cover herself with. They couldn't even go to church in such shape; no one would welcome them in rags and tatters. She sat down to write Victoria who had managed to send five dollars toward the rent. If they could hold off a little longer perhaps something might break. Cliff was talking only yesterday to some insurance fellows who talked big. The trouble was big talk was cheap.

"Hush, my dear, lie still and slumber," she sang softly, hunting vainly for paper and finally drawing the ads from the Modern Grocery Market toward her. The backs were clean and a pencil was better than a pen; she wrote fast: "Thanks thanks for the timely help. Will Durant was here last night to give a talk on Russia but not for his health so we did not get to hear him. Walks are about our only pleasure and we can't always take them together on account of the children. This house is warm, thank heaven, and the kids cheerful. They even talk about going to Gramp's where they would get hotcakes every morning but I pray we won't have to come to that affliction. Paw Radford is real childish and at his time of life deserves his peace. We used to live in an age when groceries could be charged but those days are past. Only hard cash talks and we have had weeks when rice certainly palled on the appetite. Seems to me if the future looked brighter we could all stand it better but I don't see the future, hard as I try." She got that far and put down the pencil.

It was stuffy in the room and one of the boys had pinned up his school exercise with *George Washington was the Father of his Country* written in a round bold hand over and over. When she was little, the four Wendel girls had gone off to Sunday School; little Rosamond had tiny curls and marched ahead of them all. They stood in a row and recited "Our Father who art in heaven." She had launched her life and it was rocking now, a leaky boat. Cliff was at the helm but she feared for him; she stiffened in her chair and started to move as if she must put on her hat and coat and search for him. The papers were full every day of violent deeds; men laid hands on themselves. They lost control of their lives; their lives dissolved in water or fell in blood. She got to her feet, her heart pounding, then sat down again. No sense to such nonsense: families had lived through worse. Worse was being lived through now, in parts of the country harder to bear than this, where it was bitter cold, and under leaky roofs; she was not the worst off. She was beginning another letter to one of the Hard Luck girls, a little group of old friends, whose fortunes had fallen in recent years, even as hers, when Cliff came in.

He came in, standing in a little pool of melting snow with a shining face. "Who do you think I saw today?" he said importantly.

"I'd never guess, oh Cliff, tell me right away. Something nice has happened. I just know." The darkness of a few moments before had vanished as if to teach her once again the sinfulness of foolish fears. Cliff was alive and whole; something had even turned up. "Don't keep me in suspense. Who?" she said.

"Henry Orr," he said briskly, as if he had announced the President of the United States.

"Henry Orr," echoed Nancy in a meaningless voice. She tried to piece together the Henry Orr of the days of the old Methodist church, with his rather fat ineffectual face, and the Henry Orr who had just been announced with a flourish of trumpets.

"Don't tell me you've forgotten Henry. I always said he'd make his mark. He went out West and then he came back here. I thought he had gone to Minneapolis until I saw him walking out of the bank to his car. He's one of the officers, president or something. Anyhow he's got a wonderful home. He drove me out to see it. We're invited to dinner tomorrow."

"I've nothing to wear. Oh Cliff, could I fix up my black, do you think?"

"He talks in thousands, cool thousands. Thinks nothing of taking airplanes to Minneapolis or Chicago. It's cheerful to talk to a man like that in these times. Why, I almost feel alive again." He was laughing at himself, shaking himself as if to get rain off his coat. He went over to the little mirror and looked at his face, turning sideways and patting his still thick hair hopefully.

"Maybe he knows of something," said Nancy, turning from the stove where she was heating up his supper. Could they dare to hope Henry Orr would perform some miracle? Banks were all-powerful, even since the bank holiday last March they compelled the mind with the wonders they could perform.

"I asked him, frankly. I said right out; Henry, do you know of anything? He said he wouldn't be surprised if he could turn something up." He didn't dare to sound as hopeful as he felt. He ate slowly, thinking over his record, rehearsing his faithful record in which he had always worked hard and served his employers' interests loyally without question. He could see himself standing erect, saying, "I only ask a chance to prove what I am worth." He heard the courteous reply as he handed the sheaf of his recommendations across the desk. The man behind the desk would look up with a kindly smile, lay down his fat cigar, and point to the cigar box. "Have one?"

"Thanks, I don't smoke," Clifford would answer, not ostentatiously, but firmly and with a smile to show he had no hard feelings toward one who did, but simply that he did not smoke, had good habits, and knew how to save his money.

"Cliff, do you think we could just go around tonight and you show me the house?"

"Henry's house?" said Cliff airily. "Why not?" He was astounded at his own feeling of daring. Why shouldn't they take the streetcar and just run out to Henry's place. Not go in, just look at it. He wanted her to see it, a big oldfashioned affair with real character, with two iron dogs that Henry thought a lot of in the front yard. Called them Tom and Jerry.

"I don't know how I'll hang together when spring comes and I shed my coat," Nancy said, as she struggled into it. "My clothes are falling apart, the coat is the one whole garment I own." She giggled at her own remark, as if the world were dazzling and full of amusing and delightful episodes. They rarely left the two boys alone, but she simply had to get out tonight, and take a look at Henry's home as if it possessed some refreshing power, like a fountain of youth.

She tiptoed across the hall and asked Mrs. Andrews if she would keep an eye on the place; they'd be back in half an hour or so. Out on the street she and Cliff acted like a young couple. She took his arm and he pulled his hat rakishly over one eye. They ran for the streetcar, and in the car giggled and talked behind their hands to each other about the other passengers. Their mirth cheered the

old man across the aisle who was sagging in his own flesh
with one bleared eye turned biliously outwards; as Cliff
and Nancy persisted in their smiling comments to one
another, he relaxed and pulled himself up from his inert
fat until his face seemed to lean out of his own jaws and
an expression dawned at last behind his vacant eyes.

They got out and tripped down a sidestreet. "There she
is," said Cliff in excitement, pointing, and Nancy looked
at a big rockpile of a house in the midst of a rambling
lawn with naked shrubbery around the bay windows and
thick curtains parted to give a tantalizing glimpse of
bright lights and many floor lamps. As they walked closer
they could hear music.

"They've got a radio," said Nancy.

"Pooh," said Cliff, "they probably got half a dozen."
Arm in arm, the couple paraded slowly past, and even
the prospect of trying to patch up her old black silk so
that she would be fit to appear did not darken the outlook. "I just feel our luck is about to turn," said Nancy,
"Oh Cliff." Cliff did not answer, he squeezed her arm
with his own, his mind still racing with his own witty
replies to the big black cigar behind the polished desk.

When they came home, it was hard to go in the stuffy
house. They stood at the front door, looking up at the
sky, as if they were lovers about to part. The sky was
crowded with friendly stars and Nancy remembered how
she had looked up at them the time they drove East
across the country and the retreads blew out in the desert.
The stars had seemed to follow them and taunt them as
if they shared the world's indifference to the little family's
fate. "Is his wife nice?" Nancy asked for the hundredth
time. But she wanted to hear it all over again, to be
warmed by the details of power that might radiate some
healing light.

Their own two rooms looked very tiny when they sat
down to eat the remains of the pie. Nancy let her eyes
rove over the chairs and table. It was too soon to talk of
moving, but when they got a house again, she could send
for their furniture now stored in Oregon. The old chest

was what she missed most. It was practically a crime to
have left the old chest; there had been no help for it.
They had let Aunt Trexler take the chest, and in fact,
the relatives in Roseland had been more solicitous about
the chest than about the Radfords.

It was, "Now, Nancy, be careful of the Old Chest. Why,
it's more than a hundred years old." As if she did not
know that it had come from way back East, had belonged
to the family for generations, and had been her mother's
pride. As oldest daughter she had rated the chest when
Mrs. Wendel died, never expecting not to be able to give
it a proper and durable home. Aunt Trexler had put it
in her own bedroom, with the big bed in which she and
Uncle David Trexler had slept all their married life.
Nancy's heart had chilled at the proprietary pats Aunt
Trexler had given it. She had spoken up timidly saying
that she hoped to send for the chest soon. "Of course, my
dear," Aunt Trexler had said. "And, meanwhile, the chest
has a good home." There had been many times in their
wanderings when she wished her two boys had as good
a home. The chest had always given an air even to the
plainest rooms. Of handsome old walnut, it seemed to
stand for a solid, substantial life that had more back of
it than appeared on the surface. Many a time the collector
could be stalled off by a casual inspection of the chest
with its beautiful handwrought handles. Families with
furniture like that didn't run out on you. They might
fall behind one week, but in the end they paid. The chest
was something to show her boys to remind them that
her mother's family, the Trexlers, had been Somebody,
even if they had come down in the world.

Cliff roused himself from his pleasant dreams. He had
eaten every crumb of his pie and now said again, as if it
were a formula bound to bring him luck, "I always said
that Henry Orr would make his mark."

DOME OF GLASS

AT CHRISTMAS TIME, Jonathan and Victoria sent a card to his father and one to his brother and sister but hardly expected any presents from anyone. They told one another Christmas had no meaning any more and was a sordid commercial day, better forgotten. The little town put up a few pale green and red lights and farmers went to the stores on Christmas Eve in a last hunt for something cheap for the children.

Some of the city people who had helped Tim Robb sent presents in tissue paper and ribbon to Emily Robb and although she didn't want to seem ungrateful she did wish they had sent a little money instead. When would she wear the silk blouse? And as for the bedjacket, a good sensible sweater would have been more to the point.

"Beggars can't be choosers," she said, trying hard to feel properly grateful. Victoria sent off a box of ten-cent-store toys to her sister Nancy's boys but for her sister, Clara Monroe, a card was enough. Of all the tribe, the Monroes were the only ones who would no doubt have turkey and enjoy it.

As for Jonathan and Victoria, on their trip to town the day before Christmas, Sam Bullen came from behind the counter and importantly asked to see them in the back room. They stood among the packing boxes, suddenly anxious, as if bad news had come. Sam's face was solemn as he began to stutter a little in excitement, "S-say, Jonathan, I got a letter from your father with ten dollars to buy a Christmas basket for you folks, but I knew darned well you'd be sore so here's the ten bucks." He drew ten dollars out of his pocket and passed it to Jonathan who took it silently. "He said to send a basket?" said Victoria.

"That's what he said, ten dollars' worth, to put in what you'd like, but I knew you'd want to spend it yourself," Sam said. He laughed to ease the moment and said,

"How about a little snifter?" Jonathan said he needed one, that getting the basket had knocked the wind out of him.

"But you didn't get it," Sam argued, pouring a tiny drink from a bottle hid behind a case of prunes. "Only you got to promise not to tell your old man."

Jonathan promised and Victoria shook hands with Sam gratefully. Once outside the store, Victoria said, "Nice father. Sends a charity basket. Afraid we might squander a little cash. It's bad enough we're broke without spreading it through the town."

"Sam won't tell anyone, he's got more sense than Father," said Jonathan, but he felt depressed as if he had again been led to the woodhouse for a sound thrashing. His life seemed like a ball and chain riveted to him and for a moment he had the conviction that so long as his father was alive he would never get rid of the burden. He felt humiliated again before his wife and was conscious that in her mind she was no doubt contrasting her own parents with his. Everything that he lacked seemed to have been chalked up on a blackboard before his eyes and he wondered at the farmers and their confidence in him. When he was with them, he was another person, and now standing on the curb, he hardly remembered where he had parked the car.

Victoria had tucked her arm in his and was pressing close to him. He hated being put in the position again of having to be pitied and, for a wild second, thought of being alone with a sense of freedom. His past had something humiliating in it; his wife was bound up with it, root and stock; so long as they were together he would never be free. Victoria had had to stand by while his parents had bullied him, years ago, about the house, about their marriage, and that she had witnessed his defeat seemed now to rise up against them both. He had a moment when he felt that he wanted to shake her arm from his own, and the next second the world looked so bleak without her, he said hastily, "Father doubtless didn't mean anything. It's his everlasting way."

"You're too easy," Victoria said, stiffening at once. "I'm tired of finding excuses for him. Even Sam knew it would hurt us."

Her "even Sam" was exactly as if his father and himself were outcasts, completely lacking not only in good sense but good feeling. His eyes blurred with the pain of his separateness and in that second the car swerved dangerously. She put her hand out towards the wheel but he had already righted the car. He muttered something about a cinder in his eye.

They had a tiny roast for Christmas dinner with a parsley collar and afterwards walked up and down, while music from the Hansel and Gretel opera came over the radio, talking about plans and what they could use for money in the near future. They might make furniture out of old wood, like the tables and cupboards Jonathan had made for themselves after designs from the Metropolitan Museum. With all the city people losing their heads over old furniture, they ought to be able to sell the stuff. But there would be no market until next summer. They had to get something from somewhere now. First, Jonathan would have an idea, then Victoria, and all the time the music was flowing like a too-sweet balm into the big room.

"I'm the one to go," she said. "They want you here. Tim Robb told me how much they counted on you." He looked at her sharply. But, no, Robb would not have told her. It was not even certain to happen. He wanted to decide without telling her and, if they wanted to make him a section organizer, he had made up his mind he would join the Party and go into it clear up to his neck. He did not know why he wanted to keep it secret from her, except that everything in his life had somehow been sidetracked by other people. His parents had always stuck their fingers in his pie, and he wanted for once to make a move that was completely his own. He listened to Victoria with his mind all the time running on its own plane, and he heard the music coming from the radio with irritation as if it were trying to drag him away from his purpose.

Victoria had walked away from the window where she had been digging around the roots of her favorite geranium, and he knew by the way she touched the leaves how much she hated to leave her home. She would say nothing, she would get cross the last day and scrub the floor in a fury and accuse him of not helping her, but of her real trouble no word would be spoken. Their real trouble was around them like the air in a jail. She was not speaking but, with a dreamy look, smiled at him. He was afraid there were tears in her eyes and remembered how she had looked planting their first garden, in her bare feet, with her hands in the earth as if they loved the very feel of the soil. What could she do in the city, where could she go?

The skyscrapers and towers toppled musically into the streets over the bodies of tiny people, but it was only Hansel and Gretel, two innocent children in an opera, dropping their white stones in the deep dark forest. Night would come and they would be far from home. The witch's house would glitter temptingly through the trees and their hunger would crunch the gingerbread doors, tear the sugar drops from the shutters.

"Stick out your finger that I may see if it is fat enough to eat, my dear," cooed the witch to Hansel, and the big room with the solid walls that Victoria and Jonathan now sat in had looked fit for a long life the day they first came to the country. They had set out their belongings, made others. Around them, in other homes, men like himself were trying to think of something encouraging to say to their wives. It was not that wellbeing had failed them; had he not run away from a surfeit? It was that at the dark roots of their lives the very ground fell away. What Christmas was it that he had slyly bought a rifle for his father, after his parents had expressly denied him one? The admiration of the entire family had curled around their darling boy as if outwitting Papa were a sign of genius. They had not made the slightest protest when he marched off with it, only cautioned him to be careful, that he might, uninjured, hoodwink and cajole his way to success. In this valley, the simplest, most natural gifts rotted in a kind of oblivion. Men made ingenious homemade contrivances that astonished him, bore trouble with a willingness that was squandered upon a world where cheeseparing was the great virtue, and a pot of gold the great goal. That so many virtues flourished and grew continually amazed him. If there were only some way to wake men from their slumber, but from the deep lack of faith that had made them servants, even of themselves, it was not easy to set them free. His eye had fallen upon Victoria's slipper with the hole in the toe, and he felt shamed that he had not been able to keep her even in shoes; now he was turning her from her very home. As if he did not know that he had fallen into the common pit, he deliberately thought of Tim Robb and Jake Tentman and of their cause for pride.

"Aren't you ever going to smile," she said.

"Why don't you?"

"Don't let's talk about it," she said, lightly kissing him, and a stone rolled off his chest, he began smiling for no good reason, thought joyfully of all that might happen by spring.

Going to New York seemed as crazy as setting out for the North Pole in a rowboat, in this day when practically all their friends were taking cuts or trying to get on relief. Victoria tried to put herself in the mood of her first jobs when she had walked recklessly into offices and had come out with what she went in for. The old moods seemed stupid and as incredible as the stories the aged told about how *they* had managed in their early days. Less than fifteen years had gone by since she had first looked for a job as a young girl; it seemed a lifetime.

In spite of logic, she took the train and wrote Jonathan on the way to be sure to watch out for the cats

and to look in the oven for the rice pudding she had
made.

Her old clothes looked seedy and many months in the
country made her timid and doubtful. Her hands were
smart and able; her head was bright but she could not
even get a job washing dishes. Everyone was talking of
relief and at night people, huddling in doorways, terrified her. She longed for the country, the sound of the
brook under the layer of ice; the hard work of making
fires seemed clean and a delight.

One of her old friends, Esther Whittaker, had started
a little tea room in the corner of an old rooming-house.
People had to eat, was her theory, and the only other
thing they seemed to patronize without failure was the
beauty parlors. She and Vicky had a good laugh over
food and beauty, and in the evening people congregated
and they went to different apartments where everybody
discussed the social revolution loudly. Even frivolous
women like Mary Godey held parties for the benefit of
the Scottsboro boys at which young men and women with
good jobs talked glowingly of "throwing themselves into
the class struggle" as if it were a tropical sea. The New
Deal was tossed about; was its intention to save the big
fellow or the little fellow and, if the big fellow, why
was he squawking? Victoria sat a little apart, feeling tired
and dizzy.

Esther gave her a lecture. "I can see," she said, "that
you haven't changed a bit. You ought to be more tolerant
and not expect so much. These people all mean well."
On the plea that she ought to make a few contacts with
people who might know of jobs, Esther insisted on taking
Vicky with her one night to a banquet. The originators
of the affair, all young men of excellent standing and
financial status, cheered a worker from West Virginia
who was, it was said, a victim of silicosis. "He's a real
worker, can't live long," Esther whispered in the tone of
one announcing the lion of lions.

When he finally rose to speak, the chatter stopped as
if a bell had rung. The room was still except for the

clatter of dishes from an opened door. The big awkward man stood leaning his two hands gently on the table before him. High cheekbones glistened as if already laid bare; the strong hands with long bones bent through the fingers as if the weight from above was slowly crushing them. A strong hopeful voice came first slowly, word by word, as if this occasion was for him a last supper and he was passing on his life to a chosen company.

"I am not agoing to live to see the day," he said simply, "when workers like me will be free men and not have to die to keep themselves alive but that day will be acoming. The day is acoming when men will think of us workers not just the profits they can get out of us. The day is acoming when men won't be asked to give their lives to earn their daily bread. Someday . . ."

Victoria could not hear all the words from her end of the table. The noise from the open door buzzed distractedly. The doomed man stood before the table with flowers. Bright lights were over him. Well-dressed men and women looked up at him as if he stood upon a stage. Victoria could see his lips move without completely hearing. She squeezed her napkin in her hands; then she got up quickly and left the table. In the dressing-room she sat shivering, dabbing at her eyes, and trying not to attract attention. The burst of applause seemed hateful as if it had come from some arena.

She felt completely cut off from the people around her, and the babbling voices of several women who had come in to powder their faces sounded like the remarks heard in the theatre. When Esther Whittaker came in, flushed with the success of the evening, she thought she must find a way to keep from going home with her. She didn't want to hash over the evening and to listen to arguments that suddenly seemed wearisome.

"Don't wait up for me, Esther," she finally said. "I've got a call to make and will be home later."

"You can't go yet. What's the matter with you? You simply have to hear Clement Gregory's speech." The women were finishing their makeup and were now ecstati-

cally clustering around the doorway like little girls to
hear young Gregory, whose father, it was said, had "simply millions." Victoria looked over a black-silk shoulder
tipped by an orange flower. She could see Gregory's face
that was angular and cool, handsome as an advertisement.
Only he was wearing a simple sack suit, and his face had
the intense expression of a believer. He was speaking with
an earnestness as real as the silicosis worker's had been.
And he was calling for a social change. The words came
bravely from one who had reaped the benefits of the world
as it is. A young man with a fierce expression and thick
lenses glared angrily at a nervous woman who began a
spasmodic cough. The poor woman struggled vainly,
smothering herself in a big handkerchief; someone poured
a glass of water for her. A girl in coquettish curls leaned
forward enthusiastically. America, said Clement Gregory,
America. The word emerged again and again, like a bright
hypnotic bead dangled before their fixed eyes, and the
full land, the rolling prairies, the thick forests, and the
little houses dazzled the group as the familiar images
were held up, one by one. "And we must not deceive ourselves with an inverted snobbery. We are not workers.
The majority in this country are the little men who own
homes, small businesses, clerks, the middle class whose
humble aspirations are familiar to us because we share
them and are part of them."

Victoria moved a step forward at the unexpected words.
The silicosis worker was looking at the speaker with a
puzzled expression, but Gregory was sweeping on, calling for a bloodless revolution of the white-collar class to
save the world from the onrush of what had happened in
Germany. Students and intellectuals were urged to join
forces, but with whom? The workers were not mentioned
again, and in fact, the silicosis victim who had said his
piece, now sat like a neglected stage prop with a puzzled
expression on his painfully drawn face. Bloodshed was
not the path, Gregory was patiently saying; the path was
evolution, not revolution. A Labor Party like England's
was the vehicle that would gradually accomplish the new
work of the world by peaceful legislation.

The silicosis victim sat ignored like a poor relative who is lucky if he finds a plate set for him at the foot of the table. A bitter loneliness for Jonathan was as real as a taste in Victoria's mouth. The need to touch something certain and known was as painful as a broken bone. She longed for one of her cats, for the amiable and comfortable Mrs. Gummidge to jump into her lap. She felt Esther touch her and heard her whisper, "Whatever is the matter? Are you sick?" Victoria shook her head violently, said briefly, "Only homesick, I guess," and could not explain that sinking of the heart, as if she were again a child at the Peavy Grand, sitting in awe before the big drop-curtain painted with mermaids and an obscene Neptune, only to have it lift upon a stage that was the same old stage, ill-concealed under clumsy paper icecakes meant to beguile you into thinking Eliza was crossing an honest river.

She heard the sizzle of applause crackle around the table, then catch fire like a chain of matches. Only ten years before, Esther Whittaker had railed bitterly against what she called "the stupid philistine middle class who cripple the world." The others at this table had been like her, up in arms, no doubt, at nothing more than parents who had bad taste in pictures and were shocked at free love. Now they were fondling the rejected ones as if they were a fairy godmother in their midst, perhaps a little feebleminded, but with a heart of gold. Doubtless she had lost the clue to the people who were once her friends and she listened to the talk as if it came from a country whose language she was only partly familiar with. The whole world was chopped up like that, it seemed, and Jonathan's father from his little kingdom sent a goodwill basket that had only pierced their hearts.

Clement Gregory was finishing his speech in a burst of applause. He sat down and she looked at him steadily as he looked at his plate, then, shyly, at his table companions. He was, she concluded, much too good for his convictions. "What I like about Gregory is that he is sincere," someone was saying, and with relief, she heard a male voice chime in with, "My dear lady, sincerity with-

out a program isn't going to make a social revolution.
What's he proposing? Another British Labor Party, without labor, the most bankrupt investment a man could
conceive of? It's nothing but a slightly less tainted Social
Democratic party of Germany. Bound to end doubtless in
the same way unless it is forced further to the left."

"But, Eugene, how can you . . ." and "Now, don't
jump on me, he's sincere, so am I. So what?" and the
room was spluttering, but on the whole "so sincere" triumphed. Victoria tried to remember what she had heard
about Clement Gregory and struggled as if she had known
him personally once long ago, finally resurrected the description someone had told her of Gregory's energy and
time going into his work, his devotion, his complete giving, like a saint. Looking at him, she could well believe
it. Then she remembered a girl in his office talking about
him. She had been deserted by her young man and had
gone to pieces. Gregory had tried to comfort her, had
talked soothingly to her, and had told her how he used
to play Chopin and duets years ago with his little sister. He had given up music for something sterner, his
beliefs, and the girl in talking of him had the glowing
look of a disciple. The memory only made Victoria more
unhappy, as if Gregory were completely fortified and the
silicosis victim had been utterly abandoned. The room
seemed stifling and unbearable. How were human beings
to live in times so troubled, how could they love?

She suddenly wanted only to love; to sit quietly beside Jonathan, to touch him would be something. Jonathan, Jonathan, oh, don't let him stop loving me, she
thought as she got into her wraps, and pushing through
the now milling crowd, made for the door.

The cold street seemed less deserted than the over-
heated room with the polite applauding people. She
began walking and turning into little streets she had not
seen for years. Years ago when she first came to New York

from the West, she had walked these little streets. Every stone and shop window had seemed fascinating as if in a new bewildering land where anything might happen. She was passing Julius's bar now and remembered coming here one night to find Jonathan. Her anger that he had drunk up so much of his salary now seemed petty and a little comical. She even thought of it with a pleasant glow as if it were an impossibly romantic, bohemian past, like the party they had given one Christmas with a big bowl of powerful punch, rounds of ham and platters of chicken, a Santa Claus stuffed with dates sitting on the mantel, and all of them dancing. Jonathan had bought her fancy underwear with deep insets of black lace and she had felt like a chorus girl tossing her legs and having the time of her life. It all seemed crazy and beautiful, as if it had happened in some dream.

She had actually stopped in the street and was staring, as if fascinated, into the bar, and with a swing of her hand had pushed the door open and entered. It was not as crowded as in the old speakeasy days and the faces looked completely strange. Her own face as she perched on a stool and stared into the big mirror looked back at her unfamiliarly, the cheeks too white, the hair in windy locks. She tucked at her hair self-consciously and someone in the mirror stared at her reflection. Their eyes met and, without recognizing the rather tall skinny man who began coming towards her, she tried to search her memory for his name. That funny way of scowling. Feeling his hand on her shoulder, she turned, startled at the thin face so much older. It was Lester Tolman. "Imagine finding you here," they both said at once, and he began babbling as if he could not wait, squeezing her shoulder with his arm, tears suddenly standing in his eyes. "Oh, how glad I am to see you, you don't know how good it seems, I tell you this is the only place to be. Europe is in splinters."

"I never thought to hear you say that. Wait till I tell Jonathan."

"Say, how is he? I wanted to ask but, Jesus Christ, every couple I used to know seems to have split up. The Cochrans. The Baileys. Jess and Dove White. What a world. My, it's good to see you, Vicky. You look solid. And real. And Jonathan, how is the big stiff?"

"I never thought to see the day when I'd hear you rave about America. Last we saw you, you were shaking off the dust for good. Remember?"

"Sure," he grinned, pinching her cheek. "A lot of water has gone under the bridge. Let's see, that was about the time of the crash. My father caved in on that. I've got to make some dough, I don't know how. It is the last thing I feel like doing. I couldn't stay anyhow. One of my friends is in a concentration camp. They might have nabbed me if I'd stayed. I've been trying to find out where you two were. Let's sit down over there. Hey, let me have the same. And what about you, you'd better get off beer. You used to be good at this once."

"Not me. You're thinking of Jonathan. Another beer, no, make it scotch and soda."

They took their drinks and went back to the table and sitting down stared thoughtfully at one another. "Almost five years," said Tolman. "What are you doing? What's Jonathan up to?"

"It's a long story," she said. "You'll see. Come out to see us. Lots of things went wrong, they did with everybody. No money, no jobs, and only lately we've kind of gotten second wind. Especially Jonathan. I'm looking for some kind of a job now."

"But Jonathan—his writing—did he quit? Jesus, Vicky, he had stuff."

"He still has, but it got awfully hard for him to do. He hated his past and he couldn't seem to make friends with the present. You'll see when you talk to him. He's going to be fine, he's working with the farmers in our part of the country. But you, you look thin. Tell me."

He gave a quick look around and hunched forward over the table, then laughed uneasily. "I can't get used to it. I'm back in God's country and still peeking around as if

I expected the police. It gets you. I'll never know if they had their eyes on me or didn't. It comes to the same thing, I suppose. You wake at night and think you hear steps coming up the stairs, you hear the rustle of someone outside your room. You go on the street, stop to look in a window, and a man stops, too. You don't know who he is, you begin to turn gooseflesh, you think he's following you. You cross the street and turn suddenly, ha, there he is, picking his teeth. You turn cold all over, you begin to whistle, you saunter slowly with your hands in your pockets, your heart pounding. Hell, he can't touch you, you're an American, but the next minute you remember the Englishmen they picked up. You know names. Addresses. You whirl at the corner, pretend you are losing your hat, he is gone. You can't believe it and your legs turn to water you're so relieved. You decide to sit down and get your breath. Go to a beerhall, ask for *ein helles,* someone drops into a chair at your table, and you don't dare look up. You don't say anything, and finally when you raise your eyes another fellow is looking at you, miserably, and he mutters a thin *Guten Tag* and you mutter *Guten Tag,* relieved and shamed. He is just a simple fellow, scared as you are. You sit there, side by side, taking little sips. In the restaurant you are safe. But you can't talk. He isn't talking. He isn't wearing the emblem of Work on his lapel and although he carries the *Angriff,* he doesn't read it. He has eyeglasses and every now and then he takes them off and rubs them with a very clean pockethandkerchief. His hands are trembling a little." He swallowed his drink, and leaning over shouted, "the same." Then he looked at Victoria. "Care if I pinch you to see if you are real?"

"When did you get back, oh, I'm glad you are here, really here," she said. "What's going to happen?"

"I don't know. No one knows. They are still shaking their heads and asking how it happened. Listen, in Paris there are a lot now who got out with their skins. They are still wondering how it was that the German workers got so fooled. They keep saying—but they were the most educated working-class in the world, they knew Marx, they understood the ideology. I want to tell you, they can't get it through their heads how it happened. They got caught with their pants down. I'm kind of in a mess myself. My head is buzzing, all I know is that I'm out of hell."

He took her hand and, putting it to his lips, kissed it. *"Küss die Hand, gnädige Frau,* and *Komm gut nach Hause* and *Grüss Gott,* all those are dead, but we're living. *Prosit.*" He tossed off the drink; his eyes had begun to inflame and now she noticed for the first time the gray in his hair. He saw and touched his hair, "Getting gray? We'll all be white-headed soon. But don't let them tell you it isn't a good time to be alive. At least, they've waked up a little over here. Last time I was here you couldn't talk anything but cars or who was sleeping with whom. He drummed lightly on the table.

She said, "What happened to your life of Balzac?"

"Oh, that," he laughed, then turned serious. "I don't know. I still think I have something, but ask me again in six months. I'm just crawling back to life, on my hands and knees. You wouldn't like a boarder out in the country, would you?"

"I might," she said, "and I know Jonathan would. We'll see. The house isn't very big but I think we could manage." He looks sick, she was thinking, he needs a little care. She touched his hand. "Yes," she said. "You call me up and maybe we can fix it. I've got to run along now."

"Don't go, Vicky, don't go," his hand had reached over and grabbed her arm. "Please don't go." She gave him a long steady look. "All right," she said, "one more drink."

But it was very late when she finally got home. She pushed open the door and went over and pulled back the covers on the couch. The light from the street shone on the white spread on Esther's bed in the next room, and she slipped out of her clothes in the chilly room, shivering with the cold and with the memory of Tolman's face and his shuddering way of speaking. Even in bed, she shivered, pulling the covers up over her head to make a little cave as she used to when she was a little girl, but the cave was full of light and sound; the evening with faces dissolving and reappearing was bright in her mind. When the cave grew a little darker, the worker with silicosis stood up with the bones shining through his flesh. She could no longer count sheep as she used to when she was a little girl, put to bed before dark; her mother's voice floating up from downstairs, "Now be good and go to sleep, just count sheep," came from an impossible remote past, sweet and fragrant and innocent beyond belief. She longed to be beside Jonathan, to touch his long sound body, good and real as the earth. One should not pray for love, but to be strong, and she still felt Tolman's fingers grip her arm.

They were standing in a New York street but the Reichstag had gone up in smoke and fire. The heavy glass dome had crashed and the tunnel of fire had shot up to lick the trees, the sky, the stars. Red had tinged the city; loud blows had sounded late at night on quiet doors. They had sounded on the door where he and another American, Linn Swift, were talking to their German friends. The apartment belonged to a Communist doctor whose brother was a member of the Reichstag. They had had modest *Abendsbrot* together, and the Americans, in what now seemed to Tolman a callous triviality, were talking about skiing at Partenkirschen.

As Tolman said the names, Victoria could see the dazzling slopes of snow, the inns, the happy faces of the chosen. The chosen skied, they drank hot mulled wine beside open fires and had *pfanküchen* and *wienerschnitzel,* dishes that Tolman rattled off as if he were remembering childhood toys. He was going over the scene, as if the familiar places, the dishes they ate, the impossible huge statues on Berlin streets of gods and goddesses, the fiery horsemen that were about to leap from buildings, the Brandenburg Tor, and the palace where Frederick the Great had wept when Voltaire went off in a fury without saying goodby, could somehow help him to believe the incredible night. Victoria tried to think of that night as related only to Tolman, part now of his existence from that time forth, but what he had said stayed with her as if with the grip of his fingers it had been bred into her bones.

"They came in," he had said, speaking in whispers, even on the empty street. "What I remember was their boots, shiny leather, and their leather holsters where the guns were, all brand new. Ernst stood with his hands in his pockets facing them. He seemed to know that it was serious but we kept thinking it was some joke. Then they began hitting him; his head bounced like the dummy we used to try the gloves on in the gym. One of them began kicking open doors and spilling the drawers of the desk over the floor. Ernst said, 'You can't do that. Where's your warrant?' But they had one, all right, all in ink. They must have fixed it up ahead of time. The next time Ernst tried to speak they yelled pig at him and hit harder. His head was red on one side and Linn Swift and I kept bawling it was an outrage and we'd fix them and they couldn't get away with it. Linn tried to use the phone but no one answered. They looked everywhere, even behind the portrait of Ernst's father, the old professor. They left it tipped at a crazy angle; I remember staring at it. We'd always thought of the old gent as a true German, one of those sober honest faces, incorruptible, with the stiff high collars and damned German lapels, and now they had left him tipsy on the wall, as if they'd shamed him in some deep revolting way. Ernst stood there, his eyes racing over everything as if he were trying to tell us something. Then she came out, his wife; she'd been sick and was lying down and she came to the door and stood there, all white like Ophelia. I'll never forget her eyes and the way her hand went out and they took Linn and me off, too. We could see the dull light in the sky and toward Moabit heard the crackling. There was a lot of glass in that dome and it sounded like all the test tubes in all the laboratories in Europe when it fell."

Tolman had shuddered; his deep shudder had passed into her arm, and now in bed, alone, she turned hot, then cold, tried to fix her mind on the country and Jonathan. He would be lying stretched out with his feet on her side of the bed. In the morning the light would come in a square of honey on the walls. The thought was no consolation and, when she searched frantically, even the memory of their closeness frightened her. In their closeness they had been alone and the night had been black and threatening around them.

But Jonathan would not be alone; perhaps he had not yet gone to bed, was talking late with Tim Robb and Jake Tentman. James Honeywell would be sitting with his thin face sour and deceiving, hiding his shyness. They would part only late at night and the light from the porch would shine out to the road and Jonathan would fall asleep as in the company of friends. She too tried to draw that company around her, and remembered the night Tim Robb made his first speech at the schoolhouse, and the time the men had come back from keeping the Widow Shlag on her farm, so boisterous she had first thought they were drunk. She held herself very still and heard the noises of the street; someone coughed from an apartment nearby and Esther talked in her sleep, a few brief accusing sounds as if once again she had loved in vain.

He had had a brave face, that man, and the silicosis worker rose up again before her, his martyred bones glowing faintly. He knew how to play the violin, they said, and in her drowsiness she thought she heard music and remembered how she and Jonathan had danced the waltz together, years ago at a country dance, and all the couples had dropped back to see them.

BOY IN THE CELL

UNTIL the day he began bumping up against the world on his own, Steve Carson always thought of his old man as a daydreamer who might have made good if his head had not been in the clouds. Until then he had no idea of following in his father's footsteps. He did not even want to stay on a farm, like a bump on a log, and from the time he was a little tyke he tinkered around machines making a pest of himself. He was after his father to get rid of Rock and Bess and buy a tractor long before neighbors in that part of South Dakota owned one of the machines. When he was twelve years old he could draw the inside of a steam engine and demonstrate a dynamo like an old hand. But once he got a plow all set, he could make as straight a row as any hired man his father ever had.

The Carson hired men had been mostly Wobblies and little Steve got fight and fire along with his first milk. He could pipe up, "There's a strike in Colorado for to set the miners free, from the tyrants and the money-kings and all the powers that be," along with the best of them. The stiffs made a lot of the kid and gave him ideas about the country better than anything he later learned from a geography book. There were so many little brothers and sisters that Steve had to be a man almost from the start and live up to his mother's, "Don't cry, you're Mamma's big boy who never cries." The time a nail ran clean through his foot and the hired man Gus pulled it out, he hadn't whimpered, and he remembered yet his mother's white proud face as she had snatched him up after it was over. Even with all the babies she was always finding time to drop everything to play with the children, suddenly squatting on the floor with them to help build blocks and picking dandelions with them for wine. The gorgeous green and yellow of the field, the blue sky like a shiny platter, was one of the last pictures he had to remember of the family before the cyclone came. Of that fatal day he remembered very little until a long while after.

It was not until he was a young man and in a cell at Yankton, South Dakota, up on a murder charge for shooting a scab on the road that the farmers had picketed, that he let himself sink back into his past and began to piece together that dark day. As a little boy he had not understood why he so often woke screaming in the night and could not bear the bedclothes to rest with' too soft and heavy a pressure on his arm. His mother's voice that had first spoken faintly after the timbers crashed down on the family in the corner of the cellar under the new house, had become whispers, insistent like the tiny steady trickle of a certain kind of rain on a spring day. He wasn't to cry, he remembered, shifting himself, and holding still, his face drawn and the tears soundlessly falling, drying like stains of mud on his cheeks. His little sister had been soft as a rabbit at first, then he had felt her cold stiff cheek with his own numbed hand. The broken bone in his arm had pounded and throbbed like a clock but the ticking in his mother's breast where his head had pressed, gradually stilled. His pain and fright had turned to darkness, and when he saw the light again his father's face was bending over him; he was in a big soft bed in a strange house and he had begun a new existence.

Then his father had put up a tarpaper shack and the two of them had slept together that first long hard winter. After Teacher-teacher came to live with them he didn't wake up screaming anymore. Teacher-teacher didn't like to have him hunt but she was all for having him make something of himself and, from the time he first began to understand, he was planning on getting away and moving around and seeing the world. He didn't want to be stuck on the land that was so bright and luring and took so much.

Little Steve had never gone to a Sunday School, never got a gold star or a colored picture card of the young

Jesus in the Temple. His new mother believed in the power of prayer but Walt Carson had said gently, "Don't give the boy that old bone to break his teeth on. Mankind is good enough for this world, more than we've ever been able to handle." Steve had stood proudly beside his father, only half understanding, but at night when Teacher-teacher had put him to bed, he raised his head to hear the sound of her skirts rustling down the stairs, and lay back suddenly terribly lonely and very much a little boy longing to call after her.

He never told that the time he skinned his first muskrat he himself had been sick all over, like any baby. He had sat back on his heels, contemplating the mess, more astonished than ashamed, as if he had learned his first great lesson, that his body and his head might not always work in tune. It was as if he had faced some secret and subtle enemy against whom he must always be on the alert from that time forth. He skinned more muskrats, facing the job stubbornly, did heavy chores all that winter and lay at night on the grass-green carpet Teacher-teacher had laid, looking into the red eyes of the coal stove, dreaming of riding on the range and conquering cities and becoming somebody that everyone would look up to.

Other boys grew up hearing talk of Granpa did this and Aunt Nellie has bought a new washing-machine and Uncle Hi has put rye into that twenty-acre strip but Steve Carson heard about Gene Debs and our martyred brothers and during the big steel strike he put all his pennies in a little box to send to the strike fund. He had two uncles and an aunt back in Nebraska and an old granpa on his father's side who had been a great Bible man until he read it so much and suffered so much he made up his mind religion was just a blind to lead man into the wilderness.

Walt Carson had taken Steve to see the old man when he was flat on his bed with his leg gangrened from hardening of the arteries, they said. The two uncles and Walt had stood aimlessly in the yard, trying to talk and make sense and the womenfolk had run things inside. Walt Carson had a sister who was a great hymn-singer and, on one of her trips to the yard, one of the uncles called out jokingly, "How's God?" She had whirled suddenly upon them and looked with a tense savage white face full of defiance at the men. Her mouth had opened, then closed, she had shivered, holding her arms together across her belly. Then she had turned and put another clothespin in the washing; they saw it was the frayed underwear of their old father. The right leg had been cut off and dangled helplessly in the wind. The three men hung their heads and she had turned as she started toward the house. "God's dead," she had said, shortly.

Steve and the men had not found a word to say. The windows of the house looked blankly at them. Lem Carson had taken a big chaw of tobacco and had damned lightly under his breath. Pete Carson had opened his mouth, said, "It don't make sense when a man works so hard all his life and suffers so." Only Walt had said, faintly smiling, "Well, so Sis has got off the Hallelujah bandwagon. She ought to make a good fighter for the cause. She's a fiery woman."

Steve heard so much about his class brothers and the day all men would be free and equal that he didn't rightly sense the true meaning of the words anymore than other children brought up religiously could tell you about heaven. He became a fine debater in his highschool years and got his picture in the papers and went around with the debating team to Mitchell and Yankton and even up to Pierre. Teacher-teacher cut out every scrap in the papers about him and began pasting it into a big book and he rehearsed his debate at home, with the door to his bedroom shut, *Resolved that the United States should enter the League of Nations.* Walt said that was a dead enough issue to debate about, but the schools always were a century behind. It was edging up towards the peak of prosperity then with only the farmers scratching their heads and beginning to wonder why they had lagged so far behind.

Mr. Ellery Benton, the editor of the Mitchell paper, came out to dinner and had a long harangue with Walt about the *Congressional Record,* back in May, 1919, when the farmers were plowing to plant corn and were sold down the river by some big shot. "He said, you can read it to this day," Benton said, "that farm prices must be lowered for cheaper food for industrial labor. Said the banks must call in their loans. Then somebody spoke up and said it would ruin the farmer. Farmer be damned, says this fellow. He's getting rich and lazy and soon won't work. The other guy says the move would ruin the little banks. This fellow says, Too damned many banks anyhow. Yes, sir, just the same the move was made and ten thousand banks closed out in the West in the next five years."

The two men had sat talking and Steve edged on his chair listening and not saying a word but he had reached the age when he was credited with the men and belonged with them, not in the kitchen with the girls. That men had the power to manipulate and ruin others fascinated him more than anything his father had ever told him. He couldn't help but feel that some of the songs, like "Come, ye weary toilers, We'll not cease our labors until victory is ours," were as pokey as the hymns his aunt in Nebraska sang. His father was a dreamer too and was always talking about the future in a remote lazy way that seemed at one and the same time to expect everything and nothing.

The old farmhands, the Wobblies, had always talked against the Moneykings and the bloated Capitalists and little Steve had imagined them in his mind's eye like so many monsters of no distinct shape and in fact in his early days the word "capitalist" was not even associated in his mind with the word "man."

Men were like his father and the other farmers who talked against the city fellers and how everything drained out to the cities and the eastern bankers, but later when he got to Vermillion and began to mix around with the town boys they had a chip on their shoulders too and

thought if it weren't for the big industrialists and city
workers always crabbing for higher wages times would
certainly get better. By that day, times had darkened all
over the country.

Walt Carson would have got a good crop in '28 except
the hail got it and in '29 the grasshoppers started as if
they were in cahoots with all the dark forces getting
ready to gobble the human race. There was no crop in '31
and that was the year to sell the cattle but everyone held
on thinking next year would be better. It was about that
time that Steve began to think of his state as the best
next-year country he had ever heard of.

It was always, hold on, times will get better and although times had supposed to be top all through the 1920's
yet he had never heard a single farmer talk during those
years except in terms of the next year's expectations. They
would have had fodder but for a killing frost; corn if
there'd been a little rain. They began to realize the ground
was drying out, and something had gone wrong in a gigantic way. Walt talked all the time about the moisture they
used to get back in 1914 and even up to 1918 when he
got forty tons of alfalfa off 20 acres after pasturing the
hogs on it. The golden age seemed to have gone by, leaving them saddled with a huge debt and land that blinked
at them, hard and unyielding in the hot sun.

In '32, when crops were bumper, oats went to seven
cents and hay brought $2 a ton. A man felt a fool for
sweating in the burning sun, for having given his life
for such a puny mess of pottage. Then the bankers began
hauling in fast, trying to grab the fish before the holes
in the net got too large.

Steve had never spoken his true ambition out loud. He
had no distinct notion where his intention had found its
roots. Perhaps he had taken to heart some of the sage
headshaking that had gone on when he debated in highschool. "He's got a gift of the gab. A real lawyer. Make
a Senator someday, Walt. Better send him to Congress
perhaps he can put a word in for us folks." He had
blushed, turning his head not to show how proud and

certain he felt within himself. Again, he felt that sharp
anger at what he called his weakness; blushing was a
weakness. But riding on his pony toward the Missouri
during high flood he danced her clear to the edge of
the buttes looking down coolly into the boiling water,
yellow and muddy and wild with rage.

Whole sections tore off in the jaws of the river and
floated, bobbing like bloated bodies down on the rough
and jagged stream. He would hold the quivering pony
back, his own body taut and excited. "I'll make it, I'll
do it," he said without any faint idea what he meant to
make or do, only that the fields back from the river were
wonderfully fair and the brazen sky was over a part of
the country that he loved. When the bobolink rose suddenly in the spring, when he rode to town and saw the
farmers come clumping in, timid and yet bold with a
kind of ignored strength and worth, he made speeches
in his mind and wrote fanciful addresses to no one in
particular and when he fell in love with a freshman girl
he was bewildered at the way her image crowded out his
plans.

He gave into love hotly and hung around her boarding house like a sick calf, feeling set up when they walked
out together and wild with importance when his father
kidded him about "having a girl." But when she went
with his roommate to the big dance of the year, he felt
scalded in his heart, and vowed he was through with
women forever. He even went around with the spiked
beer crowd and began talking rough. One night when
the gang went to a cathouse he pretended he had passed
out and sat in the corner of the car slumped down and
miserable. He could see the empty street and the lights
under the shades on the windows; he was lonesome for
the farm and his girl seemed to be behind the shades,
laughing up her sleeve. His father was writing that things
were going from bad to worse. Unless he got a feed loan
the cattle would starve. Steve went back to the farm and
found the place in bewilderment. His father was deeper
in debt than he had imagined, Teacher-teacher was be-

ginning to turn gray, and his young half sisters were bubbling helpless girls. He gave up college. Not for good,
just "until things picked up again," smiling wryly to himself as he slipped into the age-old alibi.

Then the insurance companies began closing the bag.
James Tyson, their next-door neighbor, was scheduled to
go. Tyson's father had broke sod on that land, the son
had been born in a sodhouse. The present house was
of his building; in it he had reared sons and daughters.
He stood around with his hands dangling down as if he
had been hit over the head like a steer. If anyone asked
him a question he answered with a smile and made them
go into the house with him where he pointed proudly to
the acetylene fixtures hanging useless as old cobwebs from
the ceiling. There was the room that was to have been a
bathroom but they never got the plumbing in. After the
children grew bigger, his wife said it didn't matter. It
was when they were small she had counted year after
year on having a real tub to wash them in.

Teacher-teacher went into a crying fury over the business and on the day of the sale a bunch of farmers from
the lord knows where put every stick of furniture back
in the house as fast as the sheriff and his men could haul
it out. It was a comical spectacle and a couple of farmers
doubled up with laughing back of the smokehouse. Nothing could be done about the sale and toward evening anyone passing could see the smoke pouring out the chimney
of the Tysons' kitchen where some of the women had
laid a good fire and had put a first-rate supper on the
stove to cook. "We ain't going off our own land, none of
us," Teacher-teacher had said, using the homely language
of the folks around her in her desire to be close to the
people she trusted.

As for Steve and several other young bloods, the proceedings went to their heads and they wanted to tear
around the country like Paul Reveres. Nothing would do
but they must get themselves down to Sioux City where
the farmers were tieing up the roads until prices boosted.
Tub Johnson's old man said it was all nonsense, no doubt,

and would be blown over and he made Tub take in a
load of hogs that were ripe for the packing house. They
rode in on the truck and the men came walking out in
the road toward them as they neared the stockyards. "Jeez,
they are stopping things, all right," Tub said, putting on
the brake.

So far as Tub and Steve were concerned, there was no
need of any argument and Tub said he had told his old
man the roads were tied up, but his old man wouldn't
believe him.

"Hell, we don't want to go against you boys," he said.
The boys in their blue overalls crowded around the truck
with the big cornfields pressing up to the rubbery
macadam and the corn growing way over their heads. It
was a bright blue night with the sky like indigo and a
full harvest moon. Steve got out and Tub pulled the
truck to the side of the road. They sat down with the
fellows beside their fire. You could hear the pigs grunt
every now and then and the long sing of the last katydids
hanging on until frost time.

An old man kept talking about all he had learned and
how he never would have thought to live to see the day
when farmers would get together. His slow calm voice,
the men bunching around, the night in its waiting stillness and their listening as if for danger, gave Steve the
cold shivers and when they asked if the boys wouldn't
like to ride in the parade the next day Steve pounded
Tub on the back and said he had to do it. They hauled
Tub's hogs over to one of the farms and Tub and Steve
slept in the hay in the barn and had ham and eggs in
the farmhouse with a man named Olson and his big wife
and six kids. Olson kept shoveling eggs into his face and
when he was through he wiped his mouth and said with
a wave of the hand, as if he were mentioning the weather,
"That there corn is as good a place to fire from as to
hide in." His wife had turned sharply and Steve and Tub
had not blinked an eyelash feeling the stern resolution
in the man as if they had suddenly shot up into responsi-
bilities they had never dreamed of a fortnight back.

In the parade Steve and Tub rode with two boys from Jefferson City who talked about the time they had planned to go to Ames College but there wasn't any price for wheat that year so they stayed home. They all craned their necks out of the car to see the length of the line as it wound down Fourth street in front of the Hotel Martin and the Jefferson City boy at the wheel swore you could see the four governors, who were meeting in the hotel trying to solve the conundrum, peeking out from behind the big potted palms. Later on, a big guy went over to the window after the parade had broken up and the farmers were strutting up and down and knocked on the glass.

"Hey, bring out the National Guard," he yelled. "We're here." The rest of the farmers had laughed and it went up and down the street how one of them had made fun of the governors. Newspapers were screaming at them, the Chamber of Commerce met, businessmen went into a huddle, and the farmers enjoyed themselves. For the first time in their lives they had scared the town fellows out of their sneering ways. They guessed they were somebody, not just to be told to go here, to go there.

For the first time in his life, Steve began to make sense of his father's sayings. Some of the boys from the packinghouse had come out to the roads to help picket. His father made a lot of this when Steve got home but Steve told him it wasn't true that the packinghouse boys had been solidly behind them. Some of them had, but the rest had begun to get ugly and make trouble. They'd begun to blame the farmers for shutting down the roads and the packinghouse managers were pretty quick to tell them that if it weren't for the farmers shutting out the stuff they wouldn't have to fire so many of them in what might have been a fine season.

Thinking it over, after he got home, Steve began to feel as if he were making his way over the map of his own mind for the first time. He was amazed at the variety of life and the whole event took the sting out of his father's troubles. Steve could not rightly feel the troubles. He thought he saw who was being sold down the river and he even thought he was beginning to understand why, clearly, as he had understood from the cradle up that when the sun shines it is a good day, when you are hungry, you want bread.

Midsummer Night's Dream: Vineland, New Jersey, 1935

*I*t's raining. Bring them mules in. Don't let no man fall
on them mules. Men, get shovels and dig trenches.
Can't work in the row on a rainy day but keep yourselves busy. No standing around here, you lazy hunks. Get
shovels, keep moving.

The lean long boy sticks in the shovel. In she go, out
she come, in she go, out she come, shubbel, shubbel, keep
movin. Now they're cutting a trench around the mule
sheds. Don't let no water drop on me, boys, I a first rate
mule, got to keep my feet dry. Shubbel, shubbel, keep
movin. There's the dump. Can't set fire to no dump today.
All them good things throwed away. Them peaches ain't
half rotted. We could make us a fine mess out of them
string beans. That there asparagus, yum, yum.

Shubbel, shubbel, keep movin.

Look at that peach. See that tomato. Ain't more than
specked. Market was low, food must go. Shubbel, shubbel,
keep movin. Hey, don't tech that peach, you might eat
the stone. Member the kid who snitched the fruit off the
dump. Thought he was smart, thought he wouldn't have
to heat no old beans in no old tincan that day. Out he
goes. Forward march. Down that road. Don't want no
thieves here. Hands off garbage. Hands off food. Hands
is to work with. Shubbel, shubbel, keep movin.

Too tired to feel the rain. Too tired. Lay yourself down
pore boy 'fore the bugs begin their pickin. 'Fore the mos-
quitoes get to itchin. Lay your bones down. Night's for
you. Sweet dreams for you. The rain leaks through. Tat,
tat, on skin, a warm soft spot, then a cold spot, turning,
twisting, can't get rid of that there spot, it's a burnin. Don't
you light no lamp, pet, the dark is kinder. Member old
man Beaseley that cooked in his hut. Smoked hisself a
cigarette layin on the straw. Went a snorin and straw was
a burnin. Up goes Beaseley in a bright red flame.

Boy, ain't you heard the boys call your name?

Oh, oh, that smell, that man smell burnin. Shubbel, shubbel, dig a big grave.

But not for the boys that's a diggin in the rain.

Boy, don't you hear the boys say it again?

Sleep, sleep, the cradle rocks, soon it's five and you'll have to get up. Beans, peas, asparagus, and cucumbers. The garden spot. The wondermaking garden. Shubbel, shubbel, keep movin.

WOODEN FACE

THE TIDE of city people slowly ebbing into Bucks county brought business. It might be disturbing to an old family selling the family farm of generations to visit it a few months later and to watch lawns spring up, old stones pointed in glistening white, shutters painted deep and suggestively rich blues. In their best Sunday clothes the one-time owners would stand a little off, timid, wondering at the fancy casement that had sprung into the old kitchen wall. The missus would feel pride at her kitchen thus rejuvenated before her eyes. The family would even bring relatives to gape at the miracle of this modern age that in the twinkling of an eye gouged out bathrooms, tapped the earth for sparkling water. The long years when Mamma bathed the babies in an old zinc tub became tortuously unreal when a peek in a window revealed glistening tile and a bath big enough for a family. The outhouse was gone, simply wiped off the face of the earth and as for kerosene lamps, who wanted to bother with dirt and muss any longer?

A fine tingling shame crept over the head of the house as he recalled the long bargaining that had gone on, how he had finally scaled down on the price, assured that this was the chance of a lifetime to get rid of that old hulk, and now with his money already half gone to the old mortgage saw his one-time home a regular palace and the value staggered up to an unbelievable figure, so folks said. "From the way that fellow talked you would have thought he was risking his shirt, and now look at him," his wife would say, flinging out her hand and looking pitifully surprised as if they had auctioned off for a song a dirty piece of land that shortly afterwards turns out to contain an oil gusher.

And although farmers gradually caught on and stubbornly held out for a better price, for some time people like the enterprising Mr. Murdstone did handsome business. Mr. Murdstone was simply a newcomer with a dark sinister face that looked merely handsomely mysterious to the innocent. Mr. Murdstone knew a good thing when he saw it and with a nose for disaster smelled out trouble almost before the family itself was aware. Mr. Murdstone was the inevitable follower of the undertaker and the minister and in the bereaved parlor Mr. Murdstone had a way with widows and widowers that was winning.

He rarely left without the owner's name gratefully inscribed on an airtight, foolproof, dotted line, and the assurance of Mr. Murdstone that he would, at great sacrifice, devote himself to digging up a buyer, even from the bowels of the earth. The option purchased for the nominal fee of fifty dollars ("You can see," smiled Mr. Murdstone revealing the tombstones of his teeth, "that I don't want to put you to any unnecessary expense and therefore am asking just the smallest possible guarantee that you are serious about this business") was hardly in Mr. Murdstone's pocket than he wired the anxious purchaser to hustle himself down to the country and, in a twinkling of an eye, the price as stated in the option rose to Mr. Murdstone's exclusive benefit anywhere from one thousand to fifteen hundred dollars higher. Mr. Murdstone simply would not have considered it worth his while to handle the transaction for chicken feed. With an eye to the future, Mr. Murdstone had cornered a neat section of Bucks county and by slapping a little cheap paint on the optioned homes, raised their value even more. The final price, always in Mr. Murdstone's pocket, was a matter of surprise to the vanishing farm family who, turned out bag and baggage, were obliged to take on, with their burdens, the conviction that the man of the house had been a poor simple fool.

Of course, there were exceptions to this way of doing business. But it must be said that the banks favored Mr. Murdstone whose sharpness appealed to their sense of humor. Mr. Burdick, a mere amateur, on the other hand, was as unwelcome as an early frost. He was apt to drag into the bank in a muddy overcoat trailing a faint aroma of spirits and his fees were mere awards, almost on a par with the bangle the porcelain mills presented to their employees of twenty-five years standing. Mr. Burdick spent too much time in the mud hoisting the rear of his car, changing tires absolutely rotted away, installing parts that were practically defunct. He did not inspire confidence in the bank, and strangely enough, even less confidence in his farmer clients, although he toured the countryside almost for the love of it. Mr. Burdick's efforts to reconcile a skeptical unimaginative city man with a long narrow house reminiscent of a boardinghouse for railway men seen in faroff mountain states, roused even a timid bachelor to consider the possibility of immediately marrying in order to raise progeny to fill the rooms with gay laughter. In his mind's eye, cunningly implanted by the glib Mr. Burdick, he saw big groaning tables, Yule logs blazing in what appeared big drafty lonesome looking fireplaces. As for the front porch that strung so long and forbidding, narrow as a string bean, why, simply rip it off, Mr. City Man, and restore that fine chaste classic appearance so characteristic of a dwelling made completely of stone and several hundred years old into the bargain.

Mr. Murdstone who used the gloomier aspects of the future with such effect on his city customers, painting that day when the bottom having fallen out of things and a man might at least retire to the soil and in his little fortress barricade himself with fruits and vegetables raised on his own land, used with equal effect on the farmer clients the gloomy present that awaited the farmer who was practically wiped out in an economic way with no chance ahead of him. A few thousand in the bank became a giddy dream to a man so impressed and so in debt as to be glad to escape the stone around his neck. Where he went, how he fared, few seldom knew or cared. The city people pouring in created certain small jobs. A man good with the pick and shovel, a man with the skill to do carpentering was simply in for a good thing and what amazed the city people was the apparent reluctance of the local gentry to rush into jobs that Nature was providing.

Time speeded things up in its inevitable way, and city people liked to think that natives who continued to live in such orderly-looking dwellings carrying on their farming or chicken business were really putting something away in the old sock and bettering themselves.

Certain it is that a farmer near the Delaware Valley road drove to Florida every winter, and if another simply sold his cows in despair, that was neither here nor there. There was also Henkle who had bought a combine and was able not only to tend his own fields, but at a price, the fields of his less thrifty neighbors. The factories were more and more settled in their ways, and no one heard of any trouble. When Willy Blaine Jr., the storekeeper's son, got electrocuted in the mills, simply pulled off the mat like a wet postage stamp, the valley rumbled with rebellion. Some men stayed away saying it wasn't worth your life and the mill thought more of saving money than installing proper machinery.

Even the Tesh boy got a word in at last, haranguing in front of Blaine's store to the little group of hangerson who were kept from their crackerboxes by the mourning that required the gas pump be looped up, the shades drawn. "You take it in the neck," he said angrily, "why don't you get together and do something like the farmers." And for the space of a few days a few rebels actually talked darkly of a "strike" but the land was so poor, the winter so hard, the farmers actually willing to follow Jonathan Chance on a march to Doylestown to demand "relief" jobs, that final shame, that in a few days talk

subsided and the men went back to work occasionally
to chat about "unions" and was there anything to it that
a union could really help or would it simply squeeze
dues out of you so some other boss might ride around on
your back.

The banking crowd and the substantial retired business crowd, whose homes in the little towns of the county
or in the nearby countryside presented such an appeal-
ing air of well-to-do tranquillity to passing cars, developed
a lingo of their own, in which Roosevelt was simply
damned as practically worse than a communist and a
greater danger because he came from a solid family that
should know better . . . and the farmers developed their
own philosophy according to their traditions and their
present state in the scale of things. Jonathan Chance's
army, as Willy Blaine, embittered by his boy's death,
called the little band who marched for jobs, stirred up
a surprising amount of attention. Straggling through the
streets of Doylestown, doors were slammed in their faces
and hostile housewives looked out curiously, complacently
certain that thrift and better brains saved their men from
such a fate.

Jonathan, in a cap with earlaps, thought he too looked
liked a farmer and he towered a little in his tallness as
he walked at the head with Tim Robb. The farm women
who trailed in the rear were timid and giggled a little
with each other, but once in front of the door of the
relief administrator, who, warned of the invasion, had
fled the courthouse, they stiffened and sang loudly, "Soli-
darity forever."

Only Tim Robb and Jonathan penetrated that well-
painted door with the shiny polished brass handle, and
they came out grinning, waving "All right" and the little
army cheered, gratified that the Marston family, who had
been denied, were now going to be fed. They got in cars
and whirled to Bristol for more confabs, this time with
the head of roadwork jobs, but this official, being a politician, treated them all to the manners of a diplomat and
sent them away with the blissful assurance that he was

going to take care of them and allow them to work on the roads at the regular rate in the near future.

Perhaps it hurt them to be called "road hogs" by the more fortunate or those who merely imagined they were more fortunate, and Willy Blaine took the attitude that the money was really coming out of his private pocket to pay them. "All these taxes," he grumbled, "it comes right out of *here*," and he slapped his pocket as if he had, at that moment, been robbed. Most farmers did not take to meetings except in a crisis that threatened to deluge them, and Jonathan was obliged to accept the proposition that men are unwilling to avail themselves of an opportunity to progress except along the grooved line.

He clung to his little group of hardheaded men and if they did not always agree, they nourished themselves on the big events in the world that struck them as manifestations of their own potential powers. The big strikes, the struggles in China, the hope that the workers in Germany and Italy would throw off their chains, were their private doxology. And when Jonathan despaired of rousing those farmers from gratitude whose wives took home piece work from the mills at Pipersville, making endless cuffs and buttonholes "in spare time they don't miss, it's a gift to them," he believed in a kind of challenge that was being flung to the world by the simple advance of science that made a machine do work that, less and less, required men.

Considering the yeasty ferment bubbling in the heavy dough of the countryside, Jonathan should have gone to sleep each night and in the morning been pleased to wake. But often in the night, he woke in a sweat. The sheets on Victoria's side of the bed were icy cold. His father seemed to have prodded him over cynically with his foot. He would lie rigid, half asleep, thinking of answers to his father and wondering at the causes that had shaped his father's life. He tried to imagine himself in his father's place but it was easier to see himself as one of the shabby men who darted out from nowhere asking, have you got a dime, while men in good overcoats parted hastily with something snatched guiltily from pockets or with faces set and wooden rushed on angrily as if someone with the plague had breathed infectiously upon them.

In his own house he could feel the tenderness of the wooden beams above his head made so long ago by a workman's hands, could see in the halfdark the rough expert hewing of the adze and in the friendliness of matter, he gradually· quieted but toward morning, the tide in his blood rushed again. He was wide awake as if his father had shouted some insult from the doorway.

Old Mr. Chance had not the slightest idea how his son regarded him. After Christmas he kept waiting for a letter thanking him for the lovely Christmas basket but none came. He had never received an answer to his letter about the well but that was not surprising.

He felt a little upset when he thought of the well but argued, sometimes out loud in the bathroom as he shaved in the morning, that in the long run Jonathan would thank him for not treating him to a namby-pamby existence. Work was the salvation and he could not believe that his son worked. He never had worked according to Mr. Chance's ideas, except during those periods when he went out on the road and sold profitably for New York concerns. It did not matter to Mr. Chance what his son sold, so long as it was legal and above board; what counted was the extent of the operations. Jonathan had made a very good salary and had even shown up occasionally in his home town looking very prosperous and energetic.

Yet even work did not reconcile him to his son-in-law Ed Thompson. On Friday night the Ed Thompsons came to his house to dine and on Sunday he went to their house. The ritual was absolutely fixed and Margaret Thompson had to argue with her husband on those occasions when an invitation might have prevented them from dining with her father. "He simply won't understand. We have to have dinner with him, I tell you. He's all alone, it's little enough."

Ed Thompson had snorted and finally rebeled. He began going off on his own and leaving his wife to eat with her father and their two boys. He never went without having first completely vindicated himself by a quarrel and, so successful was he, that, in her despair, Margaret accused herself of having driven her husband from his home. Lately she had begun picking up the pieces of his talk, wondering as to their exact worth. That he accused her of not loving him, of caring more for her father than she did for him, was hollow and false and she finally did not even bother to deny his fiery accusations.

"Fizzle away," she said scornfully. "You know it isn't true. I hate to think how often I have torn myself inside out trying to answer you. You know I love you, worse luck for me. What has come over you, I don't know. Oh Ed, what is it?" and suddenly melting she rushed to him, grabbed his shoulders and tried to look straight into his eyes. His face might be full of lather, he might have the razor poised in his hand. In her sudden terror, nothing mattered except that her husband must quit all this nonsense and speak to her, really and truly out of his heart.

Confronted by her in that way, with the tears rolling down her cheeks and her hair all in disarray, Ed fumbled for words. He even had a moment of positive pleasure in realizing how much he meant to his wife. She was a superior woman, handsome and intelligent, and she was looking at him now, weak and imploring as any child.

"Now, baby, come, come," he said, patting her arm. "I just don't like these damned family conclaves. I won't be dragged to dinner all the time. If you persist in doing it, all right, why keep arguing? What's to prevent you having dinner with your father now and then. You have me all the rest of the time, hey, pet?" He patted her arm and turned to his own image in the mirror. The sense of his remarks quieted his wife. After all, why not give up two evenings a week to her father? She did see Ed all the rest of the time. He was in the twin bed beside

her every night. Married people became regular dogs in
the manger, not wanting to share themselves and she
wiped her eyes gratefully.

"You're right, Ed, I don't know what has got into me
lately," and she smiled at him. But even when she had
driven off with her two boys, looking back at the house
where Ed alone, in black tie, waited for his brother to
call to start out to some shindig, a curious disturbing
doubt hurt her vision.

"Mamma, keep to the right," little Richard was saying,
and she brought the car into line sharply, her eyes pain-
ing her, her thoughts going round and round, trying to
solve her own terrible sense of insecurity. No, he wasn't
running around with women, of that she was sure. Ed
wasn't the type. Besides, she would know. Nothing had
disturbed the regularity of their life together except the
curious prickling sense that something was wrong. Ed slept
restlessly, too, threw himself around, called out in a loud
voice frightening her.

But when she got to old Mr. Chance's the regularity
of his house made her nervous. Her own irritability could
hardly find a place to rest a second in a house wiped clean
of everything except the ritual of order. "Papa, you're a
regular old German," she often said and the old man
was not unpleased to hear this commentary. He had an
instant swift vision of his mother in her starched lavender
skirts presiding at the foot of the long table. Her kitchen
had smelled of cookies and spice and nothing his wife
ever cooked had quite come up to the old mother's
hasenpfeffer.

Through his daughter he kept a sharp eye on his son-
in-law and even on his son Tom. Although he wanted
to discuss Jonathan he resisted, a little afraid that her
point of view might not coincide with his own. Her own
father-in-law had divided part of his fortune with his sons
but old Mr. Chance told himself scornfully that was merely
to get out of paying inheritance taxes. He believed all
such evasions to be strictly immoral and he even regarded as highly reprehensible Ed Thompson's and his son

Tom's continual attacks on the President of the United States. Much as he might disagree with what was going on in the government, he abided by the decision of the vote. He knew that Ed and Tom were finagling with a set of rascals, as he called them, in the hope that in a new election they might throw things over a bit. Since Ed had made himself solid with his company, there was not so much talk of politics as formerly and Mr. Chance, in those rare moments when he occasionally came truly awake, began to smell a rat. What was Ed up to? How was it that the Thompson clan got the gate and only Ed had somehow been retained in the new setup? Whether his own disturbance came from the profound worry that had become chronic with his daughter, or what occasioned it, he did not analyze.

He had never pried at the whys and wherefores and even despised those who did. That most of people's assumptions about life were completely unfounded in anything except their own prejudices and the luck that enabled them to sustain them, never occurred to him. Money in the bank, payment of debts, property saved with an eye to posterity, work properly done and regularly adhered to, day after day, were the laws of life. For the vague and terrible uncertainties, there was religion.

His conscience had never troubled him about his treatment of Jonathan. On the contrary, he felt grieved that his son had not panned out exactly to order. If a fine piece of leather in the shop had curled up after it had been made into an expensive handbag, he could not have felt more blameless or justified in reproach. He had fed, nurtured the boy and the boy had not turned out according to pattern. That the world around him was also crinkling around the edges and the pattern warping into terrible upheavals had not yet completely dawned upon Mr. Chance.

He simply felt that Ed Thompson must have something to feel ashamed of or he would not stay away night after night from the family dinners. A man who does not want to look his father-in-law in the eye must be a crook of a kind. At the intrusion of the word, Mr. Chance cringed slightly as if, this time, his own quickness had taken him by surprise, even embarrassed him. Then he wiped his mouth on his napkin and looked long and searchingly at his daughter.

"Aren't you getting a little thin?" he said.

"Mamma don't eat enough to feed a bird when she's home," piped Theodore.

"Theodore, how can you? I eat all right. Anyhow I was a little overweight," said Margaret, hastily gulping down a piece of roast beef as if she was ravenous.

"What's Ed up to; we never see him around anymore."

"Father, don't pay any attention to Ed. He's busy all the time or running around with that fool brother of his, Glen. Glen gambles all the time I heard and is simply worthless . . ." At the words that she had not meant to let slip, she choked a little and added at once, "Of course Ed is all right and simply trying to straighten out Glen. That's it." She was astonished at the reasonableness of this view and kept repeating it in various degrees of certitude until Mr. Chance looked at her suspiciously as if he thought she might have had something to drink. She took the hint and became silent at once. He cleared his throat and said that he hoped Ed was really solid with his company again.

"He is," Margaret said. "He doesn't tell me anything. You know Ed. I feel as if I might as well be in a harem sometimes for all I know." The words said wildly plainly astonished Mr. Chance in their excitability, and he said, "Come, come, Margaret, you're all wrought up. Now you want to have a good long talk with Ed, it isn't good not to know just how his business stands, not that a woman always comprehends but still if you are like your mother, you have a shrewd eye for business. Your mother would have made a mint of money for us once if she had had her way but, no, I took the bit in my own teeth and bought stock in wagons instead of the new-fangled car."

Margaret had heard this saga over and over and to avoid its repetition, she rose from the table. They went

to the other room where the boys had scooted before
them and the radio was already letting out shrieks under
the inexpert direction of Theodore. She turned the dial
congratulating herself that Amos and Andy would be off
the air by this time.

"Don't stop at one of those crooners," said Mr. Chance.
"How people can listen to them day after day beats me."
He himself would like a little religious music now and
then, not too much of it, but a touch after dinner and
then later in the evening a Strauss waltz, maybe "The
Blue Danube" even. Those old Viennese waltzes reminded
him of his Uncle Toby in his fancy waistcoat waltzing
his sister Emma around the kitchen and humming like
a big bee. Uncle Toby had a "past," it was rumored, and
there were times when Mr. Chance felt that Jonathan had
come at his nonconformity honorably. But weak excuses
were not in Mr. Chance's line. He heard a ragged gut-
tural, then high soprano punctured by the rip of jazz
as little Theodore senselessly moved the dial and Margaret called out sharply, "Hold it, Theo, let's hear what
he's saying," and the commentator's voice came oily
smooth, laying down the patter like gold leaf on a tomb.

But a sharper note sounded. Mr. Chance had wandered
to the hall and heard his daughter call out, "Did you
hear that, Papa? They're fighting in Vienna. The workers
have put guns in those nice houses we saw pictures of
in the papers. Wait, Theo, let that dial alone." Mr. Chance
came to stand in the doorway. She was leaning forward
straining to hear. "What's the world coming to?" she said,
looking at him. "I can't make sense to it. Theo, let it
alone, now you've spoiled it and Mamma didn't get what
he was saying." She looked with frenzied irritation at her
child who was proving to old Mr. Chance the way children nowadays got out of hand very young in life indeed.
A complete mistrustfulness of all his offspring and their
progeny was like a poison in his blood; he looked sadly
at his daughter and her child and resolved to tie up everything in a sound trust fund so that it could not be squandered by thoughtless generations. He had a complete sense

of virtuous intention in this proposal and thought with
the deepest conviction that the world was becoming de-
praved and his children were part and parcel of the degeneration. He must save them, if he could; so watertight
was the compartment of his mind, that he would have
been doubly indignant had anyone suggested that his
course was dictated by considerations for which he had
no more personal responsibility than his little grandson
had for his childish preference for jazz.

When Steve Carson got back from his Sioux City trip
the routine of farm life got under his skin almost more
than he could bear. He snapped at his three half sisters,
and Teacher-teacher sometimes looked at him steadily as
if she were trying to see through smoked glass.

Nothing on the place went fast enough. His father
moved too slowly and his sayings seemed no more than
tiny explosions of harmless firecrackers. Then he was
ashamed at his impatience and remembered how his father
had spoken out during the War. His barn had been
burned in consequence but it seemed to Steve a lonely gesture almost without meaning. All the fine militant
speeches of the farmers beside their roadside fires had
petered out too and he raged to his father about the way
they had allowed themselves to be sold down the river
by Milo Reno with nothing gained.

Walt Carson had looked at his boy and tried to talk
sense to him. History wasn't made in a day. And no strike
was lost. The men had learned their strength. It would
all show in time. Steve shrugged impatiently. Patience
seemed a defect not a virtue. They had all talked big on
the road but what did they get?

"Steve, this ain't a bargain counter. You don't hand
over a nickel and buy back what you paid. You're not
in business in this game, remember that," his father said
with unusual sternness. Even his stepmother had frowned
at him. To make amends he tried to dig into the work

on the farm but here too his ideas jibed with his father's. Steve said they kept too many cattle for the feed and Walt only shook his head and said if he sold off his cattle he'd lose his base and then where would he be? Going over his father's books he began to think the farm was hopeless whatever way you looked at it unless the debts were scrapped and they could begin all over again as if they were on grassland.

His three sisters seemed to him like little humming-birds harmlessly and foolishly going about their business. He would sit on the front porch after midday dinner watching Henrietta run to the henhouse with scraps, and coming in at night catch Nellie fold up her little square of embroidery with her hair in great placid braids wound around her head giving her face a strange tranquillity. He pitied the girls and during supper twitted them about their busy work as he called it. After supper he began going over his father's account books hammer and tongs as if he could somehow get not only to the bottom of the farm failure, but discover what made the wheels go around.

Teacher-teacher put two kerosene lamps on the table beside him and often stood near him for a minute or looked at him anxiously from the doorway as if he were uncovering old bones and at any minute some terrible skeleton might arise and shake its skull. The boy bent his alert face closer to the pages, making notes, muttering sometimes as he added figures. "He shouldn't have touched that quarter section," he said one evening to his stepmother. She stood over him, apologetic and humble. But she defended her husband stoutly.

"How were we to know? We did it for the best. That was the year, 1919, that the railroads were sending special trains around with demonstrators to show you all kinds of things. It wasn't only the land. We bought machinery, too. They said the only thing wrong with the farmer was his trying to run a fullsized train on a narrow-gauge track. They didn't call it gambling then. They said it was individual initiative." She began giggling as she said it. The words sounded funny to her. It was crazy, the way things had turned out. Steve looked up and laughed with her. You had to laugh at the way the tables had turned. But when he uncovered the new mortgages put on only two years before, he began to feel guilty. That was the very month he had first talked of going to Vermillion. Teacher-teacher was sitting at the table and had laid down her mending. The two stared at one another.

"He shouldn't have done it," Steve said, angry and hurt as if he had been a baby from whom the secrets of life were being kept. "Why didn't you tell me?" He couldn't bear to think that his father had put that much money on him. He wasn't a horse to win a race. College was too much of a bet for people who had no money to begin with. His stepmother listened to him spout away impatiently. She kept shaking her head. What words could she find to tell him of their hopes that were still fresh and green for him? College had not meant much to the boy, but maybe that wasn't much of a college.

"Steve, you weren't spared from the cyclone that time for no purpose," she said, looking at him intently, and he felt his scalp crinkle as if his dead mother's whisper, telling him not to cry, had again sounded in his ear. Her voice had the tingling prophetic quality that made him long to distinguish himself. He did not know what he meant. It was in his hands and feet, that seemed to him just a burden, to get him nowhere. Only when he took the pony and rode toward the buttes, his body seemed a piece with the horse and he knew that happiness was more than a wish. But the very next day he had a big fight with his father over the cattle question and when he got news that a new farm strike had burst out, this time near Yankton, he was off.

He wanted another chance to look at the farmers close up, as if he were examining his own future. The bunch at Yankton was a little more grim. They had the look of men who stare too long at the sky for weather. Perhaps men who followed the sea looked like that, with mild faces and their thoughts always running on a new day. It's hailing, god help the corn. Too much sun, the wheat is withering up.

Snow had begun to fly and the fellows on guard sheltered in an old boxcar on a siding. They called it their calaboose and as Steve clambered into it, he remembered the last light on the tail of a train moving across the prairie and himself as a little boy, closing the barn door, standing with lantern swaying, watching the light wink out in the darkness.

It gave him the feeling that he was going places at last and he felt lighthearted as he modestly leaned against the door and listened to the older men joke about the days when they had their pictures taken in store clothes and stiff new hats. Now their feet were in broken shoes, their workshirts were a faded blue, the overalls patched and frayed at the edges. They looked at one another, puzzled, groping, trying to make out what had happened to the country of their childhood. Once, every hired man saved to buy a little farm and every man who owned a farm figured on selling out and getting to California before he died or sharing with his kids and spending his last days looking at fat cattle and good acres tended and cared for all his life like his own children. Their bewilderment sizzled up at the words "monopolies" and "finance capital" and Charley Dawes stuck bitterly in their craw as if he had been thistle. Hell, he could get eighty million, but the farmer got a moral lesson shoved down his throat and the very men who had egged him on in 1920 shook their heads and called him the biggest gambler in the country, who even beat Wall Street.

At night they lit a lantern and it swung with the stiff cold air from the crack in the door where they kept an eye on the fire by the road and the two men guarding it. If a call came, they would all go out and throw in, in case of trouble. They would stand together, Steve thought, and the next minute looking at them, he wondered just what he meant.

When War had come, his father's barn had burned. His

family had been driven out. In his day, would that happen once more and where could he go then? He squatted on the floor, looking out the crack of the door. His mind felt tight and bright under his cap and in the car behind him the easy breathing of the men, their slow voices, were gentle and reassuring as if this were a stockcar routed for market. He had the uneasy feeling that the farmers were too easygoing and their spurts of energy would dwindle in the milking and the haying and the seeding, bog down in the inevitable chores of their livelihood. They were all older men; he thought of them tolerantly, counting on his youth.

A slow freight crawled along and in the darkness against the evening sky he could make out the black blotches of men and boys riding on the flatcars to godknows what country. Where had the sellout come in, he wondered, watching the cars as if he had seen himself ride by. Who had squandered the land's inheritance? To such questions he had only his father's answers. His father's ideals had not plugged the gap. The older men behind him were using the same words, with the same fiery intonation, "monopoly" and "trusts," and he could remember those words, spat out bitterly, from the time he could tell one sound from another. Talk had not stopped the big War and, ever since he could remember, people said another war was coming.

He heard Mike Nolan tell with a kind of relish, "Looks like a conspiracy to me, boys. I tell you the government toted out the whiskey. The banks got the gold and they had to unload. Buy, buy, they kept saying. They's more where this come from. When we woke up we had about drunk ourselves to kingdom come. Down to our last button. Looks to me, boys, as if the government and banks had been in cahoots with the insurance companies. That way they could edge us off the land, then when they got it, hire us for a nickel to do the work. That's what it looks like, boys," and Steve, turning, saw the uneven circle of faces flicker, and then at Mike's laugh and his "Well, they ain't going to do it, boys, we've got some say yet," their chuckling laughter filled the car as they thwacked with their sticks on the hollow-sounding floor.

Yes, sir, thistle was better than a snowbank, but if a cow can get grass or clover she won't touch thistle. Figure a cow eats herself up in eight months if she ain't worth more than $20. And Hank Cram spoke wistfully of the time he could have sold his cows for a hundred. Remember the year we got dollar wheat, boys? They remembered, wondering over it, chuckling, telling what they had done that year, paid off the binder, bought a new horse. By god, remember the year we bought the gramophone? In the chilly boxcar the steamy vapor of their early dreams rose like the smell of good cooking in the kitchen during dollar wheat and the morning-glory voice of the gramophone sang go ahead, this is America, bigger farms, bigger machinery, bigger crops, the breadbasket of the world full to bursting.

But when the crack came, wheat had dribbled to the grain elevators and men behind shiny desks in Chicago, with yachts on Lake Michigan and winterhouses in Miami, bought hogs cheap and sold pork dear—grain was low while feed and bread soared. The farmer was watching the weather, figuring on putting that quarter into winter wheat when the barometer fell.

Ralphie Toole got his mouth organ out for a tune when they heard gears grinding and someone shouted. Luke Anderson and Steve were first out of the car. They were running toward the road when a truck ground past the fires and the two men on guard yelled, "Stop, truck." The truck went on up the grade and Luke yelled, "Stop the bastard." Steve was behind and heard a shot. Then two cars slid out of the dark end of the road tailing the truck. "My god," someone said in the clear cold air. "It's deputies," Ralphie said, stumbling and falling on all fours. Steve ran behind Luke up to the truck. It had skidded to the side of the road. Someone was saying, "Who did it? Who did it?" over and over. The man on the seat had fallen sideways and the fellow with him was leaning hard on the brakes. Even in the ditch the truck rooted and grunted like a big sow. The cars had stopped and the deputies poured out around the farmers. They began rounding them up. Luke said, "Go look in the woods if you want your man. I tell you we were in the boxcar." No one paid any attention and they were herded into the cars and the doors slammed. Luke was on the front seat. He said backwards, "Steady, fellows," and Steve felt hands tighten on his arms. Then the car was sliding past the fires and one of the deputies was stamping out the blaze. The road looked empty as they shot on up the hill.

"What's up?" Steve said and the fellow holding his arm said, "Shut up. Don't play possum. Guess you know all right, buddy." The fellow beside him was solid as beef suet. When Luke turned, Steve saw a smudge along his cheek as if he were hurt. "You hurt, Luke?" he said. Luke shook his head and the fellow next Steve said, "Shut up, if you know what's good for you." Luke looked very stiff and straight in the front seat and when he turned his head, Steve could see how stiff and stubborn his long upper lip looked—old wooden face, they called him.

III. FATAL SPRING

ALL THAT winter Victoria kept thinking of the spring. She was lucky enough to get a job doing research for a magazine Tolman was connected with. Lester Tolman had landed on his feet. She could not help but contrast his fate bitterly with Jonathan's. Jonathan seemed never to have got anything for himself. Tolman was a glib talker and a pusher and his experiences had only quickened his ability to impress people. He told over and over about his terrible night in Berlin and added many details as time went on. Sometimes through the opened door of his office she could hear his voice saying "and the glass dome fell" so that the horror of that night, terrible and true, seemed to become diluted with the histrionics of Tolman's voice. He had had money to rush away from America in the 1920's, now he had only to come back, to present himself, and the doors stood open.

Once a young man in the office came up to her and asked her if she wasn't Jonathan Chance's wife. Nodding and blushing a little, she had listened to him tell about a story of Jonathan's he had read years before. "I remember it to this day," he said, looking at her with a warmth that seemed trying to convey remembered excitement. She bit her lips. It was actually possible that she might begin to cry. To prevent it, her eyes opened wide, she stared at the young man, hardly able to thank him, and alone had written a headlong letter to Jonathan. Tolman had at that moment emerged from his office, well-groomed and smiling, off to lunch at a fashionable restaurant, and she thought of the two men and their beginnings in Detroit, her heart tightening with pain.

When spring came she planned to go to the country every single week. She was getting a mere pittance but sent six dollars to Jonathan; four she put away in an old leather pocketbook hid in the bottom drawer, taking it out now and then to count her little hoard. Heavens, it was to be hoped she wouldn't get miserly. But on fifteen dollars left for herself it was barely possible to get along, even though Esther had allowed her to stay until she caught up with her life.

Lately a new source of a little extra money had come unexpectedly. A friend of Tolman's, Kurt Becher from Germany, had agreed to take three lessons in English a week. It did not amount to much money and his English was much better than her German, spare and ragged from college days, but she began to look forward to the evenings and to run home breathlessly to take off her suit and put a dress on before he came.

Esther was usually away and they sat opposite one another at a little table. Every session he brought some difficult exercise for her to correct and she would go over it painstakingly, frowning, with her head bent. If she looked up suddenly his eyes would be looking at her warmly and with a kind of eager curiosity that she explained as an expression of his loneliness in a strange land. When she thought of him as driven out from his country, alone and facing bitter thoughts, she spent some of the precious money for firewood and took joy in the way he stretched out his hands to it like a child.

"He's just a child, really," she told Esther. "And takes the most childlike pleasure in little things." The thought pleased her and seemed to give the lessons a harmless and joyful quality. She listened to him recite German poetry in return for having made him learn the Gettysburg address. The words of the address seemed to come fresh and new in his foreign accent. When he came to the words, "dedicated to the proposition that all men are created free and equal," he said them slowly, stopping for a second and smiling as if he heard an echo. They would talk a great deal about Goethe and, as she had promised Tolman not to talk politics with him, she found herself telling Kurt Becher about her little professor, a plain spinster, with a passion for Goethe. She had studied German with her for two years and Miss Ferris had even invited her to her rooms where a beautiful deathmask of Goethe hung over her bed. They had read *Faust*, and Miss Ferris, for all her limited experience in life, had conveyed the reality of passion with delicacy and intensity. The way she had said the word, *Sehnsucht*, pausing after it, using its translation "longing," for the stupider, who might miss it, discarding longing as not quite right, mystifying them all by insisting it had no equivalent in the English language, still sounded in Victoria's ears.

Shut up in the little apartment they would think up German words and adequate translations for a much longer time than she had bargained for, until Kurt's vocabulary grew and flourished. He would look at her, saying, "And then—" if she so much as stopped, so that easily and happily she found herself telling him about her childhood and her sister Rosamond, about almost everything except her own baby. He liked best of all her stories about her vacation in Florida and pretended not to learn the names easily so that she would repeat, stringing the names of fish together like a lot of bright beads. "There was bonita, yellow tail, kingfish, pompano, wahoo, amberjack, grunt," and he would demand at once an explanation of *grunt* a fish, and *grunt,* to grunt, a verb. Then there were mullets that led to the story of the mullet man who sold fish to the big fishermen who went out for kingfish, tarpon, and sailfish. He ate mullet three times a day and never tired, as who would of a decent clean fish but it was nothing to yellow tail that you could cook fit for a king. Then there was turtle, she had almost forgot that, and the turtle steak, cooked to a turn, with black beans and rice. If you left the food realm, there were sponges, and she quickly made a motion as if washing her face. "Sponges," he said delightedly. You could go out in a little boat, as they had, and see them growing straight up through the water alongside beautiful purple fans and branches of coral spreading like the antlers of a deer. But the best were the flowers dripping over walls, sprawling into gutters. At night if you walked along the street the scents drenched the air as the night flowers opened, the big white moonflowers, the white oleander pushing up through broken bits of wall, then the lime and orange trees, the flowers in pots as if people were bent on lavishness and any crack and cranny could support life if you wanted.

Once they had walked on Sunday night past the cemetery. You never saw a moon so high, the sky bluish in the lightness, the old houses standing discreet and dark with slits of light from long shutters. A man and his girl sat looking at the cemetery from behind moonflowers. From inside the house, an oldfashioned phonograph squeaked, "Because I love you." One big tall plumy palm had shivered as if, up so high, there was a breeze, while below all was stillness. She remembered how further on two churches, both for Negroes, were holding sway. They had stood outside looking through a window at the shabby stand with the lettering, "Christ is Coming," on a faded cloth. The reverend was haranguing a few nodding souls, "What the men of Key West need is to wash away their sins," and of course, next day, they would all have to scratch for food. The tobacco industry was gone, the sponge industry, the fishing except for little stuff, belonged to the rich.

Kurt would lean back listening to every word, sometimes he would say, "wait," and write a word down. All the new words went into a little book that at the end of the week he would proudly recite. Sometimes, at a shockingly late hour, he would spring up, "I'm keeping you," or Esther would come in and sit coughing in the next room to remind them of her presence.

When he left, she would sing as she combed her hair, the bright light of that high moon still over her. She breathed softly as if again she were partaking of that warm and luscious air. In bed, she heard the sharp and shrill noises of the street and thought of those other gentle sounds, rasped only by dogs barking, that had meant sleep. The rustling of palm leaves, the sound of water lapping on the lagoon, the voices and music coming so freely from tumbledown houses, sometimes had seemed to dissolve into one vast murmur; they had walked home in an unbearable intimacy of sound and smell as of human beings turning in bed, swallowing, throwing an arm over bodies, sleeping.

She was so busy that she had no time to be troubled about Jonathan's letters that lately were painfully matter-of-fact. She would try to be satisfied with the few words but during the day, she often thought of him with a troubled sense of something gone wrong. Before going to bed, she would hold his letters in her hand, reading over his last phrase, *with all my love darling, always.* She would put her finger on the always as if she were blind and must trace the letters to believe, and in bed, afterwards, would repeat the *always* with a glow of reassurance.

Time went very fast. Before you could turn around, the week was over, then the fortnight. She would never thrive in a city; she was a woman for the country as her people before her. Esther had a great deal of company and the arguments and discussions were endless. People who had never before thought of communism argued incessantly. Many of Esther's friends talked of the revolution as if it were, like prosperity in the Hoover era, just around the corner. Victoria sniffed at them often enough and at what she called "Marx, fifth-hand," and she said a revolution was never fought by "paper revolutionaries" with a feeling of pride that, though she herself might be working at a job in the city, Jonathan was actually putting his hand to the plow, for better or for worse.

Her attitude annoyed Esther. It was hard to live with someone who acted as if she had an inside track to history and treated everyone else as an outsider. "You ought to be glad everyone is waking up at last instead of being so superior about it. After all, we can't all be organizers." It was true enough and humbled Victoria only so long as she was still in the room talking over the evening with her friend. Once alone, she came back stubbornly to her earlier opinions and thought of Esther's friends as a flock

of birds who would fly away when the weather disagreed
with them.

When she went home Jonathan would be at the train,
looking as natural as if they had never been apart. She
would praise his attempts to keep the house clean and
could hardly wait to get her hands on the broom and
mop. He would come in from outside and look at her
in astonishment as she turned in the midst of a cloud of
dust, a blue handkerchief covering her hair. "Didn't I
do things right?" he asked, wounded that he never seemed
to come up to her exacting demands. She stopped then
with a guilty look on her face, ready to cry for shame
that he had caught her. She realized that something more
than the cleaning was involved and that his pride had
gone to so low an ebb that even this small circumstance
had in some way hurt it.

It would take almost the rest of the day to clear up
the cloud between them. Her lavish praise for his work
with the farmers seemed to him just a recompense for
her guilt, and he did not know if she really believed in
him that much or not.

But his triumphs were real enough. Si Greenough had
come down from New York and had praised the work
to the skies. They had written up the march to Doylestown for relief and had pictures of the marches in the
farm paper. The very lack of the spectacular in their
achievements pleased Jonathan. He had seen big enthusiastic meetings fade away into nothing. It was his conviction that whatever was accomplished must be done with
infinite patience by men who were not out to put on a
big show. The farmers around him seemed to be living
in feudal ages and to have taken for granted their position as underdogs to the little bankers who in turn took
their orders from the city. When he heard a little man
on a half-hundred acres talk about keeping his independence and not being in chains to a government program,
it was a grim travesty on illusory freedom that had led
them, with rings in their noses, to the slaughter.

They had air and water and they could talk up to a

certain point, and that seemed to Jonathan about all. Everything else they grubbed for with their hands and their feet, shelving it precariously against the deluge. To the west toward Lancaster, the big fat farms had held up during the whole black time but they were grounded in a solid fatty background of substantial capital earnings, bulwarked by Mennonites who lived frugally, asked for little. Arty Sturmer was a sport of this group; a man left on the outskirts when the richer had already moved further off, away from the hill country. Arty was a man rich in love and the narrow confines of his church had split him off. Tim Robb never should have tried to farm; he was probably a good agitator because he came from the shops and the city. It takes a city man to use his tongue.

Jonathan's thoughts were pretty much wound up with the men and, even with Victoria in the room, his mind would be going round and round some problem, the Tesh boy and his quarrels with Jake Tentman, Tim's love of the spotlight, Arty's passion for long speeches, making excuses for the slowness, the timidity, and dragging out of the past the reassuring flashes of their little victories. It was only in fiction that men jumped forward in leaps and bounds; in life they moved blindly with a hand out, stretching forward to feel. Once they got over the rocks and down to the path, they could walk to the sea even in a fog.

If he broke a cup and Vicky whirled suddenly with a look of tragedy and "Oh, that's my favorite cup," he had a moment of terror as if he were to be dragged back to those hideous doubts that had made him the butt of his father's humilations. The look on his face terrorized her in turn. She seemed to feel she had done him a wrong and, too late, tried to mend it. But alone she too found excuses for herself. She worked all week and could not always be amiable. When she came to the country, it was not lightly as a bird, but with all the weariness of long hours and loneliness. They should have had the happiest of weekends, but life was not lived, it seemed, in sec-

tions, cut plainly one from the other. The days over-
lapped, trailing to a new day, the broken past, and it
seemed to Victoria sometimes that evil was the more powerful force. She could not understand otherwise why Jonathan seemed to have suffered more from his father's doubts
than to have benefited from her believing love.

But after they had planted the big avocado seed that
she had saved from the city, and had watched Mrs. Gummidge and her new kittens, five this time and there was
nothing for it but to name the two ugly black ones, Mr.
Mellon and Mr. Ford, and to drown them, they both felt
their natural love for one another lighten and sweeten
the air.

By evening they would have forgot the bad start in
the morning and, when Jonathan set out for one of his
meetings, it was with a fortified complacency that Victoria remained behind determined not to feel lonely. She
would press her nose against the window, watching the
car slide slowly past the house with little honks of the
horn to say farewell, then sigh happily, looking around
for something for hands to do. With one of the baby
kittens on her lap, she reproached herself for her mistakes and resolved to keep a sharp watch on her tongue.

Jonathan was thriving, what more could she ask? It
was plain that he needed action as a body needs red blood
corpuscles and she remembered him sailing the boat on
their holiday and his tranquil happiness. Everything he
had ever done with his hands had been good, the furniture that was as substantial as the thick walls of the stone
house, the hedge of trees transplanted from their own
hills and now unmistakably thriving along the border
of the road. Everything flourished, and from a flighty thin
nervous girl she had become a woman with her feet on
the ground. She wondered at herself for becoming fussy
over little things. What if a cup broke or the house fell
down around their ears, so long as they had each other.

But when she went to the kitchen to put away the
dishes, she saw the meat he had bought with a quick
flash of anger. A dear piece if ever she saw one. Resting

her flushed cheek against the icebox she stared at the big round sitting firmly on the plate as if it were responsible for all her trouble. Everything seemed to be leaking away and no one to save it but herself. But she had only to stand on her two feet and give the thing a second's consideration to realize that she had fallen into her own pit again. A wholesome piece of beef is never extravagant and, what was she trying to do, make a mountain out of a molehill? Soon she would be picking pins from the floor and saving bits of string. And the thought of the string reminded her of her own mother who had never thrown string away. She had died with an attic full of things too good to throw away, with bags of old old letters hanging from the rafter like beheaded corpses as if the written words of the dead somehow pledged the family to immortality.

Her own attic was filling up, too. Only the other day she had noticed the bags and boxes, the lampshade that was broken but could not be lightly tossed aside because she had painted a picture on it of a clipper ship for Jonathan. Even the toys of her own childhood stood in the attic where they had waited for years for her children to play with them. There was a little trunk full of doll's clothes with tiny dresses for a very little doll fashioned in exactly the same style of her own small dresses as a child, and she remembered the Christmas that her mother must have sat up late every night stitching away to surprise her daughter. Nothing had been too hard for her mother. Victoria had only to go up into the attic now, to sit down with the boxes of her schoolbooks around her, to feel as if her mother had been looking at her again from across the table.

It was winter and her mother's long hands with the blue veins and heavy wedding ring had looked chapped and bruised under the green shade of the reading lamp. Victoria was working on an algebra problem. Her father had gone to bed after a last pipe in the kitchen. The book her mother had just looked up from was one Victoria had brought from the library. "How true," her mother had said. "How true that is. The exquisite burden of life." Then she had repeated the phrase, slowly, separating each word, "the exquisite burden." Her daughter was at that period of her life when display of strong feeling arouses only a quick panic of embarrassment. Something in the face and voice dissolved the contemptuous youthful "sentimental" that she was about to brandish at her mother. Her mother had earned the right to speak such thoughts. She was speaking now with a kind of intensity that made her daughter shiver with expectancy.

Mrs. Wendel had given a deep sigh, a faraway look had revealed the delicate brows and oval face that had never lost their early suggestion of perpetual calm expectation of romance. The bright red hair still rushed off a clear high forehead with a girlish lack of restraint. "If one could only live longer," she had said timidly. She smiled at her daughter who from the other side of the table stared at her. "You'll have to be my eyes when I am gone," she said gently. A lump of terror in Vicky's throat brought a rough answer. "Don't talk silly, Mamma." Stealthily she had watched her mother, seeing her as a human being perhaps for the first time. Trouble then did not quench life. She had tingled with a curious excitement as if her mother had passed some secret to her across the table.

There were times when the consciousness of the dead and gone was strong as a hand at her back. They had been a powerful folk enduring through wet and dry, from horseback times to the stagecoach and the first steam train. A few summers before when she and Jonathan had gone back toward Emaus and found the old Blue Church with the graves of her people, she had looked down on the two little moss-covered stone lambs over the dust of Albert and Hortensia and heard again her mother's stories, transmitted through dear knows how many mouths, of the little Hortensia sitting on a tiny stool crooning, "I'm agoing to California." The child had not gone to California with the goldrush; a plague of scarlet fever had scooped her tiny bones and flesh into the earth, but Victoria was alive to look down upon her grave. They had gone West and South, to Wisconsin and the great plains, and in South Dakota her Uncle Joe had lost his mind and failed to find gold. Sometimes the thought that she had no children to push on for her made her feel almost an outcast. Ah, lucky for her, she did not believe in the judgment or what would she say on that day to these fertile and hardy ones? She had only beliefs and her hopes that she shared with Jonathan as if they were their little children.

She was in bed and had dozed, then woke again. He had not come home yet. She seemed wide awake and had been lying that way only a few minutes before a light shone on the wall of the room where the reflection from the car struck it. She liked to think that some definite premonition made her awake at exactly that moment. It seemed to bring them into a closeness that time and space could not rupture. Now she heard him on the frozen ground, then on the porch and her hands that had been lying tightly closed, opened softly.

He was calling up, "Here's your boy" and coming up two steps at a time. Now he was sitting on the edge of her bed, she could just make out his cheek in the light from the moon outside. "I did it," he said quickly. "Si Greenough was there tonight and wanted me to sign up with the Party. They've made me section organizer. Here's my book," and he was sliding it to her across the bed. Their hands touched, his firm and cold from the night. She took it in her hands and turned the leaves as if she could see it in the dark. It would be terrible not to share his joy. She swallowed hard and said faintly, "That's fine but I thought, I always thought we'd do it together; this is the first time we haven't been together."

He wasn't listening. "They all want me for organizer. I've been doing the work as it is. Jake and Tim and all of them kept telling Si. I feel kind of set up to have them trust me so much." You could hear it, bursting from his voice. In the dark room he seemed to shine.

"Of course, they trust you," she said brokenly, choking over the memories of his father's doubting face. "Why shouldn't they?" She flared up again, sitting straight up in bed. They had trusted him but she felt betrayed as if they had taken him from her behind her back. She sank back, said faintly, "It's so strange. I just thought we would together."

This time he heard her. He got up from the bed and she could feel his disapproving look. "If you're going to talk like that. It's no way to feel, Vicky, I'm surprised at you. It's sentimental to talk like that. Even silly." He seemed to be stiffening, separating from her as if to save himself once more from her disappointment.

"I didn't mean anything by it," she said humbly. "I only thought . . ." But there was no use saying what she thought. He had already started downstairs, returning to his happiness, whistling in the kitchen. When he came up again he said, "You know they want you too. You can sign any time. That's all there is to it." But she did not answer him this time. She was staring roundeyed into the darkness, angry at herself for feeling so frightened and forlorn, as if she were a foolish bride jilted at the church.

Nancy Radford wrote her sister, Victoria Chance, that so far nothing much had Materialized in the way of the Great Expectations they had expected from their old friend, the now important Banker, Mr. Henry Orr. Victoria saw in the flourish of the capitalized words, her sister's brave attempt to make the affair sound humorous and not too grim. Even as she shook her head over the facts, she had to smile at Nancy's picture of the self-important Henry stuffing Clifford with False Hopes.

"Henry means well," wrote Nancy, "but so far as I can see is as powerless as the rest of us. He has enjoyed himself, no doubt, dangling hopes before Cliff, and perhaps he believes them himself. He twinkled an insurance proposition before Cliff's eyes that dazzled us until we sat down and soberly looked at it. Just another boon for the shoe manufacturers. Then he wanted Cliff to peddle tickets to the World's Fair in Chicago but with most of us trying to scratch along as it is, who would buy them? Cliff is a changed man these days and has talked to the Unemployed so much he is downright Radical."

Poor Nancy doubtless thought that this bit of information would please her sister and might even elicit a little solid help. Not that they wanted to take help, but who could let the children go hungry, and heaven knows Cliff had helped enough people in his time. True enough, when Victoria wrote, a couple of dollar bills fluttered out from the letter and Nancy snatched at them, laughing unreasonably and telling her two boys, who stared thoughtfully at their mamma, that it was "welcome as the flowers in May."

They were good boys and went to Sunday School with little Woolworth bibles under their arms and had signed pledges never to use alcohol or tobacco. After the children were in bed, Nancy and Clifford discussed their fortunes trying not to let their feverishness get the upper hand. The little boys were like ballast in the house and steadied the couple as much as meat and drink.

But when they got a letter from a lodge brother in Oxtail offering twenty dollars for a clear abstract to the fine lot they had sunk three thousand in, they did not even want to look at one another. For one of them to see the other would have been as upsetting as the mirrored reflection of his face is to a sick man. Clifford gravely went on reading the paper, ignoring the letter sprawled on the table with its shameless news exposed to the world. Twenty dollars.

Uncle David Trexler had sagely advised them to buy real estate and own a home, on the occasion of his last grand tour East before his death. They had taken a flier in a nice residential section at an auction and it had looked like a substantial buy. No one could say it had not gone up in value. They had paid several times what they had expected for paving and water assessments. Taxes had gobbled up considerable until that day when they could pay no more. Now it was sold, for taxes, and

they had to see it slip away. It was the same lot as it
had been originally. Only its value had mysteriously improved without any benefit to them. A few good cottonwood trees and an elm were growing as they had in the
first place. Rank grass covered the soil. Nothing had
changed except their expectations.

Nancy began to laugh. A clear bubbling laugh came
uncontrollably from her convulsed mouth. She stuffed
her mouth with her handkerchief as she had years ago,
when she was a child seeing for the first time a dead body.
It was a little playmate who had died of scarlet fever,
and Nancy with other children lined up to walk on the
front porch and look at the poor little quarantined body
behind the big glass pane, and to see if the roses the
little band had collected pennies to send were in an honored place. They had marched up solemnly and Nancy
had been terrified at herself and the giggles that had
come bouncing up through her throat. In shame she had
covered her face as if she were crying and had peeped
from under her convulsed arm at the unfamiliar face
of the dead.

"Nancy," said Clifford sternly. "It's not exactly a laughing matter."

"I know it. Only too well," and here she went off into
a gale again in a way to raise the hair on Clifford's head.

"Nancy," he said in alarm. "The boys." But she was
looking at the door of their room in terror and struggling with herself and in a few minutes showed a bleary
tearful eye over a face still convulsed with distorted mirth.

"It's only that he asks for it so casually, will you let
me have a clear title for twenty dollars, please, just like
that, as if it were please pass the butter or give me a
transfer to Pierce street car. I can't get over it. What's
it about? Where did that money go, first for the lot,
then hundreds and hundreds of dollars? Why didn't we
throw it down the sewer? Or get drunk? We could have
taken an airplane ride. I always wanted to go up in the
air. I remember that dress with the fur trimming I
looked at every day in Seattle until it was sold from

under my nose. Nothing ever became me better. But of course I couldn't have it. Why not? Why didn't I get the new wash machine instead of pulling my arms out every week with the old one. Who got that money?" And tugging at his arm, she threatened to go off again, so that he got up briskly and, with his usual presence of mind, brought her a glass of water.

"Nancy, drink this," he said firmly, and she looked up at him, smiling brightly with her eyes swimming. No man could have spoken up more forcefully or determinedly than he had the day they were married standing among the mock orange and peonies. "With all my worldly goods I thee endow, in the name of the Father, and the Son and the Holy Ghost," he had said in a loud clear voice, slipping the gold ring proudly on her finger. She knew then that she would be taken care of and protected and loved all her life.

And indeed, until very lately, when owners of businesses suddenly took over all the duties of employees in order to retrench and many other mysterious things happened, Clifford had never been fired. It was only that the structures on which he stood had turned into rotten wood, the timbers had cracked, and Clifford had been lucky, as she now saw it, to escape at all.

Clifford looked at his wife intently. He could not explain the monstrosity of the city lot to his wife or to himself. It was as if they had been unwittingly the parents of a thriving idiot child whose immense head had misled them into notions of genius. Suddenly the child tips the ink bottle over playfully, sets fire to mamma's dress, and turns the soup into the bureau drawer. "Nancy," he said desperately, "Nancy, dearest." At the unaccustomed dearest, she cocked an eye at him archly, with a new alarm beginning to tremble in her eyes. "Nancy," he pleaded. "Don't let go so. It's not only us. Lots of other people, too." And he was comforted by the thought of the lines of unemployed that he had known. He thought of their shoes and their eyes and their attempts to make wisecracks as they waited. "Listen, Nancy, we

aren't alone," and as if she too was comforted, she began
to smile, reasonably and as if her old self had once more
gained ascendancy.

But Clifford was not one to take fright for nothing.
He presented himself at Henry Orr's office the next morning and would not take no for an answer. It took time to
be admitted but finally he stood before the expansive
desk suggestive of so many lucrative transactions. "Listen,
Henry," he said without preliminary comment on the
weather. "I must have something, some job. Now. Nancy
is going to lose her mind if I don't." He trembled suddenly. His lips shook and he bit them looking at Henry
fixedly. He would have found it easier to take a gun
and face an enemy. To march off to the tune of "Over
There" seemed at that moment like child's play. He
stared fixedly at Henry as if to nail his desperation firmly
upon him so that he too might hang upon a cross. Henry
turned his eyes frantically to the side, his hand shooting
out vainly to fumble with papers. A spasm crossed the
lower folds of his fat face. Then he got up briskly and
came around the table.

He wanted to scold Clifford. The idea coming in like
this and frightening a man. He wasn't a magician to pull
jobs out of hats. The business of saying, no, no, day after
day was bringing him to the brink himself. Besides, my
God, he wasn't any big eastern potentate, linked up with
these International Jew Bankers. He was taking it on the
chin, believe you me, like anybody else. Because he had
a little front, they thought he was made of granite. A little
more of this, and he'd be spitting blood himself.

"Listen, Cliff," he said, grabbing Cliff firmly by the
arm and compassion and indignation struggling in his
face. "Listen, old man, I got a propo under my hat,
just give me a chance, will you?" He tried to pat the
arm that shook itself from him.

"Henry," said Cliff in a terrible hollow voice, "I don't
want a proposition. I want a job, anything. I've given
money in my time to Community Chests but there's none
for me. We've moved around too much for the relief

people, and why did we move? Just to try to get work, that's all. I want anything, digging, anything, I tell you. I'm a man," and his voice broke as if he had suddenly doubted if he were, in fact, a genuine human being.

"Listen, old man," said Henry, squeezing the reluctant arm again. "Let's me and you walk out a bit." He was suddenly afraid. What if Clifford were carrying a revolver and suddenly began in a fit of insanity to shoot the place up, the way that fellow out in Michigan had done. Things like that happened out of a clear sky every day. A man might be sitting behind his desk, harmless as a child, the tellers would be at their windows, a few people making their deposits or more likely drawing out their savings. Then bang, bang, some maniac lets off a gun.

The two men walked out on the sunny innocent street. It had a vacant dead look as if everyone had gone to bed for a long nap. Henry said, "Listen, old man. Let's get this straight. I'm not on Easy Street myself, see. This government interference with business is tough. What's happening to us? Take us. We're in the midst of farming country and actually if it weren't for relief these towns would be dead. Is that business? Land values are scaled over everybody's head. All the juice goes back East to mortgages and investments. Trouble is, the stores are just about nothing but big tents to cover eastern sideshows. Take Randolph's Big Store. Why, sir, that isn't but a front for half a dozen eastern businesses and they're just keeping Randolph for good will and as a kind of floor manager. Take the government now. What's it doing? Putting hornets into the factory workers so they are hollering for shorter hours and more money and all that is doing is to boost prices so the farmer can't buy anything. Ties us up worse than a binding cheese. It's terrible," and he had so worked himself into a lather that for a second even Cliff had been distracted and had let out a few little clucks of commiseration.

Encouraged, Henry pressed his arm, "My own brother can't get a loan. He's got a farm without a mortgage on

it, worth according to land values a few years back around
twenty thousand. Say, I wouldn't give him a thousand
on it. It wouldn't be safe." But the reference to un-
mortgaged real estate was unfortunate and reminded Clifford only of his lot.

"Henry," he said firmly. "I don't want a loan. I'm not
asking for money. A job. Anything. You must know of
a job, Henry." He looked at his friend's face that suddenly looked blankly at him, empty as a teacup. *"Now,
Henry,"* he said, standing still and planting his feet as
if he meant to grow there if he did not get an answer.

Henry ran a finger under his collar and coughed nervously. Suddenly a light seemed to hit his eyes, he stopped
dead. "By George, Cliff, I think I've got it. Let's see.
You say, you'll take anything? Now I've got a little pull
at one of our institutions. They sometimes take on men
to help work around. You'd have to live there, is all. It
wouldn't be much, I warn you."

"Where? What?" said Cliff. "We can manage. Nancy
and the boys could go to my father's for a while until
we got on our feet again." The delicate blond skin of
his face was flushing, even his ears were red.

Henry said, "Well, sir, that's the spirit. I warn you it
won't pay much. The Medbury Institution."

"The insane asylum," said Henry with a peculiar look.

"Well, yes, but you'd be a kind of orderly. It's a very
up-to-date place, I'm told. Dr. Alsbruch is a very intelligent man. And he accommodated me once before.
Gave a job to a young boy, whose mother had worked
for Eileen. The boy had been in a reformatory and the
Doc took him on to give him a chance. Very broadminded
man, Alsbruch."

"Well, I haven't been to a reformatory but maybe I'd
do," said Cliff, feeling almost like joking. "What money's
involved, Henry," he said in the business-like tones employed in important transactions.

"Well now, I believe it's forty a month clear, and of
course your keep." Clifford was not dampened by this
news. He was already making lightning calculations. He

beamed at Henry. "Find out now, Henry," he said, his voice shaking with impatience.

For once, everything moved fast. Dr. Alsbruch, a man with shrewd dark eyes behind glasses, showed him around. He would be an orderly, he explained, and perhaps later they might find something for him in the office. He might even find the work interesting. It was too crowded now and that was why he really needed extra help. The clean long halls, the shiny windows, and the professional air of the orderlies who might even be taken for internes reassured Cliff. He tried to imitate the matter-of-fact manner of Dr. Alsbruch and his heart lightened as he found he was equal to the sudden apparition of a strange dead face, rising like a bloated fish out of a corner of a room or menacing the quiet of a garden.

In two days his little family had packed up in the shaky Ford and were jiggling over the roads toward Boone. As Nancy almost at once wrote Victoria, their Uncle David Trexler wanting to rule the roost was a small potato compared to Paw Radford. Paw had gone to the Civil War as a bugler and could still enforce complete silence upon his household for the reception of his oft-told war tales. Nancy squirmed when she saw the big bony man come lumbering down the path, dominating the very air. Cliff seemed to shrink behind the wheel and she was horrified to see him emerge from the vehicle with the cringing humility of a badly licked twelve-year-old. As for Cliff's mother, the two women exchanged swift commiserating watchful glances. Cliff was like his mother, Nancy at once thought, and squeezed the old woman's hand with a hard sympathetic pressure. She gave an answering little flutter with a frightened look out of the corner of her eye. Her mouth twitched a little.

"It beats me," Nancy said, in a last-minute talk with her husband as he was about to depart, "how all you grownups have been under his thumb all your lives. He's only a man, like yourself. What gets into you, I don't know. Uncle David was rich but he isn't even rich."

"He's got a pension," said Cliff, grinning, "and a hundred dollars is a hundred dollars. Don't let him get under your skin, remember, it's only for a little while," and he kissed her fondly. He really loves me, she thought, with a relieved happy feeling. I should never hold it against him that he asked after the car first the time I ran into the cows driving alone near Leeds and broke the radiator. It was a brand-new car, you can't blame him. Men are like that. And she smiled after him as he tooted off, with the boys yelling like a couple of wild Indians.

"Can't you keep them boys piped down? You want to raise the roof," said Granpa looking at the boys fiercely. They promptly wilted and sheepishly went toward their mother with their mouths drawn down.

"You two," she scolded. "Can't you act better than that? Yelling so. I'm mortified to death." But her hands on their shoulders gave them little reassuring pressures and looking up at her slyly, they smiled happily.

Heavens knows old people deserve their peace and quiet. But it was a terrible nerveracking job to be on edge all the time dreading the moment when the boys would raise too loud a shout. She feared she would spoil them with her continual nagging and, to win their affection after her scolding, bought them lollypops and foolishly gave them to the boys after they had gone to bed. Indeed, she had to sit with them in those long evenings as the house grew silent as the tomb after nine each night. The little town seemed in league with the old and rang a curfew briskly at that hour. She would tell long rambling stories to the boys until they forgot the tempting twilight and went to sleep at last. Once she thought she might slip out for a little walk. She might even get an icecream soda at the drugstore. Her heart actually fluttered as she tiptoed down the stairs and prayed the door would not squeak as she opened it. The gentle little street was soft with early spring and trilling songs from radios twittered like birds. One was actually playing that old tune and she stood under a big maple tree to listen to "When you wore a tulip, a big yellow tulip, and I wore a red red rose." Her body lightened with the music, her head went up, swaying and smiling. Cliff had worn a new straw hat and she had that big floppy tan with the pale green lining. Her diamond engagement ring had twinkled in the Sunday sunshine, as they had walked in the park. Some girls and boys across the street were singing around a big piano and they had sat on a bench, smiling at one another, his tan shoe had nudged her tan slipper. People had looked at them fondly as they passed and Cliff had brought her a little framed picture of a Madonna and Child.

Oh, don't let anything happen to him, she prayed, holding her hands together under the big tree, and the next minute a door swung open and she moved on. The ice-cream soda tasted like her childhood, and she sat perched on the high stool looking with interest at the bottles and the pasty face of the young clerk who stood nonchalantly behind his little counter. The big glass bottles with the striped candy were gone, but Cliff was still a child in his father's house. At least her boys would never grow up in fear, if she could help it.

She took off her shoes on the porch and tiptoed up the stairs. But not without Paw hearing. He roared out, "Who's making that noise," as if an elephant had bolted through the front parlor. Ma came out swiftly in a long hard-looking nightgown with a bone button under her chin. She stood in the hallway with her hands clenched together watching Nancy as she switched on the light in her little room. "Oh, Nancy," she whispered. "You poor child. Don't you mind Him." She clutched out at her daughter-in-law, almost at once shrinking back. As Nancy shut the door, Ma took fright and backed off. "He'll be yelling, I got to go, Nancy. Cliff's got a nice nature, ain't he?"

"He's got a wonderful nature," said Nancy. "Like you." Tears blurred the old woman's vision. She opened and closed her mouth. Nothing came. Her lips felt dry. She looked imploringly at Nancy. She wanted to tell her that Cliff would make good, she knew he would, but she could only swallow hard. Her eyes filled, she twisted her hands. Life had made an old fool of her. She stiffened for a second, waiting for him to yell, "Ma, what's gone wrong in this house?" and when the bellow came, she stood her guns for a whole two seconds, not answering. He had to yell a second time, amazement tinging his voice with a kind of terror, before Ma with a little daring toss of the head, deliberately opened the bedroom door and stepped out to her lord and master.

After that, the two women tittered and had little jokes to themselves in the kitchen. They developed a whole series of variations on eyebrow-lifting, mouth-jerking, winks, nods and grins, that communicated their mutual esteem. Nancy listened to Paw by the hour and took dictation from him as he indited letters to his ancient comrades-in-arms in a loud pompous voice. He even began trying to trace his lost brother and sister, not seen or heard of in thirty years, and in fact as his life seemed nearing its end, he frantically tried to piece together the human fragments.

There were times when Nancy pitied the old man so much that she could sit at the little organ and with one of the boys pumping away manage to beg Paw in song to come to the church in the wildwood, oh come to the church in the dell. Paw would sit with his features softened, his great head hung down, his stockinged feet propped up authoritatively on a little stool with a crocheted top. But at supper he would begin laying down the law and reminding Nancy that in his day, men managed things better than to go chasing off and leave their families bag and baggage for other folks to tend to. A man with gumption could get along today, he asserted, looking hard at his two grandchildren who paused as they raised the food to their mouths, staring at the old man's front teeth that wobbled sometimes as he worked himself up into a fury. He liked to cite the example of the enterprising man who had cleaned up in Boone simply by going around and cleansing old cisterns. In his opinion, his son had missed a golden opportunity.

Nancy listened politely, trying not to be troubled, coaxing the boys to eat with little inaudible urgings and nods and quirks. I'll be taken for a deaf mute if this goes on much longer, she thought despairingly, but she wrote long funny letters to her husband and encouraged him to think he was quite a fellow to brave it out there all alone.

Cliff in turn wrote amusingly about the "crazies" as he called them affectionately and assured her that some of them were as sensible as lots of people you met on the street every day. He said nothing of the dead and lumpish ones who sat in the sun staring blankly or the ones who thought they were getting better only to break down again, seeming to dissolve as he had once seen a snail go when he had watched a busy boy cover it with salt. For almost the first time in his life, Cliff pondered the nature of life, feeling very humble to be alive and with all his faculties. A kind of terror lurked around the corner and he tried not to be disconcerted at so often fancying he heard his wife's voice or laughter.

He had to hold tight to himself and keep his nerve and then everything would be all right. The outside world was more formidable than this little walled city of the living dead, from which so few ever escaped. Walking down a long and shiny corridor in the evening as the lights went on, the sudden illumination made the passage seem a series of reflections and he could see his own shadow pass the mirrored darkness of a window. He took pride in his upright carriage and even began to think in terms of advancement. His manner, his very gesture, and the unassertive look of the man, helped him. If only Paw would not get too many tantrums. He could do an A-1 job here and maybe get a good recommendation to some other job. Many patients had rich relatives who might someday hear of something.

He lived in a little dream and said his prayers each night. Now and then a word, a look, a laugh dropped from one of the crazies, broke the bubble of his dream. The world that he was planning to rejoin swam, a remote mirage, beyond some impassable mountain. The old man in the garden, gobbling, "they'll get you, they'll

get you," had uttered the terrible word of truth, and
Clifford listened with a sudden trembling as if from the
crevice of a broken brain he had learned the meaning of
his life.

He would hurry then through his duties and, during his
noon rest, begin a feverish letter to Nancy, thinking
of her at ordinary chores, washing, mending, or the two
of them in the old days going to a dance at the Chinese
Lantern. The old world would sway back again, and he
reasoned once more beyond his material chances. A
miracle must happen; there was no other way.

The appearance of Sir James Bass stabilized the nervous tremor that reached Benton from the outlying shocks
of strikes and disturbances that summer. Old Mr. Chance
thanked God that Benton was a good oldfashioned conservative town. He had no idea of what was going on
in the automobile industry and took his sons-in-law's
words for it that they were perfectly capable of jockey-
ing along with the government until this crazy recovery
program blew up or was declared unconstitutional as of
course it would be.

Ed Thompson was in no need of backbone other than
provided by his own anatomy but he recognized that
other men, notably Spencer Gibbons, old Rhinegold's son-
in-law, needed a bracer in the form of a little English
conservative opinion. Good old Britain had weathered the
storm for hundreds of years, had played even with its
socially minded prime ministers who obligingly had
turned out more conservative than the conservative,
thereby illustrating the well-known adage that give a man
a little rope and he will invariably make a noose.

The Spencer Gibbons as owners of perhaps the most
sophisticated establishment in Benton were the hosts for
Sir James, and were giving a little dinner party. Following what Mrs. Gibbons understood to be the English
custom, the ladies had left the table to the gentlemen who

were rather hilariously making the most of it. Tommy Goodwin had just come back from Europe with a few corking stories about Hitler to which Sir James was listening with a rather humorousless face. He cleared his throat and the men fell into a polite silence, all except Fred Krieger, cousin of Tom Chance. He was continuing to whisper loudly to his cousin and Ed Thompson, and Sir James was obliged to clear his throat again. "In fairness to Hitler," he began in his precise voice, "we must remember that the man preserved order in Germany at a moment when anarchy threatened. A very considerable business. And they seem to be getting ahead there. Unemployment has been reduced materially and all that nonsense of agitation put down."

Prof. Clegg from Mohawk College leaned forward, nodding importantly. "Exactly, Sir James," he put in, but Fred Krieger glared at him and, putting both arms on the table, said rudely, "We kind of like a little freedom in this country, your Honor." Ed jerked Fred Krieger's arm down and hissed, "Not your Honor, it's Sir James," and in a side whisper to Tom, "For god's sake, if he is lit, take him out."

"Let him alone," said Tom goodnaturedly. "He's a big man too. I'm not so hot for old Albion."

"Freedom," quizzed Sir James. "Yes, to be sure. I presume you don't intend to imply license. As between anarchy, such as communism, let's say, and order, give me order. In an ordered society, you approach what you want. In an anarchist or communist society, you don't. Quite naturally. Why, Mr. Gibbons. Do you know the happiest people I ever met in all my travels?" He looked at his host, then, with what he fancied a tolerant benign manner, at the other guests. "Looks as if he were going to tell a bedtime story for little children," muttered Fred Krieger.

"In the wilds of Canada on one of my travels, I ran across a little town where everybody was contented and happy. They weren't haggling over affairs in Europe. The sun was setting and men were peacefully playing with their children. If it were Sunday the churchbells would be ringing. God was the concern of that little town; the priest was still the man of authority and the guiding light. I don't believe they had a newspaper. Schools for the children, a few books. I saw magnificent trees growing around this little village and it seemed to me sacrilege that such fine trees are cut down for woodpulp for newspapers. Let me tell you, you'll pardon me, Mr. Knowlesworth," and he bowed toward the one representative of the press who was puffing morosely on a big cigar, "but people would be better without newspapers. Newspapers merely confuse. Give the people churches and priests. Build houses of trees." He eased back in his chair and Rex Short was the only man who seemed inclined to take up the conversation. Short regarded Sir James not so much as a phoney as a dangerous man. He wondered who was responsible for his presence in Benton at this time, and his eyes needled each of the men in turn. Whose interests would he benefit? The automobile industry was the big thing but the really big shots were not present, except Marvin. Ed Thompson was hardly a big shot although there had been rumors lately of his moving up.

"What about the violence attending Hitler's reign of order?" Short said. Not that he personally intended to get into an argument. It was merely that the civilized point of view, as he saw it, looked upon the world as through a long spyglass. "Nothing to what it was in Russia, and it's all over now," said Sir James.

"Plenty are killed all the time in Germany," said Knowlesworth quietly.

"What do you think of our Civil War, Sir Bass," insisted Fred Krieger. "Sir James, not Bass," said Tom in his ear. Tom alone of all the company was enjoying himself. He would be married to a lovely girl, who was, moreover, rich in her own right, in ten days. He was ready to live and let live but instinctively he suspected Sir James. His clothes were not nearly so good as Tom's own. His manners were peculiar to say the least.

Sir James merely shook his head lightly at Fred Krieger. "Oh, you Americans. You can afford not to be serious," and he chuckled in company with Prof. Clegg as Marvin opened his mouth for the first time and said briefly, "With the big strikes tying up this country and more to pop any moment, it seems to me that Hitler solved something." He did not look at anyone as he spoke, certainly not at Ed Thompson.

Ed Thompson shot a swift look at his boss. He felt contemptuous of most of the men present. His wife's cousin, Fred Krieger, though a plant manager, had lost his grip. He was still fanatic enough to imagine that wages were a relative factor in good times. Cars were not bought by men in factories, or if so, it was an unimportant minority compared to the millions available elsewhere. Fred had not been called "an old red" for nothing. He was a tough egg and knew how to handle men and he had jockeyed along with them, man to man stuff, in a way to be envied. But new methods were coming into use. This man to man stuff was no longer of service. The plants were too big. Parts were made one place, bodies put together in another. It was a gigantic enterprise and the business at Toledo showed you what the industry would be up against unless it kept a tight rein.

His small brilliant eyes with their curious round shape were staring rather insolently at Sir James who seemed to him of no particular consequence except to serve the purpose for which he was invited. The conversation would do better to get around to the kind of legislation Britain had so wisely put in after its big 1926 crisis when strikes had demoralized the country. He opened his mouth to begin a question, then shut it. The host was making a motion to rise and he thought that, after all, the truly serious talk would take place at lunch tomorrow.

Ed Thompson thought of himself as a man of vision, tunneling the gloomy present. A life and death tussle with the union question, only a symptom of a more grim reality, was bound to hamper the industry. The industry had to win before a fight, not after one, when it would be weakened. "How's business?" said Fred Krieger, drunkenly, as they went upstairs side by side.

"Fine, fine," said Ed genially.

"So's your old man," said Fred, making a face.

The ladies looked up brightly and the little Wentworth girl stared at Ed boldly, letting her eyes flicker at him, her chin up. He went over to her, feeling himself to be cool and collected. One of Mrs. Gibbons' young protégés, a young man with a violin, was tuning up a soulful number. Susan Wentworth made a face at the music, lifting her eyebrows, and shrugging at Ed as if of course he shared her feelings. "You don't care much for music, I see," he said, smiling and nodding toward the little group hovering around the young violinist.

"Yes," she said, "I do. More than they do, probably. They are only trying to please Mrs. Gibbons so she will invite them to her important parties. I know *them*." And she bit the word sharply, looking suddenly malicious and hard. Margaret never had learned to tease and he liked the ease he felt with a girl who so evidently knew how to take care of herself. "I don't like milk and water though," she was saying now, jerking her head toward the music and with a lift of her hand as if to include the company. "In music, *or* men." She laughed pleasantly and he knew he was being flattered. What of it, at least she had chosen him rather than someone else. They stood side by side listening half attentively and Ed could see the long line of his wife's green silk gown, following it up to her breast and neck that was still the finest in the whole room. She suddenly caught his eye and looked at him in her still way with something of an eternal reproach in her glance. He felt sorry for her but did not allow himself to indulge too long. Life must be lived not dreamed and he wondered what might have happened if he had a stronger woman, less poetical, more ruthless like himself. He smiled at Susan who was looking at him soberly. If she were stupid she would say, "A penny for your thoughts," but she only said in a matter-of-fact voice, very quiet and assured, "I know what you are thinking."

"Yes?" he said, lifting his eyebrows and enjoying the sensation that had carried them to a greater intimacy than if they had spoken the truth. She knows nothing, thought Ed, but what of it? She is a very smart young woman. And when a second later she proposed looking at the flowers in the garden, he gave himself the luxury of not answering, but smiled in a way that he flattered himself was cool and possessive. They started toward the garden and above a bowl of fern and lemon lilies he had a last glimpse of his wife's pure and brooding face. Perhaps the color of the flowers, the music, an expression, reminded him suddenly of the time long ago when they were engaged, and he had recklessly broken a date with her to go to a stag party at Ann Arbor. He had sent a wire very late and all dressed up, she had sat patiently at the piano bench playing little songs with her head half turned as if listening for a bell. About ten-thirty the wire had come. She had read it without a word, shut the piano and walked upstairs. She had never reproached him but somehow the suffering he had caused her had brought about their early marriage.

He walked silently in the damp sweet-smelling garden, responding mechanically to Susan's little pressures on his arm. He could see her face in the light from the house; she was slim and shining like a little trout, fresh, too, as from some mountain stream. Should he kiss her now or later? He was almost ashamed to think how faithful he had been to his wife. And he had not been rewarded for it. On the contrary, Margaret had more and more hidden herself from him. Perhaps he was a clumsy lover. Once in a friend's house he had surreptitiously read a few chapters in a sex book. Some of it seemed to him pretty raw, he had felt uncomfortable as if he were in some way inferior and it had given him an angry attitude that made him want to challenge the guy who could sit down and write that kind of twaddle. A man could tell if his wife were happy, couldn't he, but, oh, that was just it, he did not really know.

He was even angry at Susan at this moment for bringing up these allusions in his mind, all unaware, but the course of association is no straight line. A mature man, deeply engaged in business has no time or energy to mull over his private affairs, and yet at this moment it was just his private affairs that were insisting upon recognition. Better to stay away from evenings like this that only gave a man ideas! Even headaches. Margaret loved him. And he remembered deliciously her submissive face, when he had come home only the other night. He had fallen over the lower hall step and she had rushed to the top of the stairs, holding her hand over her heart, calling, "My God, Ed, what is it?" He had got up, perfectly sober, and had scolded her for frightening him like that. She had started to ask him what he had been doing out so late with that gambler Glen, but she had said nothing. She had looked at him sorrowfully, instead, and he had taken off his tie with the question in his mind of what he would tell her if she quizzed too long.

Everything he was doing was aboveboard. But he wished he could have found some more respectable fellow to handle the business. He had to build up a squad that would be capable of heavy work in case of a tough strike, but it was a pity Nat Johnson was the only man available. A fellow like Stauffer would have been the ticket but he had, in some strange way, disappeared. He had simply beat it. He wondered what woman could appreciate all he was going through. What would Susan think if he suddenly began to confide in her? She was a strong and willful girl, would probably have made him a better mate. He had his arm around her now and his heart, of its own self, without any prompting, began pounding. He was pleased at his own capacity; he suddenly pulled her to him and kissed her roughly. When she let herself go limp in his arms, he had an instant of triumph as if it proved he was in the right and his wife was in the wrong.

When they returned to the house, the movement in the long room had heightened as if someone had given a spin to a bright top. His wife's green dress had moved over to another corner where Tommy Goodwin was holding forth to a little group. Susan had almost immediately held out her arms to Prof. Jessup who, enthralled, was wafting her away in what he fondly imagined the latest possible dance steps. He believed in being modern and a good mixer, and in sophisticated company, such as he took this to be, no one would be ahead of him.

Ed avoided Spencer Gibbons' eye. He wanted to postpone Spencer's nervous premonitions. Tommy was better medicine. He had gone to practically all the places mentioned in Odd McIntyre's column and in fact had inside dope that many of them were not as painted. He had met an editor of a big-selling woman's magazine and one of his contributors, a lady with a knowing look, and he had been assured by the editor that she was really one of the great writers and got paid as much as four thousand dollars for a single story in his own magazine.

Sir James laughed unpleasantly and looked at his hands. Spencer Gibbons flushed and hoped that Sir James had seen his library with all the very best things in it, and in fact he took pains with his books, and even went after the new young writers as he believed it was the duty of responsible people to encourage art of the day, not only of the past. He hoped Tommy would not talk too foolishly because Sir James would tell a story about it doubtless elsewhere, and would make them all look like amiable monkeys. Spencer believed we had just as good in this country as in England, just as sensitive, appreciative people and as cultivated. He nudged Ed, and in a corner said, "This Sir James stuff is all right. But what's the game?"

Ed at once dropped his voice and leaning close said, "Listen, Spence, I've said all along we have to play a deep game. You take too lightly the whole business of the government interference. It's like feeding fire not to fight it. We have to begin work now to block this stuff. Sir James is good publicity. Why, my wife will tell you how the ladies eat up every traveling lecturer with the British trademark."

"Not anymore," said Spencer. "I'm not so sure since the last War."

"Rubbish, Spencer, you've been listening to a few nuts like Rex Short. He's a man with a private income and hobbies. He can afford to indulge himself. You know as well as I do that in the last analysis England has only to whistle. I want you to get Sir James to tell you about the way things will line up there in the next few years. The trouble with this country is that it is too lightminded. Everything's been too easy. Look at the strikes. And we sit back complacently on our hams. Now it's gone so far, we have to tread softly. But, Spence," and Ed nudged him softly in the ribs, "we've overlooked one of our big assets. The public. Rich and fruity." He cupped his hands as if to catch the juice. "We have to begin working up to a climax. Get our own men to play our game. We've got loyal boys; get more and use them. Give them some privileges and then create an organization that in trouble ties right up with the public. Give it a name. Organization, Spence. It works in the industry, it can work here. I see a big future ahead but a lot of trouble. We have to visualize the kind of society we are aiming for. Spence, you know as well as I do that no more pernicious doctrine was ever foisted on the world than that all men are created free and equal. Plato's state was ideal. He recognized that you have to have a slave population." At Spence's guilty look, he squeezed the man's arm. "A word, Spence. We already have the slave class, you have to admit it yourself, only not adequately controlled. If controlled properly, recognized, and accepted, it benefits that class itself, just as slavery before the Civil War undoubtedly was a more secure state of being to many a nigger who, once turned loose, was lost as a bug in a briar patch."

Spence could not prevent the chill of shock from paling his eyes. Ed laughed and dropped his arm. "Can't take it? All right. Then prepare for the end." He shrugged, impatient at these milk and water souls who want everything without a price. Thank heaven there were plenty of guys with guts. He whistled softly and Spence cleared his throat, reacting a little to the man's preposterous confidence. Ed thought contemptuously that a really big man is all of a piece, not a divided person, and he severely squashed his own nebulous emotions that had troubled him in the garden, his doubts about his wife, his life with her. The little Susan was a good stiff cocktail, a man had to be strong or get crushed.

"Listen, Spence old man," he said, easily. "You don't read enough." Spence bristled but Ed laughed comfortably. "I only mean that I want you to realize we aren't playing a lone wolf game. I see a nice clean future, with big aircooled factories, machines mostly doing the work. The land like a wellcombed horse. Everything in its place, people, materials. Order." He breathed out the word as if he had been his father-in-law, old Mr. Chance, and his assurance was contagious. Even Spence brightened as the two men walked toward a little group discussing business prospects with the intentness of men who had stop-watches in their hands to time old man prosperity.

Margaret looked up and her glance wavered for a second, then she smiled at him. He wondered if she had seen him go in the garden.

THE MOURNING DOVE

W HEN Tom Chance and his fiancée came to New York to be married at the Little Church Around the Corner, Jonathan dug out his best suit from the closet, got a shoe shine at Pennsylvania Station and went to the wedding with Victoria. No one else was present except a wealthy aunt of the bride's who was in nervous excitement due to her experience near Grand Central Station the night before.

She had managed to get a cab, in spite of the strike,

and the driver tried to break through the lines. A great mob of people churned and shouted and Mrs. Engelman felt a new kind of terror as she looked upon faces that, to her hectic imagination, were capable of anything. She did not trust the driver who obviously would simply abandon her. Her story, told tremblingly to Jonathan and Victoria in the suite at the Waldorf taken by the bride and groom until the next day when they expected to sail for the Caribbean, was still going through Jonathan's mind as he stood with the others and looked sharply at the slender figure of the middleaged woman in the rich dress who had tried to communicate her fright.

He had looked at Victoria during her recital, both smiling, the same thought going through their minds as they realized that Mrs. Engelman's enemies were their friends. Something of the dim hint of the great break that might someday happen, brought the two very close. They had taken hold of hands, looking at Mrs. Engelman with an interest that seemed to her purely sympathetic. The idea was involving Jonathan throughout the ceremony as he saw his brother and his bride stand together in front of the altar and caught a glimpse through a sidedoor of other couples waiting to go through a similar performance. The bride, an orphan, had come from Detroit to marry in this church, fulfilling an old girlhood dream, gleaned from the pages of magazines. There was something touching about her as she stood in a dovecolored suit with a little bouquet of scarlet camellias and white gardenias, and Jonathan remembered, without the slightest remorse, his own marriage to Victoria, that had been forced upon them by his lawabiding parents. Their two rebellious figures, standing before the City Clerk, seemed to him superior to these two, infinitely better placed from a worldly point of view. He was glad that his marriage had begun in rebellion, it seemed to indicate the larger and more important rebellion that was to absorb his life.

The whole ceremony, so foreign to his tastes and to Victoria's, had a pathetic tenderness that made him want to reach out his hand and touch his wife. She was looking straight ahead, and her modest brown suit and green blouse showed something of her indifference to dress that gave her, in his eyes, complete distinction from any woman he had ever known. She seemed always to be involved in some passionate inner contemplation, wrenching herself away only long enough to put on clothes carelessly and it was surely only chance that gave her natural grace. There were days when she looked awkward and plain but this was not one of them. She was flushed and excited and had kissed him with her old ardor, her mouth almost at once disturbingly turned from him. He thought with delight of the night when they would be at last alone together; they had taken a room in a modest downtown hotel where they would go when the wedding supper was over.

His brother Tom and Henrietta Glaser were going through the ritual seriously and seemed not at all aware of the businesslike briskness of the Rector who was no doubt all too conscious of the other couples in the anteroom waiting their turn. Had his brother told his bride of an early romance that had almost ended in marriage? He was almost certain that Tom had escaped from this really passionate experience a virgin. He had saved himself, in a way that seemed to Jonathan alarming, for this. The factor of his business career had always involved him in caution and he had skidded through his youth and was presenting all of it to his bride. As for Henrietta, there was no question as to her state.

He looked at the couple curiously and with a little envy, pondering their chances of happiness, and then sideways at his wife, whose early life before he met her still seemed shrouded in mystery. She had never hidden from him that she had loved, really and truly, before she had known him. His own experience had been cluttered with casual and light affairs that offered no guide to her emotion. A jealousy of some profound feeling she had felt was carefully guarded as disdain for jealousy. He had even persisted in certain light affairs since his marriage as if

to test his wife's capacity for enduring love. He stole a
look at Victoria but she did not turn her head. There
was a terrible composure about her that was frightening.
Turning his face resolutely toward his brother he found
himself wondering about his father who would probably
be looking at the clock in his office with a lonely eye.
The significance of the time would make him uneasy; he
could see the old man get up and walk to the window.
He would seek in his mind for some reassurance to bulwark his loneliness and find it in homely little associations of long ago.

The wedding was for the first time absorbing him.
Coming in on the train he had not been able to think of
it. He had automatically dressed and the motion of the
train had released him from the little daily pressure of
events and duties. He had gone over the argument he
had had with Si Greenough.

In Jonathan's opinion Si's nose was too close to the
little petty day by day struggles. So far as he could see
the big spontaneous outbreaks among farmers had de-
generated into battles for relief and what he longed for
was some bold program that would lift them up and fasten
them together.

Si had pointed out that in the Dakotas there were
groups who met for talk as if a wall were built around
them and he had had dinner at a farmhouse where a
sensible young farm wife had actually told him that she
wasn't going to have another baby until "after the revolution." They had both agreed that this was a kind of
sickness as devastating as its opposite, simple trade union-
ism without a sharp political perspective. Jonathan had
introduced study circles among his groups and had been
disturbed that they had chosen as their first booklet for
study, "What to do in case of arrest." The arrests in
South Dakota had no doubt influenced them but there
was a peculiar immediacy about their needs that baffled
him.

He could never get used to their immensely practical
natures and there were times when it seemed to him that

to be assured of their own bit of land was all they wanted. It was because he was so completely convinced they never could be so assured that he wanted now to open up their view to the future. Already many of his group had settled down to relief in a disheartening fashion, scared of any further militant efforts for fear of losing the crumbs they had secured. Jonathan looked with envy at the industrial plants where flareups proved that something real and alive had actually begun. It seemed to him that in spite of all their efforts to prick holes in the government's program of scarcity the farmers had yielded to it, while in industry the workers had used the government's promise of reform to wake up to their own powers.

The whole business began to shift in his mind now, pushing out the thought of his brother and his bride in a strange way. He found himself moving closer to Victoria as the words were repeated that had once seemed offensively binding and now sounded so moving. "To have and to hold, to love and to cherish, in sickness and health, for better, for worse . . ."

He had continued to argue with Si, urging that they make more attacks on the government policies and try to break into the obsessions of the farmers who had voted for years without realizing any political distinctions. Questions of money and tariff had befogged the farmers and their outbreaks had invariably been followed by long periods of acquiescence. He was thinking of his last argument with Si now. Victoria had been present. She had jumped into the discussion arguing that the farmers of Germany had not followed the trade unions but had followed Hitler, won by promises of loans without interest and cement cellars to store vegetables. Promises that the oldest boy would get a college education; it would be a little heaven.

Si said only demagogues promised easy victories and Victoria had insisted that men lived by dreams as much as bread. He had been pleased that she seemed siding with him in his fight with Si against a too drab steady program which lacked flashes into all the corners and niches of the world, until she began quoting Kurt Becher, repeating his name many times. Jonathan had been disturbed and uneasy at the repetition of Becher's name and fancied her voice changed each time she said it. He had said curtly America was not Germany and she had left the room quietly. He could hear her in the kitchen washing the dishes and later she began to sing. She had started *"Du, du, liegst mir im Herzen,"* then had fallen silent. The silence had been as terrible as a confession but she had come in a few minutes later with a rosy undisturbed face and had kissed him as he sat poring over a leaflet with his mind only half on it.

She put her hand on his arm now as they all moved forward toward the young couple who had turned to face them. Everyone kissed the bride who seemed suddenly the most composed person present. Then they all went out into the vestry to sign the book. Another couple immediately took their place. From the vestry they looked curiously at the other party of witnesses who were standing around the new pair.

After the dim light in the church the sunshine was harsh and ugly. They blinked and walked slowly along the street. They would have dinner at the Waldorf and afterwards go to the St. Regis roof where dance programs were broadcast each night. Some of Henrietta's girl friends would be tuning in on that night's broadcast imagining their friend dancing in her new husband's arms.

Jonathan took charge of the rather hesitant little party and at dinner ordered wines, preventing his brother from swamping the party with champagne. He had tipped off the Waldorf to the newly married state of the pair and when a huge cake appeared with heavy icing of flowers and leaves, and the words, *Congratulations, Mr. and Mrs. Chance,* Henrietta blushed and smiled. She cut pieces for all her friends and little boxes appeared to pack them in. Jonathan toasted the bride and groom, Mrs. Engelman, his father, and finally insisted that Tom call up his father by long distance. As he was talking, Jonathan walked over and coolly taking the instrument, spoke a few words affectionately. Victoria listened with a surprised look on her face. So there was nothing irreconcilable between the father and son, after all. The deep and terrible ties of family life could be hacked and bleeding but never broken, it seemed. She put her hand on the back of her husband's head, stroking his hair tenderly as if he were a little boy and she must protect him, but he did not notice it, he was by this time very gay and more like his old self than she had seen him in years.

Mrs. Engelman wanted to tell again about the terrible mob. "I was never so frightened. I saw suddenly how it might be. I was completely alone. No one would help me. The driver would desert. I would be torn, limb from limb." She shuddered, looking appealingly at Jonathan, who again smiled at his wife. Mrs. Engelman's feverish fears seemed to guarantee the strength of their friends and, in the midst of the wine and drinking, the image of their power refreshed Jonathan and Victoria as if in looking at one another they had taken a long and secret pledge to a dangerous conspiratorial joy.

The bride was graciously inclining her head toward her aunt and, knowing something of Jonathan's opinions, now asked what he thought of all the strikes springing up everywhere. Her husband looked at her proudly and thought without regret of the other girl who had earlier tormented him. She had been, all flesh and no spirit, while his wife in her lovely dove-colored suit was already as poised and thoughtful of her guests as many an older matron. He believed that Jonathan's ideas about the future were unsound but it was not a deep conviction. The strikes seemed to be fulfilling some of Jonathan's prophecies and he thought that in some future final showdown, if something like a revolution did occur, it wouldn't be bad for him to have a brother on the other side. Jonathan might save him from the firing squad and in his mind's eye he saw his brother step over reeking bodies to lay a hand on his arm with the firm words, "Save him. He's my brother." He began laughing at the picture almost at

once, as if it were a good joke, and said in his opinion
a big upturn in business was due any day.

Jonathan said that was possible and Mrs. Engelman
said, "Goody, goody, now I can tell my little boy he can
have that trip to the Glacier National Park he's been
teasing about." The party had been at a round table at
the St. Regis and well-dressed docorous couples had been
dancing past all evening as if the world were really well-
ordered and serene. When it neared midnight the wedding party finally left and, dropping Mrs. Engelman and
the young couple at the Waldorf, Jonathan and Victoria
drove on downtown to their modest hotel. The bride had
leaned in the window, holding Vicky's hand, as if shy
to be left behind, and Jonathan thought of the couple
with envy and sadness. His words, covering his feelings,
said the simplest of his thoughts, "Did you see they had
twin beds?"

"Yes," Victoria said, "I don't understand it. I never
liked twin beds, and on a wedding night . . ." He slipped
his arm around her but as she took his hand and held
it tightly between her own, she seemed not to be thinking
of him. Even in their bedroom, she seemed to be somewhere else and looking out at her from the bathroom
he saw her sitting on the edge of the bed with one shoe
and stocking off. Her blouse had been pulled over her
head and she sat dreaming as if she were alone. He
watched her curiously, a sudden terrible sick feeling gripping his stomach. Her face was so pale that he thought
for a second, hopefully, that she might simply be tired.
He came out and said softly, "What's the trouble, don't
you feel well?"

She looked up at him then, smiling faintly. "I was just
thinking," she said.

"Yes, but what?"

"Oh, that I'd never had a wedding or a cake."

"Is that all?" He laughed and sitting down beside her,
pulled off her other slipper and stocking. She let him,
without moving, and went on talking as if she did not
know what he was doing. "I wonder if you would have

married me if your parents hadn't made you do it? I kept thinking about it. It's funny how little control we have over our feelings. It's so foolish to think such thoughts. Our way was so much better." Her voice went on mechanically as if to divert him, but he imagined that her body strained away from him as he touched her. The sick feeling came back again and he looked at her steadily. Her lips were trembling.

"Vicky," he said. "You've got to tell me. What is it?"

"Nothing," she said. "It's nothing." They looked at one another and the feeling of terror mounted to his eyes. She's gone, he told himself, as if he had seen her step into deep water. "Vicky," he said and fell down beside her; putting his arms tightly around her waist and, hiding his face in her body, he burst into tears. "Vicky," he said. "Vicky." He wanted to accuse her, but he could not bear to say the words that would condemn him. At his tears, she leaned over him, pulling him up beside her, holding him to her. "Don't, don't," she said frantically. "It's all right. Nothing's happened, darling. Don't, I can't bear it."

"Something must have happened, Vicky. You're lying."

"Nothing," she repeated desperately and she thought that if he would only pretend for a few moments, for a little while, that nothing had happened, everything would be as it was.

"It's Kurt," he said, wiping his eyes and struggling to his feet. "I felt it all along."

"No," she said, shaking her head with a sudden terrorized look. "It's nothing. I'm just tired." But he would not take his eyes from her. Their life together rose up before her, and a lie between them seemed as dangerous as a knife. She couldn't lie to him and live with him, day after day. She said, "I love you. That's the real truth. You didn't write to me for so long. I know you were busy, but even a card. It was the week—just two years ago—I lost the baby." Her whole face quivered, she put her hands over her face and waited.

He looked at her coldly as if he did not quite believe

her. "You thought I never knew," she flared up, "but I did. That the time you were in town and I was all alone when my father died and everything happened, you had a girl there. I knew."

He looked at her in amazement and then said, "I never tried to hide anything from you. It was nothing, of no importance. This is."

He thought she was trying to absolve herself with a reminder of his own wrongs, but she shook her head. "No, no," she said. "I wasn't thinking of revenge."

"Well, you've got it anyhow," he said grimly.

"There's no use if you talk like that. I never talked like that to you. You've always told me it didn't matter."

"This is different. I can feel it. You love him. I never have loved anyone but you." He said it simply, and looked at her with his face drawn painfully, waiting to hear some miracle of denial. A deep flush spread over her face and neck and her eyes seemed to leap out at him, wildly blue. He wanted to strike her. She turned pale and said, "Jonathan, you have to believe me. It's you I love."

She saw that she never would be able to convince him, ever again, and it seemed the final treachery reserved in life was in one's own body, lying in wait. She did not know how it had happened, only that the long tension of her life had suddenly snapped. She had not known it would be like this, that Kurt would haunt her as if he were in her very blood. It was with Jonathan she had made her bed, it was their life that counted, and the sudden terror of a feeling she had never bargained for, made her more forlorn than any waif. Her face, so woebegone and lost, was terrible to see. He put out the light, and in the dark they lay down together, just as they were. He lay stiffly and heard the heavy pounding of her heart. He had never found fault with her in all their ten years together. In her fear that all was lost she reduced their life to its most innocent best, remembering only that they had dug wild fern from the woods together, sat on the porch in the dark looking at the stars spread like a protecting mantle over their valley. They had lain in the same bed every night for ten years. As if she could reap time like wheat, she repeated "ten years" to herself. All the good had slipped away like water into sand. The words were useless as broken crockery. She did not know what to say to Jonathan when she did not altogether know herself. Kurt seemed to have stepped back into the room; they were sitting side by side and he had put his hand upon her throat. Perhaps I will die for this, she thought, without repentance. I too have a right to my life. She could think of no words for her husband who would only be thinking that another man had possessed her. Surely for that one did not let a good lifetime slip. She was strong, she would make it come right, for all of them, puzzling with the words that heavy as stones meant nothing.

She had moved toward him and he turned suddenly and flung his arms around her. He wanted to speak but the words were choking him, awkward and useless as a child's speech on his tongue, surely he could do anything Kurt could do, but he only gave a groan and lay against her. She put her arms around him too, and they lay so, quietly.

CREEPING DESERT

BY THE time the fellows got loose from the murder charge, all but Luke Anderson, it was early summer. Steve Carson came back home and for the first days couldn't get over how good everything looked. It was like falling in love, only better. He was pale as a potato sprout but stripped off his shirt and went around in the hot sun tinkering with the tractors and the old car. The car whined like a buzzsaw and her brakes wouldn't stop at a hundred yards. Steve relined them, he overhauled the engine and tightened the waterpump. The

tractor bucked but he fixed that. All the time he seemed
to be running on two tracks. His hands and his body
went right along but his head was somewhere else. For
days he didn't want to talk at all; he had heard enough
mealy-mouthed talk to last a lifetime. Luke Anderson
was in for manslaughter, doomed for five years, and Steve
couldn't get over how they had picked the best and the
brightest to frame. Nothing but the best would do them.

Walt Carson didn't know just what line to take with
his son. Steve had grown into a man so fast the father
felt a little timid with the boy. He and Stella talked him
over in bed at night and she said the only thing to do
was to give the boy a free rein, he'd find himself. "If
only the farm were a better proposition, it'd give him
something to get his teeth into," Walt had groaned. Steve
had finally of his own accord hunted out his stepmother
one night. She had walked down to the edge of the sheep
pasture and was looking at the ground, chewed to a coarse
brown pelt that had been singed already by the hot sun.
He came up softly behind her, stood a minute, and said,
"What would you say to me going to Chicago?"

"What would it be you were thinking of?" she said,
not looking at him but over toward the land where it
ran to a dry run choked with thistle.

"I know machines," he said. "I could get a job. I want
to get out of this." She thought uncomfortably that the
trial had scared him but, looking at him suddenly, she
knew she had wronged him. There was nothing scared
about her boy. He said, "Maybe in the fall. I'll stick by
Father till the crops are in."

"Doesn't look as if there'd be much crops," she had
said. She knew he wasn't telling her the half of it. Sometimes there was something almost stuckup about the boy,
as though he felt set up for having been a martyr to
the cause. But then there had been so many meetings,
people from all over the country had sent money—union
men from Akron and Flint, from Bridgewater, and
farmers from Pennsylvania. They had their pictures in
the paper. Steve had shown up wonderfully in the court-

room. She remembered how they always had wanted to
make something of him, a lawyer, somebody who could
fight for them. Working on the land was an all-time job.
She wanted the boy to go a long way, she could see him
traveling like a kind of star.

They had talked it over and it was a good idea, so far
as it went. He wanted to jump into things, was the way
he put it. The city was the place. Walt didn't see how
getting a job in a factory was going to get him any place
anymore than the farm. "Hell, boy, you'll have to be at it
morning, noon, and night. The speedup is a new idea
and they're taking it out of the men's hides."

In the end, Steve had just postponed it until fall. They
put in three crops that summer, wheat and corn twice.
Nothing grew. The beans never sprouted. The potatoes
cooked right in the ground. Even the wild stuff, the rabbits and pheasants, began dying on the land. The corn
grew ten inches, tried to put out puny tassels and shriveled where it stood. Only thing they had to be thankful
for was that the grasshoppers went away in July.

"By golly," Walt said, "it's too tough even for the
grasshoppers." The farmers seemed to get consolation out
of talking it over. They would stop each other on the
road and talk of the past as though they were at a funeral
and they were going over the virtues of the dead man
laid out in his Sunday clothes in the parlor with the relatives crying around. Everyone knows what a comfort it
is to talk about the good things a dead man has done. By
midsummer there wasn't anything to feed the cattle with
and men gave hogs away to get rid of them. Steve sold
a thirty-five pound shoat for eighteen cents but, one Saturday night when he and Tub Johnson had driven up
to Mitchell, they went into a butcher shop just for fun
and found pork selling for around thirty-five cents a
pound and lard was up to seventeen cents.

The farmers didn't seem to be able to stop everything
from sliding down the chute the chutes and the lord
knows the government paying twenty dollars a head didn't
help much. Most of the cattle were mortgaged to the

teeth and the banker got his divvy first, then the farmer got six dollars that didn't stick to his pants pockets long. Nobody had paid taxes for years, everything was mortgaged so there wasn't a square inch left to plaster. Steve went around soaking up the talk, putting in a word, but he was quiet and didn't rant around the way he had months before when he knew less. The way he figured it was that the farmers couldn't see the forest for the trees. They were so gummed up with their troubles the real blazing truth was hard to look at.

It was a miracle the way they wanted to admit everything but the truth. The truth as he saw it was that the damned machinery didn't work anymore. The system was screwy and there was nothing to do with it but haul it to the junk heap the way you would an old car, maybe salvage a few bolts and parts. He got encouragement from the talk that seemed to him to strip the gears bare. Soon people would realize the old contraption simply would not haul the load.

At night he would be in a sweat of tenderness for the world and rising in his bare feet would tiptoe to the window where the scarred fields were beautiful under the strange haze that rose like steam from the baked land. In the moonlight it was ghostly white and seemed another world than the one that in the daytime rebuked men for their labor. If he only knew more. But he knew nothing. The time at college had been nothing. He did not know where to begin, felt all hands and feet, was impatient that his father and stepmother for all their belief had not moved. The world had not changed for them. They kept on talking and now in cities, the rumble was beginning, even as it had begun earlier on the land. But on the land, the treachery of nature had sided against the farmer.

A man couldn't fight when he was so bewildered. A man stood around in a daze watching the government men come and stick his bony cattle and push them into a trench of lime. It was like seeing his family hanged for thieves. His hands trembled, big tears rolled down the creases of his face. They never did any wrong, why had this end come to honorable beasts?

Then the government set up a meat-packing plant nearby and packed up the stuff to give out on relief. The farmers got pieces of veal but it wasn't relief they wanted. They had worked and slaved, where had the substance sunk to? Fellow near Carson's had managed to store up some 1932 wheat and when the harvester company sent a man sucking around to get the money for the tractor, the farmer had come out with a shotgun. "Let me tell you," he says, "if you want to scale down the price on that tractor same way us farmers had to scale down our wheat, you can have it. Otherwise, git." This story he told triumphantly from neighbor to neighbor, crowing about it and they crowed with him, resting their feet on the running-board of his car, staring with hard dry eyes into the distance where the fatal sun blazed down through the steamy haze.

Steve and Tub Johnson ran around in the car as long as they could scrape up gas. They got to Mitchell, and Tub took a load of grassfed steers into the Sioux City stockyards. The boys ran into a big sale where the government was buying up stuff too bony to hang onto. The government price of twenty dollars wasn't enough for the bankers who were holding the mortgage and some of them were getting together, objecting to giving waivers. The farmers who were standing in a huddle began to get nervous. Twenty dollars was twenty dollars, not that they would get that, but the six dollars they would get was something and would wipe out their mortgage. They began fidgeting and finally, yelling and milling around, it began to look like a riot. The government fellow had made one arrest. Of course, it was a farmer. But the farmers got some satisfaction, hearing the bankers bawled out.

"Why, you sons of bitches, you're in the cattle business and you don't know it. If you don't watch your step your paper isn't going to be good for anything but to wipe your ass on." Then he had yelled at the crowd, "The government is distributing $480,000,000 and there are 120,000,000 in the country, that's four dollars apiece, stick it in your pockets and be thankful you've got a red cent."

Who gave any man the right to talk to them as if they were snotty little boys who had been up to dirty tricks back of the privy? It made Steve raging sore, and he almost hated the farmers for taking it meekly, as if the meek would ever inherit anything. Work wasn't worth anything in comparison to money anymore and money had a corner on the world. It could sneak around and make bargains and get you in the neck so that men who merely stuck to a job couldn't buck against it. Then there was the law, always ready to brandish a paper in your face. Steve would come home and mutter around as if he were the first discoverer of the grim tragedy that had stripped the gears of the world.

But he was young. He was good-looking with hair that bleached to straw-color in summer, and skin that burned red-brown. He had a new blue shirt and a tie he had worn in college. He and Tub Johnson would dress up and in the long evenings hang around Mitchell or go to Plankinton and watch the little ferris wheel that a two-bit traveling show had brought to town. Everybody was getting relief; the country seemed to have sunk back, easing back, looking at its hands and its feet. The two young fellows would eye the girls and one night picked up two local beauties and they all rode the merry-go-round and went on a tear through the country to Coleme. That part of the country was the worst sight yet, with the ground licked clean as if buzzards had finished it. Even the houses were stained with dirt clean up above their windows where the winds had whirled and splashed the stuff from the fields. Once toward Pierre when they saw cabbages growing in a garden, he and Tub got out of the car and stood looking at them as if they had never seen green before.

It was like a bad nightmare. But the Lutherans held their harvest supper over by Plankinton same as usual for the benefit of the foreign missions. (There were five churches, all with white paint peeling in great ulcers from the walls, and three grain elevators in the town.) Tub and Steve went in and laid down a quarter for a big plate of stewed chicken, mashed potatoes, and cole slaw. The men were hashing things over, calculating on whether the government ever figured on getting back its money. "Let them harness up Wall Street for a change. We been pulling the plow long enough," old Jake Peasely said, gnawing on a chicken leg and grinning.

There was even talk of revolution and Ole Grant said he heard Mellon had an airplane on tap ready to jump on board when it came. But the idea frightened them. You could see it edging up into their eyes. Naw, this country wouldn't have a revolution. Things would get better. The land could raise wheat for a hundred years and not give out, the soil was so deep. Next year would be better. A couple of good years would clean things up again.

He was almost ready to go out and get himself stinking tight with Tub. Tub took it all philosophically. "Hell's bells," he said. "Don't get yourself into such a sweat. You're only young once, make the most of it." But in sober moments Tub would try to figure out some kind of a future. Seemed to Tub the farmer's base was being taken from him, what was the use of beginning at scratch again. They were talking all that summer, especially the little town papers that wanted to egg on the farmers to hold fast so that the whole shebang wouldn't fall apart, about how the farmer was the new pioneer and the salt of the earth. It was nothing but a carrot slung before his nose tempting him to go on pulling the plow in the same old furrow. Tub said he wasn't going to fall for it, no sir, and Steve had to respect something about his friend that went blindly into drinking and carousing with a terrible thirst for life.

One night when the Carson family was at supper they heard a car snort along the road and come to a crashing stop near the corncrib. Steve got up and said, "It's Tub," and went out. Walt began pushing his chair back and the girls went to the window. Only Stella sat where she was, too tired to move. She had just finished cleaning up after the last duststorm, and already the sky looked threatening. This time the dust got the last bit of lettuce and even the one zinnia that she had managed to raise as if it were a sick chick with the pip. Nothing but the blighted blossom, wilted as if it had been singed with a blowtorch, showed. "He ran into the corncrib, Mamma," Nelly was saying, but she still sat there, heavy as lead. Walt said, "He'll break his darned neck someday," as if the news would not be altogether evil.

The old Ford had crashed into the corncrib all right, and had taken a nick out of it. Not that there was any corn to spill out. Still it had bent a fender of Tub's car. Tub was slanting down at the wheel looking at Steve with a wild white face. His eyes looked boiled. "Hy yuh," he began airily and tried to get out. He was so drunk he could hardly stay on his feet. "I got to get going," he muttered, but he let Steve lead him into the barn and ease him down into the little pile of hay. Then he seemed to come to his senses and, seeing Steve, began to blubber. "The goddam bitch, the rotten ol whore," he sobbed, his shoulders shaking under his blue shirt.

"Not so loud, Tub, the girls will hear you. What's wrong? Come on, take it easy. You're all right."

"Who said I'm not all right? I'm not drunk. Hey, lay off," and he began fighting an imaginary enemy, tears streaking down his dusty face. "I can't go home, I don't know where the hell to go. I got my ass in a sling, all right, the goddam bitch. She never told me, the ol whore," and he shook all over, his body in the loose bag of his clothes seemed to shake itself apart, bone from bone. Steve was scared. Had he gone to a doctor? Who was she?

Hell, he hadn't known. She was with one of the shows, remember the two girls at Mitchell, the little one was the one. As he began to talk, he quit shaking, sat up, his body suddenly sound and whole again. He wiped his nose on a few wisps of straw, even grinned. "She wasn't a bad piece," he said, attempting a little swagger. But then he remembered his trouble, sat heavily tired, drunk, half-conscious of Steve. "Stay here, I'll get you some supper," Steve said.

"I couldn't eat," but Steve had already left, and was coming back with a cup of black coffee. He half envied Tub who had been knocking around with the show and had been grabbing hold of the real world. "Here, Tub, you drink this up, I'll see you in the morning." But Tub had almost instantly fallen, the cup of coffee spilling on the barn floor. Steve shut the big door and went back to the house. Walt was reading the papers, Teacher-teacher was ironing, the girls were sewing. The peacefulness of the scene irritated him as if it were conspiring to keep him in swaddling clothes while the rest of the world lived. Tub was the only drama that had come his way since the trial and it roused him out of what seemed sleep. He went over to the little desk where Walt kept his bills and account books. The two right cubbyholes were his, and ever since he had come back he had been involved in correspondence to try to win an appeal for Luke Anderson. Letters came from all over, but it was only so much paper. The fighters were too far away; he felt stranded. He had come home and gone into a dopey dream like the time he thought he was going to get to be a big Senator just because he debated in highschool.

Walt sat reading back numbers of papers. Reading papers wasn't enough. He wanted to get to work, to do a job, to find out more about machines and men. When his father was a boy they didn't have tractors, they didn't even have the gang plow. Now they were putting out a combine that did away with the old threshing crew. Someway there had to be a plan to make men and machines mix and he wanted to find it. If he told what he thought, people would laugh at him, so he just drew up his chair and began fumbling with the papers too, his mind straying back to Tub with a kind of envy and pity.

"Looks like we're winning," grinned Walt, putting his thick thumb nail on the paper. The West Coast strike, textiles in the East, fireworks in Minneapolis. He grinned back. No more talk; he was going to Chicago.

In the morning the subdued Tub came meekly to the house, doused his head at the pump, and ate a hearty breakfast. Stella and the girls buzzed around as he sat at the table, his goodlooking freckled face clear and innocent. Red hair bushed over greenish eyes that looked boldly and with so frank a liking that even the little girls hung around him like a pot of honey. "Well, Tub, you're great with the women," Steve teased, half enviously, as the two got started in the old bus.

"You'd be good yourself, you ol deacon if you ever let go," joked Tub, his spirits miraculously restored. All the way toward the Bijou Hills Tub hummed and sang, *Roll on Silvery moon,* and *There's a gold mine in the sky, far away, we will find it some sweet day,* and he had it all cooked up that he and Steve would get themselves a couple of ukes, learn cowboy songs, and they'd go over big in all the towns.

"Listen, Stevie," he said excitedly. "There's a big future ahead. Take radio. Take the movies. Take the jazz bands and all that kind of thing. We can do it. Remember the time we wowed them at Plankinton. They couldn't get enough. Say I tailed this show up to Minneapolis. Why, I saw a couple of fellows do an act that ain't got a spot on what you and me can do. We got the stuff, kid, what do you say?" He thumped Steve on the back, letting out a whoop like an Indian war chief. "Listen, this cowboy stuff has got them where it hurts. We can buy us a collection at a store in Minneapolis, learn it and then go to it. The land's plucked clean, let's go where the pickings are good, what say? Save our jack, get married."

He was dead in earnest and it sounded like a fine time, until you realized what a dead end it ran into. You sang and played the uke, you cleaned up, you tailed the girls, and then what? What next?

"What next? Crisalmighty, how do I know. What next? Listen, you don't go asking what next?"

"I do," Steve said. "I'm asking what next," and he thought what a heel he was to be lazing so long at home. He felt guilty as if he had let not only Luke Anderson down but himself. He kept looking out at the deserted country as if to remind himself of what the world was like, not Tub's gaudy top. Flocks of white chickens picked away in the dirt in front of tumbledown houses. Once they passed a handsome granite monument stranded in a family burying ground in the midst of fields now gray and haggard with thistle. An old church was boarded up with buzzards roosting on the steeple. Corncribs yawned naked and shameless to the sky. Cattle sheds sagged with broken backs and now and then along the road a dazed cow, a sheep, a scrawny dull-eyed calf wandered crazily, munching the bare earth. The farmers had all quit painting anything long ago, and the falling houses looked abandoned with no one to tend them anymore. It was a relief to see the dark hills rise toward the river, to see the small pinkish boulders crop from the ground that had given up seed for stones.

No one was at home at Tub's father's place. The ground was picked clean and an avenue of cedar trees was wilted, with the crest of the tree dripping like a bedraggled plume. Some chickens were chasing bugs in a patch of dried weeds. As the animals heard the car, guinea hens, pigs, geese, chickens, rushed up from the ground toward the sound. Sheep began coming up over the hill from the far pasture. Their long dark noses and boiled eyes were disturbingly harmless, confiding and shameless. Even a simpering little dog burst out from some cranny, barking with frenzy as if announcing glad tidings. Tub groaned, "My god, look at them, hungry as gnats, I don't know what in hell to feed 'em anymore. They're ready to pick me. I just want to run." Steve had to push him out of the car and remind him that he would go over the engine for him and get that loud knock out and bring the car back tomorrow. Driving back he felt helpless and small like a boy who's taken his first clock apart and can't put it together. It was the wrong idea to stick way off here. He would leave the next day, or anyhow the next week. He thought enthusiastically that he never had wanted to be peaceful or safe; he wanted to stake his life and maybe lose it. This grand thought filled his lungs with air; he saw the family at meal time as if he were already removed from them.

CRACK OF LIGHT

I HAVE told that story once too often, Lester Tolman thought, as he heard his voice mechanically repeat, "And the glass dome fell." He stopped, ashamed at the degeneration of a tragic event to an anecdote, and the two gentlemen at the table lifted their heads to look at him. The one had been peering sideways at a woman in a pink hat and the other had been noting Tolman's face rather than his remarks, the cheek bones, the feverish clever eyes. They waited, suspending their drinks, but Tolman suddenly buttoned his lips refusing to inform the informers. "And then?" suggested Mr. Sneed politely.

"Nothing," said Lester irritably. "There's no more to it. It fell."

"Oh," said Mr. Pettibone. "It fell."

"A good deal was involved, I presume," said Mr. Sneed, not too interested. He was touchily going over Berlin in his mind and the hot streets were again rising to smack his eyes as they had during his one visit with his wife when she had made him drive around and around with her in a barouche an entire afternoon to pay him off for looking at that woman the night before. He had finally bolted from her with a furious look into the Adlon bar and she had sailed upstairs to change. It had not been their honeymoon but it was equally dreary.

Mr. Pettibone was more interested in sugar. He knew all he needed to know about that business in Berlin. This romantic young man was after all representing a very influential magazine; therefore sound. He cleared his throat. "As I told you, the beet sugar people have a formidable lobby in Washington. They are back of the ruin in Cuba. But we're Americans too. We need protection too. You get that down right and we'll get somewhere. Get your mind off the details. Sugar is sugar. We aren't in the uplift business. Who is? I don't know where this howl about poor downtrodden Cuba began. There's plenty of that sort of thing right at home. Look at the farmer. If he hadn't gambled his shirt off, he'd be on easy street. I know those fellows, I had a piece of land out in Montana myself. They're worse than Wall Street. You've got a world market overloaded with sugar, and beet sugar is helping to cut the throat of cane sugar. Sugar *vs.* sugar. Americans against Americans. That's a fact. I guess you can look into it from the figures I gave you."

"Yes, look into it," said Sneed vaguely. "We've got a Cuban manager. He'll tell you Cubans don't want things different. They want to live like they live. Try to do something for them and see what thanks you'll get. This Roosevelt is helping ruin us. We can raise sugar cheaper in Cuba than anywhere else, and the price is kept up for whose benefit—ours? No, beet sugar, with a restricted market for us. We could undercut the market and then we'd be somewhere. This way, I'll be standing in a relief line myself soon, in fact a feller there is better off than I am, he's got no worries." He sniffed and looked fondly at his cigar. Then he smiled at Lester with an ingratiating dazzling smile. The charm of his smile sweetened the sourness that had fallen bitterly upon them. It almost won Lester from his own morose inner contemplation.

He called for a check instead, but Mr. Pettibone stopped him. Lester protested and Mr. Pettibone insisted. Mr. Sneed grinned, "Let Pettibone handle it, sugar ain't that far gone yet."

"Anything in the report that they are making a new kind of explosive out of sugar?" said Tolman carelessly.

Sneed and Pettibone exchanged a flash, then poker-

faced Sneed said, lightly, "Talk, just talk. Not perfected.
If perfected, of course, we're all made." He smiled.

"Of course," said Tolman, ironically. "The one best
bet is munitions today. Better than bread."

"Or sugar," wisecracked Pettibone.

Amiably the three walked out to the street. Tolman
shook hands briskly and made off. Anything to rid himself of the two rhinos. He admired the simplicity of their
approach; they had stripped it down to sugar *vs.* sugar.
One power group as against another. They had not been
able, so much as lucky, in building their sugar empire.
Their success had even precipitated them into ruin. All
the flies in the world had been drawn to the honeypot
and now sugar cane grew in places over the earth that
had nourished nothing but dry sand. Where they couldn't
raise cane, try beets. And the government sticking in a
finger now here, now there, to satisfy everybody. It was
a nasty story and he doubted if they would let him use
it. At the thought, a terrible weariness made him think
automatically of the nearest bar. He would like to see that
picture he had got hold of on a full-page spread, the cane
cutters with their bent backs and the lifted machetes, and
the old man with the eyes that stabbed as if he were
hanging from a palm tree by his great toe.

He walked up the avenue, torn and distraught, thinking of how to spend an evening. If only there were people who sat quietly in their homes and read books. Somewhere in the world couples must still walk around in
their gardens as he remembered his father and mother
used to do, calling out to one another to come look at
the snapdragon. Although he was often consoled by a
consciousness that he was unique, hence, superior, it was
no release. His mother's voice delicately calling, "Lester,
come practice your piano lesson," recalled him to a life
to escape whose meaning he had gone to Europe. It had
come, he admitted, to a terrible impasse if he now thought
fondly of that very garden from which he had run away.

The world that he had expected to open up limitlessly,
had instead folded down slowly upon him. On that day

in the early part of 1922 when he had tried to rinse his mouth of America forever, and blissfully, fearfully, embarked for England, his mind, full of ideas from plays and books, he had known nothing of the dark continent of the real Europe. He had, of course, agreed with certain enlightened college friends that the Versailles Treaty stank, that the War was a sellout and that democracy had been for Morgan. But wandering from chilly London to Bad-Homburg, baited by the falling mark, he had walked pleasantly in the gardens and without a conscience drank the old wines for a few American cents a bottle at the Park-Ritter Hotel.

He had fallen in with two handsome American gentlemen, journalists with graying hair and fascinating stories, bound for Moscow and the Far East, who walked every afternoon under the trees with a young American girl between them. She had long slim hands and a delicate chin and from under a little purple hat smiled at him thoughtfully as she sipped a glass of milk. When the three rented a big car with a tiny chauffeur like a toy in leather puttees and a huge cap, it was she who insisted he be included in the party. The chauffeur's family came to see him off as if their man were leaving for the front, and they set off boldly through the Harz mountains toward Eisenach where Luther threw the inkpot at the devil and on up through Thüringenwald to Berlin, the long golden horn blowing through tiny villages scattering geese and women before it. The two journalists threw green plums and stones at trees along the way, making up a pleasant little game called *steinwurfing* to see who could hit with the fewest throws, but he and Cora Constance, the girl, sat talking in low voices about love and what was going to happen in Germany.

When children in cotton smocks threw stones at them and yelled *schieber* tears came to her eyes and one of the men said he would rather walk on his hands and knees than be called a bloody profiteer but he didn't blame them. "As for me," he said wildly, "this trip is a crucifixion." But they went on with their game amiably, mile by mile, and in the evenings the philosophical one quoted Goethe and smoked a large cigar, sharing a bottle of chilled Mosel wine with the girl while the other railed bitterly about indulging one's appetites while the world was rocking.

Once they all had a quarrel and he felt like an orphan not knowing the reason, only that the girl refused to sit with them and rode all day with the chauffeur on the front seat, now and then quietly and openly crying. He had notions of going to her room at night and once got as far as her door, his hand on the knob, but fearful she might not be alone or repulse him, he tiptoed back again.

Berlin was crowded with tourists eating the Germans out of house and home for a few cents and they drove all evening looking for a place to stay before they found rooms in a pension overlooking a park. In the daytime the three disappeared, but late one afternoon they took him for cocktails to the Hotel Eden and, sitting in the rich place, it was hard to believe the Germans couldn't pay their war debts. Cora Constance said he should go to Wedding if he wanted to see the real Germany and look into workers' homes or where were his eyes, hadn't he noticed the girls peddling themselves for a few cents on every corner, in every café, swarming like flies on dead meat?

He felt youthful and ignorant but strangely and continually excited as if each night it would be impossible to sleep. When the more suave of the journalists said pleasantly that this was the hotel to which they had lured Rosa Luxemburg and Karl Liebknecht in order to murder them, to say nothing of the hopes of the working class, the conscientious one half rose and spluttered, "Why didn't you tell me? I couldn't drink another drop in this traitors' hangout."

Cora Constance had set her drink down. Her eyes looked black and she slid into her gloves as if she washed her hands of this business, once and for all. "I'm going," she said. "I don't know about you but I couldn't swallow another drop." On the street she muttered as if she were talking in her sleep and he had a hard time to keep up with her. It was a shameful murder and Rosa Luxemburg had been a wonderful, complete, gentle person who loved everything, birds and stones, but, she said, turning to him, brightly, "The world can't stand such people."

Her words had seemed like a breath upon a window-pane where figures had been lightly traced long ago and slowly, as she breathed, the figures came to view, line by line. All the time he was in Germany the background of the world kept emerging, terrible and clear. Even while Cora Constance had talked of Rosa Luxemburg and how the workers had been betrayed, he could not help notice the Germans looking them up and down, accusing them for their good foreign clothes and shoes. The old faded green War uniforms, the dresses that were shapeless and neat, made their garments as conspicuous as if they had worn the stars and stripes upon their chests.

He was going over it, the past running swiftly, as he walked up the avenue in the mood the Cubans had bequeathed him. The guilt they most certainly did not feel for the ruin in Cuba had inevitably brought him again to the glass dome. He knew he recited that story with the terrible fascination of a man who harps on an evil deed he has not publicly confessed.

Like a tame minnow that has swum all its life in a toy brook and drifts helplessly like weed in the ocean, he had let himself be buffeted. He had gone unresisting, hearing the talk about the fourteen points and Wilson's betrayal, the price of the egg that rose higher every day. At the opera where old ladies and gentlemen with narrowed eyes watched foreigners crowd refreshment bars ordering *belegte Brot mit Schinken* and beer and goblets of *bole* in gay ringing voices, he too ordered. Or he stood smoking a cigarette, feeling objective and as if all he were learning was, alas, tragic, but only part of the great tragedy of history.

And as if he were helpless to prevent himself from sharing the inhumanity of the world, he too had contributed his drop of poison. With wonder, now, and not so much regret inasmuch as through such experiences he had painfully come to wisdom, he remembered paying the girl who had come with him to his room with a few postage stamps. He had had the virtuous excuse that this would teach her not to try to pull the wool over his eyes and pretend she was a virgin and respectable.

He had felt very self-righteous, tearing her pitiful little makeshift story from her and sending her about her business, even halting her to give her a slice of white bread with real butter as if again to trap her and to prove she had been lying when she said she was hungry. She had eaten it, every crumb, her eyes on the door, and then instantly had fled, looking after her as she rushed down the stairs, her face peculiarly white and terrified under the flapping black hat. His own shame had kept him from forgetting her and he had felt separated from the world, had fallen on a solitary way of life, getting drunk every day, standing for hours in old museums as if to touch an ancient honesty denied this decay.

And if he had not found, through accidental comradeship in a beer hall, the German boy with his feet on the ground, where now would he be? He had left his old lodgings, no longer saw his American friends, went to live with Germans, eating what they ate, taking a stoic delight in his ability to endure. All his Puritan upbringing of living for a purpose seemed at last to have some meaning, giving him stamina to see it through.

But, of course, he had not seen it through. How could he, protected by his country, by the knowledge that back of him, always waiting to provide, was his father? It had been only a stage play, and yet through it his imagination had at last come awake. This is what it is like to live, he had repeated as if learning a lesson, when he read in the papers, not without a sense of security that lifted him above real horror, of the daily suicides in that same canal where the mutilated body of Rosa Luxemburg had once floated.

All the constant talk, the meticulous analyzing that went on in New York, London, Paris, and Berlin had not held off the future that now hung like a great stone around Hitler's neck. Why make one man the scapegoat for the greed of the world that open-eyed had long connived at despair? We are all guilty, and I especially, he thought, because I see. What is the difference between Pettibone and Sneed, filching the juice from the land, stealing the marrow from human bones and a Hitler, who was only the megaphone for their secret dreams?

He stopped, searched his pockets for a nickel. Finding one, he entered a drugstore and dropped it in the slot of the telephone. He hoped it would not be too late and Victoria Chance would have dinner with him. They could talk over the sugar story, she might get interested in the sugar-beet end of it. But what he wanted was to see a solid real human being. When she did not answer, he hung up irritably. Probably she was running, like the rest of them, to a meeting as if humanity could be thus saved from some hopeless ditch. He had seen meetings that were something, blocks in Dresden packed with thousands upon thousands waving the red flag and then, alas, he had seen houses mutely and submissively draped with the swastika the day the order was received in the letter box. He thought of this now, walking slowly, and in fairness trying to understand what lay back of his lack of faith. Kurt Becher who had suffered so that his very skin bore the effects, went patiently to meetings, wrote for them, and translated long tedious accounts from foreign papers with a tenacity incredible to Tolman. This mole, who worked in the dark for some end no rock could turn aside, carried some light he could not see. How would he end, or more pointedly, could the world be thus remade?

Lester was not altogether proud of his position, it seemed as yet incomplete, the product of his nerves rather than his will. He stood, uneasily, trying to make up his mind where to dine—should he try to call someone else?—concluding he would keep on walking to the park and then decide.

There was, he thought, no need to hurry.

Lady, Shoes Are Beautiful: Cuba, 1935

Lady, they's a live season. And they's a dead season. In the live season we cuts cane. In the dead season we tries to get to the coffee mountains.

With us, lady, we lives to get shoes. It's a long road from cane to the coffee mountains. It's a hard, hot, long road. It's hard on the feet and we aim for shoes. Shoes is our aim. Cuttin cane we never seem to lay our eyes on money. On the bateye I hear they got money. The bosses live on the nice clean bateye with oleanders in bloom. They got little houses with real roofs. They got water to wash in. They say they got a little school on the bateye for the kids. Us men in the barracones don't see no money, don't see no light but the moon, don't see no woman in the barracones.

Hey, get up you, the moon's high. It's two in the morning, three in the morning, time to cut cane. Better cut by the moon than in the burnin day. Cut till twelve, cut till one, maybe two. Get rice, some dried codfish, cigarettes at five a pack. Then swing in the hammock in the long dark doom. The bugs bitin. Hold on, bug, wait for some sleep. Two months, three months, then come the dead. In the dead who gets cigarettes, better cut cane. Suck some cane, the good rich juice. Cook some yucca and dream of meat. Get up, lazy bones, don't you complain. The nice man wants you to have the best. Buy at his nice store. The company owns it, the company sells it, the company watches over all your days. Sign here, sign there, sign it away. Mebbe if you good boy, don't complain, a drop's left and you can buy you some shoes. You can put your shoes on your old stumpy feet, you can spread your toes, walk your shoes on them goodfornothin feet. Get goin to coffee mountain.

Then the rains come down, they soak up the ground, they soak up your great big goodfornothin feet. The worms they grow in the spongy ground, they fat and white, they

222

huntin a home. Worms, here is a pair of worthless feet.
Make yourself right to home, worms, in these here feet.
Think themselves so smart in them new shoes, struttin
the roads, hangin high in the coffee mountain hut out of
reach of the rain. Waitin for the feet to march back to
the cane. Cane, coffee, coffee, cane. March, march. Shoes,
you is wonderful.

Look up at shoes, hangin over my head. Boys, keep your
hands off them shoes less you want to be dead. These my
shoes. Boys, look at my shoes, um, um. Us poor boys got
no shoes.

Worm, make yourself to home in them feet. Too
proud to go without shoes. Humble yourself, get yourself
down. Boy, boy, is he sick. Has he got the sickness. Boy's
eyes roll, he's got it. Man, has he got it. Too sick to get
up. Too sick to pick on the wet soggy green coffee moun-
tains. He's a turnin gray. He's a swellin up. He's a goin
green. He's dyin. Who gets his shoes? He's a namin the
boy. Stand aside, boys, he wants to name the boy. The
boy comes forward, his eyes deep mournful. This is the
man with the big talk. This man tellin us. This the man
who is goin to be dead.

I got his shoes. He lyin now, cold as a stone. Soon in
earth, a dog buries his bone. Lie still, man, I in your
shoes. Walkin to the sugar cane. Make way, the big Shoe
Boy is comin. He tellin me, the dead man is still a talkin.

Don't lay down, boy, and roll your eyes. You can fight,
can't you, what you got to lose?

These my shoes.

THE LAST ROUNDUP

THERE was nothing spectacular about the Radford family. They were possessed of no glaring virtues or gifts that might lead their associates to point them out. They suffered from no ambitions that might not have had some expectation of fulfillment, judging from the standards of the world they had known as children. Clifford had never robbed a bank, or killed a man, or even coveted another man's wife. He had been as near to a contented human being as it is possible to find. His ambition had been "to work up" in his job, and find reward for work well and faithfully done.

If he had studied history instead of the Bible in his youthful days, when he had thoughts of the ministry, he might have taken to heart the observation that the great upheavals are caused not so much by the thwarting of some outstanding man's ambition as by the continual, hopeless negation of the hopes of the many. But Clifford Radford had, instead, paid more attention to the Psalms of David, neglecting even those parts of the Bible that might have informed him. He knew that the Lord was his shepherd and he took consolation remembering Job who cried out, *Where shall wisdom be found? Where is the place of understanding? Man knoweth not the price thereof, neither is it found in the land of the living. It cannot be gotten from gold, neither shall silver be weighed for the price thereof. Behold the fear of the Lord, that is wisdom; and to depart from evil is understanding.*

In the early days of his troubles, he had gone frequently to church and later when it seemed that, because of his constant moving, the new church turned a cool and indifferent shoulder upon his rather unprepossessing self and his modest wife, he had taken up his Bible. The clear beautiful sound of the words had steadied him. He had repeated them as he walked the streets, held to them as he waited in line. But after a while, whether through use, or what, their meaning waned. He even challenged the words as if they too were asking him to postpone his fate until his day was done. His children were growing, their needs were thrusting at him, hour by hour. True, wisdom was not in gold, but gold seemed to rule the world. It bought people the right to live; without it, they might sink like so much garbage into the old Missouri that year by year wandered its same stubborn predatory way. Fear of the Lord, which Clifford took to mean respect for the laws of God, he had. He had not violated the laws of God, as he knew them, nor the laws of man, as he understood them. But somehow, somewhere, some terrible law had been violated to throw the world into discouragement and despair.

He was not a man given to long thoughts. He liked to sit reading a little, thinking a little, dreaming a little. Lately he did not sit and think or read or dream, much. When he dreamed it was all too often, he feared, of foolish worldly things. Perhaps the high thoughts are reserved for those who have crawled back from the edge of the pit, or for those who are alone, and have no souls in their keeping. After the day was done, and the curious asylum-quiet seemed to have entered into his own blood, he went out into the long yard and walked a bit, looking at the sky that was so often the color of the opal ring his wife wore.

Perhaps he had had a letter from her. She thought up a hundred funny ways to tell him of the humdrum days. Paw wasn't so rambunctious in the heat; even he had piped down through that last scorcher. The two boys were in the ball park all day and both swore they would be in the big league someday. They had about a dozen badges, for everything, from *Rum is Ruin,* to *Remember Your Feathered Friends.* They were getting kind of hard to control and she feared the day when they would get out of hand with Paw ready to pounce down upon them. She had earned fifty cents baking a cocoanut cake for one of the ladies, but Paw put his foot down and said it was not enough and the gas ate up all the profit. She had learned to knit and if she got very good at it she would be able to knit sweaters and dresses to order. He was not to worry at all, just take care of himself and watch his health and not forget to drink plenty of water in this heat. So long as a man perspires he can't drop dead of sunstroke.

He thought tenderly of her concern to keep him alive, of his to keep her and the boys. To keep each other alive and in health, to hold on as a sick man holds on from day to day and thinks curiously of that tiny particle that would free him from his bed. If only his bile ran properly or if he could simply swallow food. The patient with the blood-poisoning, if he had only not punctured his hand with the innocent nail. If the woman with the miscarriage would stop bleeding. If the swollen appendix had not burst a minute too soon. And once on his rare excursions into the movie house, when he saw pictures of the gold bricks piled up, innocent and ordinary to the eye as any masonry, and read that this was the nation's treasure, the foundation upon which its security rested, his nerves were taunted by the image that for days suggested that for one small brick his life might be spared. More and more, unconsciously, instead of thinking in terms of, can I get a job that will support us all, he seemed to be asking himself, will I live?

He did not mean to be ungrateful for the job that at least kept them all alive, if apart. But it was as unsatisfactory as for a sick man to know that he has escaped death only to linger for no one knows how long, helpless on his spine. More and more, he realized that the day would come when any desperate move would be better than this. And he found delight in this sudden resolution; his system at once supplied the juice that gave him courage. They could stick it out, perhaps on the South Dakota land; they would make a new start. Do something. Anything.

When he read that farmers were drifting to the northwest, that upon deserted land the new breed of pioneers might raise nuts or Egyptian cotton, even he paused, his scalp twitching with the wonder of it all. How far would man's gullibility be stretched, when would it snap? The same papers carried news of a man in West Virginia who had shot himself because they made him plow up his cotton. Nuts? He could think of nothing but ribald crazy answers that hammered in his brain; nuts to the nutty, and nuts to you, Mister America.

With nuts he could buy that car which no up-and-coming family should be without, the vacuum cleaner without which a home is simply a dump, the furniture polish that reduces work to joy, and furniture to the sheen of mirrors. He could buy that lovely negligee, fragile and pale as a seashell, that he had seen sprawled carelessly in the shop window, as he stood, self-conscious, his hands in his pockets, looking out of the corner of his eye as a Puritan looks at the portrait of a nude. There it was, the lovely thing, lying for some glamorous creature to slip into. And it was curious that the negligee, rather than a dress, caught up his imagination as if it offered all those leisurely and forbidden pleasures that only the movies displayed to the eyes of men. He had not clothed some movie queen in his stolen purchase, but his wife and with all his heart, seeing her sit in it before a long glass, combing her short thick hair that it had given her such delight and such a youthful joyous feeling to cut, years ago.

She would have little slippers on her feet and, through a door ajar, a marvelous bath would spread itself with colors like the rainbow. If ever a man wanted his wife to have music wherever she goes, he was that man. Not that he meant anything foolish or silly, and as for bells and rings, that was another matter. But he had simply wanted her life to be clear and happy. Sometimes his dreams would take a turn and he would drive up to his father's door in Boone in a fine car in a fine suit and honk the horn. Nancy would come out, peering nearsightedly, unable to believe what she plainly saw. His father and mother would stare, and he would get out of the car, recklessly, tearing packages from the back seat and, right on the lawn, he'd open them and scatter tissue paper and hold up the lovely underthings. He'd have a present for Paw, too, so fine that for once the old man would be struck dumb.

Or they would go back to Oxtail and buy that very lot that they had been forced to let go on a twenty-dollar tax sale. As he walked through the long halls at the asylum—or listened to the tall crazy with the polite civil face explain in a carefully modulated voice that the gentleman who sat next to him in the sun parlor was really insane and something should be done about it— he thought he could build a house and (as he nodded and soothed the crazy) the roof was put on, the good sound copper gutterpipes installed, the plumbing fixtures carried in on the shoulders of stalwart workmen. By the time he had walked back to his own little cubicle, he was building other houses all along the same street, and in a new straw hat was coming home from the office waving to his neighbor, the man who had stood in line with him that long rainy day in Portland, Oregon.

Lying still on his narrow cot, the crazies shut out for the night, he might run across the street to help his other neighbor fix his radio—and again here was a man that might not be so highly thought of in the world, but Clifford in the gratitude of his heart chose to honor him with one of the best homes on the street. He had given Cliff carfare and bought him coffee, and wrote out a list of names for him to go to see, all had proved O.K. and had helped. This fellow had worked in mines, had laughed when Cliff asked about his family. "Lord, I never had any. Never had a mother either, except Mother Jones, and she was one whale of a mother, you bet."

Sometimes Clifford thought, with a tingling of pride, of the way life had opened up and how he had had hints of ways and kinds of living that took him far beyond anything he had ever dreamed of in the old days. It was a kind of consolation to him, as it must have been to the sailor he talked to in Seattle, who had sailed every sea and bragged he knew more kinds of women than you can shake a stick at. Nature seemed to have a way of making new skins for man as well as for the beasts of the field. There was a healing in thoughts like this. He would find himself easing off to sleep, taking hold of the idea that times were bound to get better. His wife's letter telling him about the neighbor's son who had lost his job on Wall Street, and was on his way to Albuquerque to be a hotel clerk, might look like a bad sign if the fellow had not sworn that a big boom was on the way and had a book to prove it.

If Wall Street talked liked that there must be something to it, he reasoned, and the day might even come when he could take that correspondence course he had cut clippings out about long ago. He was so cheerful finally that, as his mind put out the light of wakefulness, he added the last touch to his street, and installed a garbage collector who came around every day at five o'clock in the morning while the street dozed cozily and this fellow would be none other than the smartaleck who had been so snotty that time Clifford applied at the employment office in Tacoma.

NO REDEMPTION

IF ONLY they could have had a garden, if the corn had had a chance to ripen. If the grapes had grown purple on the vine and she could have pulled them off in big bunches and the fragrance of boiling jelly and wine might have sweetened the air. All that summer Victoria's mind clung to the charms of the past as if they had held some sorcery.

It would take so little to straighten out their lives, to set their feet again on a common path. Sometimes at work, she would make some exclamation that had no meaning. People would look at her strangely as if she had talked in her sleep, confessing some secret sin. She was only thinking, she would explain, of the garden that she had not been able to put in that summer, or she would recall that time they had a boat and lay out in the sun on the naked burning water in a tiny shell of wood. It was walking the water like the Lord. It was being upheld by some invisible power. Everything seemed endowed with a kind of wonderful magic and, when she went home, only Jonathan remained outside that enchantment.

She would try to woo him but her heart was often heavy and resentful of his hurt look. Away from it, it seemed easy and she would rehearse her rapturous return, that face to face, became a dream. She shriveled down into her self, curled down within as if there could be no redemption. He would give her no chance, it seemed, to be born again. Oh, let the light come, but he seemed bent on pursuing her with his own suffocation as if he had sworn to kill the two of them together.

There would be fine days and they would almost forget that anything had happened. They would talk about the future but the talks did not end so well. "You'll see someday, when I'm not here and you have another wife. Then you'll know how much I loved you," she would say, walking up and down, ready to break in two with the despair of ever mending anything between them. "I love you more than you love me," Jonathan would answer, stubbornly, and they would find themselves glaring at one another like two frenzied children. Kurt had gone to the West Coast and sent occasional letters. She read them with her heart in her throat, conscious that Jonathan was watching her. With an air of indifference she threw the single sheet of paper to him as if by reading the innocent words his suspicions would dissolve forever. But it did not keep him from accusing her bitterly of never having loved him and of always having lived for herself.

She would stand before him, like a condemned woman, listening to his words and fighting back the tears. Even as she fought to reassure him of her love, something gave way inside her. It seemed useless to fight for something that did not have the power to stand alone. It was not a strict stupid fidelity that she had craved but some deeper darker surer loyalty that might bend with the wind but not break and leave one with a broken reed. I have given it to him but he denies me, she thought bitterly, trying to reason with him while all the time he listened to her with a still stony face.

He did not rightly hear her words and she wronged him in thinking him willfully cruel. He seemed in a trance as she repeated all the details that were meant to convince him. There were times when he thought he would lose his senses and rush upstairs to the trunk where the revolver lay under piles of linen. Once he got drunk again and at the sight of his wild white face, she shrank back from the very doorway. He had come in swaggering, demanding that she go out with him in the car, and she had refused terror-stricken, but firm enough. When he had come downstairs with the revolver, swinging it around as if he were playing a part on a stage, and asking her if it would not be better to die, she wheedled it out of his hand, and dropping out the cartridges, hid it in her workbasket. But she did not soften at his suffering. She felt hard and cold as steel. He is ruining everything, she told herself, blindly opening the door and feeling her way alone up the road that was almost invisible in the deep darkness. When she came back he had gone to bed, lay peacefully with his arm stretched out and, when she touched him, sat up with so woeful a murmur of repentance that she could only sob, holding him to her.

And if he had been called to war to lose his life, she could not have felt it a greater waste than that they should torture each other so much and so uselessly. If he would only not be watching me all the time, like an evil eye, like a jailer sitting outside the cell of the condemned. She felt guilty enough at the terrible change that seemed to have taken place in her as if the spring inside some machine had broken. She was in such constant fear that their life would fall apart before it could be mended,

that her very hands seemed to turn to clay when he
touched her. "I'm no good anymore," she said humbly
but he felt that there was something willful in her voice,
that she did not regret her failure that seemed to save her
for a future he would not share.

Once she called out, *oh, help, help me,* in her sleep
and when he put his arms around her, soothing her, she
had sobbed as if she could not stop, in short sharp gasps.
It was only that she wanted him to help her to forget
Kurt but she could not tell him. The room seemed nar-
rowing down upon them like a coffin; she felt strangled as
if they could no longer be held together by mere wishing.

When one of the farmers came around, or Si Greenough
dropped in on one of his trips, the house seemed fresh-
ened by a good stiff breeze. Sitting with the company,
they would both feel at peace—nothing had happened—
and if a discussion came up, the two of them would
agree, proving to the world that nothing could divide
them.

Si had just come up from Alabama and he told about
the sharecroppers in one county who had said they didn't
need any argument to get five thousand members in the
croppers' union. " 'Ain't no argument with us,' " Si had
quoted. " 'With us they is ready and glad. They is just
waiting for the word. They scared some but they come
anyway.' " Some of them were now in jail, one of them
had been shot in the back one night when he was guarding the road while a bunch held a meeting in the dark
of one of the cabins. "They claimed he hadn't the experience," Si said, "or he wouldn't have got shot. A fellow told me about it. 'I tol him,' he says, 'to stay out
of the light. Don't let no light shine on you, I says, but
he stood there in the road with a white shirt on and the
light fell on him. He was on guard if a car came and
if there was trouble he was to sing out and we was to
come and throw in. He stepped back but they got him
as he turned. He fired at them from the road, it was

plain suicide; he was looking for it, they'd beat up his brother and hit the baby over the head that day.' "

Si's voice had taken on the very tone of the cropper and when he stopped, the three of them almost quit breathing; the very smell of danger was in the room. They could see flapping ghosts of trees, hear the call of a mockingbird, the creak of the scarecrow cabins as a black shadow crossed the sill. All the trouble between Jonathan and Victoria seemed petty and suddenly shameful to them both. They looked at one another timidly and with pardon. The vision of such danger was sharp and sweet—they swung out over some rocky ledge to drop into a meadow.

When Si left they went into the kitchen together to prepare supper as they used to do. He ground the coffee while she flipped a slice of ham in the pan. The smell of the coffee was pungent and friendly like old times and Jonathan moving happily around the kitchen hovered behind her as she dropped the eggs beside the ham. All the drawn look had left his face, he seemed to share the triumph of the croppers who had so many followers. If they had five thousand there, and someday five thousand in every county, the future need not always mock them.

"Perhaps Si is right," he said, the tension released in him. "He says it's only organization that counts. All the high-sounding ideas, life, liberty and pursuit of happiness, didn't give us the kind of country men expected. What good is freedom if it doesn't give you work and bread? That's why the Germans followed Hitler, he promised something."

He caught himself and for a second his face darkened. The word had reminded him of Kurt Becher but this time he would not let that mist get between them. He pushed back his plate when he was finished and sighed deeply. "I'm happy," he confessed, putting his arms around Vicky who stood amazed—a miracle had happened. "I've been worried. Si and I don't always agree. All this struggle for relief and so on. I don't know as I see it. When you give people just enough to eat and they get satisfied

or resigned to it, you've got a pretty heavy bulwark to re-
action. That's what scares me. You've got to make them
see the long road, all the time, make them discontented
with the pickings. Think of it, what a world we could
have. Human beings have never yet got upright, they
are still crawling on their hands and knees."

They made a fire in the fireplace and sat up late talking
about the wonders that could be as if they had been scien-
tists discussing some discovery that might save the world
from cancer or the soil experts who years before had
gravely warned against the invasion of freebooting enterprise into the West, where buffalo had followed grass and
Indians had followed buffalo with a wisdom scorned by
men driven only by the needs of their own tiny lifetime. "It's just that bread isn't enough, either," Jonathan
said again as if he were haunted. "Look at Si and me. We
both have rich fathers. Money doesn't mean that much.
Property will always be between my father and me. He's
a decent fellow according to his lights. He thinks he is
absolutely right."

"Oh, sure," said Victoria in a mocking voice.

"Well, he does," said Jonathan. "I bet in a different
society he'd fall right into it. He's no money baron."

Victoria got up, suddenly impatient. She looked at
Jonathan sitting with his hands relaxed, at his brooding
face. He can't go two ways at once, she thought, he'll
be cut in two, he'll be crucified. The vision was too painful. For a second she thought she saw him as that young
man carved upon a tomb in Italy in the big art book
upstairs, with lilies growing around his head and his
face though dead, as if asleep, shutin on each side by the
dead closed faces of his parents. She had looked at this
picture many times and only now thought she saw an
unmistakable likeness. She turned her face from Jonathan as if she had closed the covers of the book and
with her head down went into the kitchen. She felt that
she had somehow let a stray thought come that might destroy him.

She rinsed the cups and washed the silver, wondering
at the darkness in which human lives moved. They had

electrical equipment, they knew history, she thought she understood something of the workings of the world and saw through its shams, but she had no guard against these curious superstitions of the senses, these creeping premonitions of the flesh. She dried the dishes trying to think of some way to drag herself back to earth again, remembered only silly jingles of her youth when she had struggled to fortify herself against life's battles with little verses. Jonathan's mind might have been running on the same track; he began to recite all by himself, in the next room,

> And behold, thrones were kingless and men walked,
> One with the other even as spirits do,
> None fawned, none trampled; hate, disdain, or fear,
> Self-love or self-contempt, on human brows,
> No more inscribed, as o'er the gate of hell. . . .

"All hope abandon ye who enter here," finished Victoria, coming in with a cup in her hand. "Remember what you used to recite, just to show off, of course, when I first knew you? That one you made up in highschool about *I give my soul to the devil, he's the one who looks after my kind, and all my sensual longings are by him instilled in my mind, he rules my actions completely, where he leads I willingly go, I am one of his minions of evil, to all good impulse a foe.*" They both burst out laughing. But neither could remember how it ended. "All I remember is when you said the line, *'Tis over, with heart racing madly, I break the embrace of my love, do you wonder I pray to Mephisto and not to some power up above?*"

He looked thoughtfully in the fire, shaking his head and laughing as he remembered the crazy days in Detroit, the old carefree times at the Vidisichis', the drinking and boasting. He felt suddenly old and a little lonely.

The War, that had not yet come, put its mark on all the living. It hurried the farmers as they heaved stone on stone of the building that Arty Sturmer called "the meeting house." Old Mr. Willis had pointed with a long bony finger at a fine bit of corner with a few big trees. "Put her right there," he said. "I figure there's a good well somewhere around under them stones. We can drill later and have water." They would put in a kitchen, the women said, and have a place for suppers to raise money. They would get an old radio or maybe a victrola and dance, the kids said. They could get speakers from Philadelphia. Pictures could come here, as well as any place. Right up in front the whitewashed wall was as good as a screen. You could put the picture machine right in back here and throw the picture on. Maybe some of the city folks would give them some books.

"We don't want this here place to degenerate into a talking fest," old man Willis said. He had heard too much talk in his life, but once he had heard Gene Debs speak. He had been to a big meeting where Foster shook you to the bones. The young folks said maybe they could study some. They were all farm kids working now in the stocking mills, bringing home their wages to the old folks on the farm.

"We don't want this to be a darned club, just for a few like a sewing circle," Tim Robb said. "We got to branch out, get new folks, grow." The call to action had shaken the farmers down. The wheat was separated from the chaff, but it narrowed the little group and Tim was angry at the kind of isolation he saw growing up. The hall would break that down. They could hold meetings. Have speakers anyone would come to hear. Mrs. Sturmer was still wearing her little Mennonite bonnet but she had broken out of her shell. The chick had nibbled out into the world and Arty was prouder than anyone. At first when groups met in his home to discuss what to do, his wife and daughter were sent to the kitchen. If someone wanted a drink and went to the kitchen, there they would be sitting, quietly, lonely, with eyes glued on the door that shut them from paradise. Tim Robb had given Arty a good talking to. But it took time to wear that stern stuff down. Emily Robb began coming along with her husband, with a flyaway look about her as if she had just hopped upon a particularly frisky horse on some merry-go-round. "Come on in, Missus Sturmer," she had called out gaily. "The water ain't cold, it's fine."

Finally, Arty had given permission and Mrs. Sturmer and Daughter sat primly, with wide eyes astonished at their own boldness. By the time the building was going up, Mrs. Sturmer was as agile as you please. She came almost every day, running around with her skirt pinned up over an oldfashioned flounced underskirt. She brought a big basket full of good food for the men, a huge dish of her famous noodles, blushing at her husband's boast that Ma was the best noodler he ever laid eyes on.

The building rose fast, like an ark that would carry them all in a storm. They did not always agree like birds in a nest. Antagonism took a curious form. Some pulled one way, some another. Those who were out-and-out Communists were always yelling about "showing the face of the party." As the Tesh boy had insisted on being a "Face," it did not work out very well. The Tesh boy came from a brokendown farm; the "Face" should be a first-rate farmer who held the respect of the whole community. Jake Tentman finally also came out as a "Face." He had one of the best chicken farms in the whole countryside. And while he kept this enterprise absolutely on the up-and-up, he referred to the meetings and the work among the farmers as "life." He told Jonathan he didn't see how the city fellers, who had come out to this part of the country, ever could write when they were so separated "from life." Life to him was struggling toward that end, far-off or near, that he had visualized as a young boy in Odessa when he was chosen because of his innocent-appearing youth to row out to meet a boat that silently dropped a package of contraband leaflets into his excited grasp. The reeds growing close to shore, the swish of the boat pulling toward the dark land that might burst with fire in a surprise arrest, made the business of being a "Face" child's play, even with the prospect that vigilantes might

someday take it into their heads to ride again. But,
though Tentman had been on his land some twenty-five
years, Tim Robb was not satisfied with him as a Face.
He too must be a Face, one that had the stamp of old
American stock, and they could go look up his great-
grandfather who had carried a musket under George
Washington, if they pleased.

They would joke about the "Face," with all the time
the seriousness stirring them all, and those not in the
party a little frightened, concerned, especially now that
they were putting up such a fine building and it would
be terrible to have a lot of hoodlums wreck it. The kids
began scratching around for melodeons, old organs, and
one fellow came proudly with a clarinet. They made a
rule never to meet just for fun. Someone had to make
a talk about the work of the world, even if it took no
more than a few minutes, like an old time prayer. They
brought copies of the New York *Times,* the Philadelphia
Record, and the *Daily Worker.* A big bunch of Socialist
kids with armbands came down to one of their parties
and at the "talk" fired questions that almost led to a
scrap. Tim Robb gave them all a talking to after it was
over. He said if they couldn't behave better, where would
they get? Arty said it wasn't the fault of their kids, that
damned bunch had just come to make trouble. You had
to have a tough hide, Jonathan thought, to see through all
the squabbles, and not get downhearted at the gnats
biting. Anyone who expected a nice easy peaceful ride to
the future, should crawl into a coffin. As for his generation, the only peace he could see was in having a clear
conscience. Even that was not always possible.

It was one thing, mixing with the farmers, another
when he went to the city. More and more, Si Greenough
tried to get Jonathan to go to Philadelphia, to New York,
even to Washington, to meet little groups of sympathetic
broadminded people who might become interested a little
in the farmers' fate. If not the farmers, then the young
people. They tried to think up an assortment of wares
that would draw around them substantial help. Against

his own inclination, Jonathan found himself becoming what he had most dreaded to be, a "Front." He was not a "Face" coming out boldly but merely a "Front," extremely well dressed in the clothes his father had always provided him from the discarded wardrobe of himself and Tom, handsome, and in a pinch, even urbane. The city people read everything and their tortured legitimate doubts were often too complicated for his simple solutions. He did not know how to bring them his own great belief in men. They argued about the "Line" that the working people were following or would follow. Was it right or wrong? And while Jonathan realized only too clearly the terrible necessity of a clear plan of action, he was baffled at the reliance well-intentioned men and women gave to the word rather than the deed. He began to suspect that deep down—almost as much as his brother-in-law Ed Thompson—they distrusted the very people they longed to see rise from poverty.

He would come back to the country and mix around with the farmers to get his breath again. Those fellows who had run along with them when their farms were in danger had dropped off. The fellows who had expected a quick rise of milk prices had fallen away. Those who were left were men who had never traveled, had never been to Florida, and a few had never been to Philadelphia, forty-five miles away. They knew George Washington and Lincoln as heroes who belonged to all, but lately men of all stamps used these names as if they were plasters to cover their own sores. Once more Lincoln seemed to be sitting in that box, with hand shading his eyes, looking down upon a stage from whence a bullet would again reach his heart. In the midst of the bugles blowing, it was a comfort to find new heroes about whom there was no mistake, around whose bodies, alive or dead, there was no argument.

Dimitroff, breaking on Page One of the New York *Times,* defying the executioner and his ax, belonged to no one except to men like them. No one fought over the strikers who had been fired on in the Twin Cities. No one wanted Angelo Herndon except themselves. They still demanded their share in the country's great, but better to leaf this paper and see the face of the Chinese student, where death had made the lines of torture appear with the rigidity of peace. Jonathan envied Tim Robb and Arty Sturmer, even James Honeywell, the Quaker, who accepted all this as if it were daily bread. Even if the "Line" were wrong, this refound potentiality of fellowship of man for man must be real.

He warmed his hands at it, when, chilly with his own doubts that seemed to hamper him like a caul, he came back to his house and wondered at the sudden loneliness that waited inside the door. He thought with envy of those completely devoted men whose lives seemed all of one piece, who lived and died, in one suit, so to speak, with their boots on and their hearts beating to the last drop for one purpose. Was it imagination, or did such men really exist or did they merely hide (as all men hid) their troubles daily, those deep and personal woes that gnawed relentlessly at the very roots of a man's being. If such troubles gnawed, it was the act that counted, even as it counted in love or war.

He had taken off his coat when he noticed that a fire had been laid in the fireplace. Looking around with surprise, the house had a fresh, newly brushed look. In the kitchen a stack of freshly washed and ironed clothes had a note on top of it. "Mrs. Chance sent me the key and told me to clean up a little for you hope things are to your satisfaction yours truly Mrs. Wieder." He felt warmed, protected, and soothed by his wife's love, or was it her guilt? He tried hard to crunch the sharp bitter pang that had its fang ready to sting so easily, and walked around looking at the furniture dusted, the rugs swept, the neatness and coziness gradually restoring him. He picked up the note again, rereading it, smiling as if it had come directly from his wife.

AGAINST THE GRAIN

Toward fall a good many people talked persistently about the new boom on the way. Jonathan's father refused to get sail up before there was a breeze and wrote his son the usual letters about Aunt Em's toothache and the way the Melbournes let their son Harold run wild and how it was impossible to calculate the future although there were more prophets than hairs to a horse's tail.

"What he means," said Victoria sourly, "is that it isn't safe to invest anymore." Business was lifting all the same, a little uncertainly, as if an old face had had a tuck taken along the hairline at an up-to-date beauty parlor that could not be guaranteed and might even break down suddenly just when the old beauty in all her glory was hoping to prolong the sensations of early youth. Tom Chance wrote that he might be coming East on a big eastern selling trip and if Jonathan wanted a job he would take him on. Even Clifford Radford stirred up a little luck and said he had a job offered him in Oxtail that might not look exactly promising but still brought bread and butter and the chance for the little family to be together again. When Clara Monroe talked to her sister Nancy she agreed that it was about time things got better—if they didn't want the poor to revolt—but at night as she sat opposite her lord and master, she nodded yes, yes, to his tirades against the stupid farmers and the upstart dumb labor unions led by ignorant racketeers. From his language anyone would think that Mr. Monroe himself was a scintillating spark of brilliance—actually, he occasionally considered himself so to be.

Among Jonathan's people the only happy ones seemed the newlyweds. Margaret Thompson wrote her brother that she had more clothes but seldom saw Ed anymore

and wished he would make out a list of new books that
were worth reading.

When Jonathan announced that Si wanted him to leave
the farm-work and make a trip to the Middle West, then
come back to work with city people in the hope of getting more firm support, Victoria was up in arms. Just
when things were working out he must go skating across
the country. He wouldn't like the people that he would
have to talk to when he came back. They would be just
like his father.

Jonathan answered with a peculiar coldness that he
ought to be willing to go where he was most needed. And
who, she wanted to know, was to decide that? Was Si om-
niscient? Mistakes were made all the time, he wasn't going
to deny that, she hoped, and they were making one now.
You couldn't make a man over, no matter how hard you
tried; it was a mistake to do things that went against
the grain. It would work out badly, they could take her
word for it.

She would have said much more in the same vein if she
had not noticed that it merely confirmed Jonathan's fear
that she did not believe in him. Perhaps it was only
for herself that she feared, and when this thought came
to her she tried to make no complaints but to pack up
his things and close the house. They would not be need-
ing a house, it looked like, for a long time. It had suffered
in their absence; the little avocado tree had died. The
grass had grown rank and only the little trees and bushes
of the hedge seemed to thrive as well without as with the
Chance family.

She wrote Jonathan every day and followed his trip
on a map as if he were in the army. I'll be sticking pins
in it soon and moving up against the enemy, she thought.
Lester Tolman announced that he was going to dig into
sugar in dead earnest and proposed that he get hold of
a car and drive out to the beetfields. He could check up
on the farm situation; he'd been told it was brokendown
farmers who were feeding the labor supply in the beetfields. Did Victoria want to do the footwork? Did she?

She went out and bought a new hat and sent a wire to Jonathan saying, "Watch out for me, two ships may pass in the night."

The long ride to the West was as invigorating as a sea voyage but when she was in Chicago, Jonathan was in Milwaukee. In Minneapolis he had passed on to Omaha. They seemed always to be trailing a mirage and Victoria began to work hard and be very quiet except at those towns where the farmers poured out to some meeting. The big quiet figures in old overalls reminded her of her father smoking his pipe and standing around in his old implement store chinning with some farmer.

They were still talking in the same slow gentle way with a kind of consideration for one another that people in the East wouldn't understand. The little schoolrooms where they had their meetings, the sudden bursts of oratory from men who boasted that they didn't have a decent necktie anymore and as for a hat hair was a good thatch, made her skin tingle as if she were a little girl again listening to her favorite teacher, Miss Faversham, tell about the Boston Tea Party and our Brave Ancestors. Even Lester got a little excited and forgot that he had fallen in love with a New York actress and was on the verge of a great passion.

"Why didn't you tell me?" he demanded of Vicky.

"Tell you what?"

"Why, what swell people these are. They're great," and he felt flattered that they stood around talking to him as if he were one of them. "I get on swell with them, don't I?" he asked anxiously and Victoria had to admit he did. But at night there was always a battle about where to sleep. If it was a farm, they took what the farmer had, but if they landed in a town, Lester wanted to nose out a homey Tourist Home while Vicky preferred the impersonal little hotels with beds hard as nails and no chummy woman to involve them with a long monologue about the better times she had seen.

When they came to the Dakotas, he wanted to hurry to Montana where he had heard of the big open spaces and longed to get a glimpse of a wildwest town. The first town across the border was dead as a doornail with a local prohibition option that soured Lester on the whole project for twenty-four hours. The smell of dead dust began to leave the air and through a section watered by irrigation the beetfields looked luscious and as exotic as a hothouse after the stiff gray hairs of grass like the stubble on a dead man's face on the fields of Dakota. Victoria had a whiff of sweet clover as they rode along in the dark and the country seemed to open up, sweet and intoxicating as a flower that blooms once in a century.

In the beetfields they were not allowed to get near the workers and those they saw looked sullen and unresponsive. The setup was clean enough but a curious secretiveness made Lester determined to prowl around on his own. He came back with nothing more illuminating than a black eye. He'd been given a kick in the pants all right and told to mind his own damned business. He was ready to send off wires to State Senators, to United States Senators, to the Supreme Court and the Civil Liberties Union, but after a few drinks, he sobered up and simply jotted everything down in his notebook. He would not jeopardize the rest of his trip with undesirable publicity, he said, but he'd get the sons of bitches, sooner or later.

Lester began to talk about his nerves and to refer to Victoria as his secretary in a pompous commanding voice when talking to government officials. He liked nothing better than drawing up his chair for a good long talk and was continually surprised at the intelligence of the farmers as if he had expected them to be Fiji Islanders. He was somewhat handicapped by not knowing wheat from rye and being uncertain as to the process that determined a steer, but as his notes grew in volume, he cheered and said they would do some great pieces.

In South Dakota they went to a big meeting in a church

and Mrs. Petersen took them in charge. She was a big handsome woman with a tall important-looking husband who was running for the legislature. They had dinner at her house with two young people, one was Steve Carson who had been in jail and sat very shy, with bright eager eyes sliding over everything, and the other was a girl who had been a student at Vermillion. "Lorraine is a regular artist," boasted Mrs. Petersen. "Did you notice that banner painted up over the altar? Hikes Through Hardship?—that was Lorraine's work."

"That was nothing, Mrs. Petersen," said Lorraine with a kind of scornful composure. She had heavy chestnut hair that she kept tossing back with an unconscious impatient gesture that Tolman said reminded him of a little colt running away from its mother. "Nice kids," he mumbled under his breath to Victoria. "And Mrs. Petersen is simply in a class by herself." She was reading Stuart Chase and kept a copy of the *New Masses* under the big dictionary. She could rattle along like an old hand. "Trouble is," she confessed, "I'm kind of like Stuart Chase. I know what is wrong but I don't know where to go from here."

Mr. Petersen spoke up and said all the government was after was to wear the farmer down and get them all on subsistence farms. "I've been seeing this shadow coming for a long time," he confessed. "Sometimes I almost wish it was over. Let them take it all away, then there won't be anything to fret about anymore."

Lorraine's father had one of the biggest ranches on the west side of the Missouri and Lester was anxious to visit it. It ended with the whole bunch of them moving in on Lorraine's old man. Nobody in this part of the country seemed to think anything of company. Every table had about the same food and, in fact, Mr. LaRue, Lorraine's dad, set a poorer table than some of the lesser farmers who had ransacked the cupboards for tidbits when company came.

Steve Carson was so impressed with all the up-to-date machinery that Tolman said to Vicky, "Ever see anyone so fascinated with machines. He ought to be working on them, not stuck on a farm." Steve went around looking at the giant barn where old man LaRue had been able to store 1932 wheat, the sheep sheds, and fine new pump. LaRue was planning to winter through some nine hundred head of cattle. The two began talking about the future of the land. "You got to head up every little runnel," Steve said. "Put in dams."

"By gory, you're the first I heard said that outside the government men. Let me show you, I got two dams already. Planning on more." He began to look at the young fellow with interest, but Steve was off on a long plan for building up the herd. When he saw the dull-eyed animals sitting in the baked mud before a tiny pond with a few bleached carcasses parching on the bank, his eyes clouded. They looked pitiful, just hanging on to life.

"I figger someone has to hold to a base," old LaRue said. "After the government gets tired killing off the beasts someone has to begin breeding them again." The whole thing got under Steve's skin. The big expanse of land, not like in the eastern part of the state, the superb equipment; what couldn't a man do? But his face took on a shrewd look as old man LaRue said, "Americans like a fight. This is only a fight. Things ain't so bad." He thought of his own father, of the hundreds he knew of, handicapped already beyond redemption. This man had managed to squeeze out an enormous base for himself. He wondered how. He looked shyly at Tolman, a fellow from New York. When he found an opening, the two began talking about the chances of the West opening up again or of the land turning to a real desert, of the day when agriculture might be run so that everyone would get enough to eat. "They could get that, all right," Steve said. "That's not the trouble," and he looked at Tolman a little contemptuously.

When the men got back the womenfolks had cooked a big meal and Mr. LaRue was telling about his brother who sold silk in a department store out in Hollywood and often waited on movie stars. "To Mary Pickford, to lots of them. He says they're just as common as anyone." It seemed to please him, and later in the evening he praised Governor Berry. "He's as common as anyone. No airs. Has children, just like anyone's kids. He put on an Injun dance once right in front of the Hotel West in Sioux City. President Roosevelt entrusted that feller with relief, the only Governor besides Olsen that got the job. Yes, sir, he's a fine feller, a real cowman." He glared at Steve as if waiting for a denial, but Steve was talking in a corner with Lorraine who had on a bright red silk blouse and lipstick. They were all to stay the night. Papa LaRue was proud that the house would hold them. "Yes, sir, we always kept a big threshing crew, once a year, and slept them all. My wife never had a helping hand except during threshing. We had a crew of fourteen, threshed six weeks. My wife died, just a year ago. She was a big healthy woman, too." He sighed in a long tired way, and Steve's head came up suddenly from the corner, like a seal's out of water, and looked at the old man steadily as if trying to see through something that puzzled him.

Victoria wrote a letter to Jonathan by a little oil lamp that reminded her of when she was a little girl and her mother told her to say *Now I lay me,* and "I don't care about *if I die before I wake, I hope the Lord my soul will take,* it's you I'd like to see this minute. I feel asleep and will only wake when you come in the door."

She paused and bit her pencil. She could hear Tolman coughing nervously in his room and from outside two voices, Lorraine's and Steve's—they were looking at the moon. It was white over everything and a sweet pungent dry smell like spice rose up from the land that had been drained of so much richness. "Goodnight, my darling," she wrote, and sealed her letter.

At breakfast Mr. LaRue opened up and said there was no sense in scaling down production. "The way things

are going it makes out big-scale production ain't right,
but I know it's the only way." He put big forkfuls of
bacon and eggs in his mouth exactly as if he were pitching hay while Lorraine stood over by the stove looking
at her father with a funny quizzical look on her face. An
old bachelor uncle kept piping up that times wouldn't
be so damned bad if there weren't so many shiftless people
around.

"Well, sir," said old man LaRue. "I figure the government is trying to get a twenty per cent reduction on
cattle. I can't find my contract, was looking for it this
morning to show you. I got rid of a hundred animals,
just old shells, regular gummers. I only kept them because
they always raised a calf but it costs more to feed them.
In the lot there were a few fat animals. Twenty dollars
ain't cost of production but you take last year, before
the government stepped in, we got six dollars. That's
something."

Lorraine listened to the talk with impatience. She
looked at Mrs. Chance and Mr. Tolman with terrible
curiosity trying to imagine the life in New York. Their
interest in what her father was saying made her look at
him as if he, too, were a stranger. But when he boasted
how he had owned ten sections once and had been
offered twenty-five dollars an acre real money during war-
time but had held out for twenty-eight dollars and now
saw it was a chance absolutely gone forever, she could
only wink to keep back the tears remembering her mother
who used to sit, turning over the pages of women's magazines with all the pretty furniture, and wish they could
have just one decent set before she died. The two of
them would stand looking at the worn imitation-velvet
of the overstuffed chairs, the fern on its pedestal, the
bookcase with *The Little Shepherd of the Hills* and *Don
Quixote* in Spanish that one of the hired men, of all
things, had left behind him. They would put new paper
on the walls, and pretend they were having tea together
with a little table, just like they were little girls cutting
out pictures and playing dolls. Lorraine had never known

her father had much money. He was always complaining about taxes and when he said he had at one time paid as much as ten dollars every day for taxes, it had seemed to her that they must all scrape and live on crusts to meet such a terrible sum that was so unjust to poor Papa.

At Vermillion her art teacher had sighed and talked about the Art School at Chicago, and better yet, the one in New York, and Lorraine had such talent it was a pity to let it go to waste, but there was never a moment when Papa had a thought for such a venture. He put up a kick against her going away at all and said a girl had all she could tend to if she could read and write and keep house for her husband. It just made Lorraine tight and stubborn as if she never would learn to keep house if she died for it but she always helped her mother, grumbling over the dishes because they got her hands all withered and the nails broke afterwards.

All during breakfast she kept watching the table and not sitting down except in snatches but Steve got up and said he was going to take charge of that stove if she didn't come and eat. She flushed and looked back at him as if she were stunned until he began blushing, too. Before they shoved off in the car, Lorraine had promised Mrs. Petersen to come down to Mitchell and it was taken for granted Steve would be there, too.

The minute they had left, Mr. LaRue lost all his joviality and fumbled through his desk for some papers. He said he had to go over to the bank to arrange about a new loan, maybe they'd scale down his debt and take land instead of interest. He kept muttering about cottonseed cake fifty dollars a ton and began to carry on just as he used to when Lorraine's mother began to suggest doing something that might cost a little money. Lorraine just stood in the doorway watching him, feeling hard and spiteful. All he was trying to do was to beat her down so she'd never get married and be a good housekeeper.

"So's he can save his old two cents," she said angrily, out loud, as she took the linen off the beds and walked past all the rooms with their neat matting on the floor and the clean beds that her mother had swept and dusted year after year. And when she came to the head of the stairs and saw the picture, entitled, "Moonlight Sonata," of a woman playing a piano with the moonlight streaming over her, and her hair in a halo around her head, she just sat on the top step and burst out crying. She felt so alone with no one to talk to and her father always out and her uncle nothing but an old piece of dried up skin. She remembered the day she and her mother had bought the picture at a sale at Pierre and how guilty they had felt. Coming home, they had a job to shuffle it in the house without Him seeing it, but when it was hung, they had clung together, breathless, looking at it as if it represented Lorraine's future.

If only she had not been such a selfish coward and had stayed home when her mother was sick. She had known in her bones that it was serious but she kept telling herself that since Aunt Kate was there, she wouldn't be needed, and it would only worry Mamma if she didn't go back to school. If only she had stayed, if day by day she had waited on her mother. Oh, how could she ever in this life make up for such a crime. She buried her face in her lap, longing to atone but it was not her father she wanted to serve. Her father had helped kill her mother. He had never let her have help. The last day, as Lorraine was going away, her mother suddenly got up in her long flannel nightgown. In an old dressing-gown, she had cooked lamb chops for the two of them. "I just thought you and me would eat together before you go," she had said. The mother and daughter had eaten together while the father had honked impatiently outside waiting to drive her to the train. She had not dared look at her mother, all skin and bones. They had been silent, sharing food, for the last time.

"I'll go crazy in this house," she choked, getting up and rushing downstairs, throwing open the door and taking long gulps of the warm dry air, hearing far up the range the sudden plaintive wail of a cow that had doubtless crumpled at the knees, its hunt for grass over.

I'll go away, he'll not keep me here, I want some life, and she walked up and down the long porch where her mother used to stand with her hair in tight little perspired curls around her neck to ring the big bell for the men to come to eat. When she was a little girl, she had climbed on a chair to ring it, pretending it was a firebell and the house was in flames, then later that it was a ship's bell and she was tolling through a heavy fog while the captain steered for land through shoalwater.

Steve Carson looked a little like that picture of her brother in his uniform on Mamma's dresser. She could faintly remember him, smelling of the barber shop, lifting her up and whistling *When Johnny comes marching home again,* and Mamma crying. Mamma got a gold star and letters from the national office but Fred had never come back. Now they were talking about war all over again and Mrs. Petersen said that any day the slaughter would begin. As she thought this, her skin crinkled under her hair, she could see Steve's eyes looking at her. How well he talked, looking straight at you, not like her father who was always playing with something, his knife, or staring out the window. Poor Papa didn't look much like that picture taken with her mother in their courting days at the fair under a trellis of morning glories. He had dangled a hand elegantly behind Mamma's head and she held to a big flat hat with one hand while over them a sign blinked, "Love's Dream."

Still there must have been something between them, her mother would never let her say a word against him. "You'll know more, someday," she had said. "He's a hard man about money but he was never cruel to me," and her face had flushed up suddenly, wild and handsome, so that her daughter looking at her felt small and ignorant of life. She turned on the radio, her cheeks hot, the rooms were too small and the house stifling, but nothing but moans about *My man is gone and I'll never forget,* like the bleating of sheep lost on the range came over the air. It made her sick. She didn't mean to moan and wail. She squatted back on her heels, thinking again of Steve, his thin quick face. His hands weren't like that boy's at Vermillion, pawing all over you, thinking all he had to do was paw around and it would be just too nice for anything and you'd fall like a pear, so happy to be noticed. Oh, no, he wasn't that stripe. She didn't know what her mother knew, but she knew.

She'd always known. The time her mother took her to Mrs. Shield's, they had played all the records, not cheap ones, but *Tannhäuser* and *Mozart,* and she had sat on the edge of her chair, her heart thumping. The evening star came out and she was singing to it herself for someone actually in the world. At dances and at night in the car with the air rushing past her face, she was always coming right up to where that feeling was in her throat, but always she had said, not yet, this is not the man.

"Well, young lady, is that the way you get dinner?" and her father was staring at her over his glasses and fumbling through a batch of papers in the doorway. She jumped up, red and confused. "In a minute, Papa," and he went off, grumbling, "Daydreaming. In the morning with a house full of work. A pretty note."

IV. THE AMERICAN WAY

O N HIS way to the plant, Ed Thompson's car had to slow down to pass a group of W.P.A. workmen who were tearing up an old brick pavement. He slowed down, then stopped the car. Actually it was a lesson in politics to watch. If ever a man saw the decay of the American spirit. Slow. You would think they had all day. Look at that fellow scrape off the old stuff as if he were too lazy to breathe deep. It made Ed boil to watch it. Why, fellows like that weren't worth anything. The discard or they wouldn't be here. Then the nerve of them, insisting on higher wages. The worst of it was that they had a sucker government back of them. A man didn't know what to expect but business was counting on people getting sick of Roosevelt playing into the hands of the labor racketeers. All this monkey business should be read out as unconstitutional, once and for all.

He started up the car again, moving slowly and at the break in the road as he went over the bump the fellow who was lifting brick raised his head. His shirt was open and he stared straight at Ed Thompson. There was something about his stare that made Ed's flesh crawl and he honked impatiently, trying to turn his eyes aside, but the man still stared and he recognized Charley Young. God damn, he had had to fire him when he caught him doing union work and there wasn't a better arc-welder or more reliable man until he got the union bug. Ed had actually taken pains with the fellow, had him in for a private chat with a little paper all ready to sign stating that he would have nothing to do with the union. Charley said, "Nothing doing."

Ed remembered his own remarks very well. He had leaned back and tried to reason with the man. "What

did the union ever do for you?" he had said and Charley
had been ready with his lip—he had said if he had time
he could tell him a little something about the railroad
brotherhoods. Ed had snorted. "We aren't in the railroad
business," and that had ended it. Now he was being stared
down by Charley and it made him nervous. He honked
again and just to show he had no ill feeling, leaned out,
"How'yu, Charley," in a grave voice. Charley didn't answer, just stared at him, then picked up another brick.

The episode bothered Ed. Even after he got to his
office and began to sort his mail it bothered him. He kept
brushing his eyes as if they hurt him and they did hurt
him. Probably needed glasses. A card from Fred Krieger
on a hunting trip struck him as comical. It showed a
couple of game-birds hanging by their necks and Fred
had written on the back, "Too old to live, too young to
die." Business couldn't be so good. A man doesn't think
of death when business is fine. Cars were picking up
and he guessed that the farm machinery business must be
dragging, although the lord knows why when the government was feeding those babies enough pap for them
to buy the White House.

He pressed the buzzer for Miss Norris, looking at her
approvingly as she sat down primly, crossing a damn pretty
pair of legs. He dictated one to his brother Glen, en-
closing some clippings. It was a funny note that he had
to run not only his own business but Glen's. Still it
wasn't every man with his genius for ideas. Sometimes
he wondered if he shouldn't have gone into plain ad-
vertising. They made a racket out of it. Not that it hadn't
slumped but that was largely because they were still using
outmoded notions. Then to the secretary of the Mutual
Welfare, just so the fellow would keep him informed
about men from the plant who applied for aid. He wanted
it known that the plant was ready to stand by its loyal
workers and the association should not be obliged to support a family that might be taken care of by the plant.
Then to Fred. This will be funny.

"Dear Fred," he dictated, then cleared his throat, smiling. Miss Norris also smiled. "Your little proposition received and contents noted. Sorry I can't do business along those lines. Too bad you had to go out on the road again. Things were never better with us. The used car market stalled us for a time but that is being eased off and we look for big business. When you get around here, come see us, always a handout for oldtimers like yourself. Yours sincerely." He chuckled again lightly. "That will be all for the moment, Miss Norris, put on my calendar the Rotary luncheon for next week. I'm to make a little talk."

"Oh, Mr. Thompson," said Miss Norris, but there was no time for more; Mike Gustaf, one of the foremen, had come in. He frowned at Mike who walked closer and said, "Got another one," and then turning toward the door said louder, "Come in, Wright." Wright came in and Gustaf took a tool-clearance slip from his pocket and said, "Here's a fellow been soliciting on the premises."

Ed looked severely at Wright and said, "What about this, Wright," and he said, "It isn't so. I was in the restroom and a fellow there, Jim Turner says, You know I don't know what to think of this union business, and I says, well, make up your mind, it's one thing or the other, and that was all was said." Ed gave him a sharp look and said he couldn't have soliciting on the premises and they couldn't tolerate the union. Wright spoke up and tried to argue and says N.R.A. but Ed gave him the horse laugh and signed the slip and told him to get it signed at the Time office. Then he turned back to his desk. Wright said, "You haven't any right to fire me," but Ed paid no attention, just tightened his lips. If you began by letting a worker bully you, you were finished.

He had lunch with Spencer Gibbons and Spence had a good one about the new King of England, then Ed replied with one about Franklin D. Roosevelt. They got to laughing and then Spence asked about Glen. Ed resented the question; it reminded him of his own indebtedness to Spence. As one of the big shots on the board of directors, Spence had played the lead in getting the company

to retain him when they were about to give him the
boot. He had made up for it, in his own estimation, by
letting Spence in on Liberty Laboratories. One more year
like the last and there wouldn't be a sounder business
than L.L. It had been his idea to get out information
folders showing the activities of the reds. This would put
customers in the proper frame of mind to invest in munitions. As he saw it, Glen's job was to prepare his market
before a strike, not after. Just as it was Ed's business to
be all set to prevent a strike in autos or to squash it as
soon as possible. The textile strike, the mess in Cuba
with that fellow Machado, had taught a lot of people
sense, that you couldn't get the stuff when trouble began,
you had to have it ready. DM gas and CN gas literally
changed the face of labor trouble if used in time.

"What do you think of this for a slogan, Spence? I
was just writing Glen to drop in so I could go over it
with him. *Today in Europe rioters are killed. Today in
America gas reduces angry mobs to harmless tears and
saves thousands of dollars in property protection.*"

"Swell," said Spence.

"We could even have the dope. The number killed in
big clashes in foreign countries and so on. You've got to
make them realize the situation, as I see it."

"It goes all along the line," said Spence, but he was
bored, he wanted to talk about his daughter, who was
going with a kid obviously beneath her while her mother
simply refused to interfere. He couldn't understand Flossie
taking a stand like that. She had changed lately. She had
started studying voice and then she began going over to
the college to take a course in "contemporary literature."
He heard Ed's voice flow on and on without pleasure.
This was a moment in his life when he needed Flossie's
loyalty more than ever, and she was simply failing him.
He began to think some of her father's blood, and if
ever there was a rake, he was one, might be beginning
to show. He wanted to ask Ed but shut his mouth almost
as soon as he had opened it.

Jonathan Chance would have liked to stop in Illinois for a chat with his cousin, Fred Krieger. As manager of a big farm implement plant he might be able to give some tips on the farm situation. Si Greenough could not be interested so they kept on heading for Wisconsin. Jonathan took the wheel. He had driven a car since he was eleven years old, his body was part of the car, he could drive in his sleep. He liked best the early morning when they came out of the farmhouse where they had spent the night. The fields looked frosty white in the early light as he and Si shook hands with the farmer and his wife. Jonathan leaned out of the car to shake hands, looking at the eyes of the farmer and his wife, feeling that sharp eager pang of companionship with humankind that seemed to haunt man like some traveling star. The moment of confidence before the car started, the faces suddenly wistful as they were left behind, Si's cheerful voice booming away at his facts that were like so many machine gun bullets aimed certainly and with effect at a known enemy, were more substantial than his own vague doubts that seemed rooted in some prehistoric part of himself.

At moments like this he thought with longing of Victoria and, with intense surprise and chagrin, of his own petty actions. In what way had she sinned and what had Kurt from her that he had not a thousand times? When he got her little notes, he read them several times, smiling, and tucked them in an inner pocket, remembering the traveling men he used to meet on the road who kept pictures of the wife or best girl in the back of their watches or showed off a curl of baby's hair, like pure gold —and there was that fellow in the hotel in North Dakota, who, one lonely night, had shown him, as if it were some sacred token, a tiny erotic curl of his mistress in Baltimore that he had cut from what Victoria called the Venusberg.

His own letters to Victoria were short as if he could not hope to articulate what he felt. In the car, among their many passengers, it was Si who was fluent and Jonathan who was glad of his occupation. The very movement of

the car seemed to be swifter than anything they could
ever do—to be that very imagination on which slow reality
rides to some great destiny. But twice in the Dakotas and
once in Nebraska they heard of farmers who had broken
up tractors with hammers in their anger and frustration.
He and Si talked about it for hours and the meaning of
it. It seemed to Jonathan that it was more than simply
the infuriation of men who were blinded by the drought
and, even more, by their bondage to the big implement
companies. "Remember how the workers broke up machines a hundred years or so ago? As if they feared them?"
Si laughed and said not to get metaphysical, that the
workers had only understood that the machines took away
their livelihood, but the machine was destined to set men
free.

He didn't know whether to envy or resent the cheer-
fulness with which Si rattled off the proper answers. He
said shortly that a good deal might happen between the
destined event and now, a great war, even a great famine.
He was thinking of the 1920's when some of his friends
were writing poems to *Oh Machine* and others went into
rhapsodies over meat-grinders, the beauty of the multiple
lathe, the gyrations of a propeller. In their ecstasy they
forgot the men who made these tools, and in fact, it almost
seemed to Jonathan that Si was also forgetting them in his
apostrophe to the future.

The trip was reducing Lester Tolman to a state of de-
spondency hard to put up with. He demanded whole-
wheat bread where they had nothing but rye, asked for
beer where there was milk. But with the farmers he continued to be affable, listening to a long string of prices
and non-prices, of bad times and good until he felt as if
he were stranded in the midst of a warehouse of broken
furniture.

"I'm getting bogged down," he said desperately as they
drank milk in a musty hotel late one night. "It's getting

me. I don't see why you are so cheerful. I keep hearing
that fellow say, I could have had the sweetest life, and
there they were taking him off because he was crazy. Or
was he crazy? He set fire to his barn. Was that so crazy?
Did you see his eyes? They looked as sane as mine, maybe
saner. He talked funny though, kept telling about a
woman he had gone out with once in Sioux Falls. She
had a big diamond and fifteen thousand in the bank. If
he hadn't worked so hard, buying and selling cattle, and
then only five years ago he had a fur overcoat and a
Dodge, he said, over and over. I feel as if I was getting
flu."

He blew his nose loudly and the landlord came out and
turned on the radio. A faint nasal roar turned to someone singing. "From Chicago" their host said brightly, "it
comes over every night about this time with the weather
for next day," and the words blurred slightly as if the
singer also had a cold, "other arms may hold you tightly
but you're still mine in my dreams." Lester yawned, thinking nervously of New York and his girl and the great
prairies gaped naked and terrible to him as if he were
obliged to walk over them in bare feet. He looked sharply
at Victoria who was staring at the paper poppies on the
fly-specked chandelier and the calendar of a chubby boy
in a sissy blouse smiling over a bowl of breakfast food. It
was like the farm dining-rooms she used to see when a
child, only shabbier and with a stale air, and the old
man touchingly solicitous about giving them a little music
might have been old man Blanchard who finally got gored
by the bull who had always been so gentle a "critter" up
to the moment of his treachery. She longed to talk to
someone, not about the farmers or figures but about the
kind of terrible sadness that seemed to hang over the
land, punctuated by such flashes of hope and illusion that
at a moment like this, late at night, when the body is
low and tired, seemed only pathetic in their perpetual
postponement. It's only being tired, she said, and could
find no words for Lester who was breaking toothpicks
and then—rising and grumbling something about tomor-

row—had passed up the stairs, answering the landlord's goodnight in an equally cheery competent voice.

She hardly dared ask him to get off the track and let her stop at her old home town, but his curiosity about her brother-in-law Donald Monroe won the day. Clara Monroe immediately began a story about the hard luck they had had but Donald had a new car and their two girls were dressed out of *Vogue* fashions. The oldest boy had struck out for New Orleans, of all places, and Nancy asked brightly if they didn't remember the old stereopticon slides with the picture of the big banyan tree.

"Such a pretty place," she said with an enthusiasm that had not been dulled by her own misfortunes. And in fact, she and Cliff were already hoping to send for their furniture out in Oregon, especially the big old chest of drawers. His job didn't amount to much, but if it proved steady they could afford a home. Their boys were both anxious to get in the school band and were clamoring for saxophones. Clara's girls studied their highschool lessons with the radio on full blast and, when Victoria wondered how they could concentrate, the older one, Mildred, looked at poor aunty with withering condescension. "I study better with it on," she said with emphasis.

The three sisters had a laugh over it together, Clara taking a kind of pride in the perversity of her young. "It's a different generation," she said cheerfully. And later when Victoria urged fatty meat as more healthful for the children than so much hot bread, she said, "Oh, you can't get the young of today to eat fat meat," drawing broad generalities from her own special brood who were for her the Alpha and Omega. Both mothers shook their heads over the crime wave and the way the youth seemed to be so wayward but Nancy said she couldn't imagine her boys ever becoming thugs and that seemed to settle it. One night the three sisters drove around to see their old home, the White Elephant, that had been fixed up very impressively by the new owner. "Why, it even got the prize for the best-decorated house last Christmas," said

Nancy. "Wouldn't Mamma be pleased? Even Uncle David's house never got any better than that."

At the mention of Uncle David Trexler, Victoria and Clara snorted bitterly as they were reminded they had never received the speck of an inheritance left them by their uncle at the discretion of his wife. Nancy had boldly asked for her bit during one of the Radford crises, and now condoled with her sisters. "Maybe you'll get it yet."

"Not us," said Victoria, laughing and remembering the angry spurt of correspondence that had gone on between herself and her cousin Sue Trexler, now Mrs. Terence Bogart of Los Angeles. Cousin Sue had not been able to resist gloating a little over her papa. She had taken a natural pride in the discovery that his leavings were even larger than anticipated, at the neatness of his journals and account books and at what seemed to her the munificence of his many charities, carried on throughout his life. At this more recent period, Victoria thought it quite possible that he had been generous in his fashion.

"Do you suppose all those Y.M.s and Salvation Armies and so on got their bequests and we didn't, or was it just on paper?"

"Oh, I wouldn't be surprised if it was on paper," said Nancy, "but you girls should remember he was Mother's brother and she always said, my brother will never let me starve."

There was one big family meal with Lester Tolman looking on curiously and talking to Donald Monroe who told him confidentially that the town was finished, real estate had gone to smash, the hotels were empty, the former big families were washed up, the children of the big shots no better than degenerates, sucking up spiked beer night after night or dope or what have you. "Believe you me," he said, "if I could get out, I'd get out." Mildred piped up and said as soon as she finished school she was going to New York and be an actress so she could get to Hollywood and be in films. Clara groaned and Tolman burst out laughing.

Donald Monroe pointed a parental finger at her and

said if she passed her school work she'd be lucky and he
didn't want anymore nonsense out of her. She sulked back
with her slow languorous air that made Victoria think
of her mother's stories of the beautiful Madeleine Mc-
Crary and she wondered if each generation provided its
bit of fatal drama and, if so, what role would this child
play. She hardly heard Clifford who was going over his
experiences to prove how in each instance it was not his
fault that he was without a job. The business had folded
up or a relative of the boss got the job, and his voice
seemed to argue perpetually with himself to explain an
event too monstrous to believe.

But try as they might in this town and that, they did
not run into Jonathan and, as he wrote he would be East
soon, Tolman refused to go through Chicago. He wanted
to head straight for New York and seemed bitten with a
nervous need to hurry as if his life were hanging by a
thread. "I want a home," he said. "I want kids. Where
are we heading? I never felt so close to Armageddon. I
want some love before the storm breaks." But he seemed
to have pinned his hopes to a slim chance for, at every
big stop, he went first to the postoffice and seldom got
more than a long wordy telegram. "That's the trouble
with an actress, always dramatizing. Writes as if she were
sending a headline for the New York *Times*." And for
miles he said nothing and stared gloomily at the road.
But Victoria felt lighthearted now that the trip was over;
she thought of a little place she could get all to herself
so that when Jonathan came it would be like home.

Tolman did not show up at the office for several days
and had them all running around wondering whether he
was going to get any copy in. Victoria was nervously putting their notes together but she had no idea what his
main line would be since he had changed his mind so
many times. The pictures came in. They were beauties
and the entire office force stood around admiring the car-

casses and the one with the boy in the shirt like striped candy, holding a cow whose ribs looked ready to cave in. Tolman got her at her room at half-past ten that night. He asked if she would come over, and gave a new number. It was a swanky apartment on lower Fifth Avenue.

He was waiting in the vestibule for her.

"You look like the cat that's swallowed the canary," she said. He smiled in a knowing way and flung open the door of the apartment. It opened into a raspberry entrance that further bloomed into a large disorderly room with a lot of stagy white furniture standing around. Tolman waved his hand. "Well, I did it," he said. "Meet the hero. We're living together. There was a fight, all right. That lily-livered actor was hanging around but he didn't mean anything to her. He was simply a Svengali, putting the girl to sleep. I'm going to wake her up." He unconsciously posed before a big mirror, lighting a cigarette and pausing long enough to watch a smoke ring curl luxuriously in the air.

"I suppose they've been having fits at the office?"

Victoria nodded. She was wandering around looking at the place. The actress, Elsie Forey, Tolman explained, was at the theatre. He would be very happy when she finished living her part. In the corner of the bedroom, also in white, was Tolman's typewriter and a pile of canary-colored velvet to be used for drapes. The kitchen was in a clutter with a pair of violent-blue lovebirds mournfully squeezed together in a cage over the kitchen sink.

"Now to show you I've been working," said Lester. He handed her a bunch of notes, some in pencil, some typed. "If you can whack this together, we'll make it. I know it's damned hard on you, but nobody else could do it, Vicky. We got tonight, tomorrow, and until late tomorrow, in fact. Can you make it?"

"Sure," Victoria said. "I like to work like that. Why not? Nobody to disturb me."

"Hear anything of Jonathan yet?" he asked but without waiting for an answer went to the bathroom. "Mind if I shave?" he called out. "She'll be out from the theatre soon and I'm going up to get her." Victoria sat looking over the notes to see if she understood them. From the bathroom he emerged again, "She's everything I want. I'm going to write. I may even write a novel. Everything is opening up." He talked authoritatively as if he were the first man to experience the passion. "I want you to know Elsie," he said. "She's not like the other girls I've had. I've had such awful luck. Elsie is good. She's modest too. She says she knows she's not first rate, but I'm going to make her first rate."

"Yes," said Victoria sympathetically. She was anxious to get at the manuscript and waited while Tolman slipped into a coat to show her to the elevator. He pushed the button firmly and with authority, shaking hands politely before the door shut upon his face, fatuous with belief in his good fortune.

By eleven she had the beginning untangled and was piecing it together. He had left great gaps which he expected her to fit together as usual. It was like a puzzle at first but afterwards fun. When she heard someone turn the handle of the door, she stiffened with alarm and sat rigid. "Who's there?" she called out, clearly. "Jonathan," said Jonathan. She got up and rushed to the door. He looked very brown and handsome and snatched her up before she could speak.

"Oh, Jonathan, what a night to come," she said.

"What do you mean, what a night?"

"Don't be silly, I mean of all nights. I have to get this damned stuff out. Lester has been so busy bagging his actress he didn't get his stuff in until tonight. Tomorrow they go to press. Oh, Jonathan." He looked crestfallen and opened his bag. "I had a bottle of wine. I was sure we could celebrate."

"We will, Jonathan. I'll work like the devil all night and we will tomorrow."

"It's always tomorrow."

"Don't talk like that. I can't help it, can I?" She was getting excited as she saw that he meant to take the disappointment hard. He was quietly bending over the bag again, unpacking his shirts, a notebook. "I got a lot to tell you," he said. "I suppose it will have to keep. And say, I stopped at the house coming in. Si and I spent a night there. One shutter had blown off but I fixed it. There was a lot of second class mail and some packages. Couple of books and this." He tossed it out and she picked it up looking for the address. It was from Kurt. He pretended not to notice as she murmured, "What can this be?" Several bundles that looked like notebooks in German fell out. Some manuscript pages folded in two, written on both sides, and wrapped in a plain sheet of white paper, her letters to him. She stared at them, trying to shuffle them out of sight and looking apprehensively at Jonathan.

"What was it?" he said.

"I don't know, papers, it looks like. Here's a note." She read it and passed it to him. "He's going to South America. Wants me to keep these for him until he gets back."

"What was it?"

"Oh, just notebooks, papers." She wrapped the whole thing up hastily and thrust it on the chair behind her. Running a sheet of paper in the typewriter, she began to type rapidly.

"Let's see, can I?" he said in a mild voice. Victoria looked at him. Her eyes were too pleading. He thought, oh God, it isn't over, and cruelly held out his hand.

"No, Jonathan," she said. "Don't tonight. I'll show you. I have to work. This has to be finished. We aren't babies anymore. We have to think of our lives."

"Always our lives. I never knew what you meant."

"I know you didn't. Perhaps that's what's wrong with us. I just meant it isn't worth anything unless we do something with our lives. I don't know what I meant. Let's talk tomorrow, will you? I tell you what I'll do. I'll go out with you now and you get something to eat, then you go to bed in the next room. You must be all in, and I'll hurry like hell with this."

"I don't want anything to eat and I'm not sleepy." He

reached for the package and the letters fell out. He saw
them lying on the floor and remembered with surprise
how he had concluded that it was nothing and he had
been a fool to be upset. The letters only aroused an evil
longing to break up her work. He picked up a letter. She
reached for it, and held fast to his hand. They grappled
for a minute; it was like the game they used to play that
he always won. She said, "Jonathan, you can read the letters if you like. But you'll only make it harder between
us. They aren't anything. Some of them you saw. I didn't
hide anything from you."

He laughed, twisting her wrist, and the letters fell. He
would not look at them but sat instead at a distance, his
face heavy and dark. She gave one look at him then went
on typing. A kind of red mist floated before her eyes but
she fought with the words and made them come clear.
If he saw her working steadily, perhaps his mood would
go away. The letters were nothing; Kurt himself would
not have sent them if he thought they meant anything.
Why hadn't he destroyed them? Then she remembered
how he had said he looked for them every day, as if he
were still in jail and waited for the crack of sun that
shone a little upon the floor. Had they really meant that
much? She thought of him with gratitude, as if her heart
would burst, that he had cherished the tiny drop more
than some men did a treasure. Her heart hardened against
Jonathan, who had opened the bottle and was morosely
pouring himself a drink.

"Aren't you going to wait until we have it together?"
she coaxed, and he shook his head, not angrily, just firmly.
It had taken only a few minutes to change him. He had
come in the door as in the old days and now he sat,
looking at her as if he were set to spy. Perhaps she could
no longer control their life, and the dark flood came up
to her very eyes, her eyeballs hurt, and she longed to call
up Lester, to say, I can't do it, but by this time he would
be standing fatuously in the lobby, waiting for Elsie and
imagining that everyone was pointing him out.

When he finished the bottle, he put his hat on and said

he would go out for a while. She got up in a panic then, perhaps he might never come back.

"I'll come back," he said, as if he read her mind. But she couldn't quiet herself. Oh, he might be tight and wander around and get himself killed, like that time in Key West when he hadn't shown up and she had gone in search of him. Was their whole life to be like that and, if so, why did she want it so badly? It had been nothing —the trouble, the quarrels were nothing; it was like dirty dishwater that you poured down the sink. The dishes were whole and clean. You put them on the shelf, you ate off them, a beautiful full meal, and poured wine in the polished glasses. Jonathan, oh, Jonathan, and she did not know why the thought came to her like an echo, it seemed to her she had said *Absalom, oh my son Absalom,* and the shock that she might really have said a name not Jonathan's, stopped her. She clutched at her head and began to cry.

"Don't begin that," he said in a cold tone. "That's always woman's refuge. It doesn't get me. I just want to run."

"Run then. I can't hold on anymore. I've tried and tried. It isn't fair. I told you, over and over, how it was," and her voice was telling him, frantically as if it would never stop. A thick haze seemed to cloud his eyes. He could not bear the words that seemed to come from a deep unquenchable source, the source that had tried to drown him. Words. Words. It was love he wanted. He took hold of her throat that rose strong and resisting from her open blouse, and tightened his fingers slowly, watching fascinated at her sudden terror. She let out a choked terrible moan, then a thin weak cry, "Help." He had heard a woman in childbirth in a boardinghouse in West Virginia cry like that. His hand loosened. He put his hat on and slammed out the door.

She felt the tears scalding her face and, with her clothes all in disorder, rushed out after him. The streetdoor had slammed; the hall was empty. A policeman was coming in from the street and, at sight of him, she stopped, her hand on the stair-rail. He saw her and walked slowly toward her. "Did you hear anyone scream?" he said.

"No," she said, forcing her voice to be calm, but he saw her face streaked with tears.

"Was that you screaming? I got a call, someone was screaming."

"No," she said; then, looking straight at him, said, "Yes. But it was nothing."

He looked her up and down in a not unfriendly way. "Was that the man left the place just before I came in?"

"I don't know. What did he look like?"

"Tall fellow, thin."

"No," she lied. "Oh, no. This man was heavy and rather short. Wore a derby." He looked up the stairs suspiciously. She said, "I tell you, it was nothing. Just a quarrel. You can look if you want to." Perhaps he thinks there is a body, she thought, and it seemed that from behind some wardrobe door a body might fall. He followed her and looked carefully in both rooms.

"Have a cigarette," he said. She took one, and he lighted it, looking at her closely. "It was nothing," she said.

"Know the fellow well?" he said.

"Oh, very well," she said.

"A girl has to protect herself. I don't blame you. Some of these guys. I'll keep my eye on the place and see he doesn't bother you again."

"Oh, don't bother," she said. "It was only a quarrel."

"I'll turn it in, it was only a family quarrel, see."

"Thanks," she said. "Thanks a lot." He backed off slowly, cheerful and grateful for the diversion. She began to straighten up the place, picked up the empty wine bottle and looked at it, pitifully, as if it had been a headless child. Perhaps Jonathan would not come back, ever again. She could not seem to make out what she was doing and when she tried to go on with the typing, could not make out the words. I'll go to bed, she thought with terrible resolution. I'll go to sleep, and it really seemed to her that she could sleep because she must and the thought that nothing could stop her from finishing the work she had promised, calmed her. She bathed her face and fell down like lead upon the bed. Her hands and feet were like the dead, and sleep came mercifully, as it had the night her mother died, and the disordered house was suddenly still.

It was beginning to be gray when someone tried to get in. She jumped up, her heart in terror. The police. It was Jonathan. His shirt was torn. His right eye was cut and bleeding. "Here's your poor boy," he said in the tone of a sleepwalker. He let her put her arms around him and lead him docilely in. "I was wandering over by the river and a gang jumped on me. They got all my money." He turned his pockets out. "It wasn't much, a couple of dollars. If a taxi hadn't been cruising along, I don't know what would have happened."

She bathed his eye. "What were you doing over there, darling?" she said.

"Drinking," he said. "I was just wandering around, then the bars closed and I didn't know where I was. I'm not tight now." But he hardly knew when she got him to bed, and packed ice on his eye. She lay next to his hot restless body and in the night he called out in a loud terrible voice and jerked in his sleep. She reached toward him, patting him with her hand, as if he were her child and she could take away his sorrows and soothe him to sleep. There was a terrible ache, in the center of her being, and she thought over and over, the ache will never, never go now, no matter what happens.

My Old Kentucky Home, Goodnight:
Harlan, Kentucky, 1935

*H*e thought his time had come. He crawled way back into the hole. Don't know what made this hole. Looks like some fox hole. Remember the time you got the bounty for catching foxes when you were a kid?

He was talking to himself, man alive and man whose time has come.

He could hear the shots. The big bulletproof car with the mounted guns had been hunting his hide, had tracked him down. Smelled him out. He'd picked this spot. I want to go to the hottest spot, the toughest spot to organize. I'm an old line American, bound for Daniel Boone country. He had said that to himself.

A fellow doesn't know what makes him choose a certain course. It isn't so simple. He says, I'll go here, I'll go there. It isn't just that he wants to do the best job, it's something way back, like hearing about Daniel Boone and singing old miner songs and then he hears about the miners shot like rabbits and the big Chicago thugs hired by the operators like you buy peanuts, riding around with cigars in their maps, nicking off the boys like they were ninepins in a bowling alley. Nothing he wanted to do but break away from Chicago. Nothing would keep him. Hey, let go my arm. You can't keep me. I got hot feet. I know the ropes, better than anybody. I know the mountains. I been a hunter myself from away back. I can organize the boys to beat those skunks. To keep them from starving, from dying. To be men. A man thinks like that, he gets himself in a hot spot.

The sun was shining hot in the big field. Then the big sneaky car had come along the road. We were walking the road and we ducked for the wall. Where's the other boys now? Did that shot get them? A big silence. The sun's so hot at the end of this hole. A little spot like at the end of a telescope. Looking up at Jupiter. Take a peek at

Mars. I can't get back any further. It's awful still. Oh Christ, let me live so's we can go on fighting. I don't care about myself. Just the fight. They get the boys, pop them off, why not me? My time has come.

He can remember as if he were looking at a photograph, the open field, the scanty trees, the road. They can find a pin in that field. A toad couldn't hide. They're coming. They were shaking the ground. It's his heart shaking. His body's sweating in the cold cold ground. He drew himself up into a knot; heart, stop pounding, they'll hear the ground shake. They were talking, faint voices coming. "Hey, he must be somewheres near. He can't get away."

He could see out the hole the tip of the guns and the heels, then the soles of their heavy boots, walking over his grave. Goddamned boots, get off my grave. I'll be John Brown a-moldering but a-marching on. Now they were moving off, then they were nearer, pushing at the grass with their guns. They got me. They stood as if looking. He could hear the earth breathe. The grass.

Someone yelled. "Hey, here he is. Come on out." He crawled out, more dead than alive. They got me. Fell at the heavy feet, lay still. Looked up. Stared. No, it couldn't be true. Guys from his own camp. Not . . . Why you so tongue-tied? What's wrong. Hear our little battle? We didn't get hurt none.

He was alive, he stumbled as he walked, he was alive. John Brown, I'm marching on.

BREAD AND STONES

WHEN Steve Carson got back home he was more than ever determined to see some action. All the talk got nowhere. Teacher-teacher had hitched up and was out cutting late cane but the frost got the late corn and there was nothing much but foxtail and roughage. Walt had gone off to Mitchell, to get a bunch of farmers together to keep the relief head from running over them roughshod. She and the girls had been running the place and feeding the stock. "Looks like we haven't got any men folks anymore," she said, and her voice sounded downhearted for the first time.

Steve felt terribly ashamed and all the time he was hauling in the cane he thought it wasn't worth a load of piss and wouldn't keep the cattle going five minutes. He had a long heart-to-heart talk with his stepmother and she kept wiping her eyes and saying she didn't see what they were going to do for the winter but they'd make it somehow, and he wasn't to stop at home if he wanted to set out. When Walt got back flushed and excited because some three hundred fellows had met and sent resolutions to the Governor that they wanted a say in the relief work going on and weren't going to stand for the discrimination, all the gravy going to the meek as Moses kind and the fighters getting it in the neck, Steve told him he had written to their cousin Charles Egstrom in Chi and Charley had replied for him to come on.

Walt stood with his mouth open. "What's he say for you to do?" Steve said, "He says they're taking on men all around, not many but I got a better chance than lots. I'm young. I got to go," and he wouldn't look at his father but Teacher-teacher came in from the kitchen and said, "He has to go, Father, that's all there is to it. There's nothing here. My land, let's let one of us amount to something." Walt looked terribly hurt, and went over and sat

272

reading the papers without looking up, but Steve clumped upstairs and began to get his things together with a wild wave of feeling running over him as if he were driving a sixteen-cylinder car ninety miles an hour.

Lorraine came to stay a few days with Mrs. Petersen who was going to run some educational meetings for the youth but Steve wouldn't have anything to do with it. He went over to the Petersens' several times and he and Lorraine sat out in the car and talked about how it was all washed up in this state and she said she longed to get away where there was a chance to see something beside dead grass and grasshoppers.

Steve told all about his plans and she said if she was a man nothing would keep her. Before he knew it, they were kissing and her lips felt hard and cool like his kid sister's when they kissed on her birthday and then they got soft, and her body went limp and then got hard and strong. He didn't know a girl could be so strong and so yielding, it was a miracle. He felt shaky—perhaps it was a dream—and then they walked way back of Petersens' house where the full harvest moon was coming up over the little mound as if out of a sea. On the ground a warm layer of air made a cover over them and then the cooler air came down touching them like somebody's breath. He was scared she would cry the way Tim said a girl always did, but she made him lean back to look up at the sky so he could remember it in Chicago.

Then one night it rained and they ran under the trees with her clothes skin tight to her and he could see the wild sky when a cloud scudded and the light soft rain coming down hitting her white face in big drops. She kept laughing with a wild excited look and, when they fell down together, he just lay still for a second, and everything in his life seemed pounding away in his body and he wanted to lie there forever and love her.

When he saw the family in the morning, they looked strange and he tried to imagine if his mother and father had ever felt like that but of course they had and loved each other now, only not the way he and Lorraine did.

He went to Chicago on the day-coach with Walt's old cowhide bag he had taken to the legislature and a lunch that Teacher-teacher had packed up for him. The whole family came to see him off and, at the last minute, Mrs. Petersen drove up with Lorraine. He didn't know whether to kiss her in front of the folks or not, but she fixed it by kissing him right before everybody. Teacher-teacher looked pinched around the mouth and big tears came to her eyes but Walt clapped him on the back and laughed and said he guessed he'd make good but not to forget the working class.

In Chi Charley took him to their place. He was married to a little Polack girl who worked in a factory making gloves only she never saw more than the part of the glove she made—it all came sliding toward her and she had to work fast to keep up the pace. Charley filled him full of news the first night and they rode around town in Charley's old Ford. The very smell of the city got under Steve's skin, and the noise and smoke going up, the el rattling along and the big lake pounding away made him feel everything he had ever done before was nothing. Even Lorraine began to dim but he wrote her twice a week. Every morning, as he ate breakfast with Charley and his wife, he could look into the flat opposite where two girls chattered away drinking coffee with their hats on before they rushed off. They wore tight blouses and he couldn't keep his mind off thinking what they would be like if a fellow made up to them. But he wasn't going to let such ideas ride him, and all Charley's talk about the union just made him anxious to get hold and show the world.

Charley said it wasn't like the old days and they could train a green hand in ten days for anything.

"That's tough for a strike situation because you take it like that, it is easy to train anybody to do the work. That's why they put up such a howl about keeping the relief way below what wages are. They want to be sure they got some help laying around cheap enough to scab. But we'll lick them yet." When it came to hunting a job Charley said it was better for Steve to go by his lonesome, as he already had a taint of being a "disturber" and Steve would stand more show if he was just a green farm boy with nothing on his mind but a yen to work his ass off for the company.

He got taken on at the Ainsley plant and Ada, Charley's wife, groaned, "Why couldn't you do better than that? They'll murder you," but Charley said, it was just the ticket, as it was a mean situation and the more men like Steve they had there, the better. The first week took everything out of him but the second week he got second wind and they moved him up along the production line. A fellow who looked old enough to be his father worked next him, pouring sweat and too scared to take off time for a drink of water or a piss. The super was a mealy-mouthed guy who came around to have long confabs with the foremen. Nobody trusted either of the bosses but some of the men worked day and night to shine up to them and get favors. It didn't take Steve a week to spot who was who, and to see who was watching him about as sharp as he was watching them.

The nights were fine. He and Charley went to bigger meetings than ever he'd heard of in his life and swell speakers came from New York. One place they got him up to tell about the farm work, and he heard himself talking as if he was listening to another man. They pounded and pounded and Charley was all flushed up and excited and said he hadn't known Steve had it in him. One night he heard that Si Greenough and a fellow from the East were coming to hold a meeting over on the south side. It was not very crowded with a lot of blacks in the crowd who had come to hear about the sharecroppers in the South and what was going to happen to Angelo Herndon. He got a chance to shake hands with Jonathan Chance, the fellow who had sent some money to the gang in jail at Yankton from a bunch of Bucks county farmers and they stood talking, free and easy, about the country changing and everybody waking up and how hopeful it looked until he felt that, if he only lived to see the day when he could really throw himself into the struggle and do something for it, he would be a happy man.

Along about Christmas, if the bigshots didn't begin to get up their dander and it went around that the Manufacturers' Association and the Chamber of Commerce and a lot of their friends were getting really sore at Roosevelt for letting labor run wild. Charley said, "So far, he's been helping them. All the yelling at Wall Street don't cover that they've been getting the gravy. Most we've got is a chance to yelp a little and organize, but you don't see us cutting any melons and they have been tucking it in, only not so much as they are used to."

"Well, Charley, they got to have it like the style they are accustomed to, as the saying is," and big Eric Wall had a good laugh. But under the good humor, it was tightening up too, and you could see a showdown coming. Steve began to take a night course at a workers' school about Christmas and one night when he came down the stairs if he didn't see Lorraine in a coat with a fur collar up around her face waiting at the bottom! He felt strange for about five minutes but she said, "Let's go to Childs for a cup of coffee and some hotcakes," and they hadn't been looking at each more than a few seconds before it all seemed natural again and he had to begin trying to harden his heart not to be a softie and get himself in a jam he'd be sorry about later.

Her old man had finally broken down and let her come to spend the holidays with her Aunt Sarah. "You've got to meet her, she's grand and understands everything. I put her up to it and she wrote Papa that she would never speak to him again if he didn't let me come and cheer her up for Christmas." Steve looked alarmed but Lorraine flushed up and said not to be silly, of course, she hadn't told Aunt Sarah everything nor anybody else either.

She made him come up to her aunt's apartment that looked like a swell place to him. Her aunt was out somewhere and he was uneasy all the time. It didn't seem so natural on a bed as it had outdoors and he kept feeling guilty thinking they ought to be married. He was really glad when Lorraine had to go back home, not that his feelings had changed but just that he didn't want to mess around like that and she would have to take a chance with him and be his wife and live like he lived.

She was ready then and there, but he was sending money home to help Walt over the winter and besides what he got wouldn't keep two, it hardly kept him but for Charley letting him stay at their place. It was pretty cramped and he could hear their bed at night until it made him uncomfortable and hard to look Ada in the eye in the morning. He stayed out late every night and read in the library at the workers' school and he and a young fellow from Terre Haute (who had been all around, had shipped to the northwest and went on a freighter to Porto Rico) took in a movie and a couple of shows in the cheap houses.

This fellow, Joe Beam, said there was nothing like the tropic sea with the moon coming up, the ripples on the water, it sure got you in the belly, and he'd had girls but he loved his wife who had gone back home to her old man because he couldn't support her. It was the kids he missed. "The little feller used to shake the bars of his crib like he was going to knock the house down every time I came in the room. I just got soft all over, feeling he was really my kid. With the first I hadn't taken it so hard. She's a fine little girl but we had money for my wife to go to a hospital then. With the boy, there wasn't any money and we put off the doctor until it was about too late. There was only an old woman there and me, and she was such a little thing, my wife, but she gripped my hand until the sweat poured off me. I kind of felt that boy was mine, I'd made him, and then they just picked up and went to her father's home. Her dad was always trying to part us and telling her I wasn't any good and wouldn't amount to anything." He said sex wasn't just a drink of water to him, no, sir, he loved his wife and did still, but he didn't expect ever to see her again. The two went to a coffee counter and had some coffee and felt very chummy as if they had been looking at the world through a microscope and it wasn't a very pretty place, but outside the big dipper was large as life and Steve felt that just by looking at it, he had touched Lorraine's breast. He went home and wrote a long letter about how swell it would be to be together and they would have a fine life fighting for things worthwhile.

When he got a letter from her, he was taken off his feet and a cold chill went over him. She said she was awfully glad to hear from him as she had been feeling very low and didn't want to trouble him but she was afraid they were in for it and what should they do? She would come in a minute except if she were really that way, Chicago wouldn't be very good without any money, and she would just be in his way. She would do whatever he said and she loved him always and forever because she was really and truly his own wife.

"Well, by God," Steve said, and felt like getting drunk just the way Tub did. The whole thing had its funny side and he ended by taking Charley into his confidence who spouted the story out right away to Ada. Ada took it very seriously and said it was no laughing matter and Steve and Charley felt ashamed, not that they had meant anything, it was just that they were kind of nervous.

Ada made Steve sit down and write a long letter to Lorraine and tell her to come right away, they would be married and not to worry about anything. He felt kind of proud even if he was worried sick and he could hardly wait for the day when they could get a little place together. But he was already steeling himself against just making a little nest for themselves and letting the world go by. He had seen enough of that and the fellows at the works that were the least to be trusted wanted nothing except what they could grab for Number One.

When he got Lorraine's answer, he was scared stiff. Her father had suspected something and had opened Steve's letter and swore if he didn't come back and marry her, he'd come and skin him alive. He said it was all ridiculous for Lorraine to go to Chi and she would die in a dirty filthy tenement, and he had a letter from the old man too saying he ought to be horsewhipped but if he got back in short order he would let bygones be bygones. Lorraine had gone in a panic to Walt Carson and his wife, and Teacher-teacher wrote a long pathetic letter to Steve all cried up and blotted saying it was terrible but she could see no other way but to come home for the time being. Lorraine's Dad wouldn't let her out of the house and she was making herself sick over it. Steve never had such a fight on in his life. Charley told him to stick it out in Chi, after all he was ready to marry the girl, and what more could the old man expect. He would weaken rather than have a bastard in the family.

"You don't know that old buzzard," Steve said, and he wrote a long letter to Teacher-teacher asking her to tell him exactly how the thing stood. He had already gone to the first union meeting and was just beginning to see the lay of the land. Now he would have to go home like a whipped cur. It was only a federal union so far but if it worked up big they would get their international from the A. F. of L. by spring. He was going to do some recruiting and it must be just a bad dream that one old man could tie up his life into bowknots.

Walt had driven out to LaRue's ranch and had a long talk with the old man who seemed a little off his nut. The job of wintering through his animals was backbreaking. He was paying some fellow two dollars a week to help. He made Lorraine do all the housework and the poor child had a haunted look but Steve was not to think she wasn't damned plucky. He had to give as his best judgment that Steve should come back and stay until after it was over, then they could go off with a clear conscience. Teacher-teacher added a little note, "Stevie, this is awful hard, but I am telling you for your own good. She is a fine girl and will be a fine wife for you but she needs you now. This is kind of like the cyclone that time but you will see it through."

Steve stuffed the letter in his pocket and walked most of the night up and down the streets he had grown so fond of. It seemed senseless to have to go back. He was caught in wonderment that men could not act for themselves more sensibly but seemed to be snagged in some terrible fate that was stronger than their own lives. He hated himself that moment but he hated himself more when he thought how he had got Lorraine into so much trouble. Charley's wife said she thought he was lucky to be going back to a big farm and wasn't the old man rich? Maybe he would die and leave it to them. Charley and Steve just looked at each other and Charley said, "For Chris sake," but she went right on, "Well, I'm telling you, a rich man, a lot of land. What have we, my lord, you're well off out of this hellhole and don't know it."

Lester Tolman had a fight with Bill Graff, the managing editor, over the sugar articles and Lester said they could take it or leave it, he wasn't going to cut it up to suit them. Bill laughed disagreeably and asked him to grow up and didn't he know that sugar was indirectly backing them. Lester said *what the hell* and *free America, my ass,* and some more stuff that Bill said was simply childish and showed how immature he was. Lester finally withdrew the sugar stuff altogether and told Victoria they would make a book of it, there was always a book publisher ready to take a chance. The magazine was ready to use a few pieces on the farm situation, especially as Lester seemed to be criticizing the government.

His dignity demanded that he tell himself he would quit the job, if it wasn't that he had absolutely no money saved up. Elsie Forey was not making it any easier for him; on the pretext that Claude Wells, the ham actor, had jack and she needed him to back her next production, he was obliged to admit that she had to see him now and then. But, one morning when Lester was shaving, Claude came in and shouted that Elsie was treating him like a dog. Lester came out, looking surprised and trying to be polite but Claude threw a vase and broke it over his knuckles.

"The whole trouble with theatre people," Lester told Victoria, "is that they have to dramatize all the time. They can't stand to be natural. Personally I think it is obscene to care for someone who doesn't care for you. She doesn't care for him and he knows it." Victoria asked what about Shakespeare, and she didn't think you could turn off feelings like water in a spiggot but Lester insisted that it was dreadful for a man to cry and Claude had shed tears. After all, there was a code about things, he said sternly, and then stopped, looking a little astonished as if he were surprised to hear his own opinion, and indeed he had come a long way since the old days when he had understood why a man might very well shoot himself over a woman. I must be getting older, he thought moodily. But his satisfaction with himself did not keep him from fussing continually about Elsie. He complained that she too was a victim of this ceaseless dramatization that hampered theatrical people. "Why, I believe even in bed she's thinking of her audience on the other side of the footlights," he admitted, and then as if ashamed, added hastily, "she's lovely, she's tender, she's all I want," monotonously as if he were repeating a ritual.

He insisted the sugar articles could be worked up with a sense of drama. "It's not that I'm so interested in sugar. Sugar is just the fulcrum. It's one place where the methods are completely feudal and ruthless. Steel and your big automobile crowd would like to run things in the same way, only they've got American labor to fight, not a lot of half-naked Cubans and imported blacks from Jamaica that they want to ship out again now they've no more use for them than an old shoe."

Lester saw a chance for her to go down to Camden to get some stuff on the shipyards they intended to work up later, and she was able to stay with Jonathan a week. He was in Philadelphia in a little room and working up his own trip for the farm paper. He was very quiet and it was only when they were in bed together that he seemed like himself. But one day it was raining and she came in with her clothes all wet and drops dripping off her hat. They made tea over a Sterno and she sat wrapped up in his bathrobe. Did he remember his Turkish coffee outfit he had brought from Detroit and the little thin cookies they used to eat with the thick syrupy brew that made them feel as if they had traveled to another country? He remembered, laughing, and wondering where all those guys in the Turkish restaurants were now, and how they used to sit playing dominoes with their dark faces lighting as he came in. As the dark came on, the reflection from the lighted windows of the big plant across the street melted like candlelight upon their faces and they felt very tender and scared of one another. When he finally turned on the light, she had tears in her eyes and shook her head at him, whispering in a funny little croak, "Oh, Jonathan, it is all so strange." She was thinking of him as he had stepped off the train after one of his road trips the first year of their marriage. She had been waiting in the crowd at the gate and spotted him coming, a head taller than all the rest, hurrying with the new black briefcase he was so proud of, under his arm. She looked down at her hands and feet crossed under the old bathrobe and wondered what her sister Rosamond would have made of her life if she had lived.

It was a terribly noisy street and trucks rattled by. Some woman in the next apartment sobbed monotonously all night. In the morning she had to go back, but they promised each other that at Christmas they would have a real vacation together, they would go to the theatre and buy presents and have breakfast in bed.

Lester took her to luncheon with Elsie Forey and a young man who had just come from Europe and he looked very serious even after cocktails. Elsie was painted up to the eyes but Lester was entranced at the impression he

thought she made and fancied her affected voice was cap-
tivating all the waiters as it had him. Paul Willard was
very discouraging about Europe and didn't agree with
Lester who insisted that Hitler was shaky, that the army
was conservative and only tolerated him in order to get
Germany rearmed to the teeth. In the end they would
toss him out.

"Or he will toss them out," said Willard, and said
that it was a mistake to continue to imagine Hitler was
a nobody simply because he wore what looked like a cap
and bells to most people. It ended with all of them talking very pessimistically and as if the dark ages had really
begun. Lester said the clue to contemporary society was
in the past, and proposed studying ancient history. "Better stop at the middle ages," smiled Willard, shoving his
lip out in a stubborn way that made Elsie insist afterwards that he was really a sensualist in the guise of a
moralist. "I know those men," she said, shaking her locks
in a knowing way and giving Victoria a patronizing little fleck on the cheek with her fingers as they parted.

A week before Christmas Victoria bought a fountain
pen and a wonderful woolen scarf for Jonathan. Jonathan
wrote he would be in Washington but would start back
in the old car and get there two days before Christmas.
He would be there on Friday evening.

A fine snow began to fall and the air was clear and
early in the morning, a dazzling blue bit of sky shone
highup over the tall buildings. She bought big bunches
of firm reddish grapes and polished the apples until you
could see your face; she had a bowl of walnuts and Jonathan's presents were tied up in paper in the bottom
drawer. The day he was to come, she quit work early,
feeling very happy and in a flutter. She bought a silk
blouse with a plaid pattern and beautiful green-glass but-
tons made in a little basque that looked like the blouse
her mother had her picture taken in when she was eighteen at the height of her youthful beauty. Then she washed
her hair and put a little touch of perfume on it. Everything in the little place was clean and sweet as wax.

She mailed presents to her sister Nancy's kids and even sent cards to Jonathan's father and to Tom and Margaret. That very morning, she had the first word from Jerry Stauffer, her sister Rosamond's husband. She sat turning the card over, the writing as firm and familiar as it had been in the days when he used to add a line to Rosamond's letters. It was from Detroit; he hoped she was well, he was the same, and wished she would let a fellow know how she and Jonathan were now and then. He had married again, several years before, and Victoria wondered how it had turned out. She stuck the card on the mantel just as they always had at home and stood a long time staring and seeing her sister Rosamond as she had been as a child, with little curls and great wide eyes. The first Christmas Rosamond had ever picked out a present for anyone it had been for Victoria, and it had been a great secret. The little girl could hardly wait for Victoria to get off to school so she could get on a chair and sitting on the table set off the beautiful colored clown who spun round and round on a delicate toe. Victoria heard her parents laughing about it, and pretending to slam the door and leave the house, had tiptoed back, peeked through a crack in the door at the wonderful present, so soon to be hers, watching her little sister wind it up and make it go. It had, alas, been the only time she saw it go. By Christmas day, it was a broken toy, and good only to look upon.

The snow kept falling and when Jonathan had not yet come at ten o'clock that night, she decided to go to Esther Whittaker's party alone. A good many people were standing around drinking a rather strong punch. Most of the men soon jammed into the kitchen for a confab about politics and why didn't the *Daily* get real writers and what role politics played in a writer's life. The women were left stranded and began to talk among themselves and finally Victoria decided to go home. Jonathan had not come but a telegram under the door said he was at Mountain View, New Jersey, and would arrive early tomorrow. The car had doubtless broken down and worrying a lit-

tle for fear he was in trouble in the snow, she went to
sleep with the snow gently stuffing the crack along the
windowsill.

In the morning she again put on the blouse and waited.
There was nothing to do in the few rooms but perhaps
there was time to darn a few socks. She had just begun
on a big hole when Jonathan seemed to tumble in the
door, very big and fresh. He kissed her and said at once,
"I've been on the biggest bust of my life. Say it doesn't
matter." Her fingers seemed to turn to ice as she helped
him off with his coat. Dear god, was there never any luck.
He looked as he always did and she did not want to say
what she heard herself repeat disapprovingly, "You're still
tight." He shook his head, in good humor, and she picked
up the mending again. But she could not get on with it.
She said she had got his telegram and thought he had
had trouble with his car; apparently that had not been
the case. She had gone to the party and told him who
was there. He fidgeted on the bed, smoking one cigarette
from the other. She asked him if he wanted anything to
eat. He said he couldn't eat a bite and she looked around,
thinking, what can I say now so that I won't have to
hear what is really wrong?

She got up and went to the bureau and brought out
a little package. "Here's something I made for one of
Nancy's boys. It's just a little story about our lamb, Bud,
want to hear it? I thought I'd show it to you before I
sent it."

"Read it," he said, lying back and touching her dress,
coaxingly. She began to read, hearing her own voice with
surprise. It went on evenly but with an unfamiliar note
as if from another room. Jonathan listened attentively.
It was about a little lamb they had one spring with two
older sheep. One day the dogs got it. In the account, she
told about the dogs pouncing upon Bud and then, in the
night, after the big sheep had run away in fright, Bud
had come home all by himself, and let out a quavering
cry.

As soon as she began reading it, she thought this is

too sad for a child, whatever was I thinking of. Her voice seemed about to break and she remembered now with a rush how they had gone into the wet night together to look for the little lamb, and how it had stood with its feet wobbling in the wet grass and how Jonathan had picked it up in his arms.

He had carried the dying lamb to the house and the day he had stood beside her bed and told her their baby had been a boy, she had lifted herself up and asked to see him. Jonathan had brought him in, wrapped in a little shawl, like a doll. Her voice broke and she dropped the book.

"I shouldn't send it, it's silly of me," she said, wiping her eyes. "I don't know whatever has come over me." Tears stood in Jonathan's eyes. He had the little book in his hands and was turning it over; she had painted little pictures in it, made a little cover.

"I want the book," he said in an indistinct mumbling voice. "It's too nice for that kid. It's a beautiful book," and she wanted to thank him for saying that, for his tears, for his love, but she said instead, in a low bitter voice, "It's a woman, isn't it?"

PRINCE OF PEACE

IT'S A pity," Margaret Thompson said, staring down at her husband, "that you had to celebrate so hard last night that your own poor children won't get anything but the leftovers today. I can see right now you won't have the strength to carve the turkey." Ed opened one eye and looked at her. She looked cool as water with her head sleek and shining and he lifted one heavy paw out from the sheets to touch her hand. "Baby, don't nag me," he said.

"Nag?" she laughed, in anything but a pleasant way. "Oh, of course not. But I couldn't help but think, last night after I'd waited and waited for you to come home so we could fix the children's tree together, what it was all about. When I got the star out that was on my tree when I was a child and had to put it on myself, I just thought I'd die." Her voice had faded to a gentle melancholy. She wasn't even looking at him but staring out past the nice chintz-covered furniture to the snow-covered appletree in the garden. "Baby, don't carry on," he begged. "It was for your sake. Glen had one of the salesmen from California here and we were all going over things. If you only knew how I worked and was continually worried." His eyes crinkled with self-pity and she stooped suddenly and kissed him. He looked so red and swollen next to the white sheet—the boy she had married had completely vanished. Only around his eyebrows something of the same boy lingered.

Nothing tasted right for breakfast and the horde of invaders would soon be on them. "My God," he sighed, "wouldn't Christmas alone be nice for a change."

"Without Granpa?" said Theodore brightly, but Margaret said, "Eat your cereal. We should be glad we have relatives to be with on Christmas. Think of little orphans all alone without anyone."

"They have other orphans," said Theodore, crunching his toast in that annoying way. Ed frowned at him. "Don't grind it. Chew it quietly. Margaret, can't you teach them better manners?"

"Don't take out your own ill nature on the children," she said, flushing and looking ready to pounce at him. "All right, all right," he said, swallowing his food that tasted like ink. His head still ached from squatting on the floor while they all crouched around the tree and listened to the boys yell while they tore their presents open. A sudden vision of a hunting trip he had once made with Fred Krieger rose before him. They had gone into the north woods and the hut had been deep among silent trees. A roaring fire, frozen deer on the ground outside waiting for Fred's man to dress, hot punch—how had he made that—and long peaceful smokes. He was wearing the

new housejacket his wife had bought him and its color
embarrassed him. It would do for a pansy but, if he said
anything about it, Margaret would be hurt.

Even after breakfast there was no peace. Wasn't he
going to shave? How about clearing out from underfoot
with the boys for an hour and getting some good fresh
air before company came. If she had to listen to any more
complaints she would go crazy. Hell, what was a wife
for if a man couldn't open his mouth now and then.
Nothing but a billfold and scurry around to get money,
but although he took satisfaction in this martyred picture, he knew it hardly fitted him. Margaret wasn't ambitious enough. She would turn the boys into mollycoddles
if he didn't watch out.

He went upstairs and fiddled around with the victrola
in the upper hall. It was a long while since they had
played the damned thing. Look at the money he had sunk
in expensive records and now you can get it over the
radio for nothing. Practically for nothing. Nothing was
given away, at least not to him. For handouts you had
to be worthless. If a guy was worth real dough and earned
it, he had all the misfits of the country hounding him
as if he were Simon Legree. This hinged on just what
he had been talking over with Spence Gibbons. The value
of propaganda. Not obvious stuff, such as the reds poured
out, but indirect stuff, made by tactful contacts with newspapers, businessmen, especially those in a position to influence others.

The company had already begun trickling in when he
was still shaving and of course he had to cut himself. He
could hear Glen's voice and then the slow voice of old
Mr. Chance. Wonder what presents he had brought the
boys. Good bonds would be to the point, but it would
probably be some wacky toy. The old man couldn't get it
into his head that the boys were growing. He ran the
comb through his hair and looked at it, reminding himself of the ads for hair tonic. Just the same too much
hair came out and he would have to begin getting treat-
ments. Worry did it. Who ever saw women go bald? Not

that he'd swap his man's life for the best of them. Still worries did thin the hair. He was just going to stick up here until they were all there, then there wouldn't be any need of talk. He could carve and they could eat. That would keep them quiet.

Then Spence Gibbons' voice. He had forgot Spence was coming but his wife had gone off to Havana, of all places, taking the kids with her for Christmas. Something was beginning to smell rotten in that quarter, no wonder Spence looked harried. He winced every time he had to face a good hard fact. Take Glen, he didn't wince, he just took another drink. He felt uneasy at Glen's going to Cuba. But the damned Cuban the company had last year had messed things. A soldier had actually passed out from a stink bomb exploding in his lap and the papers had howled about poison gas. People couldn't shut up about it. The company had hastily had conferences, then put over some counter-propaganda about the humane effects of gas.

Good old CN gas, nothing but harmless chloracetophenone, a nice liquid chemical for lachrymating purposes. Then old DM gas with a jawbreaker name, diphenyl-aminechlorasine. He loved to cuddle those words on his tongue, it gave him the feeling of competency, of power. Power. Without power, where were you? DM not only brought tears but a guy who got it tossed up his cookies pronto. What harm was there in that? What he wanted to get into Glen's head and into Spence's head too was that it wasn't only the physical effects that were important. Even more devastating were the infinite possibilities of the moral effects. Back of a harmless gas you had to have guns because you had to create the idea of fear and respect for force. There you were treading, too true, on dangerous ground because you had a ridiculous contradiction among people who wanted law and order without paying for them.

This wasn't before 1914. My god, he could remember his father telling how they turned the hoses on out-of-works. Now they pampered them and kept them at home, warm and cozy with their stocking feet in the gas oven and the radio turned on getting the news of the world. No wonder you had cocky workers who didn't give a damn if they got fired or not. Then all the Christers going around, bleating about peace, peace. They had to be worked into the plan and convinced that peace could only be had by the use of Liberty Laboratories products, gas and grenades, backed by the reality of machine guns. Then you'd get the cockeyed workers in line. Loyalty was the finest thing in the world and when he thought of how disloyal those guys were to the plant that was feeding them, he could cry.

He actually had a tear in his eye now and wiped it out with a newly furled handkerchief as Theodore came bounding in. "Mamma says hurry, everybody's here and the turkey's done."

His shoes creaked a little. He wondered why and the possibility of inferior leather, even in expensive shoes, bothered him as he went down holding Theodore's hand presenting a nice picture of father and son. Old man Mr. Chance did not get up, merely nodded, his feet in tissue paper scattered from the gifts the guests had brought. Glen's wife looked pretty with big blue earrings and Glen himself had managed to get some color into his face. "How did you like Web Fuller?" he said, as the two brothers stood side by side.

"Good guy," said Ed. "By the way, when are you starting for Cuba?"

"No hurry. In a week. Maybe two. Web got me all pepped up. But then he's been in good territory, just as he says. The West Coast was full of juicy strikes all last year and what did we get?"

"Well, don't hurry things. I don't want to bring Jonah on our business. Let the other fellow get it. I'm fixing up to break it before it happens but you and me and Spence need some more confabbing today, hey, Spence?" Spencer Gibbons nodded in a sickly half-hearted way and Margaret called out, "Now no shop. I'm so sick and tired of hearing all this talk of mobilized units and so on. I tell Ed the trouble with him is that his nerves are over-mobilized, that's all." Everybody laughed, and Margaret on the pretext of fixing Ed's tie came over and whispered, "Try to cheer up Spence. Nettie Gaylord just called me on the phone all of a twitter, it seems there's a rumor around that that professor at the college left on the same boat with Flossie Gibbons."

Ed had only time to raise his brows. The room had become suddenly silent. "Come along, folks," said Ed as the maid stood politely in the doorway and announced dinner. Then there was the battle to please everyone. "Enough whitemeat here to feed a regiment," he said, "so don't hesitate to ask for more." Actually he was worn out before he got to helping himself but he loaded down and began. Margaret had got Leroy, the boy who washed windows, to dress up and he was now pouring wine with all the air of a trained European servant. Ed looked at his wife with admiration. She flushed with a sudden wild look of happiness as he said, "Nice work, baby," in a tone of voice that meant he loved her. Old Mr. Chance's sourpuss would take away your appetite; he thought of something to say to the old man and called out, "What do you hear from Jonathan?" Immediately he realized he had put his foot into it. Margaret frowned and Mr. Chance merely cleared his throat and said he had not had the honor of being informed.

The three men, Glen, Spence, and Ed, wanted to talk shop but the minute one of them began the women began moaning, so they had to string along about the dance the Liddels intended to give New Year's Day and wouldn't it be nice if they could all go on a cruise together. "Where would you want to go, Lydia?" asked Margaret, turning to Glen's wife.

"Oh, Egypt. I always wanted to go up the Nile."

"Another Cleopatra," said Spence, ironically. "Only where is Antony?"

"Give me Bali," said Glen, crunching a big piece of white meat with a wicked look.

"That's a man for you," said Margaret.

Spence was leaning around Theodore to get a whispered tidbit from Glen who wanted to know if he had heard about the time a fellow was giving a talk to Rotary and got all worked up telling about Bali. He said the camera man had taken miles and miles of film, all tits, but it fell flat on the old boys. Not dignified enough. Spence choked and Theo pounded him on the back. "Mr. Gibbons's choking, Mamma."

Everybody's attention was directed to Mr. Gibbons who, scarlet, sat back with tears in his eyes. "Gosh, that's good," he wheezed, still struggling for breath. Everybody wanted to know the joke but Glen said it was for men only. Lydia smiled wisely at Margaret. "We'll get it out of them, later," she said and Ed sighed. "That's the worst of it, they do. A married man is never fit for anything."

"Oh, I wouldn't say that, Ed," said Margaret, hurt.

"Well, I mean he isn't able to keep secrets and there was never a time he needed to keep secrets more. He gets worn down if he tries to keep a few things to himself and finally it's a toss up whether he wants to make a man of himself and hold on to what he's got in a home with a woman who is always looking as if she were nailed to the cross, or sink back in comfortable mediocrity with a happy wife." His oration only added to Margaret's unhappy expression and he pushed back his chair irritably and they all went into the other room for coffee. Leroy came around with some lovely little liquor glasses and Ed's mellow mood again descended upon him. He went over and twitched his wife's ear, then leaning down whispered, "Listen, I wasn't talking about myself. Don't you get it? That was for Glen. He's too soft for anything and Lydia is just a tattletale." Margaret pressed his hand gratefully and Glen called out, "Hey, no spooning."

Then the men were in a huddle and things began to liven up. Ed went over and stood with his back to the fire. He threw out his chest and looked with pleasure at the little group. The two boys were playing under the piano. Damn it, they were too big for that sort of thing but that was Margaret's influence again; wanted to keep them babies as long as she could. "Well, there's nothing like Christmas," he said. "The plant took care of a lot of the men this year, just a special little remembrance to the loyal men. We sent big baskets of fruit and candy."

"You didn't tell me," said Margaret. "How nice."

"Well, I tell you, fellows like Mac and Jim Ferguson, tough guys who would lay down their lives for us, it makes you feel like doing something for them when all the time all you hear is whining and see fellows going behind your back to join a union that is only going to rook them."

"Just the same," said Spence seriously, "we haven't seen even the beginning."

"Exactly what I was telling Glen. I said last night you haven't seen the start, didn't I, Glen? Those fellows are getting encouragement all along the line. The government and the professors, the colleges are honeycombed with pinks or worse." As Spence's face flushed up, Ed shut up, remembering suddenly Mrs. Gibbons' alleged escapade with the professor from the college. An awkward silence lasted several minutes.

"Can't we have a little music," said old Mr. Chance testily. "Mamma and I always had singing on Christmas. The old German songs, most of them. Don't you remember, Margaret?"

"Yes, I do," she said softly, suddenly touched by the old man sitting alone. "I'll play something if the rest don't mind." She went over to the piano and put her hands on the cool keys. Ed watched her profile, the head lifted, her warm round throat. Something stuck in his own throat, as she began, *Oh, little town of Bethlehem, how still we see thee lie. Above thy deep and dreamless sleep* . . .

Mr. Chance sat with his eyes closed. Spence bowed his head. Even the little boys came out from under the piano and leaned against their mother as she sang. *The hopes and fears of all the years,* they chimed in, opening their mouths wide.

Ed cleared his throat uncomfortably. "Hey, you'll have us all crying," he said after she had finished.

"The Prince of Peace," old Mr. Chance said. "Remember, Margaret, how Mamma always said, this is the birthday of the Prince of Peace? I wonder how she made those little white cookies with sugar, I don't suppose you remember." Margaret hung her head. "No, Papa, she never told me."

The day before Steve Carson was to leave the Chicago plant, one of the fellows got fired. A story was cooked up that he had scrapped fourteen cases and the boss told him he would have to fire him. He said he had not scrapped fourteen cases but the fellow working next to him, who didn't belong to the union, said he saw him scrap them. This fellow was ready to sign an affidavit saying he saw the cases scrapped. The union fellow had been on that job four years and out he went without a chance to defend himself. The union men in the shop buzzed that spies were at work thicker than thieves and it was tightening up so they wouldn't dare meet, let alone wear a union button, and the very day Steve left another fellow was picked off his job.

The boss came in and said it was too bad, but the fellows didn't want to work with Wesley Feeney. Wesley Feeney said he guessed that was a mistake, he'd been on the job two years and knew all the men, and he stood up with his tools as the line hadn't begun yet, and called out, "Hey, Bud, and Harry and Shrimp," and the fellows who were along his line and all knew him, answered very friendly and he said, "You see, Mr. Whitcomb, they all answer me friendly." Whitcomb just shook his head and said he hoped so, and he didn't want to keep a man from working but he didn't want any trouble and Wesley had better go until this thing could be smoothed out. Wesley began to argue and a fellow named Waite that wasn't regular on that job and worked about five hundred feet off on the other line called out, "Feeney, you are a rat, we don't want to work with you."

Wesley spoke up so loud everyone could hear but he tried not to be excited, and even Steve got it from his line. "Why, you lousy loafer, you. You have a nerve calling an honest man, who fights in a union for your rights, a rat." Mr. Whitcomb was waiting and grabbed hold of him pretending to be afraid of a fight but Wesley shook him off and spoke up, "Listen, men, don't let these people pull you around by a Pinkerton spy. Come out in the open and show yourselves as men. What kind of men are you who will keep quiet and let them say you are no friends of mine when you were friends?" The men all the way up the line grabbed at his hand and arm and yelled they wanted to work with him but Steve rushed from his line as if he were on fire and grabbed at Wesley too and said, "Sure we want to work with you," and he kept holding to him and walking along with him forgetting all about his line that was ready to start up.

It didn't do any good because Mr. Whitcomb claimed it would only start an ugly fight and he regretted it very much but couldn't blame the men who didn't want to work with him for feeling the way they did. Steve wanted to yell out that they weren't men who were holding back the job but just stoolpigeons but Wesley was giving him the wink and jerking his eyebrows and he suddenly got very self-conscious especially as Whitcomb gave him a very sharp look and asked him what he was doing so far away from his line. Steve took a long chance. Hell, he had to leave that very day, and he spoke up and said if Waite could drift five hundred feet away from his line to pick on Wesley, he could leave his line to stick up for him. Some of the fellows looked at him with long secret approving looks but the fellow next him shrunk down between his shoulders when Steve came back and his lips got tight and he wouldn't so much as speak to him.

It's all right, old monkey face, don't speak, Steve thought to himself, and he seemed on fire. They were doing forty-five jobs an hour on his line and he had had all he could do to work up to it but that day he was actually waiting for the job. The whole line seemed to spin before him. He could hardly wait for a chance to talk it over, but none of the fellows would talk at noon and it wasn't until night that they thrashed it out at union headquarters to see what could be done about Wesley's job. They decided to make a fight for it, but already a lot of the men were getting cold feet, the thing appeared to be dying on its legs, and Steve could hardly believe his ears when one of the older men yelped that if Steve had a wife and a lot of kids he'd get dry behind the ears quicker than you could say scat.

He would have felt humiliated and downhearted about the whole business if Charley Egstrom hadn't wised him up when he went home that night. "We got so many stools, we don't know our own men, that's fact. The union has to begin doing something for the men or we'll lose them. So far we ain't had much more than failures and a name. But I can tell you this, Steve," and Charley's face got sharp as a blade, "if that don't work, we'll find something that will. You can put that in your pipe and smoke it. We ain't just dependent on the A. F. of L. or on anything, we can make something that will work. It'll come because it has to."

He said the words so surely that Steve felt a great weight go off his chest. He felt he had got hold of something he could carry back with him. He talked it over with Charley. Charley said it was rough on rats to go, but Lorraine was a swell kid and after all it wouldn't take long. Steve could come back and things would be further along than now, or he'd eat his hat.

All the way back on the train, he sat up in the day-coach and heard the wheels grind out, *it'll come because it has to, it'll come,* and he felt happy and proud and when he got off the train and saw Walt and his step-mother looking anxious and a little timid, he waved to them with a big grin busting out, and Teacher-teacher's face lit up. She hugged him so her hat fell off backward. "Oh, Steve," she said, "I was almost afraid to look at you, but it's going to be all right."

Even in a few months Walt looked thinner and sort

of transparent around the mouth, but he had a lot to say about things not exactly dying on their feet there either. They were beginning to talk about a third political party and one that would grab in a lot of people and he was all for it, but Steve could see his heart was not in it. Walt had seen parties come and go and he was set for something drastic coming along that would lift them all from the dead level.

The biggest surprise was Mr. LaRue who gave him one sharp poke in the ribs as if he were getting ready to fight, and then let his eyes twinkle. "Had my eye on you all the time," he said. "Between us we can put the whole deal through." Steve got a little set around the mouth and hoped LaRue wasn't planning on him making a lifework of his ranch but he decided not to bring up any controversial stuff now. Lorraine had a new blue dress and had insisted on a preacher to marry them because she knew her mother would hate it any other way. The preacher came and stood in the bay-window and he and Lorraine faced him with the parents and Steve's kid sisters in the rear. Tub Johnson and a couple of the young folks in Mitchell came and acted kind of hysterical as though they were getting. married.

It was an oldfashioned affair with a big cake with whipped cream and Papa LaRue had dug up a couple of bottles of wine somewhere and there was hard cider for those who liked it and a little corn likker, but not much as LaRue didn't want a lot of monkeyshines getting started. They had a big spread with preserves and rounds of cold ham and chicken and potato salad and slices of pie for old Mrs. Percy who came in with old lady Ridgeway. The young folks danced and Papa LaRue led out with old Dan Tucker just for old times' sake. Steve thought he never saw anything so lovely as the way Lorraine pranced out, proud and still, as if only her feet were moving and her body held straight and her head up. She looked to him just as if she were dancing with a rose in her mouth, and he thought he was a pretty lucky fellow. After all, it was all turning out for the best. When it came his turn, he stamped an extra step and gave a whirl just like the fellow he and Charley had seen dancing in the movie in Chicago. They all clapped, and Teacher-teacher ran around looking about sixteen years old and did the Highland fling she had learned off an old neighbor when she was a girl in Nebraska.

When they got out to the ranch, he got a stubborn fit when it turned out old man LaRue was only to pay him two dollars a week but Lorraine whispered not to fuss, Papa would do something nice for them if he was patient, and he melted at the look of terror she had, and just went ahead. The up-to-date setup got hold of him, and he began to figure out how to lick the chances of drought the coming spring when they put in the crops. He and LaRue would talk it over after supper, with Lorraine sitting in a chair with her feet on a little stool.

"I got 'em all licked around here, even threshed three hundred bushels of wheat last year. Sowed rye too, but cut it for straw. Machines is the answer. We can get out there and buzz around night and day. We got deep plows. We got searchlights and if there is moisture we get the advantage of it." He smacked his lips over it, but Steve felt ashamed of his solitary position. Still he had to admire old LaRue's endurance and, before the winter was over, he got to like chinning with him when they went on the range to speculate on the deep snow that might give the moisture. LaRue went around in a cap that looked like a Daniel Boone coonskin with no tail, and at night, in his big stocking-feet, he would sit making little drawings and figuring on the number of cows that would be dropping calves, with a kind of burning interest in the fate of each one.

"That old Maud, she's a regular gummer, I should have sold her with the lot I turned in, but she gives a good calf, every time." And sometimes he would throw his head back, give a shrewd look at his daughter, as if he saw her naked, and shout, "Well, I hope you have more chicks than Mamma and me had. Two ain't enough to butter anything." His head would hang down, and he'd talk along about what they would do with the boy until Steve and Lorraine, in bed afterwards, giggling together, would hope and pray it was a girl just to feel they weren't being bossed all over the place.

He had it easy, in spite of the hard work, but the chores took the life out of him. Even the excitement of the baby getting nearer and the way Lorraine's body swelled out, like a big juicy pear, wasn't enough to lift his spirits. He had a scrawled letter from Charley Egstrom, near spring-plowing time, saying that things were kinda black. The men had been scared pissless with all the spies making trouble and the union had fallen off something terrible because the good fellows were scared of losing their jobs and getting blacklisted.

"But, mark my words," wrote Charley, "where there's a will there's a way, as the saying is. We need a union more and more. Production speeding up only makes them more set on busting the union. It has got cruel. Every time I see a new car I think how it gets took right out of our hides. One night my back got me so bad I just lay down on the floor when I got home and begged Ada to throw a cover on me and let me alone, I ached so. This can't go on forever. Hope you can make it back soon but you may find yourself blacklisted for letting off your mouth the last day you was here."

LaRue had about seven hundred tons of straw and they mixed it with cottonseed cake for a nice feed. Not like Walt who was dragging his animals through on godknowswhat. He had mortgaged his animals for a feed loan, then his crops for a seed loan, and was hoping for animal relief to stagger through. Lots of people around were using the money they got for animals for their own food and even LaRue said you couldn't blame them when the animals were plastered with mortgages so thick they'd never realize on them. But LaRue liked to tell stories of thrifty fellows who made good. "It shows you," he would say as if he never tired of it, "how a thrifty man can get ahead. He keeps off the roads and minds his business and in the end he has something." Steve began to question him and to pin him down, so he had to admit very few started from scratch but had help from somewhere. Sometimes after these long discussions that seemed to be like a red rag between them, he would look so fagged out that Lorraine had a terrible feeling of panic, as if a train was coming too fast for her to get off the track. But she soothed him when they were alone. "I know how you feel, but it won't be for always. Just hold on a little longer. We'll go away together, us and the baby."

He sent away to the agriculture stations for the latest bulletins and sat at the radio at night when there was any kind of talk on. Once they listened to the Firestone hour all about rubber tires, rib tires, ground grip tires, tires for wheel barrows and lawn mowers. The possibility of rubber on farms was overpowering, the speaker said, the use of tires on the small tractor would have a far-reaching effect on leisure and drudgery. American farms had made more progress than were made in a thousand years preceding. . . .

Steve's ears got redder and redder and suddenly he switched the radio off as if he were going to slam it to the floor. He felt ashamed to be sitting in his father-in-law's well-stocked house. He had suddenly remembered the farms around his father's and his father's own place without light and never a convenience. Edgar White had it so cold his wife had made a dugout with her own hands, just a hole in the ground, and the last winter she was alive, she had gone in there like an animal to keep warm. He gave a kick to a chair and LaRue looked up and said, "Whoa there, whoa now," kind of laughing but Steve slammed out of the house. A cold stinging wind hit his cheeks and felt good to his face. He wasn't going to sit there and listen to any more lies. Leisure? Who was going to get it except the rich and the out-of-works? Leisure and starvation, not leisure and rubber tires.

He walked clear up around the big cattle sheds and stood inside near their warm flanks. The quiet munch-

ing noise and their deep dark silence soothed him. He
thought he was going to cry. He was homesick, not just
for the city and the work and the men and the hope of
making a union and the fight coming on, but for something deeper, it was terrible, and made him feel as if
something were sticking in his throat.

Only that day he had read about a new discovery;
they had found new hormones to feed plants to increase
production on an unheard-of scale. None of the nursery
people would touch it. No wonder. They had plowed
under, not produced. A kind of craziness pounded in his
very temples. He leaned against some harness and the
sharp buckle dug into his skin. If he knew of a gold mine
under his feet and couldn't reach it, had no hands or
feet, must just stare at the dull ground and know that a
handbreadth away the earth crawled with bright sparkling metal, he couldn't feel worse than he felt now.
Godalmighty, thousands had been driven from the land
to godknowswhere. The soil had nourished the bloody
flux not men. He didn't know of a darn thing his father
had bought for years, since he had the brainstorm to send
him that semester to Vermillion, except interest. He
went out in the wind again and saw the light in the
house as if it were a long way off. The ground dipped
away like a dark wide expanse of deep water and the light
looked lonely and high. As he neared the windows he
could see Lorraine sitting with a troubled listening look.
But the old man was reading a Sunday funny paper. He
gave a short laugh and went inside.

Jonathan Chance had expected to tell Victoria about
his experiences with the different groups in Philadelphia.
After she said, "It's a woman," he admitted it was and
they stared for a second at one another. He had gone
into a few details, that they had met a few nights ago,
she had driven up with him to New York because here

was where her people lived. She had been married and had just left her husband who was much older.

He had expected a shrewd withering glance from Victoria at this point, half aware of the tinge of complacency that had crept into his voice. She had not looked up from her mending. Her face had grown as still and white as wax as he waited for her to burst out at him. She was a fierce creature who knew how to use her tongue. Her freezing silence wore his nerves; his resentment felt confined in the room that had become much too small. She looked calmly for her scissors, could not find them, and put the awkward mending to her mouth to bite off the thread. He saw her hands trembling. Once when he had come home drunk, long ago, she had hit him with a quick blow that had been healthy as a splash of cold water. Nothing came from her now and although he had not yet begun to admit that he already thirsted for a sight of Leslie Day's face, he was reminded that he had begged Victoria "not to mind" when he came in the door and she was most certainly and heartily minding. She would not even do that one small thing for him, and he got to his feet bitterly. She looked up then, her whole face quivering with some deadly inner convulsion. In a funny flat voice he heard, "Oh, when is it going to end?" He did not answer but decided he had better go out for some cigarettes. He said as much, since she made no resistance.

She heard the door close. He has gone, she thought, and will never come back to me, and this time she felt that she was powerless to run after him. His words "not to mind" hampered her thoughts like a foreign tongue. The landslide had been held back long enough; let it come. She would have to run for her life if she were not already buried and now among the beaten dead.

When he came back, she was sitting in the same place as if in a trance. His breezy false attempt at high spirits was inflammable; she flared up. "So you couldn't wait. I suppose you were telephoning her." Trapped in her terrible clairvoyance, he started. Would there never be any possible escape? He said angrily, "Why not?" She tried to hold her tongue; she could not bear to see them make fools of one another. After all, he was in the room with her, not with some stranger, and forgetting her own history she simply labeled the other woman a whore. As if she had spoken the words out loud, he had wheeled upon her, but she had drawn her feet up under her dress and sat rocking herself. In the mirror of the dresser she could see their two selves; she did not know in what way they had changed. The terrible inexplicable nature of this moment cramped her so that she could not get to her feet. What awful expectation had led her now to feel that a dagger had been put in her very vitals. Her father and mother had never quarreled, and childishly she looked at Jonathan as though the heavy ring her mother had worn to her very death with the word "forever" engraved inside, had been put upon her own finger.

Her heart was beating steadily louder to gain momentum for its future life. If she could only laugh and put on lightheartedness as one might a lovely dress, wind herself around his neck and make him feel he was her life, her all. Oh, but he is, my life, my darling, and she choked, trying to speak, and not able to, sat like a judge, sternly, picking at her mending. If she could only rise dramatically to her feet, say decisively, "choose between us," but the role did not become her. She had not annexed Jonathan like a piece of land; he was a whole human being with lungs and heart, and it was too true she had wronged him. She too belonged to herself, she thought proudly, and the words seemed part of some unearthly bargain that had witlessly betrayed them. Their two selves that had thought to melt at the very sight of one another, stared coldly now, each out of its separate shell, and Jonathan thought with a sinking of the heart that a man could be annihilated by so much hatred as he now persuaded himself poured steadily, wave on wave, from his wife.

Lester Tolman did not spend his vacation wastefully. He was convinced that a positive change must come to his life and that Elsie was part of the transformation. Although they had been in the apartment for weeks, order had never emerged in any true and living form. The drapes had been put up at one window only. His typewriter seemed always buried under a flood of her clothing. He could not budge Elsie from her own selfish way of life. In vain he pictured the country and the pleasures of a home. She would fairly weep over the picture and for a rapturous hour they would furnish the place, plant gardens, entertain their friends. Her mother would be installed neatly in a wing and a wonderful cook would have prepared a meal fit for the Gods. Even perfect love reigned and Elsie and Lester, their arms inseparably entwined, walked in the cool of the evening in the scented gardens. But in the end, she would wail, "But how? Who is to pay for it?" and a deep cold silence lay like a tomb between them. As if he did not know she had money saved up. For what was it rotting? Not that he wouldn't do his part. He would continue at his job and then, when he had something saved, break from it for country life, to write at last, what he pleased. This pleasant vision of writing what he pleased taunted him and gave him all the satisfaction of achievement. He told himself that the substantial work was done by men over forty, he still had a few years to prepare for his task. But he was not going to tempt fate. Only this vacation, to reprove those laggards who let life go by, he had slipped a sheet in the typewriter, had written his name and address in the left-hand corner and had begun, Chapter One. When Elsie came home he showed her a fully completed first page and she had almost wept. They saw themselves as creators, continually renewing life.

If the theatre were not so exhausting. If Elsie had not had so hard a life. She was continually wringing her hands and insisting on her struggle. He had to admit it was only too true. He admired her for it. He had no intention of taking her from it. Oh, didn't he, and how did he think she was to get to the theatre stuck off in the country? Did he want to make a man of her that he put the burden on her back? No, she was thinking of his own good. He would have to take care of the rent, it was a man's role. He had promised her to pay for the repairs on the car; was he going to do it or must she shame him by paying it from her own pocket.

He did not know why his dreams always seemed built on sand. In his bed, with her body curled submissively beside him as if to soften the blow of their true relationship, he could feel his former lives pound their way in his temple. When he had taken this job, he had promised himself a new decisive firm character, consistent with the experiences he had had in Germany. He was a man sobered by a look at history from a front-row seat and that sobriety kept him even now, when some feebleness in his nature clung to Elsie like a limpet, steadily looking at his whole life, edging around it, measuring it up like a tailor trying to get a man to stand still long enough to get a new suit properly fitted.

If only he did not fall for flashy temperamental women! But even as he cursed his luck, he took a secret gratification in his choice. He was, he sighed, like his uncle, whose life was checkered with the fair sex and who had never been faithful to one woman. And the knowledge that infidelity was his fate was not torturing. It even seemed to provide that base for suffering without which the experience of life drifts over a man like water rushing down an impenetrable and rocky hillside. In moments of true misery, he wondered at himself. Why was he somehow entangled with a woman who loved herself better than anyone else? Why did he not have children? At such moments he uttered the humblest queries. If only he had a home and something to work for. He curled up inside himself and died a dozen deaths a night, but in the morning he bathed, shaved, and in a bright tie and fine matching shirt, was that competent, slightly bored, sophisticated person whom visitors in the office always noticed with respect as if he had been a foreign duke or lord.

He seemed perpetually struggling in a murky fog, waiting for that blinding light that would illuminate everything in his life as, for a few strange moments when he fought to come out from ether after his appendicitis operation, he had felt himself floating in some translucent cloud with a complete knowledge of all life, past and future. He had awakened calling "I see, I see," in ecstatic tones that had frightened his mother who appeared like a dim cobweb that had somehow trailed his comet flight.

The holidays devoured so much of Elsie with the extra matinees that he had half a notion to rush down to Cuba to do a little spying around about the sugar. When he called on Victoria to ask how much time outside the office she could give, he found her down in bed with bronchitis. The doctor, who had turned out to be an old schoolfriend in the University of California, had come. Jonathan had gone out somewhere, and she looked peculiarly flushed and ill to be left alone.

She had insisted she would be all right and Jonathan would be back at once and anyhow Lester's nerves would not let him alone. He wanted to wander. A number of parties were going on. There was a feverish density in the air, he could not sit still. A few drinks here, a few there, and the same perpetual talk of people earnestly trying to resolve their lives, even as himself. A visiting Englishman of repute was at one of the houses and the talk revolved around communism and the danger of the rightists in France. His head ached. Oh, for a good oldfashioned home with dogs, cats, and children, a Christmas tree ten feet high and some nice motherly woman to beg him just to drink a little more of the eggnog, it wouldn't hurt a fly. He would be half-seas over but it wouldn't make any difference to anyone, and he would drink more of the warm rich stuff, sinking into a bliss of joy that came from sitting where people had not forgot to love.

To love. Was that it? Did he mean a woman? He had had little happiness there, only strange false flights. His foot was on the lower step of another house, on Tenth street. He looked up at the windows. One tier blank. One tier with curtains down, the third with tiny wreaths. The second was his station. He pressed the bell and toiled up. Why was he coming here? Only that he had to go somewhere and Anne Pond had told him never to stop on ceremony. Probably he would get a cold look or interrupt a love scene. His own love scene was now going on in Act Three before an audience of lovethirsty citizens uptown.

Anne was really glad to see him judging from her warm handclasp. There were several people in the room. One was an Irish Catholic who in the 1920's had tried to forget his salvation. The other was a Jewish Catholic who had made a long and circuitous journey through a Jesuit college to, of all things, communism.

These details were whispered hurriedly in his ear by Anne as they stood near the table where she was just then measuring out very generous highballs. She did not want his progress impeded by strangeness and, looking at him brightly, suggested he would like both men. Tolman took his drink and straddled the hearth rug. The newspaperman, Collins, was a warm personable fellow, a little on the mellow side. The Jesuit was indescribable. An impetuous glowing manner seemed halted by some recollection of the proprieties. Collins and the Jesuit had once known each other very well; in fact, they had attended the same Jesuit college. The Jesuit was now speaking of that period, interned for six years, a cadaver in a tomb. His present buoyancy made his recital of his past life unreal, as if he had merely dreamed it.

Collins laughed a good deal at the recollection of Thomas in his college days. In an aside to Tolman, he said it was gratifying but disturbing to find him repeating all his own arguments of former years, which Thomas had then opposed. Collins seemed to have opened a door, from which Thomas had exited, only to exit through still another door which he now held wide for the reluctant Collins. For it was quite clear that Collins was disturbed by the exuberant warmth of his friend's acceptance of yet a third philosophy. He had had an early Hebraic education, then a Jesuitical, now he was turning in a third direction.

Thomas shook his head benignly. He was barely swallowing his drink and he began excitedly calling upon Collins to remember Thomas Aquinas. There was no irreconcilable contradiction between catholicism and communism, he said. Both centered around the brotherhood of man. Even details of their early beginnings had the same overwhelming solicitude for the spirit rather than the flesh, for the cult even of poverty, as witness the early disciples and the present-day organizers who went out with empty pockets, starved, hitchhiked, and were shot and beaten like martyrs.

Anne said, "You make me uncomfortable. I don't think it is like that. Religion is sickly to me. It rests on a concept of immortality and of a belief in God that only hampers us. Religion has always been used to belittle man, to humble him, to make him small and docile." Both Collins and Thomas jumped on Anne and Collins asked indignantly what present-day character could even compare in spirituality with Joan of Arc.

"Sacco and Vanzetti," said Thomas, his eyes widening and Tolman said that he would like to present Sophocles. Sophocles had died for all time. For liberty of opinion. The only way he could save his life had been to lose it.

"What did he really die for?" said Thomas, walking toward Tolman and looking as if he meant to back him into the fire. "He believed in the state, didn't he? Sacco died for Justice." He pronounced it tenderly, "joostice," as he imagined it had been said by Sacco himself. He would like to make clear that actually the consciousness of the rights of the individual had been growing all the time. There was no comparison between today and the Roman Empire or a Greek City state. Only a few individuals had great power then, the masses were slaves. Tolman tried to edge in "Germany" but Thomas did not give him a chance. He kept repeating "joostice" until Collins began to imitate him.

"Joostice, joostice, well, what about Joan of Arc. She died for not only this world but the next, the most complete spiritual being. The circle, above and over life."
Thomas said coldly, "She died because the priests betrayed her and she was burned at the stake."

"All right," said Collins heatedly, "then Sacco and Vanzetti were plain murdered."

"The spirit in which they died is important," said Thomas, and the two of them had practically forgot the others. "They were not resigned, meekly accepting. They fought it. They said it was a crime to the end." And suddenly aware that he had shut out Anne from the discussion he now went over to her and slipping his hand through her arm, said, "She's a true Catholic, no matter what she calls herself. Her life is an act of faith. Oh, Collins, you are the old, we are the new."

Collins shook with a kind of deep laughter that was not mirth. He said, "Look at them. They make me sad. They are like the honeymoon couple going off on their honeymoon. Those on the platform wave and cry. Why? The revolution is a long, long way off and they act as if it were tomorrow."

Tolman had been waiting to get a word in edgewise but in spite of his lack of participation, he felt happy and excited. He was mixing another round of drinks, and everyone in the room looked charming and delightful to him. He thought how puny a man is to let himself tie up his life to one person, to one fate. He had a second's uneasiness as if he heard himself declaiming something he might later disown, but at the moment he wanted only to discuss spirit and matter and that the two were one and indivisible. Pavlov's experiments in animal behavior intrigued him; did they not in a way illuminate even the problem of catholicism and communism?

Anne was trying to get the talk on a more realistic plane but when she mentioned strikes and organizations, Thomas merely looked helpless and confused. "He knows nothing except a theory," Anne said to Tolman as Thomas went to the bathroom. "What a strange person.

He seems to me to be trying to put some ballast into his beliefs by widening his religion. It is all so strange. When he came in, he said he and a friend had come to New York from a midwest college and they could find no place in the modern world as Catholics if they wished to continue to use their heads."

The two Catholics now began discussing church history and Tolman was thinking that Elsie would have returned long ago; she would look at the empty bed, perhaps with a pang of alarm. She might even wonder if there were another woman; this perpetual game of hide and go seek was suddenly distasteful to him. Anne said in a low voice, "What happened to your sugar articles?"

"They didn't want to use them, the bastards, but I'm going to work it up, in more detail later."

"You ought to do it now," she said, speaking still lower. "I heard, don't ask me how, that a big strike was to be pulled in the sugar harvesting season this year in Cuba."

"You did?" He looked at her sharply. He felt a tingling along his spine as if he were coming to sudden compelling happy life. He wanted to ask questions but remembering Kurt Becher, remembering many things he had learned in Germany, he preferred not to ask. He said simply, "If that's so, now is the time to do it. Even for one of the papers."

"That's what I thought," Anne said. They turned back to the other two as if they had said enough to one another. He did not want to leave the strange crew that continued talking until near dawn. A little dizzy they all went out on the street together. At that hour Tolman was always recalled to his earliest expectations of adventure as if the cobwebby silence had restored his full illusions. Going to a restaurant for hot cakes and coffee appeared as a momentous decision that in some way was to change his entire life.

When he reached his own apartment, Elsie reared up in bed but was actress enough to coo, "Darling, where on earth were you, I haven't slept a wink." He kissed her eyes absently, wondering for the first time if she dyed her hair. He looked at his typewriter; some chiffon underthings covered it. He tossed them off brutally, and looked at the page that was still in the typewriter. Page one. He ripped it out. For some reason he said firmly, "No more dreaming."

Victoria and Jonathan Chance had tried to treat one another as civilized beings. After the first two days when Victoria had lashed out with a fury that would like to take the skin off a man's back, she had subsided. She sat as if stunned at their Christmas dinner, smiling as if a little demented. Their thoughts seemed to mingle in a confused painful attempt to touch one another. "This is our last Christmas," she said, not accusingly, but as if she had said sadly, the snow has fallen especially heavy this year. He said, "No, don't say that," and tried himself to believe it. He did not know what was happening and because he found it impossible as yet to think of a future life without her, he still persuaded himself that what he now experienced was nothing more than the chicken pox and soon over. He had seen Leslie Day again at Victoria's own insistence after a telegram had come asking him if he would telephone, she was very ill with the flu. Victoria had been all scornful commiseration. "Phone her," she said. "She's doubtless sick on your account. You got yourself into this." Afterwards, waiting for him to return had been too heavy an offering. She had walked in the cold biting wind up to the Park, her coat open and the bitter air striking her bare neck heedlessly.

In bed the next day, she thought guiltily she was no better than the weakest woman who sickens in a last effort to keep what is going from her. They had sent for a doctor, someone Esther Whittaker knew. He had come in busily, peering at her through thick bright glasses. "Well, what's wrong?" Jonathan had stood around; he felt sick himself as some men do when their

wives are going to give birth to a child. He meant to
ask the medico to take a look at him, too. "Where did you
get those circles under your eyes," the doctor began,
stripping off his gloves and looking stern.

"I always have them," Victoria said out of her fever.

"You didn't have them when you went to the University of California." She raised her head painfully. "What
did you say?"

"I said you didn't have them then," he said, smiling
mysteriously.

"Who are you?" she asked. Jonathan looked on pleasantly. Anything for a diversion from their troubles. *"Now,*
my name's Jensen. Then . . ." He shrugged. "You don't
remember me? Oh, well, I'm not so handsome as I was,
my hair has thinned." He waited, his vanity hurt. She
thrashed vainly in bed, struggling to remember. These
men. If she could only think; he would feel wounded.
Was it possible he was the young Pole who used to come
to Barney Blum's for long talks about socialism and the
War, and then had finally been drafted, had come to see
her in Seattle in a brand new uniform? Or was he that
bright young fellow who had called up to make a date
and used to wait outside classes to walk as far as the
Campanile with her? If she made a mistake, he would
wither. He was withering already. What babies they all
were. He said pointedly, "I remember you. I even remember things you said."

"My eyes aren't always like this, I've been crying,"
said Victoria.

"I thought so," the doctor said, not looking at Jonathan, who cheerfully volunteered, "We were talking of
separating for a while." The doctor turned and looked
at him.

"So," he said shortly. "A tragic mistake." He had stuck
the thermometer in Victoria's mouth and with hand
firmly on her wrist tried not to see the wave of red that
had colored her face and neck as Jonathan spoke. "Marriage is good for people who want to do things in the
world. It's far from perfect, but it's something to put

your roots in." When the thermometer came out, Victoria asked if he weren't the one who had come to Seattle in a new uniform. She even remembered his name but was afraid to say it; it had a ridiculous sound, like "popcorn." He seemed hurt that she did not recall him clearly and with the same intensity he had remembered her.

"Such is life," he said. "We all change. I am fatter, not romantic anymore," and he quite evidently thought of himself as a gay handsome blade in his youth, whereas Victoria preferred him as he was, a good solid man with shrewd eyes and quick deft hands. He now advised her to go to a hospital. A temperature, 102°. Nothing to play with. She needed care. Jonathan said he would be around as if frightened at the thought of her leaving him so soon. She said firmly from her bed that she was very well where she was. She wasn't to be prancing around, he warned, or she'd have pneumonia.

Then she was alone. Jonathan had gone out after drawing the shades. He had tiptoed back with big pears and two red apples. Does he think I can eat, she thought angrily, but tried to be grateful, even to speak. He had always hated sick people and he did still. She could see it in his eyes roaming around, trying to think up a decent escape.

"Go and see someone, go see your old friend Gus Hight." He said if she could manage all right, he would. He'd come back in a jiffy or phone. The room was big, peaceful, and empty now and she could go back to that time in California. Six months before she had met another man from those days whom she remembered very well. "You were just like blue flame," he had said. She pulled his words to her, as if the doctor had said them. That he had remembered her all these years melted something hard in her breast, it spread its delicious pool around the tight confines of her heart.

So she had really been lovely. She shut her eyes as if in the darkness she might again find that slim girl and they might once more attempt life together. It was a long hard way back, and she did not know how it was possible to come so far and not to change. Worry changes a woman, and you can't bear children, her mother always said, without losing your youth. Not that the baby had been a big one, he had been very tiny, no bigger than a shoebox and she had put up a lot of preserves that fall, cleaned the cellar and attic. Always have things ready, never go out on the street in dirty underwear, her mother said, just think of your shame if you should have an accident and be taken to the hospital. The place had been in apple-pie order, always had been, births or no births. In the night she would wake, feeling the bliss of a bed of her own with her own true husband and a house roof over her head and good acres of land. The smells and the sounds would steam up in the dark. A clinker would fall in the stove at night and she could hardly believe her happiness. Soon the strong sunshine would pour in the window to wake them to a new day.

Where are you, she said, curling down in the bed, and she could not find herself. She had gone in search of her sister Rosamond, instead, who was dead and had just left to marry Jerry before he went to war. She must hurry or it will be too late. Oh, hurry, hurry. The train is coming, but the order to move will come first. He will leave Camp Funston, then he will be put on a ship. She'll never in the world make it, and the ticket had been endless, a great yard of a ticket that guaranteed nothing but a never-ending journey and no time for love. And then the train had come puffing into the station, importantly, and the two young girls had run for it. Rosamond had stood on the steps with a bunch of violets on her blue coat. Her hair had curled out softly from under her little hat. Oh, if she only doesn't fall off that step, but they were shoving her up the steps now. The white arm of the porter was closing the door and through a moving window she saw Rosamond, crying and waving.

She was alone.

I thought we would go on writing to one another forever, she thought, miserably cheated, and now it is over. We were each to have children and write back and forth about how little Peter had the croup and little Anne is taking piano lessons. Where is she? And she was listening to old Papa Blum with his plumy white hair, saying in his wise voice, "No good will come out of this war. It is all evil." It was taking a long time to bear a new war; it was being born now in the world, and what a painful thing it is to struggle and then bring out a dead child. Oh, if she could stay for a few minutes at that one place where she had had it all before her. But nothing was ever still. The light under the windowshade cut like bits of sharp glass broken against her eyes. She shut her eyes again, and her mother was telling her not to move until she was well. She had brought her hot chocolate and was holding out the steaming cup with her hands around it. I can't drink it, my throat hurts too much. Oh, but she had had scarlet fever harder than anyone. It had fairly crippled her. Several children had died in their neighborhood but Victoria had pulled through.

"You were meant to live for something," her mother had said, tenderly, and she felt ashamed to notice the broken nails on her mother's hands. "Well, your mother's nursing pulled you through," old Dr. Marvin had called out, smelling fresh of antiseptic and cold air and always a curiosity with his thumb sliced off and still so agile at measuring drops into a glass. Oh, mother, mother, and she was running down a long corridor that had no end, yes, this was her old home, the very kitchen with the cook stove and funny brown paper, and her mother very bright and living was pressing at the ironing board. She saw it was a dress for Rosamond, not for her, and said in a hurt voice, "Why, you are using my green dress to press with," and indeed her best green dress was being put to no better use than a pressing cloth for Rosamond's dress.

"No, no," her mother said. "This won't take a minute or hurt anything."

"But I just pressed my dress," she cried, deeply offended as if nothing that belonged to her would ever be in the least regarded. But then, ashamed not to be gracious, she burst out, "Oh, never mind, only I'm so tired," and it seemed as if she were completely done. Everything in her was drawn out, and she could only repeat in a nightmare, I'm so tired. Everything that had failed her stood around like so many empty boxes to be lifted and put on shelves too high to reach. There was no baby for the clothes and old Mr. Chance had not kept his word about the well. The wall had broken in at the cellar and water was pouring over all the good preserves and help, she called in a loud voice, mother, mother, help me, help me, but she was alone again and her mother busily walked past her at a distance with a glance that neither saw nor heard.

Victoria opened her eyes with great effort. Someone had come into the room and she saw the substantial trousered legs of two males. They walked toward her and she raised her eyes and the faces blurred. Poor Joe, her mother had said, and poor bird, a wild bird in the house means death and, "Jonathan, take out that bird."

"She's delirious," she heard a voice. It would be Gus Hight. "Nonsense," she said in a clear sane voice, and felt a hand on her forehead.

"She's pretty hot," said Jonathan.

"Stop all that cackling and get me a drink," she said clearly and Jonathan chuckled. "Nothing wrong with your temper is there, Vicky," and she knew he would never call her darling again. Help, oh, help me, but it was useless to call upon the dead. "Get Lester on the phone," she said firmly as Jonathan held her head to drink.

"Better wait till you're better," he said as if to a child.

"I know what I want. Now," and Gus said, "Better humor her." She heard them rattling around with the phone, complacently. That would show them she knew her own mind. When she said now, she meant now. Jonathan said, "What do you want to tell him?" What did she want to tell him, she was going down again but struggled hard. "Tell him I'll get started on that piece he wants, I'd better go to Cuba myself. No use trusting any Tom, Dick,

or Harry." Jonathan said, "You can't think about going
now. You're too sick."

"I'll show you if I can go or not," she was saying or
whose voice was that, was it hers or did it belong to her
Aunt Hortense and had she just then read it in a letter from Nancy telling her that Aunt Hortense was just
a shell, with a big lump, and they had told her she didn't
have the strength to go to Portland for the radium treatment and she had got right off the bed. "I'll show you
if I can go or not," she said, and on her last legs she
had actually ridden down, a two-hour ride on the train.
Oh, but she had been a misunderstood woman in her day
and Victoria begged that she would forgive her for her
harsh judgment, poor soul, it had happened a long time
before, way before Victoria was born or even thought of;
she'd never had a fit life and her own mother had got
the man Aunt Hortense had wanted.

Jonathan was talking over the phone. "He says all
right but you must get better," he said in a troubled
voice. "I'll get better," she thought, and aloud she said,
"I know my own business I guess." She wished they
would get out of the room again. It was no use to go
back to the dead; they had failed her, but she could doze
a little, couldn't she? No one had taxed sleep yet, had
they? She could get her strength. Unless someone would
be waiting to grab it from her the minute she got it.
They'd find out if she was one to stand on one leg waiting for death. There must be living faces somewhere.
"Go away," she ordered in a loud voice, keeping her eyes
tightly shut, and heard the two men blundering around.
Finally, they took themselves off and good riddance.

She felt her face working, tears oozed out from under
her hot lids and, bitter with salt, stung her cheeks. She
kept her face rigid as death. God knows, she thought,
God knows what I'll ever do in this world without him.

THE GUNS BEGIN

Lester Tolman imagined that if Elsie Forey were not an actress she would be a wonderful woman. He was continually irritated by her need for an audience. On Sunday nights when she could not corner "worthwhile people" the apartment filled with nondescript young men and women of small talents who were devoting tremendous energy to painting or to writing or to acting that was meaningless. Elsie would drape herself in the doorway and hold forth passionately on the integrity of the theatre and how she would never never sell out to Hollywood. It was thrilling to hear her describe the lowbrow clever race who had simply taken over the movies that could never be redeemed until people woke to the value of art in their daily lives.

No one had a chance to put in more than a word and even the young writer in hornrim glasses was obliged to shut up and fumble impotently for another cigarette. From his position in the kitchen, Lester listened to Elsie's pronouncements on unfamiliar subjects with amazement. She spoke in a tone of authority upon international politics and alliances as though diplomats lunched and went to bed with her regularly, telling her all they knew in exchange for her favors. Lester stood up from the icebox, his mouth half open, the cheese and crackers unchewed upon his tongue, and listened to her hypnotic voice. He snickered to himself and, drawing back, chewed the morsel and swallowed it. Even Horn Rims could not combat her but sat with face flushed, scowling at the stories of others.

Lester sympathized with him and coming out from his hiding place shook hands with the guests, selecting Horn Rims for particular attention. Horn Rims immediately launched into a scholastic appraisal of the labor situation that smelled of the midnight lamp. Lester nodded politely and tried to keep his eyes on Elsie and her trained mice.

He felt constantly degraded by his own situation and every night resolved to break with his life and begin again.

The moment he lighted a cigarette and began his announcement Elsie, by some terrible instinct, knew how to make herself small and charming, infinitely tender and touching. Abandoning her role as a great woman, she became a little child bride, crouching on the floor at his feet, tying and untying his shoes, rubbing her face like a cat along his knee.

His decision melted to nothingness. He upbraided himself, told himself he was doomed to a lonely old age in his mania for perfection, that Elsie was just what he wanted, that she had a right to her life and he was a lucky man. He would hear himself call her "his Diana" in the beseeching tones that he had listened to from other throats with a feeling of humiliation and despair.

"You're the only man who ever understood me," she would say in a low voice and he did not know why he was cursed with the suspicion that she was listening to her own words and purring over the perfection of their delivery. Once he gave her a sudden push as she crouched at his feet and as she fell backwards, a wild look of furious comprehension crimsoned her face and neck. She staggered to her feet as he laughed helplessly. "Beast," she said thickly. "Beast." He sat tiredly looking at his hands wondering why he did not let her sweep off the stage in a final breathtaking farewell performance.

At night when he could not sleep he made up scenes in which they fondly said good-by forever; it was usually a snowscene on a street with cars plowing noiselessly through drifts and the lights flashed blindly into their faces preventing them from a last deep embrace. They held to each other's hands instead and her face worked with a terrible effort not to cry. When they parted, he watched her tottering off in a whirl of snowflakes, her slim blackclothed figure dissolving into night. He would go to sleep with the exhausted feeling of someone who has listened to music that once deeply stirred him, and

waking in the morning would feel relieved to find that
he was not in some hotel, alone.

Although he had taken Page One from his typewriter
with the firm decision of a man who is remaking his life,
he continued to make notes on the edge of letters and,
as he rode in the throbbing subway, composed a chapter
that was dully interrupted by his own station and left
him in the bewildered state of triumph of a man who has
glimpsed a goodlooking interesting face in the corner
mirror of an elevator and with surprise recognizes himself.

If he so much as brought up the question of the ham
actor, she immediately gave in to him, admitting her hopeless slavery that but for Lester would condemn her to
a barren hideous life that even his marvelous imagination had no idea of. Lester was forced to submit to the
flattery, succumbing to a role he could not absorb. He
would occasionally look at his hands that felt numb and
cold as if they had been plunged in icy water groping for
the pearl that always lies so clear, so pure, so disguised
within the oyster far below upon white sand.

When Victoria Chance proposed that she leave at once
for Havana and begin collecting the material they needed
for their work on sugar monopolies, he was as relieved
as if someone had bought a ticket for him and put him,
bag and baggage, upon a fast-moving train. He recaptured
his sensation of swift decision that had so moved him
the night he had stayed out talking with the Jesuit,
Thomas. He went over to her place and found her sitting absently, very pale and thin after her illness. She
was half packed and had only stopped, she insisted, to
sip a little coffee. Jonathan had left that morning, and
as she said his name, her eyes had the still fixed look of
someone watching another begin a perilous high dive that
may end in a broken neck.

"Anything wrong," said Lester briskly, at once uncomfortable at the threat of having to consider another's trouble. She shook her head quickly, got to her feet and they
went over the details. She was to get what she could

and he would come down for a week to do the big por-
traits and to land, it was hoped, a long story from Batista
that would fix the political angle of what appeared on the
surface a harmless study of an industry.

He had dinner by himself, continuing to be vaguely
upset by Victoria's look of a sleepwalker as she got on the
train. He had shouted after her to take care of herself and
even demanded her assurance that she hadn't under-
taken the trip too soon after her illness. She had nodded
brightly, her face lighting for a moment, and he had gone
off content, planning his own trip down on the boat,
champagne cocktails and moonlight, yet vaguely disturbed
by the way he always selected leisurely images when he
longed to be moved by danger and action.

When he got back to the house, he was surprised to
find all the lights on. Muffled sobs came from Elsie's bedroom. The show had closed and they had gone into re-
hearsal for a new production only a week before. He
supposed she was tired out and giving way to a little
legitimate hysteria. Tiptoeing to the door he looked in
on the crumpled bed; her face distorted with tears rose
rigidly from the pillow at his approach. She let out a
wail as he came closer and burrowed into the bedclothes
with so real a semblance of despair that he wondered
what the act meant.

When he tried to touch her, she shivered and mumbled, "Go away, I can't stand it, I can't bear to live, let
me alone. Let me die," all the time shuffling with shaking hands for the smelling salts that had slid under the
covers. He saw it was real and propped her up. She sobbed
hopelessly. He patted her on the back and tried to push
the hair from her hot forehead. "What's happened, darling, tell me, poor baby," he soothed, and she clung to
him, sobbing, unable to speak. At last it came out.

Lester could not help it; he grinned silently and ma-
liciously even as he soothed her bleeding pride. The
ham actor had humiliated her before everyone. She had
never expected anything like this. For years she had
been his ideal, on a pedestal. She was the motive of his

life, for her he produced plays, sank money into productions he had no interest in except that they provided her with a good part. If he could also play a tiny role, just to be near her, to say, "Madam, the car is waiting," it was all he asked. He was, she had always considered, a man of ideals. Today he had actually played up to a shameless girl, before everyone, a society girl, very young and beautiful, who had newly and suspiciously been allowed in the production. If there was one thing Elsie hated, it was a rich dilettante who had never worked, suffered, or lived. Elsie had given up everything for the theatre, she had lived the life of a nun, he could believe it or not. Now she was ridiculed before everyone.

She was burning up with shame and Lester sitting beside her could feel the heat consuming her flesh. He was deeply absorbed in her grief, the most genuine feeling she had ever displayed. When she could not be quieted and continued to sob, he sent for a doctor who gave her a sleeping draught. He saw clearly that his whole relationship with Elsie was bound to change and foresaw that he would be sacrificed. Curiosity as to the role she would now assign him quieted him. He had to wait two days before she could talk connectedly. In a brokenhearted voice she said they could no longer live in the same apartment. If it came to choosing between Lester and the actor, there was, it seems, no doubt of her choice. She wept a great deal and swore that Lester had been the only poetry in her life for ten years. The actor was a dope; she only slept with him a few times in a whole year. She was dead inside, actually frozen, when Lester had come along. He had warmed her veins, he was a breath of life.

She burst into a loud wail as she reluctantly gave up the breath of life for the sake of her career. What would she do without Claude? He had money; influence. He had built her up. Lester was, alas, poor. He had a good job but he was a wasteful boy with no idea of the future. They would have to be sensible at last, but they would never stop seeing one another, would they? He understood, didn't he?

Lester unfortunately understood too clearly. He wanted to ask her brutally how long she thought she could keep on eating her cake and still have it, but he soothed her instead. "I think you're making a mistake," he said. "You let fear rule your life. And what for?" He couldn't help but add that she would simply dry up.

They took a long last ride in her car up the Hudson feeling that they were very much in love and terribly unhappy. He was surprised that the alteration in his life made it almost impossible to decide anything. He stood for minutes each day trying to select a tie and when he read the papers dreaded that moment when news of a big strike in Cuba would necessitate some action. Victoria wrote short notes saying it was next to impossible to get the dope she wanted; that the people who should trust her didn't, and those who should be suspicious took her to lunch and practically put all the cards on the table.

Elsie had moved out to a big hotel apartment nearby, where the ham actor also resided on a different floor. Lester missed the canary-colored drapes and suffered when one of the lovebirds died of neglect. The place began to get on his nerves. He would walk past Elsie's house with his heart ticking like a clock and, completely exhausted, fall into a chair in his own rooms. Putting a record of Beethoven's *Seventh Symphony* on the victrola he lay back, suffering, until his cigarette burned down to his fingers. He made up his mind a hotel would be better. He moved to a large room in a quiet hotel and stuck a new sheet in his typewriter. He numbered it page 100 for a change and began a conversation that sounded vaguely witty.

He tried to think of the most admirable character he had ever known. He remembered a country doctor in northern Michigan who drove in blinding snowstorms, delivered babies, got up at all hours. The man's big red face under the fur cap rose up before him, surprisingly vigorous and alive although the doctor had been dead for years. Lester wished he had gone in for medicine or the sciences. There were actually people who thought he had got somewhere by being on a prominent magazine. At certain moments, when he was dictating letters to his stenographer or answering the phone, he felt a busy sense of importance that deceived him. Alone in his apartment there was no pretense. He began to study the history of the Middle Ages and to question the motives that led the human race to faith or to doubt. As he had never believed in anything, he shifted from despising those who had faith and in feeling chagrin at an emotion he had not experienced. It was not religious faith he envied but that deeper surer thing, such as led Galileo to his death muttering, *the earth does move*. It was the faith of the Curies, burning their furnace fires for years in search of radium, and finally he thought of Kurt Becher, and admitted that it was his faith, too, that he envied.

One night he picked up Chekov's *Notebook* and idling through it came across, "Faith is a spiritual faculty; animals have not got it; savages and uncivilized people have merely fear and doubt. Only highly developed natures can have faith." He read it several times and marked it with a pencil. Then he got himself a scotch and soda. The sentence heavily depressed him with a sense of his own inadequacy. He tried to tell himself that faith, the kind that mattered, was built on the constant sifting of many doubts and that the doubters were the little polyps that finally allowed the island to rise above the sea. The notion did not truly comfort him. He lay on his side in bed aching in every bone. Perhaps he was going to be ill. He ticked off on his fingers all the miserable faiths that have brought their benighted curse upon a world, faith-healers and rainmakers, führers and medicine men. But he knew that he was only fooling himself. It was not that kind of faith that he missed in his own life. He tried to reach down to draw another coverlet over him; when he found none he lay for a chilly hour debating whether to get up or to try to keep warm without one. He finally went to sleep.

When the phone rang he jumped out of bed as if he had been shot. Stumbling over a chair he unhooked the receiver and said, "Hello." The radium face of his mantel clock showed three-thirty. Elsie's voice said, "Oh, Lester." He waited and coughed. "What is it?" he said briskly.

"Lester," she said, and he could see her lying back in bed; she might as well be on the stage with a thousand eyes upon her. "Lester," and the word had all the coaxing quality of a great love scene.

"Elsie," said Lester in a businesslike tone, "why do you do this? I have to go to work in the morning. I can't lie around. Go to bed and don't call up again." He started to hang up but curiosity prevented him. In a flood of words Elsie was telling him she couldn't sleep, she thought only of him. She was so lonely. Couldn't he come to her?

He could not and would not. He thought that had been settled once and for all. "I want peace, Elsie. P-e-a-c-e" he spelled insultingly. "You want me to be an abject little dog like Claude. Well, I'm not. You've done enough damage," he hinted darkly, "now let me alone." He hung up this time flatly, and sitting on the edge of the bed, saw the sheets stretch white and endless. He lit a cigarette but the image of Elsie, no longer an actress, simply a woman but beautiful and shining, newly risen from some foamy sea, put itself into his very hands. Her arms were spread and he ran his hand under her arm, around her right breast and with his other hand gently parted her legs. He gave a hoarse sob and scrambling for his clothes began to pull on his socks. When he got to his underdrawers, he stopped, his throat was dry, his eyes hurt. Damn, damn, the bitch, the whore, all she wanted was a beauty treatment and he fancied her standing before a mirror examining the little line near her right eye, pulling her hand down her throat. Perhaps she needed a massage, or only love? He rushed to the bathroom and filling the tub, got in.

He soaped himself and using the brush scrubbed away at his hands and feet. He even soaped his head and standing under the shower let the water run first hot then cold over his head, tickling down into a final icy stream. Drying himself, he mixed a stiff drink and sat down. He was wideawake and the drink had no power over the rushing burning anger that jostled his desire. Why not telephone a callhouse and have an honest woman who knew her business and traded her wares? He had his hand on the telephone and was fumbling for his address book but as he started to dial, he shook his head, hung up. The thought of the wait, the monotony, the stupidity involved was too much for him. He was frightened at the violence that demanded nothing short of blood, the raping of a virgin, Elsie beaten and bruised, every bit of actress knocked out of her.

The images that ran into one another like a movie run off at breakneck speed sobered him. He walked to the table, picked up a book, examined his typewriter. The roar of the city streets that lulled during the night was tuning up for a new day and the big trucks began distantly booming, heavy and steady as continual bombardment. He held tightly to the table, staring out the window that looked down into the pit of the street. His fingers stiffened along the edge of the table and as he quieted, sweat poured over his skin. He felt that he had barely escaped some terrible fate. His breath was coming hard as if he had been running with the pack whose deep humiliations could only be assuaged by blood, one of the living dead who with sticks and guns had so horrified him that fatal night in Berlin when the glass dome fell.

He sat down to look this vision straight in the eye. He continued to tremble but he was happy as one who has triumphed over evil.

Jonathan had looked back at Victoria, looking very small and crumpled, sitting at the top of the stairs where she had come to watch him go. He did not want to look anymore, and had turned very rapidly, holding his hand above his head and waving as he used to wave when he drove off in the car at home with his eyes on the wheel. His eyes stung and he walked off with his head down. He did not know how to tell her. He did not know what to tell her because he did not know himself. The point at which his life had veered was in darkness and he must stumble on now as best he could.

He held tight to his duties and fixed them firmly in his mind by glancing at a notebook. He must be in Philadelphia by seven. Without knowing how it had happened, the last days with Victoria had slid by without a chance to tell her about the difficulties in the new work. He felt irritated as if he had cheated himself and could not account for the casualness of their separation. They had been unable to say a word except about the house and did he pay for the new license plates? Everything had retreated into some terrible frozen silence that could not be warmed in a hurry.

He drove badly, and dreaded the faces that would flock around him that evening. Leslie Day's face, small and gay, peered at him in the reflection of the windshield as it had the day they drove up from Washington together. His foot automatically pressed the gas and the car shot forward and he could feel that quick racing eagerness that was close to happiness. He let his mind rush over their reckless three days together, the night they had met in Howard Hackett's apartment, the skeptical remarks of the munitions man who had looked through and through Jonathan as if he were a romantic specimen, but authentic, the old woman with the gold chain to eyeglasses who kept tapping her neck and demanding details of what she called the "poor and oppressed" as if only the most miserable items could refresh her withering spirit.

He thought of the gathering now, pulling it around him as if somehow an accusation of it might wash from him his guilt about his wife. He did not know at what point in the talk he had suddenly felt hoisted upon a rostrum as he and Terry Blount, young sprouts still in highschool, had been given a hand up by dignified elderly

gentlemen with rounded vests and watch chains who listened with beatific smiles while he and Terry spouted
away about the Huns and helping the boys "over there."

Certainly what he was now saying was not of that rotten cloth, and yet the very glibness of it chilled his marrow. He had somehow, without his own desire or will,
been ripped up from his place among men. It was the
farmers and workers he had chosen; it was a simple straight
path without glory. Of all things he had wanted not to
be, it was a "Front." Somehow, in some manner, for some
far-off event, he had become that which he abhorred. In
his fine clothes, with his good looks and charm, he was
an ace of a "Front." He realized that it was his but to
do or die, his not to reason why, and he repeated the
words wondering at their aptness. When it was proposed
that he leave the country and make what Si called "important contacts" to help broaden the work among farmers
and to unite it with all progressive movements, he had
been vaguely flattered. Its face value had seemed important. If he was worth more as a "Front" than as simple
Jonathan Chance who daily mixed with farmers and directed their needs and tried to hoard a kernel for a
future that would bring to men of spirit more than daily
bread, then he was willing to be a "Front."

He had not calculated so sharply upon his own equipment as Victoria who shook her head and prophesied
no good would come of it. It was not that he did not
respect the people he met, worthy and full of good intentions. True, their ideas were split in as many direc-
tions as a piece of soft wood timber that has not been
properly cured, but they wanted peace, and as he said the
word he could see their mouths softly rounded, enunciat-
ing it as if they were blowing some bugle. They came
with sleek, properly nourished bodies, with generous
pocketbooks, with upright notions, with imaginations
teetering fearfully upon a tomorrow that might bring
them down in the wreckage. To circumvent that disaster
they hemmed and hawed, they played with watchchains

and asked the time, and gave their mite to the cause that their rights might not perish from the earth.

He had no reason to doubt them any more than he doubted himself but perhaps it was exactly himself whom he doubted. His very manner grew rigid as he fancied some hostile eye fixed upon him; his words came firmly as he painted that hell in which they would all cheerfully burn unless they awoke to their danger. The smell of brimstone seemed often in the room; he was roused by his own language to remember its far-off early echoes born of the World War. Long ago he had rejected with shame his boyish speeches and accepted the proposition that the War had not been exactly for democracy.

The new war brewing was all too real. Sometimes he thought he saw Kurt Becher's face with the shining eyes and mouth that could look so grim. He would remember Lester Tolman's recital of the night the glass dome fell and his voice took on the pain of men who had lived through terror. The room with its solid citizens would look unreal; he would feel slightly ashamed as if he had again played the part of Dr. Higgins in *Pygmalion* on the college stage and were contemplating an early success on Broadway. His constant sense of uneasy embarrassment at being forced to a robust role that did not fit him, unnerved him. His doubts boomeranged; from criticizing his audience he began to heckle himself.

He told himself this was a job that had to be done; the world was an Augean stable, why should his hands remain clean? But he seemed to have lost some touch that he needed to keep himself whole. He had always despised what he had termed the "word twisters," those verbal acrobats who seemed to delight in their own agility as an end in itself. Now he heard himself use words too easily. He began to debate what he meant by "peace" and to feel that it was a mockery to use a word that meant one thing to him and another to the people to whom he spoke. Was it peace simply not to be engaged in war? The stereotyped answers clogged his brain; he had no time to work over such stones, and only thought of his own wordiness when alone.

It was in a sweat of discomfort that he had talked with Earl Bradford, the munitions man at Howard Hackett's, his eyes sliding around for someone who would look at him simply, honestly, with the complete confidence of Tim Robb or Jake Tentman. He was lonely for Victoria; his loneliness crept into his voice in a tone of uncertainty. Mrs. Hackett was worming through a long harangue with an amiable woman in a violet silk blouse about the similarity between Hitler and Mussolini; the old lady was snatching bits about the sharecroppers from a pale and harried government employee. He should bless them for their good will but he saw them only as hopelessly divided.

He began to think of his little group of farmers as unreal, a tiny island in a great sea. Had he simply been lulled to a sense of unreality and if so, what purpose were these meetings at which he now officiated so unwillingly, serving? For what was he working, if not for the disinherited?

He had the uneasy suspicion that the present company wanted only to keep things as they were. To be sure, the edges were ragged and should be trimmed and the humanities should be strengthened and preserved. It was just at this point that his very mind gave way, suffering a schism of irreconcilable hope and fear.

In a way he understood better Ed Thompson who did not believe one could improve the human race as you improved a model of a car. A plan comprising more sunshine, heat, air, food, to say nothing of dignity, for the human race was simply a nutty notion to Ed. These people sitting so cozily together and so full of the milk of human kindness seemed to Jonathan like mercury that may run off the table and hide under a chair. If they could only have a saner world. But it was, he was convinced, merely a renovated 1929 they wanted, not a dazzling newly created 1950. They had put a reluctant bet on a horse that they would rather see win than the vicious

animal with the black rider, but their complete selves
were not in it. They would be upset if the cream was not
in the coffee. They hoped to walk from the world they
knew to the world to come on feet that were never without shoes. Let the stones be put down in the mud by the
workers and they would promise to step across, lightly,
firmly.

His eyes clouded as he almost at once accused himself
of being unjust and narrow. He began coughing in a kind
of helpless impatience. "Sorry," he gasped, "too many
cigarettes." Mrs. Lundel put a motherly hand on his
shoulder. "Young man," she said, in a concerned voice,
"I've been watching you. Don't you know what too much
smoking does to you? It cuts down your life, that's what
it does," and her words were so measured and solemn
that he found himself looking at her to decipher the special significance she attached to her own life, now so
frayed and worn. He thanked her, involuntarily looking
for a drink. He remembered Si's warning, never to drink,
to remember his responsibility, and he held himself back
from the bottles that he saw ranged temptingly in the
next room. The effort made him rigid; he stood stiffly
like a clergyman at a wedding to which the bride is tardy.
His eyes dropped and upon looking up met the wise
black stare of a girl in the doorway.

She was somberly watching him and did not move as
he unconsciously stepped forward. Her smile was secret
and confidential, meant only for him, saved through an
entire evening, perhaps an entire life. Mrs. Lundel had
followed his glance and, clucking, introduced them, "This
young lady has been dying to meet you. Mrs. Day, Mr.
Chance." Someone put on a victrola record and they were
dancing. He felt that he had left the room and, light as
air, was a boy, up in Michigan, whirling around and
around at the gay evening parties with the black lake
outside and tomorrow only a path of sunshine leading
to the water where one might dive to soothing darkness.

She had not said a word and, after all the words spoken
that evening, the silence was beautiful. He could feel it,

alive and whole—he held it in his hands, it was good, like something a man can make out of wood or stone. It was one of the good sound dependable things in life, like bread, and he told himself that her body that yielded so gracefully, so effortlessly, went where his went, accepted without quarrel or question his terrible lonely need.

V. THE CITY WITHIN

VICTORIA CHANCE had taken the train rather than the boat to Havana with the idea that she must hurry. The shock of leaving made the inevitability of a strike seem close at hand and in the small hotel she turned around in the emptiness, placing her few articles, adjusting herself for a temporary moment. There would be no time to rest, she hoped, not feeling rest in her bones but some terrible urgency to move before it was quite too late.

She had followed Lester's instructions implicitly; had gone first to the big tourist Hotel Plaza, had telephoned the Cuban who had hurried down to see her, all in a fresh white suit with his desperate dark eyes looking only tired and dissipated in the bland evening light of the great square outside. She would have to be very careful, he urged, and probably not see very much of him as he was too well known a figure on the island. His own pleasure at his conspicuousness, that doomed him to some martyrdom his heart seemed set upon, interested her more than his talk. They agreed to meet at his own house, out in the fine residential section of the Vendado. "My parents," he smiled wryly, "hate all this, and fear constantly. They will think you a nice bourgeoise and be very happy."

She herself had been anything but happy the next day. The interview yielded nothing but generalities and the confession that he longed to escape the island. The room in which they sat was airy and full of sunshine. Watercolors by some not too well-favored artist hung upon the walls. Shelves of books reached the ceiling. Everything was terrible; it was worse than under Machado. The students at the university were out on strike and the island had nothing. Everything drained outside to foreigners. Ah, if he could only get to New York. Last year he had been in Paris and had hoped to go to Hollywood. She looked at him in astonishment; that drooping poetical face was only too earnest. She stirred uneasily asking crisply for details. How did the workers on the sugar plantations live? How could she see the harvest?

The *zafra*. He shrugged hopelessly as if she had asked for a trip by plane to Paris. She would have to work it through the American Embassy. He was powerless. They could get her anywhere, if they chose. He spread his hands, each finger expressing total cynical acceptance of his shame.

They agreed to meet again; she wondered vaguely for what. Already she had determined to plunge in without him. It was not the state of the intellectuals in Cuba that gnawed one's very nerves; at that moment she did them a grave injustice, completely distrusting them as if they were clutching at her dress and had just refused to give up her gloves. Crippled they might well be—in this air they could never have come to full strength—but they were merely one poor limb on a terribly mutilated body that, although she had been in Havana less than forty hours, was already beginning to smell to her like a badly concealed corpse.

The Cuban had obligingly telephoned a friend, the proprietor of the small hotel, and she had a room and her meals at a ridiculous figure living among Cubans, who chattered in the elevators and convinced her that an ocean rather than a strip of water barely seventy miles wide separated her from the homeland. She felt indeed separated not only by space but by endless time that had no beginning and no end. No letters came from Jonathan and she did not want to understand the significance of his silence. Now that they had parted, the parting seemed a dream. She postponed examining it as if it were a dear body in a morgue that it were better not yet to view. She had work to do, she told herself sternly, holding herself up each day with a resolve that was braced by some impending terror.

Every day she stood childishly at the desk in the hotel, stunned at not receiving so much as a paper. Rushing upstairs she would forget her mission in Cuba, and in burning language write Jonathan just what she thought of him. He was a stone, with a heart of wood. He had sent her off, like a servant, without the courtesy of giving notice. Get out, I don't need you anymore. She would stop in the midst of her letter, her eyes blinded, her arms would fall upon the table, she would lay her head upon her arms, her heart softened with all the memories of Jonathan's pure goodness to her. Forgive me, my darling, it was all my fault, but if she so much as stood up, washed her face, made up carefully as if for some longed-for lover, she was again sounding off her deep and terrible trouble that could not be appeased by forget-me-nots of memory.

Every morning she rushed out, went about blindly, sniffing the air, her mind catching up this and that, ticketing it, putting it away. For what? There was the bench in the hot sun and the palms would gently rustle overhead. The bright blue sky would open its mild eye above the city. Her eyes, shielded from the sun by the brim of her hat, saw the feet of the passersby, in good snappy shoes, in torn rope-soled sandals, bare and scarred. The bare toes scraped and scratched aimlessly in the dust, the roped soles turned their piteous torn fragments to the light of day. On the benches, rest for the weary but for her there was no rest. Not here. Not there. The ceaseless eternal preparation of life must be now coming to some great secret; it would presently be revealed.

The seed is planted in the soil; it grows in darkness even as love and is born. But life had come to this island only to die. Behind that very façade, the smell of death. The old man wrapped in papers on the doorway of a bank, such a funny sight to a group of drunken tourists on the hunt for romance that had been so positively promised, so absolutely guaranteed at the big tourist agency in New York. One does not look for allure among ragged bums and they pushed on in gay bands peering into faces; are you there?

But it was a very bad season for tourists. Madam, there was never a worse season. So much trouble, the bombs, have driven away the tourists. You can see for yourself, madam, that it is peaceful. A tourist lives in the past, madam, and does not know that time changes swiftly. Each day the shopkeepers shook their heads, standing like sleek eels in their doorways, waiting to glide out to clutch at the unsuspecting tourist who, idling by, stopped a second to look at the tiers of perfume, at the rows of shoes, the array of pocketbooks to hold heaven knows whose wealth. The rows and rows of stores, so distressingly empty, the cafés with their clean and bouqueted tables, for whom were they waiting? Who bought the cakes that languished behind glass in the stiff showcases with the bright yellow-and-green frosting of flowers and darts ready to pierce some expectant and fond heart? The bacardi and the malaga, for whom? And the great white capitol building, spoken of so bitterly by the boy in the elevator working his way through medical school—so that he might join the half-starved medicos serving a population too poor to pay—for whom had it been so proudly erected, sugar loaf on sugar island?

For what sacred guest did the island wait, even as she waited every day for a letter that did not come. Oh, show some sign! But there was no sign in the sky that beamed bland and pitiless upon bare heads. Lady, miss, please, lady, and the pale hands of old men holding their eternal lottery tickets. Oh, take a chance for our sakes whom luck has deserted. Lady, miss, and the bright sidling eyes of men whispering. She turned to look them full in the face, unhurried, unfrightened, shamelessly comforted by their desire as if they had thrown her a rope to drag her once more to the shores of the living.

But where were the living? The city had the flat surface of a bright and gaudy postcard. The police in bright new uniforms with guns in black holsters sallied up and down the wide streets. On Sunday nights, a little life seemed to bulge out of the deadness. The empty cafés played music to streams of pedestrians who walked around and around, arm in arm, blissfully, the girls together passing boys in twos and threes. Middle-aged and young faces, women sticking out before and behind, thrusting themselves brightly for the open whispers of men calculating their charms. Almost alone in a sea of empty tables, an elegant girl, escorted by a youth with lacquered hair and tiny line of mustache on a pasty superior face, looks serenely and contemptuously across the street where in darkness the dirty white suits of loungers sit sprawled on the curb for their crumb, as an audience waits for the movie star to take off her negligee and lift a bare arm from behind a transparent screen. She bends toward the young man, her face magnolia-pale with glossy dark eyes, the white patches of her flesh gleaming through the slits around the shoulders of her lacy black dress. Now and then she lifts her tiny hands with the velvet black bows tied around each useless wrist and across the street, the silent breathing row strain forward, as if a rocket had been set off in the sky.

"But I tell you, Mrs. Chance, reciprocity has saved Cuba. Cuba would be finished without it," and the good-looking young man with a fresh rosebud in his button-hole from the Commercial Attaché's office, shows her beautiful charts to prove there is positively a rise in prices.

"Where does it go, the money?" she asked stubbornly, her hat resting a little lopsided on her head, a cigarette held firmly between her fingers. "Have you a chart to show living standards are going up? Just show me that."

He looked at her sharply but, no, she was smiling with a bland innocence. He cleared his throat. "Well, of course, we can't furnish that as yet. But standards are bound to rise. Rents have gone up already. The wage scale is fixed by law now at eighty cents and the mills are glad to pay it because they can afford to."

He believed. Belief was in his earnest gesture, in his controlled confusion and anger at her prodding questions.

Safely entrenched in his cage, he did not mean to be annoyed by the tickling straw she had thrust, it was to be
supposed frivolously, between the bars. What was she
after? It was common sense that if Cuba got a better
price for sugar, if more sugar was sold, the island rose
by its own bootstraps. The money went somewhere,
didn't it?

She listened patiently and fumbled over the figures,
the charts, the clean sober outgoing office, with its foundations built upon that rock of ages, the government of
the United States. The gentleman from Pettibone and
Sneed's Havana office, so glad to see her and so anxious
to help Mr. Tolman in his useful work, was more cynical.
Sugar was sugar, he repeated like a formula good not only
for this life but for the eternities. You competed on a
world market and the reciprocity treaty favored whom?
Trade with United States but not sugar. What sugar
wanted was an open market, catch as catch can, with its
chance to beat the world trade. "We can raise it here as
cheap as anywhere, cheaper."

The faces of the informers bent toward her; she saw
herself rise, heard herself answer, laugh, refuse a cigarette, take a cigarette, smile, wait, agree, shake her head.
Like a puppet, she saw the body of Victoria Chance move
sharply and swiftly through a doorway, hurry purpose-
fully down a street as if it knew its sure and certain destiny. She would enter her hotel and the anxious figure
in white would rise up from a corner chair, come forward
hesitantly. They would shake hands and the sharp warm
pressure that denoted trust aroused her from the contemplation of her other life. She would ascend from some
dark pit and listen warmly to the story poured from a
mouth that had learned caution. The languid young man
she had met the first day had not been idle; his friends
streamed toward her. Teachers, university professors, doctors, lawyers, came with their stories, their eyes melting

with pride and happiness that she was not simply an American lady, a tourist, but a "friend."

At night she gave in to the powers of darkness and lay on her bed as if stunned, asking herself why everything came too late, why the vacation she and Jonathan had needed so badly had come when it could no longer heal; heard again her mother's voice, when dying, rich and tender with longing, as she stared at the bright sun beating on the floor by her bed, "One should always do things, if I had only gone to New Glarus, the town my father had founded. I always wanted to go there, and was just getting ready, when *this* had to come along," and at the word *this,* her arm was flung out as if to touch that imaginary dark shadow that waited to take her by the hand and lead her, not to New Glarus, but to death. In the morning she got out of bed and ate her roll and coffee, sustained by the voices that were waiting, even at that moment, to pour themselves into her ear.

"Burn this corruption," her mother had said fiercely, her head in its tangled hair reared out of the bedclothes, her eyes firmly facing the horror and indignity of her own dissolution. But her father of less stern stuff had wept and would not have it so; the poor shell had been gutted, the veins tapped, the cheeks nicely painted and stuffed with cotton and her father had looked upon that lost doll who had been his wife and whom he could no longer honor except by shortly placing over her the largest possible stone. Perhaps its durability might atone for the fugitive haste of living.

We were going somewhere, my darling, surely not to this, she thought as she inclined her head to the bitter story of rents too high for people too poor. Eighty per cent—that's it, eighty, and the eyes of the man in white had flashed in triumph as if he were presenting her with a rare gift—of the landlords lived across the water, in Spain, and she was not to think it was only Americans in the trough, no, on the contrary, this was a feast of all nations. She had only to check on the railroads, the banks, the various sugar mills. Sugar and its subsidiaries, all in the hands of someone who sent money somewhere else. The vegetables and fruits? Raised by little men, head over ears in debt to the commission men, your pardon, lady, Americans, who sold the produce at god knows what price and paid what the devil pleased.

Sometimes she went with one of them to the university on the hill and talked with some spirited student, and all the time, every day she left herself standing by the desk in the hotel, patiently waiting for a letter, for a cable, for an old newspaper, folded up with the word "hello" written upon it in Jonathan's hand. There were moments when the sun, the talk, the strange tension in the very air, made her fears childish and stupid. She had only to finish her work, to take the boat, to go home, to find Jonathan and he would catch her up in his arms, laugh at her trouble and she would not even mind that he had put her to so much needless pain, they would simply put it behind them and love each other as they always had.

Sometimes when Steve Carson came in from his father-in-law's barn, he would hear the radio going, and soft music float out to the kitchen. He pumped water on himself, scrubbing away at his hands and face, and walking to the door would catch Lorraine dancing all by herself with the baby held blissfully under her chin. She would look up startled, her face flushing but continuing to dance, only slowly, apologetically, as if it were somehow an accusation against him. He thought a woman couldn't look more lovely; his throat ached watching her. He would go over and putting his arms around her start them both off, in tune, all three dancing around and around the room. If LaRue came in, they would stop short, Lorraine would pretend to be fixing her hair and Steve would walk over and pick up the paper and glance at it casually.

LaRue would snort a little. "What about supper in this house? I expect his highness is the only feller around here needs to be fed," and he would poke his big finger into the baby's face. The baby would catch at it, chuckling. Steve had to turn his head to look; that was his boy, and the way he ducked his little head, cooed and made noises was something to watch. Lorraine would dart to the kitchen, and at night in bed, they would feel alone and happy again. The baby's crib was beside their bed and the heavy snores of LaRue only mildly disturbed their whispers.

"He'll never be hungry, that's one thing. Papa has to leave it to someone. We don't need to worry, that's a fortune in itself." She sighed and Steve beside her stiffened, his mind alert, his body on the defensive against his wife's cuddling.

"I guess we didn't make him just to be like your old man," he said in a flat voice. "One pattern like that's enough." He swallowed hard, the resentment against LaRue cropping up in the darkness. "Oh, Lorraine honey, it isn't just for him to be safe, I'm thinking about. He ain't just a porker. Don't you want him to be more than just not hungry?"

"I want him to be like you," she said. She was sometimes afraid of Steve. He had a talent for drawing out life that made her worship him as if he had already distinguished himself in some rare way. She did not know just what he meant or where it would lead him. Sometimes an icy fear came over her that it would take him away from her. She knew he wanted to go away now, that nothing on the ranch really held him. If only her father wasn't so dirty mean, but the two dollars every week just burned. Even that had gone to Steve's father, who had been on the rocks that winter. "It never rains but it pours," Steve's stepmother had said when she had to tell Steve that Walt had come down with what looked like rheumatism. He was doubled up with it, and all that winter hobbled around while the girls and his wife took care of the stock. The two dollars was only a drop in the bucket, but it took away Steve's hope of getting away soon.

"He's got me by the balls," Steve said. "I can't go without something. I'm just like a slave here, come right down to it. We got plenty to eat and our clothes, and the baby's fine, so we don't need to worry too much, it's just I fret to be here with no outlook."

It wasn't the life he wanted. The winter went into him hard, with the cattle just barely making it through. At times when he wanted to tear loose and run for it, he held back, trying to pretend that he was just taking a new kind of course at a college. He sent off for all the booklets and pamphlets he could lay his hands on and even old LaRue's hardshelled practical farming had to give Steve credit for bright ideas. Science could fix things in the future, if mankind gave it a chance, was the theme of many a sermon Steve let loose night after night as they sat around the long evenings. Look how the sulky plow gave way to the gangplow, and the steam thresher to the new-fangled combine outfit that a couple of men could run. Look how wheat had improved, and you take corn, they could breed even better if they put their minds to it. Sometimes during that winter he brooded over the chances of making a new breed of corn that would stand up in drought and in marshy weather and make a bigger fuller better ear. He would get down to work, making charts and fooling away, tormented with the notion of inbreeding corn the way you did cattle, until you finally bore down to a few hard and fast kernels, then a few hard and fast ears, then a field that bore up under any shock.

But he had no sooner thought of it than he had to begin working away from corn to men, and because he was so downhearted that winter he had to think that disasters were just inbreeding men so that they finally got a hard fast kernel that would stand up and lick the world. They would make a new race of men, strong and big, with will and power and they would just about remake the damned old earth. He would have to laugh at himself and the way corn and men got mixed up because his cousin Charley Egstrom was writing him that maybe he wasn't so bad off where he was. Things looked kind of black and the bosses had it down in the books to lick tar out of them. They needn't think it would be so damned easy, they would find out, but it looked like a bloody day edging up on them. The bosses had learned some new tricks and tried them all the time, like scaring the shit out of a man by making him learn a new guy his trick, and then they had spotters everywhere and favorites who followed you around, so you couldn't take a piss without someone peeking at you . . . "but don't think Stevie old boy that we ain't learned a few tricks of our own, and all I say is that more of this and the boys will be ready for anything because between you and me, kid, there is worse things than death. It is all right for the bosses to not like to lay theirselves down in a fine casket with a lace pillow when bed was so nice but if you get mixed up in the speedup so you don't know if you are checking in your guts or your tools, that's another song, and don't you fergit it. The boys is all asking for you and remember how you spoke up that day for Wesley Feeney. Feeney got the black mark all right and is on relief and his wife took it cruel. She nags the life out of him until it makes your blood run cold. My old woman is a good sport if I do say it and says for me to keep my pecker up, she will stay by me thick or thin. So long kid and come back to us soon. We sure would like to see the baby, hope he is a chip off the old block."

Steve read the letter again and again and could see the faces of the men and how they looked when they checked their tools and how they looked in the morning when the line was starting up and the foreman came along with his false voice, pretending everything was fine and dandy and they were all good fellows working for the fun of it, and he felt darned lonesome. He would have been ashamed if he hadn't felt lonesome. He hoped to Christ he wasn't ever going to be one of those fellows who all they wanted was just a wife and little home and baby and let the rest of the world go hang. If he thought his kid would be like that he didn't know but he'd go in now and take a necktie and choke his life right out.

Tub Johnson began driving over toward springtime when Steve and old LaRue were going over plans for plowing and sowing. Tub had got him a regular cowboy outfit with a red neckkerchief and chaps and a big hat and he would strut around in LaRue's parlor and sing a cowboy song that he claimed to have made up himself. "You take a song like this, Stevie, it would go over big. Listen yourself to the radio. Ain't mine as good as they are? I tell you if I could only get someone to write it down for me. Then I got to get me a copyright and then get someone to buy it. It's a cinch." Steve had to laugh and yet look at the fellow, he had only to sit down, to begin strumming his damned little cigarbox that he'd fixed up, and everybody around wanted to stand and look at him. Half the time Tub would have along a girl, or maybe two or three, who just sat looking at Tub in an itch of happiness. He would tilt his big hat back on his red hair and open his eyes wide. The fair lashes on his greenish eyes made his stare wide open as a baby's and his voice was a melting persuasive voice that even got old man LaRue fiddling around with his legs as if he longed to get up and do an old time polka.

One night they had a dance at LaRue's. Walt and his folks were there and Teacher-teacher was in one of her highflung moods like she was a filly. Tub just twanged away and everybody was dancing and screeching and having the time of their lives. LaRue broke down and made Lorraine make coffee for all of them and even went down the cellar and dug up an old bottle of brandy. Everybody gasped when they saw that brandy, like the world was coming to an end. But LaRue bit the cork out with his teeth and poured everyone a drink that would stagger a blind mule. Nobody got nasty, it was all good fun, only the next day LaRue looked sheepish as if he had been caught back of the barn doing something he shouldn't.

When they got the plows in, the soil was dry as bone underneath and they just groaned at the tail of dust kicking up behind. The top soil had got very little moisture but they worked night and day, getting it in, trusting to a little moisture coming in time so the seed could root. The first big dust storms had begun toward the south when a soft green fuzz showed, and they looked at it as tenderly as if it had been the baby's hair. Everything was suspended on that fuzz; they had it in their minds when they went to bed and it was there the first thing they got up. Seemed as if their breaths were going softer not to disturb it but it might as well have been different, it was all wasted.

The sky got black and the dust was whirling down on them. It fairly blinded the animals and smothered all the green. The baby lay choking under a soft white cloth soaked in water with all the lamps in the house looking murky as if some bad dirty fog had seeped through the keyholes and cracks.

LaRue came in and sat with his head hanging down. They had to live through it as though a plague had taken the country by storm only there was no doctor. The doctor had cut out and run; they were orphans alone in the world. They were on an island with only the sly eye of God looking at them through the boiled clouds like the dim light on an old car stalled at night with the brights out and one dimmer gone dead.

"This is no time for mooning," said Ed Thompson, slipping relentlessly into his light overcoat. "You don't think I'm woman-chasing, do you?" He patted his wife's cheek lightly.

"I almost wish you were," said Margaret. "It would make you seem more human."

"Human? Baby, how can you talk like that? Who could be more human than I or a better husband? I don't have to bill and coo to prove that to you, do I?"

"No," said Margaret, coming up to him and removing an imaginary fluff from his coat.

"Did you find a long golden hair? You're my only girl," he said, kissing her and taking up his gloves he hurried for the door, waving as she called, "When are you coming home?"

"Don't wait up," he said, and he did not know why it was so unsatisfactory to be a model husband. He only felt vaguely that he had missed something. He did not know just what. And there was no time to mull over such notions. Thank God his life was crammed to the brim. He drove slowly following the streetcar track then turned toward the college. John Stock lived somewhere on this street. He'd done a good thing to get a key job in the Community Fund drive. Especially now as he was no longer officially with the company and looked as free an agent as ever stepped the earth.

Stock came to the door himself. Ed shook hands warmly and called out cheerily to Mrs. Stock who was disappearing through the hall. He and Stock sat down together. "How does it seem to be working?" asked Ed, taking off his overcoat and eyeing the gas logs in the fireplace.

"Fine," said Stock. He was a red-faced man and made the mistake of wearing a too florid tie. "The relief manager is very glad to co-operate. I gave him the card you suggested. I had in fact a lot run off with the questions as we had gone over them. He said he thought it was a very good idea to get all the data possible on a relief case like that. I checked with him the questions we were most interested in. Of course I didn't bring you in. I don't know if he knows I was ever with the company."

"There's no reason he should know," said Ed. "This is a new fellow. Comes from Grand Rapids."

"All the better," said Stock. "I said the questions we thought most advisable to get information on were the applicant's attitude toward unions. Did he belong to the A. F. of L.? Or any other workers' organization. Such as the unemployed workers' council. Then, is he an officer in any group. Well, he took the cards and I got back some of them today to look over. I said it would help us in our community work because often these fellows can get help from their mutual aid societies and just don't, they stall around and try to leech off the government relief, see?"

"Sure, sure, did you get any names for us?" Stock handed him the cards.

"May I ask how you'll avail yourself of this information?" said Stock. He could not get rid of the language that during the day had become habitual. Ed looked surprised at his stilted manner then shrugged his shoulders. "Why, you see, John, we may be able to use a fellow who is out of work. Maybe we fired him even for union activity. It's not always clear who will be able to hold out and fall back on savings or relatives and who has to go to relief. A man who goes for relief is hard pressed. Sometimes they change their minds. If we bring them back, and let them go on in their job with the understanding they can be of service to us and by a little loyalty to the company, help themselves, well, such a guy sometimes listens to reason. These aren't fellows who have been in unions twenty years. They're new. It doesn't mean anything. And once they learn a lesson and get a pinch of being out of work. Well, they ain't so dumb." He was thumbing through the list and checking several names. "Of course, I don't see them myself."

"Well, no," said Stock. "That wouldn't be a good idea."

"We got a man. Golden. He's done some nice jobs for us. He goes around to call and sometimes he gets them one way, sometimes another. He can make a fellow think he is just reporting for the government. The N.R.A. He says the government wants a little checkup on how things are, is the company protecting the men and have the men any kicks. The fellow is out of work. He is crazy to get back and thinks it is o. k. Then he gets his first paycheck and after that we got him by the balls." In his exuberance Ed Thompson had waxed eloquent and did not notice Mr. Stock blanch slightly. He immediately ducked his head, yes, yes, and Ed finished and stood up. "Thanks, old man. Go on with the good work."

"I was just going to tell you. One of these men has

been talking. I mean one of the men who applied for aid. Two fellows came in today and protested. They said the relief had no right to ask such questions and so I thought I'd warn you, we may not be able to keep up."

"The nerve," said Ed. "Ready for a handout and then not want to co-operate." There were times when he believed what he said. Certainly, he thought, as he walked back to the car, started her and drove off on another mission, he believed firmly and positively in the righteousness of industry to be given a free rein. Under a free rein the country had been built up, and power went into the hands of the natural survivors, those most able, most fit. He believed that today as much as he had when in college and other fellows were talking socialistic nonsense. Of course, many good sound men began that way but they outgrew such childishness. Life was short enough in accomplishment.

He had profound contempt for the union that was inadequate, quarrelsome, self-seeking. How could they cope with a strong able organization such as industry was able to master? He could tick off on his fingers the different devices by which he hoped to guard against the union virus. He realized he was looking ahead, but wasn't that fellow Hitler planning on a thousand years? The next few years would count more than any time in the last fifty.

Then he was stopping at Grant's place and there were a lot of cars parked around. Grant sure drew the boys in. A nice little game, drinks but no girls. A clean straight place that was open as a baby's eye. Mike Witlow was in a pit of smoke in a corner with a couple of guys that Ed had never seen. He came out in the hall, holding his cards. "Anything up?" he said.

"No, no," said Ed. "Ain't you interested in pay day?"

"Sure," laughed Mike. "Since when you turned keeper of the dogpound?"

"Oh, I'm just pinchhitting for Barker," said Ed and slipped his hand in his pocket. "I'm on my way to Glen's. What report did you get from Mac about the boys?"

"He swears they don't even meet. I tell you, you got the spine busted. They're all rats. You can scare shit out of them. Buy them like gumdrops. Mac claims they aren't more than a hundred men left out of thousands. He swears they all dropped like hot cakes last month when you began firing."

"Good. Now, on the other side of the fence. How's your credit scheme working?"

"Fine, Ed, fine," said Mike, fingering his cards. "I'm getting some swell contacts among businessmen. They'll be a great help, just in case."

"Well, anything that gets the boys co-operating. Later they'll co-operate on more important things. All in the same boat anyhow, as I see it. Sound out any of them on their labor policies?"

"Yes, Rex Short is kind of wobbly. Seems to think unions are in the cards and he'd rather play ball."

"The damned rat," said Ed, flushing. "He's got a juicy income on the side. And his wife has money. He can afford to go soft but what about the rest?"

"That's what I said," said Mike, looking at his hand uneasily as someone called out, "Oh, Mike."

"Aren't you going to take a hand tonight, Ed?"

"No, I'm moving on. Just wanted to look in. A quiet evening."

"Sure," said Mike, moving away. "Well, see you later."

"So long," said Ed, giving a quick look around the place. A nice quiet club. A retreat from homelife and the prying nosy public. He walked over to the bar and looked tenderly up at a mounted sailfish. A stuffed mallard brooded in a corner. "Hey, Wills, a scotch and soda. Make it Haig and Haig."

"Right, Mr. Thompson," said Wills.

In case of future trouble, Mike's little credit association could co-operate on the law and order question, a matter of prime importance, and it was a good thing that Glen had such close connections with the police. Through Spence he had been given a nice little bit of protection business to the local cops and was teaching them how to use the stuff. Glen was feeding them the whole line about the danger of the times. "Good scotch, Wills," said Ed Thompson.

Lester Tolman had not seen the last of Elsie. She called up the office the next day and in a little penitent voice asked him if he wouldn't have lunch with her "once more." He said cordially, of course, and they arranged a meeting for the following day. They had lunch, Elsie coquetting across the table, but he was embarrassed at her familiarity with the waiters and her new-found ardor for the working class. When they took a drive to the Park, "just a quick run," Elsie had promised, she roguishly asked the attendant at the gas station if he belonged to a union. Lester listened in astonishment; Elsie had not changed. It was he who had changed. Her ways were simply not cute anymore. But she was so determined to extort his old feeling from him that she would not let go easily.

"We can't talk here on the street," she said as they stood outside her apartment house and he had firmly turned to walk away. "We can't part like this. Why need we part? Lester, come up and let's talk."

He looked at her quietly. He wanted to smile but he didn't want to hurt her, in fact, he only asked to leave as quickly as possible. "Listen, Elsie. I know you smell nice. You think if you could only get me to bed with you, everything would be as it was. Perhaps you're right. That's just why I'm not going. There's no sense to it. I want one thing out of life, you another. Why torture each other? Say good-by, Elsie, that's a good girl." He held out his hand and she struck at it frenziedly, her face flaming. "Damn you, you're just a brute, I never saw such a stupid insulting man. This is the first time in my life any man has let me down like this."

"Well, Elsie, it ought to be good experience. Just think, next time you have to play a part of a woman who gets the cold shoulder, you'll be able to put your whole soul in it," he said. He smiled but he did not want to; he was unreasonably saddened. He turned and walked off, feeling sore and tired as if he had gone to a country where they had promised fine mountains and there was only flat desert land. Elsie had steamed inside, almost knocking down the big doorman. She would no doubt fling herself on the bed; sob. He took no pleasure in the grief he was causing. But it was only her pride that would be hurt, probably that was as painful as if one suffered from real love. He was surprised at the way his own mental image of "real love" had made him utter the words, though not aloud. He had known, he was thinking, almost every kind of love except that kind that one authenticated by giving it the name "real." It did not depend on time or place; it was valid only by its creation. He should know it, they said, if it ever came.

It was a relief to find a note from Victoria Chance on his desk. It was written in the crazy hand of someone in a tearing hurry. She was off, she wrote, to Santiago and to a place in Oriente she would not even mention by name. He had better shake a leg and get down. The strike was coming. He ought to get in touch with the bigger sugar men first, and certainly get to talk with Mendieta and Batista. After the strike there might be no Mendieta.

He debated whether to go by plane or boat, but plane cost too much and anyhow Victoria was an alarmist. He would get there in plenty of time; this was really his vacation he was taking and not on company time. The weather turned out vile until they hit the Florida coast. Then the sun blazed out and pale and wormy specimens crawled out on deck looking bedizened in their summer outfits. He had dinner at a table with an old gentleman and his wife who was deaf but did not like to admit it. The old gent was full of a long story about his friend Mr. Miller who had gone every year for seventeen years on account of his sinus to the same place in Florida. The old gent was not going there but to Miami where it was livelier. Mr. Miller had a foundation to handle his affairs, that showed you how well off he was. The wife spoke up and said, "Mr. Miller is always so busy."

Her husband wanted to know at what as he had the foundation to take all care out of his hands. He himself was fascinated by the idea of all care being taken out of anyone's hands. His own business had gone to pot; the printing business, that is, they made the machinery that did the printing. They sold presses to Mexico before the insurrection when that man was killed and the bandit became a leader. The bandits destroyed all the machines, and his firm never sold anymore. They had done business with Switzerland, Peru, Buenos Aires, Japan. Just as they were expanding the War broke out and finished their business. He had not yet got it into his head why. It simply happened that his kind of business was no longer valued in the world and so, although he had traded in an honorable way, he had to fold up.

"The way I sold a man was like this," he said, his face lighting up, "I'd say, now a man is judged by his clothes and the company he keeps, isn't he? The customer would agree, any fellow would. Then I'd say, just so, and a business is judged by its stationery. Then I'd put the question, if you got a letter on a nice engraved heading, carefully typewritten and another on a printed heading in longhand, which would you answer first? This used to sell the stuff. Woodrow Wilson was responsible for our business being done to death. The White House and government used to use engraving but he cut it all out. Now only the White House and the cabinet use it. Why, sir, people used to think you small potatoes if you didn't have your wedding invitation engraved, now only the very wealthiest have engraving. An invitation to a party wasn't worth anything unless it was engraved and people used to make calls and leave cards. Every hall had a card stand with a bowl for cards. Now they don't make calls and few even have cards. Society has collapsed," he said sadly, and Lester looked with interest at his firm apple face, with a good thick head of hair and bright eyes still alert for every goodlooking woman that passed.

"Yes, sir," he said, "taste has gone down. The stage used to be fine. I remember Daly's theatre. The scenery was real, let me tell you. A door slammed like a real door and Daly went to Europe to get real French furniture. Ada Rehan and Mrs. Gilbert were fine actresses; who can hold a candle to them today? The son of a friend of mine married the daughter of Mrs. Gilbert but I never realized it for years. Mr. Drew was always a gentleman. No matter what part he played, he was always himself. The same goes for the others. I tell you only a return to Victorianism can restore this sense of values."

His wife had apparently imagined that they were still discussing Mr. Miller because she now asked brightly what phosphates he had sold. Her husband looked irritably at her, muttering to Lester, "Can't hear, deaf as a post," and shouted, "I don't remember, dear."

Her inquiry turned him back on Miller who it seems had been out of a job for a while, simply out, proving beyond the shadow of a doubt that all this unemployment was no new thing and a man who had it in him could rise above it. Miller had been out before the War. One night Miller and his wife went to a party. When they came home and she was taking off her garter, zip, like that, it fell to the floor. He said, "That's it," and immediately got the idea he'd been working on for the contact of the sparkplugs. "Don't ask me how, I'm not up on the mechanism of the thing, all I know is that he got the idea then. Now they can be put right in and pulled out but not then, and it was Miller's idea that made the difference. He made a lot of money out of that. Sometimes a man oversteps himself. Take my cousin. He wanted too much for his invention and lost the whole shebang. He invented a lock for a mailbag, a new type. Before, they used a leather strap on a steel hoop or something like that, now he invented one that could be closed with one movement, locked and everything. You could do ten bags like that in the time it took to do one of the old type. The government offered him ten cents a bag and he wanted a dollar, so was turned down. The government later had another bag offered and took it. My cousin never got over his disappointment. If he'd taken that offer it would have meant ten thousand a year at least and later more; now he just sits calculating what he might be making. It embitters everything."

The old lady excused herself and the two men went out to walk the deck. The stars had come out and Lester felt a strong sympathy for the little outmoded man. What would time do in his own life to maroon him in his old age? He hoped a great deal. He hoped even that the day would come when the great gap between men's vision and their works, between "we, the people," and their practices, might be bridged. Would that day ever come? He was thrown back again upon his recurrent pessimism and was dragged up by the busy voice at his side. "Women dress very indecently now," the old man was saying. "Once I got on the subway a few summers ago in New York. It was a very hot day. A woman came in and sat opposite me and I swear she had nothing on under her dress. You could see the whole works. To cap it she sat leaning far back. I could see everything she had." He said it right- eously and Lester wondered if he were a religious man. He said he was; he was in fact a vestryman in his church.

"When you say, lead me not into temptation, you mean it, don't you?" Lester couldn't help saying but the old fellow could not get the point, only shook his head in judgment over the woman whom he still no doubt saw in the flesh. At such a price, desire was not worth keep- ing, Lester thought, pitying his companion at the same time that he honored his zest.

When the old man left, he walked around restlessly or stood and looked moodily at a few couples dancing. They looked very weedy and the women too eager. He got into conversation with a steward who said they had just had a wireless that trouble was popping in Cuba. "I got a brother there. Cuba is fine for tourists, he always says, but try and live there. I don't know, he's in the to- bacco union. They busted his union, broke all the chairs and beat up the fellows who were around. My brother wasn't there that night, his wife was having a kid, see, so he missed out, pretty damned lucky, I'll say. One guy got his jaw busted so he can't eat nothin but soup. Another guy is still limpin around. They were at my brother's place, see, last time I was on the island. You ought to heard them lam out at the way things are. But next minute they are laughin, they're funny fellows. I don't know if I'll get to see my brother if there's trouble. If there's shootin they'll likely not let us guys off."

Lester tingled with a chill that he could not control. He went to his cabin, looked at his bags. The ship's orchestra was whining above but he thought he could hear guns. He was astonished and told himself he was damned yellow. Then he gritted his teeth and lit a cigarette. Finally he threw the cigarette away and brushed his teeth. Everything inside of him seemed sloshing around like bilgewater in the bottom of a boat. He took a big nip of brandy and crawled under the covers. He'd give anything just to stay on the boat but he could never face Victoria again. Or himself. He was afraid, but there are certain conditions a man makes with himself beyond which life is impossible. He took another big shot of the brandy. He felt better. His head spun a little and he began to hum. He even imagined himself running at the head of troops, shouting; they were going over the top, no, it was a valley they were running in. Death Valley. The valley of the shadow of death, he said, I shall fear no evil. Thy rod and thy staff. Oh, for faith, any faith; a man who knows why he dies is not lost.

But he is dead, said Lester firmly, sitting up and staring at the bright light over the washbasin. He is very very dead. He can never speak again or know a woman or hear a bird. Lester, who had not heard a bird except the machinerylike chirps of the lovebirds in Elsie's place for some time, thought particularly of the bird. He remembered the birds singing in early morning when he was a boy; their sweet trilling sounds that made life seem to gush in new broad bands of water down a rock. He thought of the birds, everything in him sharpened, quickened, as his preoccupation with death transformed the hollow slaps of water against the ship's sides to distant guns.

My country 'tis of thee; Wo ist das Land?: Paris, 1937

So they got Roselli at Fontainebleau. They are international in their little methods, aren't they? They like a quiet spot. How many of us fell at Wannsee out of Berlin with only the trees where lovers used to walk as witness? Keep step, eyes ahead, they let us walk today for the dead.

We are the comrades of this brother; the German exiles have come out of their holes, marching with our Italian comrade to his last home. Leave the Arc de Triomphe to the unknown soldier, the procession winding through the back streets where the poor salute from their windows and a girl hangs out a red shirt, past the old mighty dead, Balzac and Abélard and Héloïse, past the two-year Barbusse to old Father Lachaise. Bury him now.

He was quicksilver for a long time, his last stop before Paris, Spain. Guadalajara was his answer. Italians fought Italians on that road and which were better men? Those who followed the lie or those who followed the word and the deed? It's down in the books now, laugh that off, Mussolini.

Heads up, shoulders straight. Show Paris streets that life still beats and waits. Dark may come but there's sure to be morning. Dead we may be but there's more to live on. Links, links, links. They stole our words, they stole the tune. Now they're all marching back home as if touched by the moon. Yelling Sieg Heil as if they knew what they said, singing Heil Hitler for their daily bread.

Their mouths are shut, their ears are sealed. No, comrades, the dead are not here. Roselli will live though his feet turn clay. His heart still beats for another day.

Our Goethe loved your Italy too. Where the citrus blooms there's a long dull noon. They've got guns and they've got hate. We've got the future if we don't break. Links, links, links. Thaelmann is buried in their jails; it's not finished till the last man fails.

THE MOUNTAIN

A T LAST Victoria Chance had broken through the ring of United States government employees with their charts and figures, rosebuds and patronizing, through the circle of Cubans in white suits and briefcases to the workers who drifted into the office of the radical paper, *Trabajadores,* to tell their stories.

Even the editors on the paper had looked at her with suspicion as if they had some goldplated copyright to their revolutionary ideas and meant to keep them intact. There is no time to convince them, she thought desperately. She was not going to run home with lies and slanders. They had heard it before, too often, and listened warily, suspicious of her. Did not the little book on spies warn in particular against women? The student Manuelo came down from the university and argued with them, long and ardently, his ears growing red, angry words spouting from his mouth while she sat self-conscious, trying to appear agreeable as they picked her to pieces.

Then one day she lifted from the desk a copy of their paper, turned it over. On page two suddenly Kurt Becher's name leaped out at her. He was arrested, in Brazil. A few lines, nothing much, the usual fiery denunciations against a government that was no respecter of persons or democratic rights. He had been caught red-handed they said, with propaganda. He would be accused of fomenting "revolution." She sat still as stone. The student came over, sat down beside her, began to joke a little. She looked at him quietly, still holding the paper. "A friend of mine," she said, pointing to the paragraph, and then she pulled Kurt's last note to her out of her pocketbook and handed it to the boy. It was about going to South America, leaving his things with her, his name, Kurt, that was all. The boy got up and went to the editor who had looked so glum.

The two read the letter, their heads together; they
turned it over, held it up to the light as if it might contain hidden writings. Time is going so fast, will they
never make up their minds to help me, she thought, but
they were coming toward her together. The editor, Vincente, pulled his tie straight over his wilted shirt and sat
down on one side of her, Manuelo on the other. When
had she seen him, how was he? They looked at her with
warm glowing eyes as she talked. Word seemed to spread
through the long room; eyes looked up and heads bent
together, whispering. As she talked about him, she remembered the time she had brought him two neckties
scarcely worn from the assortment Jonathan's brothers
and father had sent him. He had been pleased as a child,
admiring the heavy silk and manufacture. Now he would
be sitting once again, in a cell, in a prison shirt, but when
she tried to see his features, only the eyes were plain to
her.

They let her talk to some of the secret members of the
union who worked on the sugar plantations. She came
every day and sat waiting as Vincente led the men forward, one at a time or in twos or threes, proudly, as the
true treasure of the island. They sat on a long bench in
the midst of clicking typewriters with the street door wide
open on the blazing pavement where a self-conscious policeman in new uniform and hot-looking yellow shoes and
a gun in a new black holster walked past, elaborately
indifferent to the scene inside. The man from the coffee
mountain sat beside her, his feet in ragged white cloth
sandals, his big dark hands nicked with purple scars. In
a quiet slow voice he told about men who cut cane, picked
coffee on coffee mountains, slept in hammocks when they
could or empty sacks on wet ground, had no home, often
no shoes. The union men came to this paper as to home,
here their stories were shelved up against time, against
death and for some end too far off easily to believe.

He was looking at the cigarette in her hand, his eyes
had become fixed, painful and tired. She held the pack
toward him and his long face that looked as if it had

been patiently carved from some fine wood, the eyes hollowed far back for protection from the rain and weather, smiled faintly. His big long fingers fumbled, then gracefully extracted the cigarette, poised it, looked it up and down. Smiling deeply, he put it in his mouth, lighted it slowly as if shielding the flame from a great wind, and took a deep puff. "Take it all," she said, ashamed to be owning a full pack. "Please take it."

He looked at her quietly, shaking his head. No. He would however take two more, and he took two, carefully, thrusting one above each ear where in the shelter of his hair they gave his face the curious wideawake appearance of a bird. "American?" he said with a question, looking at the cigarette he had just taken from his mouth in pleased surprise.

She nodded yes, smiling, as he began again. He was answering her questions. "Meat? It was not for them. They had cane juice, rice, some beans, yucca." Once he had made a little garden but the company let the bulls into it and they trampled it to nothing. Too much food makes a man strong. Hunger makes the mills go. A man must be very hungry to cut cane. He is always in debt to the company store. What he dreads most is the dark nights. When there is a moon it is fine. If he asked for a light, it would be a crime.

Victoria simply put away her notebooks. Let Lester worry with the figures. She came every day and now and then Vincente would come over and talk to her. She was after him to tell her how to go up into the mountains to Realengo where last fall the government, at the urging of the sugar mills, had sent in troops to try to take the land from the mountain men. They had made a final desperate stand, sheltering behind the great virgin trees, with machetes in hand. Workers in Santiago had poured out in a sympathetic general strike; the government troops had been called off without firing.

Vincente said it was a very hard trip. Then he said she would have to wait until a certain friend came back from his stay there and could tell her the way. She became more and more insistent the more difficulties grew. It began to seem like a battle between her and Vincente. No one went to Realengo; it must be a myth, founded only in pride. Vincente protected it from her, while he balanced this and that, doubtful, trusting her, distrusting her. If the strike came first, she could not go. But she was relentless with him; some stubborn will seemed to have fixed on that one object.

Jonathan had gone into some dark world. Kurt was in jail. The fires the Realengo men had lighted on their mountains began to seem real to her, as if she had seen them. She pictured the giant trees, the sharp mountains, the ring of light, and far below the circle of sugar mills that pressed covetously closer and closer to the Realengo land. After talking to some of the men from the sugar mills she would walk back to the hotel as if in a dream. She would stop in a bar, and in a daze, sip her drink, unconscious of the stares directed at her.

Above the bar a lithograph of a Sidoney Indian girl looked down at her from among the bottles and fat little liquor jugs. Her mind seemed to float in a dozen worlds, like some balloon, cut adrift. Now the wind took it to the past where her father lay, all alone, dying in a hospital, with her telegram that he could no longer read on the table beside him. They had sent her his glasses in a worn case, a leather wallet with receipted promissory notes, fifty years old. She remembered her mother's boasts of the fine land her father's father had owned, of her father's early conquests in business, their going West to the "land of the free" and his final liquidation in a world that had not cared much about his meticulous honesty. He hadn't been like her mother's people who were always on the hunt for a little capital, and Victoria's own niece already had the same sharp eye, casting a longing look at the silver teapot that had belonged to Uncle Joe—it was of solid silver with real elephant ivory in the handle that came from no good source as Victoria had discovered.

In fact, the family history had some pitch in it, no more, not as much as most family fortunes. In that era,

around 1870, Joe Trexler had been a young boy in a bad
spot and Grant had quit being a failure cutting cord-
wood and had gone to the White House on the backs of
the boys who died in the war. Grant was a tired sick man
longing for peace and had a gang of politicos on his
back and sat at last up in that neck of the woods near
Saratoga, where the big racehorses tear around the track
and earn fifty grand in the wink of an eye, writing his
memoirs to pull his family out of debt and die honorably.

She would look up at the Sidoney girl, the very last
of her lost race, stranded in a bar, and think of her own
grandfather taking Swiss dairy farmers up the Mississippi
to start little towns in the lush Wisconsin wilderness. He
had had no eye for investing for the future, had passed
up Chicago as a "mudflat now but bound to be a big
city," his interest kindled, his imagination fired, but he
was no Cortez, sulking on the shores of Cuba, "I didn't
come to be a peasant but for gold." Men had been coming for gold ever since and Victoria thought of the mountain men whose labor had only brought upon them the
covetousness of the big sugar companies in the valley,
as if they signified the history of the human race.

At night she would stand at the window of her hotel
room and look down into a big apartment where a man
tossed a ball to his little girl, or up at a window where
a man and woman stood staring down at her. High up
a big square of orange pane reminded her of the window
almost identically like it that she had looked out upon
the first night she and Jonathan had ever spent together.
If she stood long enough perhaps the same moon would
rise and hang delicately above the sleepers.

They had climbed the four shabby flights to Jonathan's
room, a little tight from a wild evening party, a little
shy from their brief and sudden acquaintance. The smart-
cracks had dropped off when they were finally alone. No
one was around against whom some elaborate make-be-
lieve need be played. She had looked around her, at an
old shawl over a trunk, a deathmask of Nietzsche on the
wall, rows of books, two beautiful red wineglasses. He

was fumbling with them now, a little awkward for someone so full of ease, and poured wine from a bottle under
the dresser. They touched glasses solemnly, looking into
each other's eyes as they drank. As they started to take
off their clothes, not with the haste of lovers, but shyly,
they began to talk and Jonathan began to recite, "The
night has fallen; not a sound in the forbidden sacred grove
unless a petal hit the ground," and she had hardly dared
to breathe, watching him in her underslip, her hands
crossed on her knee. Perhaps, she thought, he does not
really want me. The whole pattern of their early youth,
bred for haste, *St. Louis woman with the diamond ring*,
since a great war had seemed to reject them for living
and design them for death, was now *Say it with music*,
to be sharply and forever broken.

There was to be time for everything.

In the hotel room she drew her breath sharply, staring
at the unfamiliar room. Jonathan, she said aloud, but
the name already sounded strange. Why had she passed
by her father standing on the corner so long ago? All
her mistakes seemed to surround her with their bicker-
ing. She pulled a sheet of paper toward her and, as a
sharp explosion sounded in a nearby street, wrote rapidly,
"Jonathan, speak to me, just once more, forgive anything
I've said wrong. Just speak to me once more, I don't
care what you say. You are so far away, I can't find
you."

The words looked bloated and deformed with her
tears. If there were something she could send him to remind him so he would speak again. She thought of the
time Jonathan had told her of the traveling man in North
Dakota and his strange love token of curling hair. She
reached for the scissors and pulling up her skirts cut
quickly. The letter felt springy and soft; she took it downstairs to mail hardly noticing the half-frightened huddle
in the doorway. As she stepped out to the street, a shrill

"Don't go out, Señora" made her hesitate but she walked firmly to the corner, dropped the letter in the box and returning heard the hotel clerk's angry voice, "Lady, there's shooting. Do you want to get killed?"

PEACE

LESTER TOLMAN went to the Hotel Plaza and found a note waiting for him from Victoria. He was to be sure to see Vincente on the paper *Trabajadores,* and they would tell him where she had gone. Then followed a list of teachers and professional people whom he might like to see. She had already talked to them but it would do him good to talk to someone besides the officials of the government and that stuffed shirt at Pettibone and Sneed's.

He was a little irritated at the tone of her note but relieved to find the city so relatively quiet. The hotel clerk assured him it was all nothing but terrible for business. Business, he gloomed, had never been so bad and they were planning a little fête to bring over some nice people from Miami to try to pep things up a bit. The lobby was stuffy and full of dead-looking palms and couples from the States with white shoes; the men in white flannels and the discontented women in summery clothes with descriptive literature filling their laps. He couldn't find a spark of gaiety and spent the first evening in the bar at Sloppy Joe's where a couple from the States and a lady, solo, joked loudly with the barman trying to put on an imitation of a wild evening in Havana.

The next day he dropped notes to Victoria's list and prepared himself for a procession of people; then decided to drop around to the American legation where he felt curiously at home. A young attaché was ready to make any appointments for him and said there wasn't a chance of a general strike. "They wouldn't dare," he said in a positive and patronizing voice, and went on to say it was too bad there was so much false rumor about Batista who was really a good guy, just a simple fellow and a man of the people. They went out to lunch together and Ed Bland, the attaché, said that the trouble in Cuba was that the people were always discontented.

"Nothing pleases them," he said in a grieved voice and yet the trouble the United States government had taken to freshen up trade ought to be appreciated. They smoked cigars that Bland chose himself; they were the best and much superior to better-known brands. Tolman listened to a few off-color stories about Cubans and their women and Bland promised to take him to see a real rumba, not the cheap stuff put on for tourists, but the genuine article, very secret and in fact a religious rite. Then he took him back to the office and showed him a lot of charts and flung out a few scathing remarks about some of the sugar crowd who were hardboiled, all right, and deserved anything that might happen to them because they were not even trying to co-operate to put Cuba on its feet.

It was a relief to get away from the guy finally, and when Lester got back to the hotel he found a little weedy dark man in very white but shabby clothes waiting for him behind a palm. He took the fellow to his room, he said his name was Alquinas and that Vincente had sent him to say that the señora had gone to Santiago and on up to Realengo in the Oriente mountains. "Where's that," said Lester, in a snappy voice, feeling unaccountably impatient of the quiet humble voice.

"Very fine place," said Alquinas, showing his teeth and elevating his brows. "Very fine. High in mountains. Can only be reached by horse, very steep, so," and he elevated his hands at a perilous degree.

"And you guys let Mrs. Chance go there alone?"

"Oh, no, very good man from Santiago will go, she must go, she say I must go and no one could stop her. Very brave lady."

"Brave, fiddlesticks, she's crazy, going off like that. I

had no idea. Why, anything might happen to her. Where's your sense of responsibility?"

Alquinas evidently could not understand what Lester said; it was convenient to shrug and yet he could not prevent a look of contempt from creeping into his eyes and that made Lester more irritated than ever.

"When's she coming back? I don't like it, I can tell you. Her husband will blame me." It sounded weak but he could think of nothing more argumentative. The island seemed sliding away from him into the sea. He could see the evening shadows tinge the square outside the window, past Alquinas' head, and the buildings were taking on the curious tones of coral under water. He felt as if he were in too deep and wished he were safely back home. The fellow was no doubt laughing at him, he should conciliate him and find out what he could about the strike. When he mentioned the strike, Alquinas simply looked innocent and said in a blank voice, "What strike?"

"Why, the strike everybody says is coming off. That is everybody except the Americans. The Cubans, I don't know what they think. Who knows anything around this dump?"

"Knows?" said Alquinas, looking pleased and shaking his head like a bright child. Lester looked at him as if he would cheerfully choke him.

"Now, Alquinas," he said, "I got off on the wrong foot with you, but just forgive it. I was worked up, that's all, and if you ask me this island is a damned jumpy place to be in. I'm working with Mrs. Chance on this sugar proposition and what you tell her you can safely tell me, see," and he smiled what he hoped was a confident and a happy smile. He had, however, the sudden hopeless feeling that it was going to end nowhere, and in fact Alquinas merely smiled and said Mrs. Chance was a nice lady.

"That don't get us anywhere, we agree she is a nice lady, but what I want to know is what the situation really is here, how can I see this Vincente?"

"Vincente very busy now." Alquinas spoke slowly and

seemed to be thinking deeply. Lester had the alarmed conviction he was about to walk out and desert him. "Here, Alquinas, don't go. We got to understand each other better. I got to see Vincente. Mrs. Chance told me to," and he searched all his pockets for her letter. When he found it he handed it to Alquinas who smoothed it reprovingly with his fingers and read it quickly. He can read all right, the bastard, thought Lester, he's just acting dumb to stall me.

Alquinas even laughed at the mention of the stuffed shirt. He put his thumb on the words chuckling until Lester said, "What's so funny?"

"Very funny lady, Mrs. Chance," said Alquinas, but he would say no more. "Better wait till she comes back," he counseled and left Lester looking out at the square wondering how he had been so stupid as to let himself get off on the wrong foot. "It's that damned Bland working me up against everything," but it was no consolation. He was actually tied up, with no one to see except the sugar crowd and the embassy people, and curiously enough not one of the names on Victoria's list came to see him except a teacher who introduced him to a doctor who sent him on a long car-ride to the far suburbs of Havana. Through long rows of little tan-colored houses and bougainvillea and hibiscus, the little street-car bounced over a track that ran between ragged grass and palms and little stores and more tan houses and swarms of children and old women with sore eyes until he came out at last to the foot of a hill.

He went up to the sanitarium to see the head doctor and director who turned out to be a very handsome hearty fellow with a lovely wife and five children. They had lunch in a cool clean dining-room, with Venetian blinds and cooling wine, and Lester began to breathe at last. Dr. Barrios took him all around to show him the newest up-to-date sanitarium only it wasn't finished and had not been finished for several years. They walked through miles of rooms smelling of fresh plaster, and climbed ladders to the roof where in a nice big refrigerator they could

keep many cadavers at one time, and then down more ladders to an operating room, and the doctor was all the
time deploring politics that held up everything and let
poverty make such holes in people. On the roof they
stood looking out over luscious country with the earth
red and purplish sprouting with vines and trees and the
roads making broad marks like the trail of a slug toward
Havana where they could faintly see the dim frosty dome
of the capitol.

"If they had poured some of that money here, instead
of into that monkey house to show off before tourists," he
complained. "All the time, costs of living go up and
people go down. They need to come to get cured but it
is not ready. I have a few beds, that is all. The island
rots with the diseases of poverty, we are drowning in
sugar, actually drowning, it is all we raise almost, the
island stinks with it, my dear fellow, and where does it
go? I can take you to places where they have no lights,
nothing. Never tasted manufactured sugar, only sucked
the juice from cane. This island is rotting, but if we
can only . . ." He stopped abruptly, looked sharply at
Lester, searched in his vest pocket for a cigar and handed
it to him. Lester bit off the end sharply, stung by the
man's distrust of him. He turned full to look at him; he
felt as if his voice might tremble and tried hard to control it.

"I wish you'd tell me," he muttered. "I didn't understand at first. I'm beginning to."

"Of course, of course, my dear fellow," said Dr. Barrios, and they trooped back to the house where a young
medical student waited with a briefcase. It ended by
Dr. Barrios and the student driving Lester back to
town. They made the chauffeur take a roundabout way
to look at the fortress where both had served terms under
Machado. "Every honorable man has been in jail here,"
laughed Barrios, bursting into a shout as they passed a
granite boulder. "Hey, wait a minute, here is where we
got the bastard who killed one of our beloved boys, during
Machado," and the student and Dr. Barrios turned to

give a long stare at the stone, while the student recited how he had put in two years in jail and had composed some very mediocre verse which he promptly tore up when he got into the sunlight. "It's another dimension," he said. "You think one set of thoughts and they seem all right but once the sun hits you, you realize how peculiar they were."

When they dropped Lester at the Plaza they looked after him with friendliness and curiosity, and Lester had a glimpse of their lively faces with the dark eyes staring back from the open tonneau as the chauffeur clumsily honked his way through the cocktail-hour jam around the Plaza. He walked in slowly, and found a note from Bland suggesting they have dinner together. Lester read the note twice, then tore it up. He told the desk to say he had not come in yet, and walked out the side door.

She took off her dress in the shell of a house at the foot of the mountains. The women stood around in a circle admiring the dress, the hat, the shoes. Their beautiful dark eyes slid over the fabric with shy looks that, without envy, beheld what they saw with the open candor of a child. Victoria slid into the workman's overalls and shirt, tied a handkerchief over her head and, going out into the bright sunshine, looked at the mangy horse. The little stout man from the union in Santiago was already sitting on a similar horse, chirping to it. The women stood around as their man in sloppy fragments of blue trousers and bits of a shirt, held the bridle of the far from spirited nag intended for her. The empty moldy sagging house would shelter this family for the night and somewhere on mounds of old rags they would lay themselves down. A kitchen must be somewhere, a few broken dishes had perched, like molting birds with one wing shot off, against the lean boards. They patted the animal, adjusted her foot, chirped to the horse, waved brightly. She was off. At last she was going to Realengo.

The hard steep mountain was ahead, a thin trail winding up its long sides to the hidden country.

The horse hung its head doggedly, nipping the tough earth with its feet and the fat rump of Salvador bounced on his horse ahead of her. It was a fine high day and she thought with astonishment of her trouble that she had grown accustomed to as a malignant disease with which one must live and finally die. It had not vanished but was as remote as the view of the sugarmills they were soon to see from the turn in the path that corkscrewed through such perilous rocks to little plateaus of safety. A light giddy happiness without rhyme or reason seemed pouring into her from no other source than the sun.

The horse plodded jerkily not like the swift running pair that used to take her father and herself and her little sister Rosamond over the Iowa roads to distant farms. The sound of the big threshing machines, the straw whistling through the sunny air like golden arrows, the tall green corn, where she and Rosamond had tried so hard to get lost like the babes in the wood, rose up before her, accompanying her with all the reality of a dual landscape. When they came to the plateaus, Salvador turned in the saddle and delivered a vituperous lecture on the sugarmills, their greed and evil, and far down she could see their tall chimney stacks belching out the molasses-scented smoke while all around pale green cane spread its sickly grasp as far as the eye could see.

Up and up they went, through virgin timber with vines thick as huge snakes, and tall ferns strong as trees. A deathly hush was in the air. The low cry of some bird, now and then a flash of wings, was startling as the report of a gun. Strange flowers dripped from trees, and the sweet fresh smell of mosses was pungent as spice. The trail was very narrow and Salvador shouted, "No one come here who can't ride. No autos. No big guns." And rounding a curve he pointed proudly to a lookout under dead branches where men had lain waiting to spy upon invaders. "Not a chance," he bellowed happily, then recalling reality, said gloomily that unfortunately no doctors or schools had ever come here either. "Much sickness," he said, as if he had described a bit of scenery to a tourist.

She rode behind him, laughing to herself, everything saturated with delight. Perhaps I'm going clean daffy, she thought, happily, not at all deceived that this would last forever. Tomorrow or next day the other world down below would have to be faced again. But up here fear seemed childish, a nightmare that lived only in imagination. They dipped, the horse skidded and righted itself. Once Jonathan had made her a little boat and it was in the attic now with her grandfather's diaries about the tall buffalo grass in Wisconsin and mint juleps, five cents, and her Uncle Joe's letters about the antelope running against the sky and the grass growing like a vast lawn as far as the eye could see. They had known the country when it was young and sweet and Uncle Joe had said, "I'll never cross the Mississippi again until I have twenty thousand dollars to give mother," but he had been led back finally, without a cent, staring out at the river as the train rumbled across, his hand playing with a loose button on his coat, his mind a lost and broken toy.

She thought of him now as, step by step, they mounted higher and higher and of the pony that the Indians had shot from under him when he stole into the Black Hills hunting gold, and of the love letters she found when her mother died that a girl Uncle Joe had loved wrote him from Atlanta, Georgia, where he had got into a jam with a lot of fancy politicians so long ago. All the lives of all the people she had known joggled and pressed as if they were beams of light and she would not have been surprised to see riding by her side a strange company of faces she had never seen, her grandfather with his straight tall figure and deepset eyes, the optimistic handsome Uncle Joe, and even Uncle David Trexler on his pony Macduff that took him to Montana the time he got his first step up in his fortune by cheating all the soldiers at the fort. Rosamond would be somewhere and Jonathan just behind her, and the boy who took her dress off back of the schoolhouse saying, "Say you love me," and she had said, "I love you," for the first time, and the words had sounded marvelous, with the hum of locusts and the ground had been hard and cold and she could hear the noises in the ground, as if the very earth were speaking, the frogs in the brook down in the hollow, and "Say it again," and she had said it, and Jonathan, I always loved you but something happened to us, and whatever has happened has to be borne. If I only had six children, like my grandmother, left a widow and their livings to make, it would be easier, she thought. The worst is to be alone. But the little horses were snuffling in the early evening air as if they smelled a house, and the path was bridging a tiny marsh and, through a wide still path of soft spongy tobacco-colored earth between banana trees, they turned toward a palm-thatched hut where a man with wild eyes squatted before a great round basket shelling corn.

VI. THE BAD LANDS

STEVE, wake up, someone's blowing their horn," and Lorraine Carson was shaking her husband's arm. He stumbled up in the chilly early gray and went to the window. "Hello, who's there?"

"Me," said a voice, muffled and far away. Steve threw the window wide and leaned out. One of the Lenertz boys looking thin and shivering in the early morning light stood by his car with the lights on and engine running. "What's up?" Steve called.

"Can you come down?"

He was pulling on his shoes and buttoning his pants over his pajamas. A cold chill of premonition made him shiver. "What's wrong?" he said, stopping short of Ben Lenertz's white face. Jim Lenertz got out of the car and stood by his brother.

"Tub," began Ben. "It's Tub. He ran into a big truck, it got him all right, right over by that bend past the schoolhouse. Some girl was with him got all banged up. They took her to the hospital. Fellow in the truck got shot in his side. His gun went off, see, when the truck and Tub's car bumped together." His teeth were chattering and Steve felt his own body cold as stone. He grabbed Ben's arm, "You mean he's dead?"

Jim nodded. "He never knew what hit him," and, his voice released, bubbled inconsequential items, how they had heard the news and how Mrs. Johnson sent them to get him and how Tub had been over to Roberts County to a meeting to give what he called his radio broadcasts, singing with his cigar box . . . when a bunch of town guys beat up some of the farm boys.

"What's that?" said Steve, coming sharply to life. "Who? What fellows?"

373

"Nielson who owns the hardware store, and Sam Stone and that big guy who runs the meat market, Finley I think he is, and a bunch of them. They say they were Legion fellows holding some get-together."

"Hold on, Jim, let me, I was there, see," said Ben, shaking himself as if to keep his teeth from chattering. "It's the same bunch made trouble last year when we were working to try to get Luke Anderson off, calling us reds and so on. They were at this joint, see, the only place with any room to meet in, and some of the fellows were there to hear a guy from Minneapolis. He was talking about co-ops and then Tub was to do his stunt. The other guys were meeting in another room and they got full of beer and busted in on us. Tub was sitting there in a corner waiting and me and Tub's girl, this girl was there, too. They come in and began swinging chairs. Some of the fellows jumped out and they got hold of Arnold, the lame guy, and told him he had to run the gauntlet, and they made a line, see, and made him go through and they each hit at him. They took off their belts and hit him, they almost put his eye out with a buckle. Ray Epping got so mad he busted right into them hitting out, and they grabbed him, and says, *Oh, you love him so much, go on kiss him, you love him, come kiss him.* And they got hold of Arnold again and began shoving the two guys up to each other. Tub grabbed a chair, it all happened so fast nobody knew what to do, and yells at me, what you waiting for, and hit out at them. They were too many for us, I see that, and Tub's girl ran out and me after her. Tub was swinging at them." He stopped, sniffling. His nose looked cold as a dog's, and Steve hated him at that moment. He wanted to hit him for running out but he said impatiently, "Go on."

"Well, they threw Tub out on his can. He was wild. He said he was going to round up a gang and beat hell out of them and I says to Tub, keep your shirt on and get going or they'll be out after you, and then I stepped on her and makes for Charley's place thinking to get some of the boys. Charley is there with his cousin Phil Towne-

ley and we headed back but by that time they had cleaned
up everything and Moe Bogan who runs the joint had got
scared and turned out all the lights. I never see Tub
again. Seems he didn't go home that night, that was
Saturday and, yesterday, Sunday, he never showed up
either. He was probably getting the girl back to work,
she works in Mitchell, early this morning because this
happened around one o'clock."

He stopped. The three figures looked small and strange
and the land in the early light loomed all around them
hard and unrelenting. Steve couldn't speak. His mind
seemed to be leaping around like a jackrabbit. To him it
was clear as daylight that Tub had been killed because
of the scrape. He said roughly, "What we standing here
for?"

"What you want to do, Steve?"

"I'd like to go for those guys," he said, and for the
first time in his life he knew what it meant to want to
bust hell out of another man. He remembered the night
in the road when the scab driver had been shot and when
deputies, fellows from town like these guys, had come
and rounded them up. A network of events seemed to
have got him and his friends into its mesh and he shouted,
"They're to blame. If they'd shoved Tub under the truck,
they couldn't be more to blame in my sight. They got
him all worked up, he didn't know what he was doing."
His own feelings that were at that moment at such a high
pitch seemed to him to have been Tub's.

"Tub was kind of a reckless driver sometimes," said
Jim.

"He wasn't," said Steve. "He drove fine, drunk or
sober. There ain't nothin we can do for Tub except
to think straight." He glared at Jim who began coughing apologetically. Ben looked reproachfully at his
brother. "Tub was a first-rate driver," he said.

"O.K.," said Jim.

"Take it easy, Steve," said Ben. "Ain't no use going
off your nut." Steve jerked away angrily. Just stand and
take it and crawl back and lick your wounds. No, sir,

not for him, anymore. He opened his mouth and said quietly, "Tell Mrs. Johnson I'll be right over."

Even old LaRue was upset at the news and started out to water the stock in his naked feet. Lorraine dribbled tears all day and the Johnson house was so full of cried-up girls and women it almost got Steve's goat. He seemed to be carrying a heavy stone in his chest and nothing would get rid of it. The tears and carrying on didn't help matters nor old man Johnson standing around with his beard unshaved and his red-rimmed eyes like a hound-dog's, asking over and over, "What's that feller mean, coming here to bother us, saying it's Tub's fault?" be-cause already the company that owned the truck were nosing around trying to smell out a chance to grab in-surance. The truck was a dead loss and the driver was lying up with a bullet wound in his leg. All Steve could think of was to get the guys who had beat up their gang, but it was making a stink and the vets of foreign wars had come out with a statement condemning the Legion and such actions. No one seemed to know how it had started except that a lot of drunks had decided to cut up. Some said that Finley had had bad luck with his store and the chain stores were cutting into business right and left so that everybody was sore and there wasn't any money but relief money anymore.

Nothing seemed to make sense and all Steve could think of was his hatred for the businessmen who were always holding back on everything that had any guts in it. They were always the bootlickers and hangerson. No matter how often they got taken for a ride down the chute the chutes they came right back for more. Their tongues were hanging out just begging for it, nice good old Morgan and fine and dandy Mister Ford, just so they could have big shots for pals and spit on the farmers and the little fellows. They were so goddamned scared of the future and if they could only grab some of that nice big heaven that belonged to Mister Mellon.

Steve drove over to his father's and Walt was hobbling around with his rheumatism with a grave face. Teacher-teacher was all cried-up but the three girls looked excited and had put on their best dresses as if they thought something was bound to happen any minute. Walt said, "Son, you don't want to lose your head. It's going to get serious in this country. You got to keep your head. And don't forget, don't get to feeling persecuted. It's bad. It just makes you want to run around with a knife in your teeth. I don't know why we all kinda feel that the fight was to blame for Tub, everybody does. It ain't the whole story though, it ain't just that fight."

Steve was impatient. He shook his head angrily. "I know that, don't lecture, Pop, I know. It was just Tub hadn't anywhere to go. None of us have. Look at me. Two dollars a week and a slave to Lorraine's old man. And I'm lucky too, and I don't forget it. I don't want that kind of luck. I'm getting out, I got to." He stood with his hands shutting and opening. It made Teacher-teacher want to cry just to look at him. He was too big to take on her lap or give a cookie. He had to do it himself, whatever it was. She could see he had to go and she was glad of it.

Mrs. Johnson was the calmest of the lot. She was white as snow and went around as if she had felt shoes on her feet, dusting and putting things to rights and not crying. The day of the funeral she was dusting the parlor where the big Bible rested on a tidy, with Tub's name in it, born and died, with all the other Johnsons. The picture of Mr. and Mrs. Johnson, enlarged, in their wedding clothes with her hand on his shoulder, she standing up behind him, hung in a gilt frame. She dusted everything, the picture of Tub as a fat baby in a dress with lace on it, and as a little boy holding a lamb, his graduation diploma from the highschool and a shell from Atlantic City and two colored postcards from Chicago. Pa Johnson was telling how Tub had the makings of a radio

genius and "a big company was after him in Minneapolis
to come play for them," he lied, forgetting how he had
opposed Tub at every move and laughed at his songs. It
was a warm day and the windows were open. They could
hear the many noises of the field, the sheep had come
up from pasture and all the geese and turkeys were circling around the house, excited and twittering, thinking
it was time to feed. The minister who was to do the reading was an old man who had lost a son in the World
War and people said he was a little cracked since.

He stood up behind the long coffin with the red and
white carnations on top and he stared down at it as if
he were seeking to look at the young dead face. His hands,
that were big and knotted from helping in the harvest
fields, trembled and he tried to steady them by holding
his open Testament braced against his big skinny frame.
In his mind a confusion of thoughts tussled with one
another for possession. He had known Tub since he was
a little boy and he had the feeling that it was his own son
he was now burying once again. His only son had been
killed in France and he had a photograph of a white cross
in a field of many crosses to remind him that his boy was
truly no more.

The fight on Saturday night had taken grave possession
of him and he felt that he must use this occasion to point
some lesson, some warning. All the time the text he had
chosen jostled with other sayings and crisscrossed with
"that these dead have not died in vain" and "war for
democracy," and then he kept being tortured by the contradictions in living that made life planless, so that the
Gospel itself became faint in his mind. The last years
had mocked at him, and although he had at first opposed
war, he had not been able to stand out against it after
his son enlisted. He, too, had been drawn in, and it was
terror to him now, that in the beginning he had been
right, and in the end, through seeking to follow his son,
wrong. The idea that his son had died in vain had never
been so strong in him as he stood behind the boy's coffin
when again another son seemed to have yielded up life

purposelessly. He could not bear the waste and tried to find some way to drive home some lesson, some idea, that might make this life a tiny drop watering the barren land.

As if a man did flee from a lion, and a bear met him; or went into the house, and leaned his hand on the wall, and a serpent bit him, he thought, his lips moving, as he considered how Tub had gone confidingly to the meeting, had been beaten, had witnessed the humiliation of his friends. He could fancy the boy driving around and around wildly, getting himself in deeper, and all the time the thought that nobody wanted or needed young men was torturing him. The old preacher could see the look of the unwanted and unneeded in the young faces before him; a terrible, half-defiant look, with the bewildered expression in the eyes. What has come over the world, he muttered, half aloud, and what has come over me, that I am helpless to save these lambs.

He began to speak, gently, he heard his own voice and tried to guide it, he heard himself begin the verses, saw his hands lift the Bible, that true great book of warning, heard his voice:

"Verily, verily I say unto you, I am the door of the sheep.

"I am the door; by me if any man enter in, he shall be saved, and shall go in and out, and find pasture.

"The thief cometh not, but for to steal, and to kill, and to destroy; I am come that they might have life, and that they might have it more abundantly.

"I am the good shepherd: the good shepherd giveth his life for the sheep."

The old preacher stopped. His thoughts were louder than his text. They were crying out at him; you are alive and are burying the young. You do not die for your sheep but stand by while they are slain.

The silence was oppressive. The old man's lips trembled but he firmed them. He went on:

"But he that is an hireling and not the shepherd, whose own the sheep are not, seeth the wolf coming, and leaveth the sheep, and fleeth; and the wolf catcheth them, and scattereth the sheep.

"The hireling fleeth, because he is an hireling, and careth not for the sheep.

"I am the good shepherd, and know my sheep and am known of mine.

"And other sheep I have which are not of this fold: them also I must bring, and they shall hear my voice: and there shall be one fold and one shepherd."

Again he stopped. The words that should follow were clear as if written on a scroll. From this point he should go on and tell how Christ was the shepherd and died to save His sheep, how His blood washed His lambs white as snow and how He led the lambs into His pasture. The love of God was made manifest by men in their love of fellowmen, it alone could bring about Christ's Kingdom. He meant to exhort them to follow in His footsteps and redeem the world through love.

The words would not come. He stumbled in his speech, coughed, holding his big hand apologetically over his lips. The thought that Christ's love had not spared the world from agony tore at his heart like a lion. Christ had cast out the moneychangers but they infested the temples as of old. He felt as if old texts were rubbing into his eyes, blazoned on the wall in words of fire. *Hear this, O ye who swallow up the needy, even to make the poor of the land to fail, That ye may buy the poor for silver, and the needy for a pair of shoes; yea, and sell the refuse of the wheat.* For what had his own boy died and had the land not been turned to refuse through greed? Of what use to preach of the Kingdom of God when the kingdom of earth was a living pit?

Sweat stood out on his head. Mrs. Johnson for the first time began to cry. Tears rolled down her cheeks. The old man began aloud, "My friends, we are all guilty. The temples are unclean. The work of Christ must be done again. There is no peace in the land. I know this boy well. He was a good boy and believed in the Lord." He stared at the coffin and the thought that man had betrayed man by going too long to God, hurt him. He could feel the hurt as if a giant fist had grimly squeezed his vitals. "Dearly beloved," he said gently, "God gave His only begotten Son that whosoever believeth in Him shall not perish, but have everlasting life," and it seemed to him that the only begotten son was his own boy. Tub's dead form and his own son became one. He stared at the long box, it was his preaching that had been wrong. The Son of Man had not been wrong. His followers had perverted His words; they had cast their eyes too long at heaven and had scorned earth and mankind whom He had come to save.

Although he had failed in his sermon, no one felt that he had failed. They saw an old man overcome with irreconcilable grief and they remembered his own son, and wondered at war that had been followed by so much hatred. In the silence that followed a short prayer, Milly Trigger and the two Olson girls stepped up and began singing, "Somewhere the sun is shining, somewhere the song birds dwell." The old man sat down with a confused look.

Steve had been watching him closely. The old man's confusion had dried his own grief and anger. He suddenly understood the preacher's trouble and when he said, *Whosoever believeth in me shall have everlasting life,* Steve understood what he meant. To him the words were direct and to the point, and never having been brought up on the Bible as a religious book, the words meant to him simply that whosoever believed in life, would live, and whosoever believed in death, would die. Death was not only of the dead but of the living and if a man's life aimed beyond his own, he lived, whether he was under the ground or above it. His head began to clear as it became plain to him what he must do with his own life. He even stopped wanting to fight the bullies who had started all the trouble. They were gnats pestering but they were not the great thief. The great thief had bitched and botched them all, why blame little men who knew nothing but selling and buying and would pick the fillings from their grandmother's teeth. Even as he thought this savage notion, he saw the kindly face of Henry Whittle, the grain and feed man, who could not understand why there was no money anymore.

He held his end of Tub's box firmly and proudly, and when it was in the earth, and the LaRue car had driven back home, he got out, and instead of following the others into the house went to the big barn. He wanted to be alone. He fell down with his face in the hay and lay as if dead. All his life seemed to die down in him and he lay still trying to think of practical plans. He could hear the windmill whining and then Lorraine rang the big bell for supper. He did not move. At last he heard the door creak open and roll back. Then he heard someone step across the barn floor; Lorraine. She was looking but did not call and then he heard the ladder creak and did not move. From the open door in the loft the last red stains in the sky promised bloodshed but he stared at it unafraid. She was coming up, and he could hear her breathing hard as she stood beside him, then she threw herself down and lay beside him. She put her forehead on his forehead and her mouth on his mouth as if he had died and she must again breathe the breath of life into him.

She didn't speak, just held him tightly but gently, and he could feel all his muscles weaken and tremble. Tears welled up from the pit of his stomach. His arms tightened around her as he sobbed, "Oh, Lorraine, oh, honey." She rocked him in her arms as if he had been her child, and he let himself be rocked. Then he sat up firmly. "You won't stop me, will you, honey, but I got to go away. I ain't doing any good here. I'd work my fingers to the bone, but for what? I got to go." And to his great relief, to his joy, she said firmly as he, "I know it, Steve, I know it."

The little dark terribly strong man had appeared suddenly as an apparition against the sky and first evening star. He stood, compact and solid, in blue workshirt,

white trousers tucked in boots, staring at the room that
faced the deep gorge and ironblue mountains. Hernandez's wife had just lighted the one lamp that Victoria
had so far seen in Realengo; she let out a cry. The men
got up and rushing out, embraced their leader. The actor Navarro came back and beating his chest with one
hand said, "It's Lino." His voice was bursting with pride
and Victoria got up and stood a little timidly. Lino came
straight to her and shook hands. He was not as tall as
she was, but his hand was strong, warm, and completely
trusting. He had been hiding secretly in the mountains
and that he had come out, simply to tell their story to
her, brought tears to her eyes. She bit her lips angrily,
telling herself, "If you cry now, I'll never forgive you,
never." The children of Hernandez who was in Havana
for "lucha" (it was always "Struggle, struggle, struggle,"
Hernandez's wife had said excitedly and "Me alone to do
everything, not that I grudge it, but when will it end?"),
were chasing the ducks and chickens out from the side of
the table where Lino proposed to sit. The boy was tugging at the little goat and high up under the sweet-
smelling thatch of the roof, white doves were cooing
throatily. The big parrot swung on its hoop calling sar-
donically, "Choo, choo, choo."

The plump Salvador from Santiago had never before
seen the mysterious leader of the mountain men and he
was very impressed. His face glistened, his warm eyes
were ardent as he leaned toward the unsmiling serious
face of the little man who had led the Realengo men
against the armed militia of the government.

"Not the government, the sugarmills put them up to
it," said Navarro, who acted as general master of cere-
monies, running around to drag up chairs. "See," he was
shouting at Lino. "She doesn't speak very well but understands everything. *Comprende todes,*" he roared defiantly,
as if once again on a stage, his mad eyes circling the serene
faces of Lino Alvarez, Salvador, and a little man who sat
by himself quietly beaming, full of the importance of
being a guard to the trail that led down the gorge. His

eye glistening like a coffee berry turned in his head toward the wide open face of the house and his ears bristled up under his dark thick hair for the crackling of a twig, the rustle in the night, that might mean an assassin.

For Lino was a hunted man. He carried two bullets in his arm where guards from a sugarmill had fired upon him. He placed this arm, a little stiffly, at his side, the hand supporting itself along his knee, the hand of the other arm rested on the table. Navarro subsided, the wife of Hernandez stood by her pots and pans, and heated water for coffee in an oil can. The little boy was crunching coffee berries with a stick in the hollowed-out log. Lino looked around at the room, tenderly, as if it belonged to him.

He just wanted it made plain to Victoria that the land was rightfully theirs. They were no outlaws. No bandits. The land had been given to them years ago for fighting in the war for freedom. They had paid taxes. They had done all the work. Then the sugar companies began trying to get hold of it. Some of the foolish ones took loans on crops. They got themselves tangled up with the companies. Then the companies began trying to foreclose the land. They said it was theirs. Lino just wanted her to know and, through her, the world—and as he said this, his face grew terribly still, his lips firmed, and he looked at her steadily as if entrusting her now with an important duty that she must by no means forsake—that they meant to keep their land or die.

As he said the word "die," Navarro sighed. He had been leaning forward with his famished face breathing in every word. The doves stirred. Outside the evening sky had shut down hard as iron. The word "die" blazed up in the room lighting their faces.

Perhaps I have heard this word really and truly, for the first time, Victoria thought, and for me and all the living it has a special and terrible meaning.

Instead of feeling depressed, she felt unaccountably lighthearted. The danger was tense in them all and they sat staring as if the enemy had come up upon them and waited without.

"Guns," said Lino, in a sober voice. "We need guns," and he said it in the matter-of-fact tone of someone who has asked for bread at a table that provides many loaves. "We are entrenched up here, with natural advantages. The trails are impossible for any but mountain men. How can the enemy shoot? They will only hit trees. Last fall we stood behind the trees with only machetes. They said, 'We call upon you to surrender or we fire, it is our orders.' And I said, 'I too have orders. To defend.' "

Navarro looked around the room proudly. Pride oozed from his every pore. He got to his feet in his old filthy trousers and torn shirt, stretching his handsome straight figure that had, so he had earlier informed her, graced the stage in towns all over South and North America. San Francisco, Seattle, Lima, Buenos Aires; he had prized the words as if they were nuggets of a lost fortune. But his dream, to become an haciendado, had shaped his whole life, guided his philosophy. She had listened to him only the night before in his own palm-leaf hut with a book of tattered clippings on her knee to prove that he had once had great powers. His wife and many children with beautiful soft eyes stood around. A piece of comb was carefully stuck behind a twig. A tiny piece of soap clung to a ledge in the wall. Pigs grunted in the dead fire on the ground hunting scraps. The rooster hunted in the pig's hide and a skinny boy staggered in with a bucket of water lugged up from the spring far below. To own land and be free had been his guiding star, and he had mixed his lot with mountain men, some black, some white, some old stock of several generations, some discards from Jamaica, from Haiti, shifted from place to place to work in sugar, tobacco, coffee, and at last here to grub for their very lives.

"Me," said Navarro, pounding his chest, "Vice-president. Lino, president." He was referring to their organization and stood with his head up as if he had been high officer of some great kingdom. Lino listened to his vice-president without smiling. He was still thinking of guns. A little stack of papers wound in red calico came from his pocket reverently. The papers that proved the legality of their claim. Lino was no politician. He did not know the language, the means, the whys or wherefores, that tormented a dozen countries. He knew his people owned their land, and meant to keep it. They owned it legally. He was bothered with legality, but legality failing him, he wanted guns.

"Water is water, whether in a drop or the ocean," said the plump Salvador, with a serious face that made him look suddenly like a caricature of his jolly self. "Here it is on a tiny scale, but in no way different than all over the world." He shrugged expressively, his shrug indicating his appraisal of Victoria and his hope that he might be educating her. His wild expectation, that in some way help might mysteriously come to the island through her, was clear as day to Victoria. Only Lino seemed hard, practical, counting on no one much except themselves. If they put up a fight, he said, the rest of the workers on the island would back them up. They had gone on strike before, they would again. Salvador began to talk of Pancho Villa, of Sandino—and Navarro, throwing himself into the conversation, warned his chief to beware and not let himself get trapped with fair promises, like Sandino. "They talk of guarantees," he roared, "and then shoot you in the back."

Lino Alvarez for the first time smiled. The smile lighted his mouth, his eyes, and seemed to vanish in his hair. "They will not take me," he said seriously, and reaching his hand toward a black holster on his hip pulled out his gun and laid it before them. It looked shiny, black and deadly, but very small. The wife of Hernandez had been brewing the coffee that now stood in tiny cups before them. The children had disappeared to bed. The deep coughing of the sick boy in his hammock racked the walls of the house. Every palm leaf shivered.

"Me," repeated Navarro as if he wanted that statement not to be forgot, "Vice-president," and again he thumped his chest that had a frail and hollow sound. Lino sat solid as rock, sipping his coffee, his hand steady and his arm with the bullets in it raised upon the table.

In the night the cold went to the bone. She lay in her clothes with her shoes on shivering, with an old gunny sack pulled around her for warmth. She dreamed and woke and dreamed again and the dreams shrouded her in old anxieties. She was at home and had raised prize roses but the neighbors came in mourning with long faces. When she woke the sun was powerful and shining as polished metal. She washed her face in icy water and sprinkled drops on the herbs that grew outside the window.

Lester Tolman cursed himself for being a damned fool and playing around when there was work to do. His head bulged like a balloon and he thought of the night before with a distaste that was real as if he had bitten old iron. Bland had taken him to see a "real rumba" in a shack on the outskirts where a tawdry altar with tinny vases of paper flowers attempted a religious background for a rite that was just dull nonsense, evidently cooked up for suckers. The brown girl in the ginger skintight dress had moved indifferently in her dress and he could see her breasts and belly, slow, hard, and provocative under the fabric now. He shoved out the image with a vicious jab of the telephone hook and ordered a pot of black coffee and hurry. This would be the time for the strike to begin after he had waited for days with a perfectly clear head.

The phone rang and he grumbled "hello." If it was that woman he had met in the bar with the guy from Michigan—who talked big as if he were in the know and then when he was tight began to let down his hair— he had his little speech all ready. Let her roll her hoop by herself or words to that effect. What was that guy's name? Industrial munitions. Glennie, the woman had called him, and his mind crisscrossed with Glennie's stories of guys laughing their heads off about business picking up. Every strike meant business and they were ghouls running after the ambulance wagon. Glen Thompson, industrial munitions. Someone had cut off the connection and he shouted impolitely that his phone had been ringing but the next minute Victoria's voice sounding rather excited said, "Can you come over to my hotel? I just got back on the last bus. They've stopped running."

He grabbed his fountain pen and rushed into the boy with the coffee. "Sorry, son," he said, fumbling for a tip and fell over a brass cuspidor. He almost ran across the square, ominously deserted. The shutters on the big bank were down. A woman was trying to duck under the shutter of a drugstore as it rolled down and Lester saw only the *Diario* on the news-stand. So, he thought, that sheet is the mouthpiece, the same gang of crooks who had backed the Spanish government against Cuba in the Spanish-American War. A solitary streetcar manned by a terrified soldier, with another soldier standing behind him with a bayonet, clattered incompetently past. Far up the street a faint haze looked like smoke and curious innocent shots sounded like a premature Fourth of July.

Victoria was in the roof restaurant eating a wizened little fish on a very big plate. An enormous woman giant who toured in vaudeville sat at a nearby table lapping up food from several assorted platters. He sat down at Victoria's table limply while the dirty dishes were being roughly stacked by a frightened waiter with his coat off. "You can get a swell view from here," Victoria said, waving her hand toward the window that looked out on the seacoast. Between the hotel and the sea, houses intervened with shutters down. On a roof, a little dog worried a child's doll and a woman was hanging up pink underwear. A man squinted at the sky where two airplanes were buzzing around and around like giant wasps.

"You had me worried," said Lester pettishly, squinting at her through his headache. "Where in hell were you?"

"How do things look to you?"

"Rotten. They can't win. It's suicidal," and he began

running through the stuff he had picked up from the diplomatic crowd, the bank crowd, the sugar crowd.

She looked at him sharply. He thought she had gotten terribly thin but she was brown and wiry. "The whole island's back of the strike. Except of course the big business interests and their yes-men."

"Listen, they can't win. You can't lick guns with bare hands. Or with little children carrying posters saying we want pencils, we want books, we want milk." He felt as if he would break down and begin howling like a crying drunk. "It's not done, Vicky." He expected a hot argument but she listened to everything. He even began talking of the Chadbourne plan, actually a lockout against labor, and of all the other tricks that had sideswiped the island for a long time. "The sugar crowd got sideswiped, too. Then the bankers couldn't unfreeze the sugar assets; banks folded up, big depositors looted little depositors. The competitive sugar-beet crowd from our own sweet little country and the Philippines put a crimp in things. Besides, get down to brass tacks. Do you think old Uncle Sam is going to stand aside and see the proper people mopped up by a strike that won't do anything but substitute something bad for something still bad."

"Gosh, you're sour," Victoria said. She looked at him for a whole minute. He lit a cigarette and stared back. They ordered black coffee and sat sipping it. "Listen, kid, I like you, but get this. American corporations control around ninety per cent of the cultivable land, one third of the territory, the rest is just about mortgaged to American creditors, the big hunk of the sugar industry is controlled by American capital. Now figure it out. Who owns Cuba?"

They began to quarrel while the waiter took the cloths off the table and a scared boy finished a glass of milk all by himself in a corner. "Where's all your friends? Alquinas and so on. They ought to pop up and tell us something." She said, if he would clear out and let her get her notes in shape, Alquinas would turn up. He said it was too damned bad her friends were so choosey, they hadn't helped him worth a plugged nickel. She looked at him again and began fumbling with her papers. He saw a cablegram fall out and asked idly, "Who's the cable from?" "Jonathan," she said briefly and stuck it out of sight.

Nearly everything had stopped running. They didn't dare take a taxicab for fear of running over tacks or worse. Tolman kept phoning to get an interview with Batista but no one would talk to him. He finally phoned the Embassy but they said poor Batista had been up all night and had just gone to bed. "You see," Lester grinned to Vicky who was sitting uneasily on the edge of her chair. "They know all about him."

He finally got sore and said he was getting nervous and wanted to get off the island. Bland at the other end of the wire yelled at him, "You nervous? What do you think we are?" but he finally promised to see that Lester got out to the barracks and got an interview. He went out and decided to grab a taxi, tacks or no tacks, and have a chat with Bland. Bland was pasty-faced and took him into another room. Mendieta was being anything but firm; the damned idiot wanted to go out to his chicken farm, afraid, no doubt, of assassination. Lester gave a loud guffaw and for the first time thought the strike might win. He asked Bland what he thought about the plain people of Cuba getting a new deal for a change. Bland stared at him and said he had no time for wisecracks. Lester tried to get Victoria on the phone but she had gone out. He felt lost. He had nowhere to go but a bar and no one to see but stuffed shirts. He didn't know why Dr. Barrios had dropped him. Lordalmighty, he wanted to see the Cubans get a decent break for once in their lives but he was a realist. He just happened to know the cards were stacked against them.

Shutters were down on cafés but he got in a sidedoor and in a funny wilted electrically lighted joint called for scotch and soda. Two men shut up and looked at him, whispering suspiciously. He began to get the creeps the way he had in Berlin. "It's the same bloody flux trailing over the world," he thought and wanted to go to bed for a long winter's sleep. The bears had it over mankind; they could snuff out the light for the long hard winter months. It. was winter now in the world and he wanted to forget it. The longing for a home and a wife and children of his own again haunted him and he thought with them around him he could stand the dark. He got back to the hotel just in time to get a call from Bland saying he could see Batista around nine that night. Victoria had left a note. "Please find out what Batista means to do if Mendieta resigns. Find out how he means to break the strike." Lester grunted as he hastily shaved and changed his shirt. "Why, how would he break it except force? Guns. He's got plenty."

It was very late. The curious milky sky might be midnight, it might be four in the morning. The taxi ran up on a curb and stopped. The driver got out and opening the door said, *"Vamos."* "What's that?" said Lester, trying to see the fellow's face that dimmed and receded to his vision. The driver repeated that he would have to walk the rest of the way; a little bomb had exploded in the next block and he didn't care to drive any farther. "That's a hell of a note, a little bomb," and once he had begun to talk Lester couldn't stop. "Just a teeny weeny bomb, well, who could have set that off, did you see anyone running?" but getting no answer he hunted for his money and fished up a dollar bill. The driver took it and without waiting, ducked into his cab, turned it around and made off with a great clatter.

Lester tried to get his bearings; the evening was swirling around him as if he were a swimmer in raging water. He had gone to see Batista, and the heavy face of the ex-sergeant bobbed up with balloon-like swiftness, then the morgue, and the stiff anguished face of the dead boy with the round black hole in his forehead. As he tried to walk, the girl in the ginger dress and without the ginger dress jostled him. He took a deep breath and saw the wide empty square only a block ahead. In the lobby of the hotel a pale porter was shuffling bits of matches and dust into a tiny brass pan with a toy broom. His legs felt bloated and carried him past his own door; with difficulty he turned the ship and pointed her toward shore. When he opened the door, Victoria jumped out of a chair by the window and rushed at him, "Lester, you had me scared to death. Whatever happened to you?"

"Nothing," said Lester unsteadily. "I was in the line of fire, that's all."

"You mean you got hurt?"

"Nope. I saw Batista, that's all. After that I went to the morgue to cheer up and after that," he stopped, remembering the ride to the suburbs, the hunt for the girl in the ginger dress, the smell of *vetiver* in the bed and a parrot croaking like a raven and dropping cracker crumbs in his cage, the obscene rattle of the bird's claws on the bars, the shrill laughter of someone outside and sounds of voices . . . but she hadn't pinched his poke, *Oh Ballocky Bill the sailor, Oh the lady whose name was Lu.*

Victoria was wiping his face with a wet towel and in the far mirror through the yellow light he saw his face, gray and crumpled, worse than a corpse, and no one had found the bodies of the two university students, only a trail of blood where they had been dragged from a car. He rushed to the bathroom and shut the door. If he could only get rid of everything and fill up again on new air like a brand-new tire. Make way for the 1950 model. Victoria was rapping on the door, damn that woman, persistent as a tick. He poked his head out. "Did you want anything?"

"Yes," she said. "Lester, try to tell me what Batista said. It's important. Alquinas is coming to my hotel to find out."

"Write it yourself," said Lester, coming out and dropping in a chair. "You read the papers. You can write the piece yourself. I and the loyal true army are one, me and the people. Papa love mamma. The bad reds. The bad agitators. Naughty naughty."

"The strike," said Victoria. "The strike."

"Strike," echoed Lester. "Of course. Why, poof, like that. It comes, it goes. The magician turns it to smoke. Nowhere can see."

"Oh, God," said Victoria, "why couldn't you keep sober."

"I'm sober," said Lester in a surprisingly sober voice. "I know what you want too. There's nothing new. I told you he'd use force and he will. He has already. He's jailed everybody he can. I doubt if you see Alquinas again. If the strike isn't broken now it will be in a day or so. Force, dear girl, force. Papa love mamma."

He saw her standing before him, she looked tired and thin and as if she were going to cry. He pulled her hand toward him and kissed it softly. "*Küss die Hand, gnädige Frau. Komm gut nach Hause.*" At the German words, her face quivered. "Don't," she said, as if he had hurt her.

He pulled her down on his lap but she struggled up. "Please, Lester, please. I wish you hadn't got tight. I've got to find Alquinas. He's counting on me." She got to her feet, straightened her hair, and for the first time he felt that he saw her face clear, a calm tragic face with eyes that looked at him now imploringly.

"Please, Lester, try to think, didn't you get the slightest hint that would help them? I don't give a damn about anything except to help them." Her voice broke, and she caught herself up, lit a cigarette while he cleared his throat. He felt suddenly ashamed and disliked himself. In a cross voice he said, "No, Vicky, nothing. I'd tell you. You know the setup better than I. Only you're so blooming hopeful I want to cry." He bowed his head and she touched his hair gently. He could feel her hand that seemed to soothe his very heart.

"Stay with me, Vicky," he whispered. "I can't bear to stay alone. Jonathan won't care and I won't touch you, just stay."

"I promised Alquinas," she said, "but let me help you to bed. See, it's easy. Just lie down and go to sleep," and he could feel his body docilely plunge forward, then the sound of his shoes dropping, she was drawing the cover around his chin.

"Shall I sing you a song?" she said softly. "Yes," he whispered, "sing me," and he heard her humming, then words, "Hush, my dear, lie still and slumber," and his eyes closed, he thought he was home again and could hear the gardener run a lawnmower over the grass in the early morning. He held tightly to her hand and when he woke she was gone. A streetcar jangled past and he thought, "God, the strike's over already," and lay listening, but no more came.

THE SHROUD

Don't let's talk of politics," Mrs. Roberts was saying in a pleading voice. "I'm so sick of materialism. What did materialism ever solve?" She looked around brightly, her head poised as if she were a cowgirl on the plains about to slip a lasso over some unsuspecting head, instead of a woman in her Washington home, talking to her guests. Jonathan Chance turned to look at Si.

"I'd like to see her picking pecans just one week. These damned lady bountifuls make me sick."

"Shh," said Si, frowning. "Don't be romantic."

Jonathan shut up and pulled himself back from the doorway. He felt the letter in his pocket that Si had brought along from the office. It would be from Victoria and he would slip off and read it the first chance he got. He must write her, once and for all. The sharp knife was best. Mrs. Roberts had turned her attention to a good-looking young man who had picked up a book. "Recite some of your poetry," she pleaded.

"I don't write poetry," said the young man, turning around slowly and presenting anything but an enthusiastic face.

"Oh, I thought you did. But you look as if you did," said Mrs. Roberts waggishly. "You ought. Someone should."

"Lots of people do," said the young man. "I just don't happen to be one of them."

"Then read us something. Read us that last scene from James Joyce's *The Dead*. It's so poetical, so beautiful. Aren't we all in the mood for a little literature?" She looked around and the young woman in the corner nodded eagerly with a sudden scared look. The young man did not move. The rest looked at Mrs. Roberts who was fluttering toward the bookshelves bent on an evening with the arts. Jonathan had backed into the hall and Si followed him.

"What's the matter?" Si asked. His pleasant composed face irritated Jonathan. He envied Si who seemed to be swimming under heavy water, happy and content. "I just can't swallow this duck soup tonight," he said. "I'm no good for this, Si."

"You got three hundred dollars from Mrs. Bond. And Mrs. Roberts will give us a handout. We got Dick Rudd a secondhand car this morning and he's off to Florida."

"I was going to ask," said Jonathan. "Any word of Williams?"

"Gone like a shot in the dark. A piece of shirt on the bush. His wife thinks the sheriff was among the vigilantes; if we can prove that we've got something. Don't you see how important it is to broaden out? We don't want all our good fighters crucified."

"I don't want them confused either by wondering if they are going to hurt Mrs. Roberts' feelings," said Jonathan. Si looked at him and shook his head.

"Don't let your nerves get you. You ought to straighten up things with Victoria."

"I know," he said.

"You'll not be good for anything until you do," said

Si. "You're the very person for these people. You know how to talk to them."

"I don't," said Jonathan. "That's the trouble. Of course, some of them, Tony Wickham and Glen Toy, but I'm tired of holding Mrs. Bond's hand, figuratively speaking. I don't know what the workers think or feel anymore. Everyone I see eats well; they own cars, have big apartments. It isn't what I set out to do." He shut his mouth. How tell Si that he felt once more as if he were just a salesman. Even if it were no longer for himself alone, or for money, the technique was the same. He had not come to that selfless point of view that considers nothing but the object gained. He did not believe he ever would.

He and Si were standing idly in the little hallway and someone had sidetracked the reading of Joyce's story, *The Dead*. He wondered how many conversations were going on in the same fashion throughout the land, or was his father still meeting with his relatives for a little center-table talk? He wondered if Leslie would be sitting in the big chair, waiting to spring up when the door opened. Thinking of her was like putting out the light and going to sleep, falling into sweet dreams. But the day finally came. He could no longer imagine that in his lifetime he would find any peace. He couldn't go back to the sail-boat days or dream over a fishingrod in Northern Michigan. Neither could any woman restore him to the world of men. He had to go that way alone and in the company he had chosen.

"And if anyone thinks what we call democracy is the final phase, he doesn't understand physics, chemistry, or mechanics. It's only a method anyhow. Did democracy under capitalism give brotherhood? Yet we all dream of it. Blake said politics is only brotherhood. The brotherhood of man. Why do we all dream of it unless it is to be?" Tony was speaking as if in a hall.

"Some people dream of heaven. That doesn't mean they will play harps when they die, does it?" It was the tart voice of the lawyer, Mr. Penner.

"It's not the same, Penner," said Tony. "I'm speaking within the realm of possibility."

Jonathan was thinking of the cellar in the worker's home years ago when his father's workmen decided to go on strike. The friendly faces were beaming upon him, he could feel the cool nose of the dog nuzzling his hand, his own pride that he had gone against his father and sided with the men.

"The laissez-faire program really meant only freedom for trade. Liberalism has always meant simply freedom for a certain privileged class. Now another ruder element realizes laissez-faire is no longer a working technique. And to oppose this rude arrogant monopolist class who want to rule without rules, you have only one strong element, the workers."

"Oh, Mr. Penner, what about us? Aren't we all for helping the workers?" said Mrs. Roberts in a fluttery but sincere voice. She almost looked as if she might cry.

Jonathan turned to Si. "I could do more good somewhere else. I envy Rudd."

"Rudd? Well, that's a tough spot to be in. He's got a tough job but don't think this isn't important."

"Maybe," said Jonathan firmly. "I just can't do it properly." He shut his mouth tightly and took pride in his stubborn resistance. How could he work with conviction when he was constantly arguing with himself? Si had shrugged and was looking through a little notebook. The entire curious pattern of Si's life amazed Jonathan. Si was a firm rock beside which Jonathan seemed only a rolling pebble. Was it a crime to doubt? The only moments in his life when he felt certain had been in Pennsylvania when he could actually see the result of his acts.

Perhaps men like himself were doomed never to become men of action. Only yearners in that direction. He did not like the picture but he looked at it steadily. He was hearing again another conversation. A young man with a stern haughty face was trying to impress everyone with the extent of his radicalism. Shakespeare had no message for this age; one man's notion of truth was unimportant and even presumptuous, organization was the only thing that mattered.

"He must feel guilty about something," said Si in Jonathan's ear. "He worked for Hearst for five years. Is that the secret?" The manner, even more than the words, astonished the little group. Penner said drily that he hoped the speaker wasn't imagining himself superior in ignoring Shakespeare; the tired businessmen of America had always been of that company. A tense discomfort tightened faces. Mrs. Roberts laughed uneasily and Tony turned the conversation toward the expectations of the Liberty League.

Talk. Would he never break free from it? He thought of Jack London whose faith had flickered and paled the longer he had remained away from the source of his beliefs. Surrounded finally by money and talk, he had killed himself. Jack Reed had burned out in Moscow. What would have become of him if he had lived? For some men talk and the routine of organization begins to seem like death. His feeling of guilt about the many vacillations of his life had made him harden his doubts into acceptance of whatever was assigned him. He told himself a job was a job but he could no longer hide his uneasiness. No wonder men rushed even to war. Bookkeepers especially thought Ford the marvel of the age. He made cars. That he broke men was for them a subterranean event, hidden from their eyes that saw only new roads, cars buzzing past, the shiny fronts of salesrooms. A fellow like Williams gets kidnapped; Rudd takes his life in his hands and goes on the trail. For better or for worse, that was the life he wanted. Instead he was only the dressed-up doorkeeper, opening the door for the rich ladies.

He had broken too much in his life and his guilt about Victoria made him conscious of the unopened letter. He reached toward the pocket and touched it as if he had concealed there the ashes of her body.

His brother Tom had burst in upon him on a selling trip, and finding Leslie instead of Victoria had tried to be nonchalant. But in talk with Jonathan he had asked frankly for the facts. Jonathan had assumed a hardboiled manner he did not feel. "Victoria and I are all washed up," he said, and had been annoyed at Tom's "Does Victoria know it?" Then his sister Margaret was writing to him as if he were a baby. His father was "furious," she said, and was changing the much-changed will.

He would leave the little house in the country, not to Jonathan but to Victoria "for life." He thought of it now in the hallway of Mrs. Roberts' apartment, leaning against the wall, and wanted to laugh. He could hear her rip out against his father. She might even burn the place down. He remembered, and knew only too well that Victoria would remember even better, how his father had promised them the place, led them on to put money into it, to improve it with their own hard work. "We worked like peasants," he could hear Vicky say, and now she would feel only a servant to a house, bound to it for life, privileged to keep it in shape, to pay its taxes, to build its repairs, in order to pass it on to the family of the man who had deserted her. As if he were saying farewell to her, looking at her for the last time before the coffin lid is nailed down, he contemplated her at her very best and most frightening, when full of revolt, she had taunted him with never being able to free himself. "Your family spoiled everything. Not by loving you too much but by owning things you might someday have. You might have flung your life into something that mattered, but no, you had to hem and haw." It was true; he had never completely given himself even to his wife and for that very reason she had given herself to Kurt. He saw it all as if he were looking at pictures of himself at school, in college and on his wedding day. He saw his father's ignorant comments about his writing that had so undermined his faith in himself but some men had freed themselves of lack of faith. They did not care for ice or snow or the heat of men's disdain.

No wonder she had loved Kurt. In this last intimate glimpse of her, before he shut the lid, he revived her, her head up, her eyes fiery mad, blazing their deadly blue. Incredible that she could also make herself small, gentle as a kitten, but the hot and cold had cracked his bones. The earth breaks in the thaw of ice and heat and leaves no ease for growing. He had to tell himself that she would remarry again, would revive, but he was already discarding the cold letter he had earlier composed to her. Sentences from it should stand, but were they true? He had intended to say, Leslie and I love one another, it is all I want, so peaceful. At the moment he had composed it, Leslie's arm was around his neck. He determined to say that it was useless to see him, why rake up the ashes, but in his present frame of mind he could think of nothing but the color of her eyes.

Si was putting on his coat. The clamor of voices from the big room had stilled. Someone was reading in a pleasant even voice. Jonathan listened and recognized the words from the story *The Dead*. Once he had almost known the words by heart but the moving scene of snow gently falling over all Ireland had been blotted out in the last few years. He thought of it with real sadness as one might remember a cherished friend from whom one has not heard for a long time. He listened to the beautiful prose gratefully as it softly stirred in him the memory of his wife sitting on the bed in the hotel the night she told him about Kurt Becher. He could see her face as he put out the light, looking so woebegone and lost, and then he saw her in their early years when she had come one night to Reading to surprise him. He had gone to bed early after a discouraging day trying to sell territory that kept books in drugstores next to bathing caps and douche bags. He looked up from a magazine expecting the boy with the icewater, opening to his loud "Come in." Victoria had stood perfectly still in the doorway, like an actress, her hair shining with newly fallen snow, snow on the shoulders of her coat and melting on the gloves upon her hands. Her eyes had flashed at him as if she had come triumphantly over mountains and through gunfire.

He no longer blamed her. If anyone was to blame, he

must blame himself. He wanted to go out and send a cable, BE HAPPY I LOVE YOU, ALWAYS WILL, but he could not do that. It would be more self-indulgence. He must cut the tie, once and for all, if he were not to be completely faithless, if he were to live. The blunders of his life must lead somewhere or he must resign himself like those lost souls who murmur, "What use is it to live?"

On the day Victoria was to leave Cuba she was up and about at five o'clock, packing her bag, sorting her papers, and looking again and again at Jonathan's cable saying a letter waited for her at Miami. The silence in the streets was more terrible than gunfire. It meant the strike had been lost. Alquinas had come only to vanish into the cell of the fortress. All her friends would be in hiding or imprisoned, and as for the other crowd, Lester could take care of them. She never wanted to see them again.

At seven Lester came over from his hotel looking haggard and with a cut from shaving on his neck. He said, "Let's have a little postmortem and then don't forget, you promised to whack all those notes in shape and send them airmail to New York when you get to Miami. I don't see why in thunder you want to go there. I don't see why you can't do them here."

She said she simply had to get off the island. Lester said he didn't want to harp I told you so, but still he was surprised that a woman of her good sense had expected any other end. "It's not finished," she said, pulling on her gloves angrily as if he had insulted her. "It isn't all over. You'll hear of all this again." And she said it so fiercely that he merely said he hoped she wasn't losing her objectivity. She gave a little snort and he asked if she knew that practically every party had been willing to concede something to some other party but the links didn't fit, at least not from up above. Down below, she had seen herself what people thought and if right made might the story would have a different ending. As for

him, after his experience in Germany he simply had to
conclude that right had nothing to do with present-day
events. Looking soberly backward one could hardly feel
that justice had ever triumphed. In fact, he had never
come across justice, philosophically speaking.

His very voice irritated Victoria who began walking up
and down. He seemed suddenly completely boring, and
the hotel clerk and the enormous vaudeville performer
who was rocking violently in a specially built chair
seemed total strangers. One minute she wished she had
money to fly to Miami and the next she was frightened,
wished to put off the time when she would have to find
out the truth.

Once on the boat, her own personal affairs again seemed
petty as the yellow island turned to haze and sank at last
into the sea. She stared after it soberly as if watching all
her friends swallowed up in a vast shipwreck that has
gone down before one's very eyes. Could no one have
saved them? Her friends behind bars might have been
looking at her with solemn haunting eyes, and beyond
the equator, in still another jail, Kurt Becher was facing
her without smiles, with grave intention.

At Miami the crowds of middleaged and old in white
clothes had the look of well-cared-for ghosts who survive
for no purpose and as she waited in line at the postoffice
for the promised letter from Jonathan the idle patter
seemed to come from the other side of a high wall. She was
on one side and they on the other. "Henry, don't you
think we should try that new restaurant in the next block,"
and his, "What's the matter with the old joint?" and, "If I
don't hear from Maud today I'll know something is wrong
at home," might almost have been spoken in another
tongue. Then the line was moving nearer the window. It
was like waiting for news of the patient who has had the
operation. How is he, doctor? Will he live? And she knew
she expected some last-minute miracle. In front of her
the old bodies in neat hats, fresh whitened shoes, spick
and span pocketbooks to match, turned away empty-

handed or laden down with their little spoils, sole evidence of their surviving importance in the world.

Now the letter, very thin, was in her hand and she had moved off with it, keeping it to the last so that she might imagine once more it would begin, *My darling*. It began instead Dear Vicky, and she read to the end, the words jumping, large and ragged. Then she was walking but she could not see where. Though Jonathan was alive, she did not know him anymore. She could not understand what he said or why.

Without knowing it she had walked toward the water, and felt her feet move sluggishly in the heavy sand. If I sit down I will never get up again and it seemed to her that she must keep walking. A storm was coming and would soon break and she must hurry home and shut all the doors and windows. When the storm broke they would have to crouch in the cyclone cellar as they did long ago. Before it came she must hurry and send all the notes she had promised Lester. Alquinas and Vincente had not betrayed her and at that very moment Lino and Navarro might be going over together the circumstance of her visit. She hurried back to the hotel and ran cold water over her wrists. A terrible pounding shook her body and she must hurry for fear something should break inside and she might drown in blood. She sat down and began hammering the typewriter keys. It was like an antidote to poison, the harder she struck the keys, the quieter she became. She pushed back everything, way back, and as if this might be the last deed she would ever do, as if the guns had already been mounted and were training upon that very room, she finished, stuffed the long envelope, put on the airmail stamp and dropped it in the box.

Then she was in the bus and it was pointing North along utopian highways already warped, past sidewalks that were crumbling before houses that had never been built and ornate lampposts with the lights broken studding ragged fields. Houses slapped together in the days of the Florida bubble cracked open to the sky. Then came the long slow reaches of pine and the dark gobbled up all objects. The stars looked too high. She put her hot face to the pane and her tears wetted the glass. Am I a wild animal that he will not see me, she thought, and she did not know how she could bear never to see him or how she was to bear to see him in this changed way. A kind of wonder dazed her. Where had their life gone? What made sense anymore? Her head drummed, her hands were feverish and, when the bus stopped and the driver called, "All out, ten minutes," she did not know what to do with herself. The passengers piled off obediently and she too drank the tasteless coffee and when it was time to go, she was the first in her seat. Where would she go, who could help her? She seemed in a circle, turning around and around like a puppy with a can tied to its tail. Faces blurred and even Kurt Becher had gone out like a lamp in a wind. Then she scolded herself and said, only think if you were a silly timid woman who never had stirred from home, made crocheted doilies and believed in the Holy Trinity, Holy Matrimony, and the Holy Mother of God. But at that she suddenly envied those who could pray. She could not pray and Jonathan had not died in her arms. He was gone without even leaving a grave.

In that return to childishness that despair brings she thought of her mother rolling the dough for pies on Sunday morning, and she was a tiny girl again whose head came just to the top of the table. They had brought her home from Sunday school and she was wearing a little plaid dress with a pocket. In the pocket there was a little handkerchief. She had curls that her mother had made the night before, winding the hair moistened with gum arabic on kid curlers. She was telling her mother the Sunday school story Mrs. Groniger had told the children. It was about Joseph and she had remembered every word because her uncle had been named Joseph too. They had cast the boy into the pit and then they had taken the coat of many colors that the other brothers less loved had envied and dipped it in blood.

She could see herself now as that child and the coat as she had fancied it made of skins of little animals. "The coat," she kept saying, "Joseph's little coat," and her mother had bent down smiling. From that great distance her mother's love only reminded her that she was alone, but she cried no more, the dried tears stung her cheeks. She pushed her hat straight. She thought she could see her life in a crystal ball and it was not the life she had expected. She was caught in wonderment as if she too were on a deathbed humbly asking, "Can this be I?" Something had happened to Jonathan, she did not know what. He had undergone some change as mysterious and complete as Lot's wife, turned to salt. I don't know him anymore and already she began thinking of him as if he had not changed, had merely gone on a long journey, had died. Then she thought she saw him with his arm around another woman laughing at her. She began backing away from him, everything in her very still, and, looking at him gravely, backed toward a cliff. But she was only in the bus and it was running very fast and all the passengers except herself were sleeping. Navarro's wife was looking at her.

"Life is hard with us," she was saying, "the children die," and her mother had looked like that when Rosamond died. "When I think of my mother's sorrows, I can bear this," she had said. Victoria thought how little she had understood then and at this moment, at the very point where her life had failed her, it began to come back to her. She seemed to have been floundering around in the dark and had just seen a tiny light on the other side of a black swift-running river. Navarro's little children, sitting on tiny stools, were again looking at her with big wondering eyes. She had forgot Kurt who had been left in a deeper solitude than she had ever known. She felt ashamed of herself but her strength did not come back to

her. Her hands still felt like stumps that were bound behind her back and she was to wander in a grove with the
pears always too high for her mouth.

I won't forget them, I won't forget them, she promised
and already she was borne up by her own pledge. Navarro
had looped his life to an entire world; was she less able
than he? She would not desert them and they would not
desert her. I have myself, she thought, no one can take
that from me. She would not try to think; the bus seemed
plunging in long waves and the shore was far off. But she
need cry no more since there were those who had shed
blood, not tears. They had fallen in the island left behind her and lay now in prisons or in death; those that
lived waited in silence to speak one day again. She sat
bolt upright and watched the bus run into daylight. The
road and fields were solid ground and the objects of the
earth like sleepy animals were rising to their knees.

If you take me to Kirkwood, I'll get to St. Louis
all by myself: Tortosa, Barcelona Road, 1938

So they think they've got us. I can just hear the papers
in Paris, London, New York all screaming, Franco
drives to the sea. Did Franco get to the Café Gran
Via to drink to his own birthday? Did he turn Madrid to
ashes? Ask the women standing in line off the Puerta del
Sol. Ask the kids peeking down at the ruined black tile
of the Duke of Alba's bathroom. Get the notion out of
your head that life has to be cushioned with ease. That a
flat tire means death. That you can't find coals in the
ashes. Wipe every old notion out of your mind and start
fresh. Right here on this road.

I'm from Missouri; one of you "got to show me" boys.
I got to see, taste, feel proof. Reading does me no good. A
book is only another's lie. Even if it's his deepseated word,
how do I know? I'm one of those fellows that has to look.
Yes, they can shuffle the cards and stuff the deck and draw
every ace but one. They can buy guns and bombs and
bring in a crew from Germany, from Italy to rub us off.
England will snuffle in a corner, France can hide her face.
Hey, I don't want to look, it's too painful. Get it over
quick, what you're going to do. Come, come, it's all for
the best. Nice Mister Franco will save the church, restore
the priests, substitute holy water for land, salutes for
bread. And keep us all safe for another five, ten, fifteen
years. Satisfy the gluttons, spread around the butter of
peace. The smell of death. The sellout.

But they haven't got one little card.

We got the living, they got the dead. There's some guys
won't sell out for a crust of bread.

See that little fellow over there. He won't stop fight-
ing until he's dead. He's only one Spaniard in Spain.
They're all over this country, thicker than fleas. It's going
to be hard to bring them to their knees. That word democ-
racy sure does stink, it means please go away and let me

think. Hands off Spain, let Hitler and Mussolini ride. She'll bounce hell out of their old backside. She'll give 'em one swell ride.

They're trying to scare the world sure enough: Paris will be blotted out, London will be blotted out. Did they blot out Madrid? I don't say they can't. But did they? Did they win after two years? The women are still having kids in this land. The goats are dropping their two cents. The grapes are ripening on the vine; wait for the wine. You can see the vines right next the shellholes, cradled in the ribs of rock, every little handful of earth so precious you had to say a prayer to get the vines going. That's what started the whole damned thing. They were telling the peasants to scrape the dust off the rocks and sprinkle it with holy water and maybe it would grow a grape in one spot, and in another, the Dukes were chasing wild boar in miles and miles of woodland playground. Take your kiddie car elsewhere. Root out the hogs if you want the workers to live. Or else give up, make a clean proposition for slavery.

Here they come, some baby. Let 'em drive to the sea. What can they do with the ocean? See that head. So, we're up against our old pals the Moors. So long, Al, I'll be seeing you.

COAL OF FIRE ON ICE

LESTER TOLMAN in a new dark blue suit, shirt the color of grapes, striped tie of heavy silk, and in a Ford V-8 drove up to New York from Washington on an average of once every two weeks. It was a pleasure to drive slowly down Fifth Avenue, especially at dusk; the tall buildings at that hour suited the picture, became properly softened, and from a car seemed only a fitting background to this modern age. He liked to catch an occasional glimpse of himself, his hair graying but the face lean and long. He had shaved off his little mustache, this was not the 1920's anymore when everyone coming back from Europe held to a mustache as the last vestige of the days now behind them. Everything about his car pleased him, the shiny metal trimmings, the little traps to hold a half-used pack of cigarettes or playing cards—although he never played and considered it a bore, gambling was another matter—roadmaps, and a woman's white glove stained with lipstick.

If he stopped at the Brevoort terrace, he could almost imagine himself back in Paris and it was practically the only place where one might hope to run into an acquaintance. Time after time, Lester drove hopefully to the big city only to find everyone vanished. The phones were dead, the doorbells did not work, the lights were out. He had simply to wander into a bar and ponder over the miserable desert men had made. Everyone had run into their holes like gophers on the prairies, they had gone out of town as he came in, they had entered the theatre as he was leaving, and a man could drop dead and a policeman would order an ambulance as if he were calling a cab for a drunken sailor. Take the body away.

He did however have two friends he counted on with fair regularity. One was Bischman, the well-known lawyer, who was practically always at home in his huge apart-

ment where he lived with his mother storing up bits of
Marxist literature, some rare items fit for a museum, paint-
ings that might one day become famous, and curiosities
in carved wood. It soothed Lester to call upon his friend
who had the undisturbed appearance of a Buddha and
handled his little objects tenderly as if they were lovely
women. Lester passing through the hall to his friend's
study would feel the gimlet watchful eye of old lady
Bischman and, daring to turn his head and bow, catch
a glimpse of a castiron coiffure and a stern face set rigidly
in the frivolous background of three old ladies in lace
who seemed always to be shuffling cards and calling out
"I pass."

The men would sink down in cavernous chairs, Bischman would offer a cigar and Lester would refuse. Or
Bischman would occasionally pour old Napoleon brandy
into big balloon glasses and in a crisp voice talk about
Washington, the New Deal, the new C.I.O. development
in labor, and the darkening of Europe. Lester would rise,
shake his shoulders irritably and shout, "It's too much. I
want peace. I tell you it's becoming a madhouse," and
Bischman would raise his eyebrows and say, "Calm yourself. Why don't you marry?" and Lester would wonder
why he did not marry, why women seemed always to slip
through his fingers, became useless just as they had become valuable, haunted him and became boring. He
talked lingeringly of Elsie Forey who had finally gone
to Hollywood, and persuaded himself that he had really
had a great love affair with her. It was too lonesome
otherwise.

Then he persuaded himself that he was really a kind
of Don Juan and he liked to call on Eleanor Tyde, a
young woman painter, and laugh with her over details
of his various love affairs, real or imagined. She would
swing her head, looking at her work with eyes half-shut
while he talked, putting a touch here, a touch there, while
he prowled around watching the white nape of her neck,
her long hands, and the shape of her face that reminded
him of Botticelli's Venus rising from the sea. His skin

would feel hot, his hands moist, he wondered if he should make love but she had a way of laughing that made him feel slightly ridiculous. He fell back more and more upon his work and its importance grew in his eyes. He appreciated his job in a department of the government whose influence was not obvious but far-reaching, in short, he fed newspapers, journals, and radios the facts about the New Deal. Every now and then he was moved to genuine enthusiasm. Photographs sent from Kentucky of young girls packing books over mountains, of young children fed in nursery schools, of theatres and music reaching millions. He had the illusion of culture sweeping the country, of light brought to darkness, and he got angry with the skeptical barroom arguments that jeered at these sound projects. He flattered himself he was in the great stream, and squabbles in New York about the internal difficulties in the labor movement angered him as if they were part and parcel of the folly of the Middle Ages where ecclesiastics had spilt blood over the number of angels on the point of a needle.

When Victoria Chance accused him of hiding his head like an ostrich, he shuddered, shouted he had a right to live his life as he pleased and was glad to return to Washington where couples sat at home in the evening and gave parties where the men played chess and chowder was served at a late hour. He told himself that Washington was the hotspot of the nation, that the fate of the very world was being dealt behind doors, but although this might be true, he did not actually see the cards or hear the remarks, or witness the shuffling of the deck. He just felt he was in the midst of things although he might as well have been sitting in his mother's garden in Vermont with the New York *Times*.

He had to feel in the swing of things and who could blame him? Certainly Victoria Chance did not. They had written the sugar articles and a series on Cuban politics for the New York *Post* that was talked about for a few days. Lester had been fired from his job and in a sulk had sat for days in a hotel room. Then he had moved to a rooming house and finally on Hudson Street he slept almost all day on an iron bed, read thrillers, and went unshaved. His mind went dead, he could hear the insects in the old plaster of the walls. On the floor above a drunk argued over and over with his wife about the fate of the world and a kid cried. He heated beans over a Sterno, imagined he might starve, and took pleasure in thinking of a corpse, found almost a skeleton, in the locked box of a New York room. Then he was bored, longed again for the sun, sat in parks and talked with men who joked about prosperity around the corner or who sat as he did, staring at their shoes or waiting to grab a newspaper left by a nearby bench. He would have liked to be taken off to a hospital, there to lie as if on a ship that is cut off from land, irresponsible to the duties of the world that could go to hell for all he cared and the sooner the better.

He began to cry easily and, rescued at last, thought of the weeks spent alone with a sort of pride. Friends saw him with surprise and asked, "Where have you been?" When told of his sufferings they looked at him as if he were crazy and wondered why he had not come to them for a loan. Now he was on sound land again, he wondered himself, a little sheepishly, but he continued to tell the story of how he had nearly starved as if he had faced some genuine crisis.

If he had been a genuine pénitente he could not have felt more purged, and when he got the chance to go to Washington it seemed to him only right that he should be compensated for what he had gone through. He even promised himself a rich book out of his experiences and it was disturbing when he was installed in the capital to find so many other men promising themselves the same reward. He lunched with congenial companions and got into a hot argument with a man in his own department over the respective merits of Chekov's *The Cherry Orchard* and Tolstoy's *The Power of Darkness,* Tolman siding with Tolstoy and clinching his defense with a vivid description of the play in which one could fairly hear the crunching of the bones of little children.

He lost track of what he had set out to do in the world, of what he hoped to become. He felt he was doing a solid job grounded in his own self-respect but he found himself unable to believe that conservation, planning, a patch here, a patch there, were going to fix up the great new world that under man's very eyes had suffered such changes. Then he soothed himself with long conversations with taxidrivers, newsboys, bootblacks, and picked up young hitchhikers whose stories he retold in Washington with excitement and indignation.

Once he overheard two men at lunch at the Carlton laughing about what damned fools they had been in their youth. One was a newspaper owner and the other had the round eyes, round paunch, oratorical manner of a politician. They were roaring over the "vapid illusions of youth" and as the scraps of talk reached him, Tolman suddenly felt sick. He wanted to hit out at them and for a second had visions of throwing up his job and romantically becoming an organizer in the new growing labor movement. They were simply putting the lid on "socialistic nonsense," consigning to the garbage pail the skins of fruit they had enjoyed consuming.

He walked slowly back to the office. Labor will stem the tide, he told himself, labor will save the day, and he wondered the next moment whether labor would really rouse in time to save the magnificent machine that seemed to be rusting. Germany continued to haunt him and sometimes, when he thought of Cuba, his feet got cold, a heavy oldfashioned clock like the one in the hall in his childhood home seemed to be ticking loudly. Uneasily asleep, he often dreamed of graves and tombstones falling down.

He listened apathetically to young Jim Agnew, lately arrived in Washington. "It's no use keeping your eye on the Versailles Treaty or asking was Wilson a betrayer or betrayed. You were too young even for marbles when it happened and now you keep mulling around in the rubbish. It happened and if anyone had lifted a finger to help democratic Germany it wouldn't have fallen like a plum to Hitler. Now all the democracies are beginning to bellow. They see the writing on the wall. It's hypocrisy. And in my opinion the democracy in Germany that fell, deserved to fall. Didn't it behead the workers? We can do absolutely nothing. Nothing. It only makes martyrs to oppose it. Stop the dam one place it runs up over the wall somewhere else. Ever see a river on a rampage?"

"The Connecticut," said Agnew.

"Well, they say dikes, dams, all sorts of scientific contrivances can control flood. But human beings, that's different. They won't submit to science. On the contrary, they are always opposed to it. They have even rebeled at vaccination, always doubt the possibility of change. I see a small and hopeful minority getting swamped with the flood. What can unarmed men of will do against arms? And arms they themselves created? It looks black. You talk about the militant worker but he doesn't act quick enough. Guns are faster." He could again hear the crackle of machine-gun fire on a Havana street. His nerves tingled and he would feel that he was only maintaining sanity to forget it, to smile and to run his finger lightly over his upper lip as if it still bore a mustache.

Then he would spend a long time in the bathroom warbling, *Did I remember to tell you that I adore you,* while he bathed and thought of the little girl in green he had taken out the night before. He would emerge in black tie, and pretending to ask for a match, show himself off to Agnew on his way to some shindig from whence he would return very late, a little wilted, a little tight, a little sour, but not too weary to read the headlines on the early morning paper that he had bought as he came in.

Forgetting his moral exhaustion he would again rouse, shout, "Christ, why doesn't someone do something? What's the matter with England, with France? Why is Litvinov the only one to speak? Why can't they let Ethiopia at least buy munitions so she can defend herself? Do they want to line the world up along the wall before the bandits?" and then he would drop the paper. His face would turn pale and in a thick and broken voice he said, "Yes, the governments do not represent the people anymore. All bandits," and he sat with his chin sunk down, unable to bear the vision. "Where are the workers? Why don't they make more noise, why do they always let themselves be sold down the river and, too late, find out the reason why. Where are the leaders? We don't want postmortems. Before the fact, not after," and he tore his hair as if he alone were before some bar of justice, answerable for the fate of the world. Then his constant burning *whys* seemed like so much useless tallow and he would be silent for days, easing his conscience by giving money to causes, his nerves worn with the bustle of constant talk. Oh, give him a book to read in peace. He at least could not swallow slogans as if they were capsules; take this, take that. Feeling better? Try this.

Even puffing himself up with hints of little intrigues did not soothe him.

Agnew was trying to save money, he did not know precisely for what. He would like to get married. He had barely escaped the fate of some of his best friends who were mowing lawns, picking up odd jobs as they could in the home town of his birth. He liked to read the papers that discounted the pessimism of certain groups and constantly printed cheerful news about business picking up and how much better off this country was than the rest of the world. *Which nobody can deny,* he sang. He envied Lester his European past, his escapades, real or imagined, and Lester envied Agnew his extreme youth. When Huey Long was shot, it was Lester who cried, "Thank God, not a minute too soon," and tore up the morning paper to celebrate.

Then it was running into the elections again and Brown Derby Al was up Du Pont's alley. Cries of America, America, rang through the land, new rallying-point of old betrayers. The Spaniards were fighting Spaniards in Irun and there's a fortune for anyone who can think up a new place for a watch. Some suggest the toe but not useful to dancers. For young men of ideas America remains the fertile land of opportunity. Look at Europe and be grateful. One hundred thousand workers in Paris stormed

to strike if France did not aid the government in Spain
and reports came in of the love feast of Alf Landon, oh,
Susanna, and F. D. R. with the old F. D. R. charm at Des
Moines where each outdid the other. Pretty good fishing
up the Potomac and if you don't call on me I'll call on
you. One hundred were seized in Vienna for circulating
propaganda for the Spanish government and Mrs. Beryl
Martin, London society woman, anxious to be the first
woman to fly the west passage was sighted sixty miles from
Newfoundland in her blue plane as dark fell over the
Atlantic and a storm broke; rains came down at last in
the dustbowl of Kansas, Missouri, and Oklahoma.

A black Italian airship put into Spain to avenge one
obscure Italian citizen, said to have been killed. Bombs
fell on women and children.

Agnew's sister's husband's uncle came to Washington
from Cincinnati. He was a Reverend and Agnew and Tolman went to the home of another Reverend to see the
old man. He was beaming and expansive. In a large over-
sized collar, stiff ministerial white tie, false teeth, with a
gentle smile on a stern and forbidding face, the Rev. Apledore presented his wife, considerably younger, in a snuffy
brown silk with frills of lace and frizzed hair. Determined to be sweet and agreeable or die, she smiled at
the two young men and they asked how the couple liked
Washington. "Oh, fine," said Rev. Apledore. "Simply wonderful," said Mrs. Apledore. The Reverend's friend, Rev.
Bainbridge, sniffed and said, "Washington is the most
beautiful American city." Then they were all sitting in
a stiff circle and the conversation was veering shyly to
politics. Agnew kicked Tolman discreetly but it was too
late, he had already boldly plunged with a question about
the vote in Cincinnati. "Oh, everybody in our town voted
for Landon. That is, the thinking people, the bankers, the
best people, the substantial people of money and means,
voted for him but of course the Negro vote was bought

and then the big relief rolls and the machine rolled up the democratic vote." He smiled sugarly and Rev. Bainbridge asked if he had ever heard the story about Dinah. Rev. Apledore said that people in their pride come down. The King of England, the most popular monarch of his day, had come down. "Yes," he said. "Bonaparte came down. I expect Roosevelt to come down. Mussolini is due for a fall, not that I don't give him credit for doing some good and cleaning up the country."

"Mussolini had to rise by burning the Old and New Testament, Hitler burned the Old Testament. You can't stay high and flaunt the will of God," said Rev. Bainbridge, looking solemnly at his visitors. Tolman stared at Agnew who asked for a cigarette. He lit it and Tolman lit one for himself. Then Agnew began looking around for an ashtray.

"You can't flaunt the constitution, either," said Mrs. Apledore.

"It's all prophesied in the Bible," said Rev. Apledore, stroking his thin hair that wound precariously around his skull like a long skein of silk. "It's all there. The pagan states will fall like the chaff from the wheat. The ten horns of paganism."

"Did you hear that one about Dinah," persisted Rev. Bainbridge. "A colored man was asked how he come to marry Dinah. He scratches his head and then he says, why, when I first saw her I fell for her because she was so handsome, and second, when I heard she was doing twelve washings, I just naturally gave her my heart."

"Pretty good," laughed Rev. Apledore. "Wonderful happy folk, the Negroes. Just naturally lighthearted and when they know their place you can't get a better servant."

"That's right," said Rev. Bainbridge. Agnew said he and Tolman had a date. "You young men," wagged Rev. Apledore, but his face became gentle as he said, "The poor king. Did you hear his broadcast? I don't believe in divorce but I felt sorry for the young man." Tolman said he had enjoyed meeting someone from the heart of America. "It is the heart, isn't it?" he said, but Agnew was already edging toward the door. Outside he said, "What did you say that for?"

"What should I say? Cry over the king of England?"

"No, but you know Cincinnati isn't the heart of the nation."

"It might be. I was thinking of something else all the time those two old buzzards were talking. I kept hearing Roosevelt. *We have a rendezvous with destiny.*"

"Yes," said Agnew. Both took deep breaths of the good fresh air. "But what destiny? The Reverends' destiny, the destiny of the House of Morgan or of the workers? Hitler's destiny? It reminds me of that poem, written by the poet who died in the War. I don't mean *Trees. I have a rendezvous with death.* It's all right for you. You're edging out of the draft age. But I'm twenty-five."

"Destiny," said Tolman again. "A wonderful word. Destiny. Only man's intelligence can connect him with destiny. Otherwise, to quote your sister's husband's uncle or the uncle's friend, Rev. Apledore, I forget which is which, man is chaff in the wind."

"He is anyhow, if he is dead," said Agnew. "Or in jail."

"You're wrong. Dead, yes. But even then don't you think the way he dies is important? As for jail, we are all in jail."

"Balls," said Agnew. "You'd know it if you were in jail." But Tolman wasn't going to take anything from Agnew. "I was in Cuba," he began. "I saw jails with women and men stuck in pens with the air so thick you gagged and the women whores were right out like birds in a cage with a pisspot in the middle of the room so anyone could watch. Don't tell me about jails. You lose everything in jail. You go to pieces."

"Dimitroff didn't go to pieces," said Agnew. He was staring at the bottles in a window, Green River, Bonded Belmont, Four Roses, Golden Wedding, what lovely names, and he could see a wonderful river flowing with canoes and girls and boys calling to one another.

"Christ cried on the cross," said Tolman. "He broke down and wept."

"He wept in the garden, not on the cross. On the cross He asked God to forgive the fools." They had both remained fixed, staring in the window, and Tolman showed no further disposition for argument.

"My dear Dr. Apledore," said Agnew. "You first."

"After you, Bainbridge," said Apledore Tolman, holding open the door to the bar.

DOOMSDAY

"FOR GOD'S sake, calm yourself, Ed," said Spencer Gibbons nervously.

"Don't make me laugh," said Ed Thompson. He was walking up and down and his face, usually florid, had grown livid. Now and then he stopped in his stride and stared steadily at himself in a little mirror hanging on the wall. It made Spencer increasingly nervous to see a man stare at himself that long. He would even finger his tie, run his hand over his hair, and, continuing to talk, watch himself as if he were an actor learning a part. Only there was nothing of the actor about Ed Thompson and his expression wasn't that kind of an expression. He was simply looking at himself as if he were staring at another man. He whirled upon Spence.

"Did I or did I not say two years and more ago, three years, that if we didn't capture the political machine we were up against it?"

"Sure," Spence said uneasily. "I remember your saying it."

"Good," said Ed. "I'm glad you remember. What's happened? Our plant, plants all over this area, Flint, Detroit, are taken over. Just like that." He snapped his fingers. "And we can't get action. Why? We got an anarchist in the State House that's why. An Irish Catho-

lic traitor. I did everything. Tried to think of everything.
We've got co-operation from every big plant in the state.
God, even Knudsen is caught with his pants down." He
began laughing. "I'll tell you why. We're still old rubber
stamps, that's why. Living in the past. I saw this flood of
sentimental legislation coming but I didn't take it seriously enough. Even the newspapers aren't realistic anymore. They've been yelling that labor had given Roosevelt a mandate. Makes them feel chesty. Why, the whole
damned country stinks with little spindly workers standing on their hind legs."

"Well, Ed, it's not that simple," began Spence.

"Oh, don't talk to me. You and Rex Short. It's fellows
like you who stand aside washing your hands who let
things get to this pass. The public? It's just a bunch of
sheep, following the winner. If we make the moves fast
and win, they follow us. Now they are actually sticking
up for the strikers. Why, they actually had a meeting saying they didn't want cars with blood on them. So the
Governor won't order the National Guard in there to
clean them out. What's the law for?"

"You know as well as I do he can't get them out without bloodshed. And I said all along you guys weren't
making yourselves popular with the public by refusing
to talk things over with Lewis."

"Lewis. There's the rub. We managed it all right until
he popped. Why, I had the plant in complete control.
We busted things as fast as they happened. Pop goes the
weasel, just like that. I don't see yet how he got started.
For one thing he pulled a strike without more than a
handful back of him. I'm trying to look at this reasonably and learn something. I don't want to just yell. It
was successful, see. He got the fellows sitting down and
the rest liked it. He worked out some wonderful tactics.
I got to hand it to him. They can make forts out of a
plant. That's another thing, and the thing works, see, so
it spreads."

"It's sure spread, all right," said Spence gloomily.

"What I can't get over," said Ed, "is that it had to

happen in the season. Just as we were picking up. They howled about hard times so long and the second we give them some jobs, they sit down and quit. Want to be organized. We got to have our union. Mamma's titty ain't good enough." He made a contemptuous face that almost immediately crumbled. He sat down at the desk and put his head on his hands.

"You know what Rex Short did this very morning? Called me up and asked if I was coming to the weekly luncheon? I didn't even answer, just hung up the receiver."

"It would do you good, Ed," said Spence. "Why don't you come around to the house now? It'll be quiet. We can have a few drinks and it will soothe your nerves."

"Can't, Spence. I'm waiting for a guy now. Thank God, we got a few friends in the city government here. I can tell you right now we can deputize a few fellows to handle this ourselves if the Governor doesn't want to act. But it's the future I'm concerned about, more than this. All my work did no good. That's what hurts me. It's just like a good general who has everything in mind. Ammunition. Strategy. And he's in the right too. Then he gets a flank surprise attack. He's scattered and everyone runs down the hill. Well, we ain't running down the hill, but I admit they've won the first round. How does Ford do it? He has an iron hand. And he's responsible to no one but himself. We're like mongrels. I've said all along, give an inch and they'll take an ell."

Spence felt completely inadequate. The excitement Ed felt had distracted him from the situation to Ed himself. They were about the same age. Ed was a little younger. What kind of a world were they heading into? He had contemplated some peaceful years. Building up a fine library and finally bequeathing it to the state college at his death. Music and growing old with his wife. Now his wife was seldom at home. He did not want to think; darkness pressed on his eyes. His daughter was gadding with a boy whose father no one had ever heard of.

"Business has been given the run around," said Ed. "I
never thought I'd see the day when our own plant would
be shut against us. It's all a European idea. Part of the
humanitarian scheme that merely sabotages business with
a lot of sentimental nonsense. When it's sabotaged long
enough, then watch out. Before that comes we have to
get control of the machinery again. Can you imagine
this happening if Hoover had been in the White House?"

The one small desk light shed a curious reflection on
Ed's face. He looked suddenly disappointed, boyish, like
a kid who has gone to the old swimming hole to find it
has mysteriously gone dry. He was thinking of his whole
life, of Margaret, of his self-denial, of his loyalty to his
home and his business. He had put everything he had,
as the saying is, into one basket. And that basket proved
to have a hole in the bottom. It wasn't even his basket.
A lot of brainless workers were grabbing it as if they
had a right to it. The world was crazy and he felt grieved,
a deep sense of persecution began to haunt him. He
wished Spencer would get out and not even say good-by.
There was a mild timbre about the man's speech that
irritated Ed. It suggested weakness and from somewhere
he must, at this crucial moment, gather strength.

THE EARTH DOES MOVE

HE WOKE with a jerk. His head had rolled off the
cotton waste to the icy cement floor of the plant.
Steve Carson pushed the waste back under his
head, stretched cautiously on the mat of waste under his
body and strained to see in the long dim room. It must
be nearly six o'clock in the morning, the hour when he
would, on other days, be gulping down his breakfast, hurrying into his coat and crunching over the stiff snow to
check in before the line started up on the first shift. A
light from outside flickered on the ceiling and the long

line of windows facing the street glittered in a dimmed glare. The soldier boys were keeping up their fires.

In a few minutes he would get up and walk over to the window to look at them. Last night before quieting down, a long line of men had stared out the windows at the huddle of young kids in uniforms stacking rifles, looking like a picture in the paper of how to play soldier. The guns had barrels, they were real. At the corner of the street, the kids had been busy playing fort. They had mounted two machine guns into place, had roped off the street and a nice tall kid could be seen strutting up and down, busy pacing off the hours of his duty.

It didn't look real. It was real. By the long window now looking at the fires in the street were Fred and Charley, keeping guard. He could see their heavy legs a little apart, the shape of their skulls, the inert position of their arms. They weren't talking, only looking. It was pretty quiet. The steam had been shut off, the electricity was off. It had been cold and dark as the tomb. This was the sitdown strike.

This was what it was like. Not like you thought, but like this. The excitement of it was churning inside him like watching a big newsreel of the world, like looking at a history of your own life. He lay still. Ike McGee was breathing hard through his mouth, Willy Benson was snoring like a locomotive. Last night the guys hoisted up on slabs looked as if they were laid out in a morgue. The rest had piled on the floor on top of cotton waste. The steam bath where you washed the acid off metal was still piping hot. They laid planks on top of the steam and the boys lay on the planks roasting the cold from their bones. Today they would make a fight for some heat. They might threaten to make a fire inside. Last night they had just dropped down where they could. Everybody wanted a turn on the steam bath. "Hey, me next," and it had sounded like a lot of kids up in a mountain camp playing tricks on each other like you see it in the rotogravure. "This is our cheerleader," they wrote on a tag and tied it around Joe Polaski's ankle when he was laid out on his slab. It was a job to quiet down. The din of the big trucks moving around, getting into place along the windows by the river, hummed in your head. For hours the big crane had swung trucks, three high and three deep for a barricade. The heavy noise of the trucks moving had pounded like great big feet.

The boys were lying all over the place now, looking flattened and empty but by the window he could see by Fred's and Charley's legs what a man looks like. A man gets smaller as he gets older in this game. Steve was twenty-five but before a man is forty he is out. Out you go. No time to spit. Here's your time card for taking a drink. For talking. Get going. If the union is so smart, let it take care of you.

The union. A warm glow rushed over his body under his stiff clothes as if he were looking out at the street again late yesterday afternoon just after the plant shut down. That was some smart trick. For two days the whisper had gone around that they would pull Plant No. 9 at four in the afternoon. All the dicks and thugs had run to be on hand. Even the boys in that plant thought they were pulling the real thing. But *this* was the plant that was important. Right here. There hadn't been a minute to lose. They were beginning to move out the machines; the old trick that always beat the union. So they had to work fast. It was smooth sailing. When the boys began sitting down, the company dicks were at Plant nine. But outside, what a commotion. The second they got wind and the foremen were kicked out, the police began coming down. Then the women popped out of the ground from nowhere, locking arms, backing themselves up against the gate.

Steve was going over and over it in his mind, the high moment when the union sound-truck began talking to the boys inside right over the heads of the police and the company yes-men milling around in the crowd like specks of pepper. What a wonderful invention a sound-car was. It had talked right out loud, and he heard again Jerry Stauffer's voice, almost as even and clear as if he

were talking to them earlier in the year in the basements
of fellows' homes, telling them not to be scared, that they
had their constitutional rights and must fight for them.
He was talking yesterday just like a general back of the
lines, giving orders like in a war, *"Watch the doors, guard
the windows, look out for the overhead passage, barricade along the river, we are with you,"* and then the boys
had crawled along the scaffolding connecting the two upper stories. Some company sniper might be hiding there
waiting to shoot. They had crawled, single file, like Indians hunting for a phantom army. But the phantoms had
gone.

The men were pushing out the foremen through the
back doors. "Hey, get going, you guys." The foremen
turned ashy. Not the boys, the foremen. Not some fellow
told to turn in his tools and beat it, he wasn't any good
anymore after using himself up so fast for twenty years.
Run along with your old creaky bones, peddle them somewhere else. Try to get on a charity list in your old age. If
you live that long. Old bones and old rags for sale. Oh,
Christ, it was bitter.

He'd seen his own cousin Charley Egstrom get it in the
neck. And what about himself? They hadn't welcomed
him with a band when he went back to Chicago, had
they? They didn't hang any roses around his neck and
say, "Welcome home." Not on your life. Nothing doing
for you, kid, beat it. We got no use for guys like you.
Go on, let your union take care of you. This plant is for
fine loyal workers willing to keep their mouths shut and
work like we tell them, we're protecting such guys. You
mean to say a guy can't work in this country? Without
the o. k. of some snotty union. Peddle your stuff somewhere else. And he had got himself to Michigan. Every
day he'd got it taken out of his own hide, pitching into
the speedup like the house was on fire and you ran around
tossing everything out the door and windows trying to
save it before the flames got it. Tearing the carpet off
the floor, the bed, the baby's crib. The baby. His own kid
seemed to be putting his spoon in one eye and laughing

at him, making faces. This is for you, kid, too. Maybe this was the way men felt when they went to war, holding all their life in one hand, like water, fearful that someone might jog the elbow and spill it so it would be gone forever. Well, they had the goods on the foremen now.

They couldn't go on saying how they never tried to get the men to join *their* organization, as long as joining was such a sin. The little cards had fallen right out of their coat pockets, the files they hadn't time to close gaped with their secrets. They had little files with all the secrets written down in black and white. They had cards to sign up the boys in the yellow organization that was claiming to represent the "good workers" who were just dying to work for their company and never ask for anything. Oh, sure, the foremen wouldn't dirty their lily fingers with a union; they'd only sneak around trying to scare guys and sew them up with promises.

As if they didn't all want to work. Hell, if a man gets wrung through the speedup wringer it's all he's good for. He's no mortal good to himself or to his wife anymore. All he wants is to hit the hay when he gets home and he's a bundle of muscles shaped like legs and arms, and the second the whistle blows, the line starts up, he begins moving like he was wound up in back and doomed to jerk up and down until the toy can run no more.

Whoever thought to see such a sight? He snickered remembering the foremen running like rabbits. Thought this was their last stand. It was all UP. No time for their lunch pails. A run for your life. The boys had cleaned up the lunch pails last night but none of the fellows would so much as touch the company canteen. They could have left money for the cigarettes and the candy, but no, sir, don't touch it. Don't buy off the company, fellows. Don't take a stick of gum or one cigarette. You'll never hear the end if you do. Such a squawk will go up as will deafen you. They're touching our property. They're destroying our valuables. Wait for the union, boys, they'll take care of us.

Then the men were clearing the decks for godknows-what action. The big crane was humping around with a truck dangling in its jaws. A jab here, a jab there, delicate as a finger and the tiny truck settled down, truck on top of truck. Try to break through that, you bastards. Shoot if you can.

Shoot. They might. The guns were real. The word die emerged cold and strange and new to his mind. Serious business was on the table. They mean business. We, the workers, mean business. Take your choice, ladies and gentlemen. The line forms to the left and to the right. On your right, a nice bit of concrete, steel, stone. On the left, only men. Here you have two assortments, take your pick. No, lady, we can't give you a mixed assortment. We can't mix the goods today. Don't crowd, sir. Easy. Plenty of time. In his mind he could see the men lined up for their tool clearance, their pants baggy in the rump, their shoulders sloping, their faces sweated up and streaked. Big guys and little guys, tough and stringy, all tired to the bone. Dog-tired, heads hanging, homeward bound. In old tin cars, straphanging on streetcars, or in second-hand cars or cars that would take a couple of years to pay off, riding around so the wife won't take it so hard. Would they shoot?

He could hear the click of a gun but that had been his own gun back home in South Dakota getting ready to pop off a fat pheasant streaking through the edge of wheat or a rabbit bounding over toward the buttes. Did a bullet going through a man tear the same kind of hole? He thought of the hole, round and bloody, the skin ripped out, the hole that looked so small and so fatal in a rabbit or a bird.

Men shot men in war. Make no mistake, we are now at war. The bright blue burning of the acetylene torches as the men welded plates over the door with openings for hoses to go through, blazed again in front of his eyes. He went over the events of the last twenty-four hours, turned backward to his whole life, full of wonder that the tools of a man's mind are brightest when he meets danger. He hears words all his life, sees sun, tables, cars, streets, and then he looks down the barrel of a gun. His whole life swoops up into his face as if he had taken off in an airplane at dawn. He can pick out the things he knows with amazement. So that's what a horse looks like. And his own life sticks out sharp and clear, as if, now he might lose it, he was privileged at last to look at it, handle it like a jackknife he'd never rightly had the use of.

"I'm a lucky man," he thought, seeing his whole life spin out, fitting itself together, wondering how a man in danger begins to look at himself almost for the first time and now he may soon go out like a light, he wants to understand how it has happened and how he came to be. He thought of himself in the cyclone cellar and his mother's cold hand growing colder, then his father's voice with its indignation against the wrongs in the world. He had escaped death from the cyclone but now if he should die, he at least knew why. He searched in his pocket for a bit of paper to write a word to Lorraine. Oh, my dear wife, my darling, and it seemed to him he had never loved her so much as now, lying on this cold stone floor with all the men around him who were thinking his same thoughts.

This is my job, he thought, and he seemed to see his job like a box that could be carried in his hand. Nothing elegant like a doctor's medicine kit or a lawyer's briefcase or a dentist's elaborate shiny tools. Just a job, like a brick, at the foundation of a skyscraper. Not a fancy job, just the run of luck that most men had. A job at the bottom where a man had to feel a man if there was to be any sense to the world. A job belonged to a man, more than a wife or child or mother. He had to have it to live and the world, much as it might pretend he was nothing to it, had to have him.

The men were stirring. One fellow was sucking the end of a pencil, hunched up over a letter to his wife. These are the facts of my life, Steve thought, fitting the last piece together. Over by the window the boys still stood on guard. Steve got up and his feet felt like clods of iron; his legs creaked as he stretched but he grinned at Fred.

"They'll be bringing us some grub soon," Fred said, and sure enough, the union would find a way. The men were thinking of the union, shyly, proudly, with all the loyalty they had. Steve's throat hurt as he thought. He could remember a dozen things, the foremen mocking at Jerry Stauffer, "You got too much piss and vinegar in your blood. Why don't you let the peaceful guys who are satisfied with their life alone?" He was seeing the fellows from Saginaw with their heads cut open by the company thugs. Hey, get back to your line, quit trying to be something. Even if they won this round, no one need think it over. It would just be beginning and the bosses knew all the tricks, could make favorites, say honeysweet things. "Why, Mr. Barker, we were planning such a nice future for you. We were just going to suggest you take our foreman's course and work up. We simply don't understand how you come to be dissatisfied and join the union. Can't we talk it over?"

The fire outside had made a big black scar in the white snow and the young guards, looking more than ever like kids at play, were passing around cups of something hot. "Wish our fellows would hurry," said Fred. "That makes me hungry." The snow was white and crunchy the way it looked in the picture at home called "Snow Scene," only the world didn't look like that anymore with a peaceful house resting on a hill and smoke like warm fur pouring from the chimney. He could see the lips of the young National Guards kidding each other on the other side of the high iron gate and only yesterday the last man over the gate had clung to the top to fling back a word to the friends of the union milling in the street. "Brothers and sisters, we're only fighting for our human rights, better to die like men than live like dogs on the speedup." Then the crowd had backed off a little as from a fort about to explode. The brother had clung there for a second and it was terribly quiet. Steve could feel his whole life pound through his body. Then the crowd began to breathe again and the brother swung over the top of the gate. He eased down on the other side and walked up the steps to the fellows inside.

AFTERWORD

Elinor Langer

I

The novel you have just finished is the final volume of a trilogy. Bringing to fruition many of the themes and characters of the earlier novels, *Pity Is Not Enough* and *The Executioner Waits*, this Feminist Press reprinting of *Rope of Gold* presents the culminating writing of the trio to the public for the first time since 1939. The first novel appeared in 1933 and the second in 1934, and Josephine Herbst had every reason to believe that when she finished the third, which she thought would be shortly, the publisher, Harcourt, Brace, would issue them in a set, at which time she could give them an overall title. Unfortunately, it never happened. Life and politics both intervened. When she did finally finish the third volume in 1939, the political climate of which the radicalism of the trilogy was such a natural extension was in the midst of transition. As the publisher quickly realized, its audience had been swept away.

The most important thing for the reader to be aware of in making the acquaintance of the trilogy through *Rope of Gold* is its overall historical authenticity. Not only in its recreation of large political and economic events and movements but also in its incidents and details, the trilogy is solidly rooted in fact. The second most important thing is its autobiographical fidelity. Though there are many qualifications and exceptions, the simple statement that Josephine Herbst's trilogy is "about her mother's family" as it established itself, divided, and made its way into various corners of American life in the period roughly between the Civil War and the beginning of World War II, is nonetheless essentially true. It is in fact in the tension between the abstract historical forces and the individual life stories—both equally "true"—that the distinctive flavor of the trilogy is to be found. *Pity Is Not Enough* is "about" a luckless nineteenth-century carpetbagger named Joseph Trexler, the fictional counterpart of Herbst's mother's favorite brother, "poor Joe" Frey, the person for whom Herbst herself was named, but it is also "about" capitalism. *The Executioner Waits* is "about" Victoria and Rosamund Wendel, whose girlhoods and early adventures closely parallel those of Herbst and her sister Helen, but it is also "about" the rise of resistance to capitalism during the 1920s. *Rope of Gold* is "about" the marriage of Victoria Wendel and Jonathan Chance, whose fictional biography is close to that of Herbst's actual husband John Herrmann, but it is also "about" the 1930s revolutionary movement. To what extent the mere emphasis on political and economic forces gives a cast to individual experience that it may not have had in fact and thus distorts its autobiographical nature is an arguable point, but in a loose sense the relationship of Herbst's novels to the events and people in her life is close enough. Indeed, what is remarkable about the trilogy from a biographical point of view is her bravado. Not only in her use of history, but also in her use of herself, from the initial pages of *Pity Is Not Enough* to the closing passages of *Rope of Gold* she was committed to a structure of which her own experiences, public and private, were the central material, and she never knew where it was heading.

II

Josephine Herbst was born in Sioux City, Iowa on March 5, 1892,[1] the third of four daughters of poor, newly transplanted easterners— Pennsylvanians—who had moved there only a short time before. Although her father, William Benton Herbst, was a kindly man who always held a place of affection within the family, he was not a particularly interesting one and it was her mother, Mary Frey Herbst, a lively redhead with a powerful imagination, who set the tone. Restless herself, and filled with longing for the wonderful "East," her stories about her family were her daughter's principal entertainment. "At least once during the cyclone season, Ann Wendel and her four girls raced through the pouring yellow rain to the cellar," reads the opening passage of *Pity Is Not Enough.*

> The littlest held to the bigger girls. . . . In the cool damp cellar they lit the lamp and shut out that dreadful sky and the red barn a monstrous red looking as if it lived and breathed in grass that was too green and living. Down there, they huddled around and Anne brought out to still their terror old Blank and his fits, the dead and gone Trexlers and Joe, the most generous brother, poor Joe.[2]

Nor was it only with the family history as stories that Mary enchanted her daughters, particularly the younger two, for the history was present as well in the material form of letters, diaries, and journals passed on from one generation to the next practically from the time of the arrival of the first Freys from Germany and Switzerland in the days of William Penn, and these hung enticingly in pouches in the attic to be brooded over and deciphered and lovingly re-imagined during long days of idleness or headcolds or rain. "The first inkling I had of the complexity and significance of people in relation to each other and the world came from these documents," Herbst once wrote. "Living seemed constantly fertilized and damned by the tragic burden one generation passed to the next."[3] In the late 1920s, settling down in Pennsylvania not far from where both her parents had grown up, she sent to Sioux City for some family treasures to take their places in her emerging household. The letters were at the top of her list.

Considering the extent of her later departures from convention, Josephine Herbst's childhood was not very remarkable. Sioux City was a town that valued respectability highly, and "Josie" was as respectable as the rest. At home she and her younger sister Helen cultivated the attention of their mother by disparaging the adolescent posturings of the older two, but in grammar school and high school she herself wanted above everything to be just like the others and, judging from the platitudes in her early diaries, she succeeded. It was not until after her graduation from high school in 1910, two years at a Sioux City college called Morningside, and a year at the University of Iowa in Iowa City, where she devoted herself as much to her sorority as to her studies, that she realized that her own nature and Iowa's were not the same. "Why do people in little towns have one of two expressions . . . either sluggish, ambitionless countenances or else eager, stingy, calculating ones?"[4] she wrote to her parents in 1913 from the small town of Stratford, Iowa, where she had taken a teaching job after her father's business failure had made it impossible for her to continue school. "The ignorance of my children in regard to things that mean the most to me—namely books, and appreciation of out-of-door things, is appalling,"[5] she told them another time. Alone for the first time, without the influence of schoolmates or home, her own interests and convictions were suddenly clearer to her—and chief among them was a desire to be a writer. She kept a journal, not the sentimental diaries of her earlier years but a conscious exercise in observation, and she began writing stories. When she sent them to a former professor and he encouraged her to continue, she was elated. "Bless you, I expect *hundreds* of failures to one success but that isn't discouraging," she wrote to her sister Helen, whose ambitions and aspirations were very similar to her own. "I'd rather fail in story writing than succeed in anything else."[6]

But the decision to be a writer and being in a position to write were different things, and between the desire and the possibility there were years of struggle. She worked in Sioux City for a year as a stenographer, tried to finish college at the University of Washington but became ill, then worked in Sioux City for another year at yet another dreary stenographic job. Even her arrival in Greenwich Village in 1919 after she finally graduated from Berkeley was more a false start than a new beginning, for though she was at last in an atmosphere she had longed for, her circumstances were far from easy. Turning instinctively to the radical political and literary circles she had first become aware of in California during World War I, she took her place in the bohemian world associated with the old *Masses* and *The Liberator;* she had a love affair—her first—with Maxwell Anderson, then a young editorial writer for the New York *Globe* and a married man with children; but she was still poor and struggling with two jobs—one as a welfare worker, another selling books—and she could not find the opportunity to write.

In the summer of 1920, following the break up of her affair with Anderson, Josie left the city to work as a cigarette clerk at a Catskills hotel. While there she discovered she was pregnant. To her surprise, she was pleased and she wrote Maxwell Anderson that she wanted to have the baby but he was not interested in any such complications in his life; he dissuaded her, and she returned to New York and had an abortion instead. That September she got her first literary job, as a reader in the magazine empire of H. L. Mencken and George Jean Nathan. In October, her sister Helen, who was married and living in Sioux City with her husband, attempting to save the money that would enable them to break away, also became pregnant and also had an abortion—but Helen died. Josie found she could not get over it. Despite her position with Mencken, despite friends, lovers, and a genuine sense of belonging, her energies plummeted. Ill to the point where a doctor forecast permanent impairment if she did not rest, she decided instead to strike off on her own again and after concentrating singlemindedly on saving money, in May 1922 she abandoned New York and took herself to Europe—to cheap Berlin—at last "to write."

The novel that Josie wrote in Berlin is a bitter study of marriage from the point of view of an unmarried woman and it follows her relationship with Maxwell Anderson so literally that it appears to have been as much the emotional release as it was the literary opportunity that she needed. While she was writing it she lived a life of deliberate sexual abandon, as if she wanted to heighten her alienation so she could begin to see it more clearly, and when she had written enough of it, she relaxed. In Paris, in 1924, she met another young American writer, John Herrmann, and fell in love. Josie's relationship with John Herrmann marks the first fresh beginning in her life. Though it had much strain and tension in it, it had much joy and tenderness as well, and it was the center of her existence for many years. From 1925 to 1926 they lived quietly together, unmarried, in a small Connecticut farmhouse, devoting themselves to one another and to their work. *Nothing Is Sacred*, Josie's first published novel, an account of her mother's death that is just as autobiographical as the never-completed novel about Anderson but much more artful, was largely written in Connecticut, as were some early stories. In September 1926, under pressure from John's disapproving, conservative parents, they were legally married and moved to New York, exchanging the life of writing for the life of writers—a life they both also enjoyed. They took a tiny sixth-floor coldwater-walk-up on lower Fifth Avenue in the Village, found jobs, and spent much of their time in a company of intermittent Village denizens that included not only such friends from Paris as Ernest Hemingway and Nathan Asch but also such new ones as Robert Penn Warren, Allen Tate, Caroline Gordon, and Katherine Anne Porter. It was a warm and sustaining community. When John's novel of adolescence, *What Happens*, was published in Paris by Robert McAlmon in 1927 and confiscated by United States Customs on grounds of obscenity, H. L. Mencken, Babette Deutsch, Heywood Broun, and Genevieve Taggard were among their acquaintances testifying in its behalf; and when *Nothing Is Sacred* appeared in 1928, it carried praise on the jacket from Ring Lardner, as well as Hemingway, and was reviewed enthusiastically by, among others, Porter and Ford Madox Ford.

In 1928, frustrated by the amount of time New York required them to spend working to live instead of living to work, Josie and John decided to return to the country and soon found an old stone farmhouse in Erwinna, Bucks County, Pennsylvania that would remain her home until she died. There her writing flourished. Working almost entirely in an autobiographical vein, between 1928 and 1930 she wrote a dozen stories on subjects ranging from various childhood memories to recent New York escapades and these appeared both in little magazines such as *transition* and major magazines such as *Scribner's* and *The American Mercury* as well. Following the publication of her second novel, *Money for Love*, in 1929—a novel that also drew on her affair with Maxwell Anderson—she was described by Sinclair Lewis as one of a group of American women novelists "at least as important"[7] as any men; she was treated as a major figure in a critique of the "Hemingway school" in *The Nation*—a critique to which she zestfully replied;[8] and so celebrated were writers in general, including Josephine Herbst, in the period in question that when she left with John on a trip across the country after the manuscript was delivered, a gossip item to that effect appeared in newspapers all along the way.[9]

In the fall of 1930, about a year after the American stock market crash, Josie and John went to Russia. More in the spirit of a private adventure than of a political pilgrimage, the trip was nonetheless an appropriate marker for the decade that lay ahead, for as they tried to settle in again after their return they saw that the Depression was not only an economic crisis but a moral, political, and intellectual one, and that the literary community they were part of was becoming very much involved. In part because of differences in their temperaments, in part because of the difference in their sex, both their responses to the situation and their opportunities diverged. Gregarious, charming, always welcomed by his fellow male radicals as an amiable and effective companion, John joined the Communist Party and became actively involved in organizing farmers in the rural area near where they lived. Josie, less welcome, was more solitary. At least as far back as her year in Berkeley, she had had an idea for a trilogy based on her own family and now, under the influence of the radical intellectual climate of the Depression, it began to take shape. As she examined her family's history for the first time through a Marxist prism she saw that the homely familiar stories told to her by her mother for as long back as she could remember were not simply domestic diversions. They had historical significance. They had meaning. The entire saga of the Frey family from the events of her mother's childhood to the events of her own was an illustration of the breakdown of capitalism. The story of Joe and its contrast with the story of Daniel, the only one of her mother's brothers who had managed, however dubiously, to succeed . . . the story of her father's struggles and her mother's endless pursuit of the little "capital" she believed would help give her daughters a start . . . the stories of the daughters, particularly herself and Helen, as they carried the burden one generation further, attempting to gain a foothold for a new and freer existence in the 1920s: they were all part of the grand scheme of History!

Excited by the possibilities before her and offended, in any case, by the male exclusiveness of the radical movement—not so different, in fact, from the attitudes of the same men in the 1920s but highlighted now by the egalitarian aura of the day—she kept her distance from much of the organized activity of the early 1930s and filtered most of her political energy through her work. Her feminism was there as well, in the form of strong female figures kindling independence and ambition and self-confidence from one generation to the next. "Don't be stupid and shut your eyes and imagine that the only things in life worth while come from men and what people call romance,"[10] says the fictional mother, Anne Wendel, to her daughters Victoria and Rosamund in the early pages of the trilogy, and it is very likely that Josie sat writing those words one evening in the early 30s after John and his comrades, ignoring her expressed desire to join them, had marched out the door. *Pity Is Not Enough* appeared in 1933. Correctly described by reviewer Bruce Catton as an American "success story in reverse,"[11] the book received the usual contradictory distribution of praise and blame from critics of different persuasions, but it was treated by all of them with respect. "Josephine Herbst has written one of the most impressive novels published this season. . . . [With] *Pity Is Not Enough* she takes her place as one of the few American important women novelists" of the day, declared Horace Gregory in the *New York Herald Tribune*'s literary supplement, *Books*,[12] and in the private commentaries that meant as much to her as the published ones, its reception was equally warm. "Josie darling, it's just too damned good 'for this world,' . . ." said a long enthusiastic letter from Katherine Anne Porter.

> Everything about it is right. The way you have got your avalanche of material controlled so it rolls down a great groove to the exact stopping place: and the way you have told the whole story of a historical period and related it perfectly to the miserable fortunes of one little, confused struggling family. . . . You know how much I have loved your work . . . but this is finer by a dozen times than anything you have done. It's a wonderful book, you should be easy in your mind about it. It will wear and wear.[13]

With the appearance of *The Executioner Waits* in the following year, 1934, the pattern continued. "The publication of this second volume . . . establishes her right to be considered one of the few major novelists in America today," said Horace Gregory, again in *Books*, dropping the qualifying "women,"[14] and once again there were letters from friends. "It is magnificent. Surely the best novel I have read in years if not the very best I have ever read," said a letter from William Carlos Williams, dated Thanksgiving, 1934.[15] In addition to her success in fiction, she was also gaining a reputation as a journalist. In 1932, 1933, and 1934 she contributed major articles on midwest farm conditions to *Scribner's*, the *New Masses*, and *The American Mercury*, and she was also beginning to review books.

John's writing too was well received—in 1932 he shared the Scribner's literary prize with Thomas Wolfe for a story about a ruined salesman called "The Big Short Trip"—but as time passed he was doing less and less of it and devoting himself instead exclusively to politics, including work in the Communist underground in Washington, D.C., an activity of which Josie did not approve. These differences were not their only problems. In 1932 Josie had become involved with a young woman painter named Marion Greenwood; John had also been drawn in, creating a triangle; and though the episode itself was over, the complications that followed from it were not. During much of 1934 they were more or less tacitly separated. In early 1935, while she was on a journalistic mission to Cuba for the *New Masses*, in circumstances very like—but not identical to—those that form the emotional climax of *Rope of Gold*, Josie understood that John had finally left her. When she returned to New York in the spring, between her novels and her reportage her name was better known than it had ever been, but her marriage was decisively over.

The second half of the 1930s was very different for Josie from the first. She lived alone, sometimes at Erwinna, sometimes in New York in apartments borrowed from friends or in hotels, sometimes at the writer's colony, Yaddo, trying to re-establish some kind of tenable life for herself, and not succeeding. She desperately regretted the break up of her marriage. Responding both to the absence of a personal life and to public events she became much more politically active than before. In the summer of 1935 she went to Germany to report on the opposition to Hitler for the *New York Post*, a difficult and dangerous assignment whose conception and execution both rested on her close Communist ties; she spoke often after her return on Communist platforms and for Communist causes; and though she tried to get back to her writing, specifically to the final volume of the trilogy, she found she had neither the singlemindedness nor the capacity for isolation it required. In the winter of 1937, moved, like so many others, by the drama of the Civil War, Josie went to Spain, an experience that was at the same time the high point of her political involvement and the beginning of its end. She went thinking that even if she had failed in her personal life, there was still meaning in political action. She came home believing that political life was far too complicated to be sustaining. The uprising in Barcelona in May, 1937, the word of the execution of the Spanish Trotskyist leader Andres Nin, the news of the purges in Russia, increasingly hard to ignore, all suggested that Communism—the Soviet Union—was not the hope it had once seemed, and just as the hopes had been high, so the denouement was bitter. Against the background of rising international tension and widespread anticipation of an approaching world war, the divisiveness of the American left was particularly disheartening. Following her return from Spain Josie continued to try to work for the Loyalist cause but with every action inspected for ideological purity by the Communist Party such work was difficult, and she gradually withdrew. It was in the negative and despairing climate that characterized the end of the decade that Josie finally finished *Rope of Gold*, which was published in March 1939. After the Nazi-Soviet Pact a few months later, she was never actively political again.

In December 1941, immediately after the United States entered World War II, Josie went to Washington and got a job in the information and propaganda agency known as the Office of the Co-ordinator of Information, or OCI. A few months later, in an episode prefiguring both the political climate of the late 1940s and 1950s and her response to it, she was fired. "I am reported to have protested against the violation of various civil liberties . . . in the 1930s," she wrote following an interview with government investigators several weeks afterward in which she was finally told the reasons.

> Good. I am reported to have printed articles in magazines known to the Measuring Stick trade as "left." I am grateful that during the last decade I was not confined to the *Saturday Evening Post* for expression.
>
> I am reported to have been actively interested in the Loyalist cause in Spain, but in order truly to damn me they allege that I have taken part in a Communist Party broadcast from Spain. . . . My answer is: I would have broadcast from Spain under any auspices, including the Communist Party, in order to have one tiny chance of arousing people in England, France, and the U.S.A. to the danger that threatens not only Spain but themselves. History vindicates this position.[16]

"History" may indeed have vindicated her briefly, but it was not a very reliable ally. By upholding the commitments of the 1930s as appropriate for their period in a new period that was interpreting them very differently, Josie was taking an increasingly isolated stand. Between her 1942 firing and her successful defense of the government's attempt to deny her a passport in 1954 she was caught up in cases arising out of her involvements in the 1930s many times. At the same time she was also losing her audience. A modest novel of rural life, *Satan's Sergeants*, set in Bucks County, had attracted very little attention on its appearance in 1941, and a much more ambitious novel, *Somewhere the Tempest Fell,* which dealt with some of the political confusions of the postwar era, published in 1947, met a similar fate. Immune from the blacklist by reason of poverty and self-employment, as time passed she was nonetheless subject to an informal "greylist" in which the number of opportunities that came her way was mysteriously small. She rarely, if ever, heard from the magazines she had written for earlier and when her last book, a biography of the early American botanists John and William Bartram, was published in 1954, the picture on the jacket, taken in 1939, was misleading as to the generation she belonged to, and not one of her previous publications was mentioned by name. She became steadily less known and more impoverished. It was a period of overwhelming diminution.

From the time of her return to Erwinna at the end of World War II to her death about a quarter-century later, Josie's outward existence did not change very much. She stayed mainly in the country, alone, increasingly desperately poor, alternating her isolation with short stays in New York when possible, and sometimes with visits from friends, and she worked—she worked continually—on her writing. Starting around the middle of the 1950s she became more active again, the center of a circle of admiring contemporary writers which included not only the poet Jean Garrigue, with whom she had a long and deep involvement, but a host of younger men such as Alfred Kazin, Saul Bellow, and Hilton Kramer, who were touched both by her spirit and by her work. Through them she began publishing critical essays on literature and other subjects in journals ranging from *Arts* to the *Georgia Review,* and she felt she was again in the world.

Of all the things that concerned her in these years, nothing was more important to her than her memoirs, an immense intellectual and artistic undertaking that was to be at the same time an evocation of the literary community of the 1920s, a defense of the political commitments of the 1930s, and above all, a claim on history for herself. The relationship between the trilogy and the memoirs, which are in many ways similar, can perhaps be stated in its simplest fashion as the difference between youth and age. Where one is an attempt to mold the material of life to fit a central interpretation—a call to action—the other is an attempt to let the material simply unfold with all its contradictions—a call to thought. Her mother's brother Daniel, for example, the very incarnation of "capitalism" in the trilogy, becomes, in the memoirs, a poignant human being. The mother herself, presented in the trilogy as so governed by economic necessity that all her efforts and all her philosophies are bent to the struggle for survival, emerges in the memoirs as an original and powerful character whose troubles by no means wear her down. An elegant blending of argument and art, Josie's memoirs constitute such a major contribution to the understanding of the 1920s and 1930s that if she had ever completed them it is very likely her reputation would not have continued its decline, and instead of reading *about* her, you would be reading her now. However, that was not how it happened. With both public and private sorrows that were painful for her to come to terms with, yet she felt belonged in her book, she was more constrained in the telling of her life than she had been in the living of it, and with the exception of three published excerpts that appeared in literary magazines during the 1960s,[17] the memoirs were never completed. When she died of cancer in New York Hospital in January 1969, the unfinished manuscript was in a box under her bed.

III

Both as the fulfillment of the earlier volumes and as a novel standing alone, *Rope of Gold* is one of Josephine Herbst's strongest achievements. Not only does it bring the politics and passions of the period to convincing fullness of life, it does so in such a way that the links between the economic crisis of the 1930s and earlier crises, and between the radicalism of the 1930s and earlier radicalism, are movingly and forcefully demonstrated. The gap between the necessity of revolution on the one hand and its unlikelihood on the other is the underlying subject of *Rope of Gold*. It is not only a partisan novel, it is a skeptical novel as well.

The heart of the novel is the story of the relationship between Victoria Wendel and Jonathan Chance and it is used to show the complexities of love and revolution both. Taking up their histories at approximately the point they were left in *The Executioner Waits*, *Rope of Gold* opens with a long, painful confrontation with Jonathan's family in his father's comfortable living room—a scene that will feel familiar to radicals of any generation who have ever suffered political estrangement from their relatives. It follows them across an essentially political-autobiographical terrain: Jonathan's difficulties in sticking to his writing, his self-doubt, his identification with the local farmers' protest, his elevation into a responsible position with the Communist Party, his dissatisfaction with being made into a fund-raising "Front," Victoria's sorrows, her isolation in the country, her gradual development of a career as a reporter, her rising identification with the international revolutionary movement, particularly during a visit to Cuba, her increasing dedication to her work. It also documents what happens between them: the recriminations that are a product of their poverty and disappointments, the complications of their conflicting schedules, their sexual and emotional infidelities, the long slow dissolution of their mutual trust and hope until their eventual, inevitable, separation. There are the near misses:

> The long ride to the West was as invigorating as a sea voyage but when she was in Chicago, Jonathan was in Milwaukee. In Minneapolis he had passed on to Omaha . . ."[18]

The long-awaited reunions that go inevitably awry:

> By eleven she had the beginning untangled and was piecing it together. [Lester] had left great gaps which he expected her to fit together as usual. It was like a puzzle at first but afterwards fun. When she heard someone turn the handle of the door, she stiffened with alarm and sat rigid. "Who's there," she called out clearly. "Jonathan," said Jonathan. She got up and rushed to the door. He looked very brown and handsome and snatched her up before she could speak. "Oh Jonathan, what a night to come," she said.[19]

The ultimate revelation, on the day he arrived late for what she already knew would be their final Christmas:

> "I want the book," he said in an indistinct mumbling voice of a handmade volume she had illustrated herself, "it's a beautiful book," and she wanted to thank him for saying that, for his tears, for his love, but she said instead in a low, bitter, voice, "It's a woman, isn't it?"[20]

> "If only they could have had a garden," thinks Victoria, "if the corn had had a chance to ripen. If the grapes had grown purple on the vine and she could have pulled them off in big bunches and the fragrance of boiling jelly and wine might have sweetened the air."[21]

If only they could have shored up the foundations of their love, like the foundations of a house, to shelter them against the world outside, but they are opposed to such shelters on principle, they want the world to come in, and soon their own foundations are lost in it.

It is helpful to appreciate the fullness of the previous characterizations of Victoria and Jonathan earlier in the trilogy to understand the pathos of their collapse. It is as if not only their own lives but history itself falters when they do. From the great large families of the previous generation whose histories have filled the pages of the trilogy to Victoria's single still-born son, from the material amplitude in which Jonathan was raised to the impoverishment of his psychological and revolutionary will, this—their own terrible barrenness—is what it has come to. But if Victoria and Jonathan are the central emotional focus of this history, they are not by any means its only focus. There is a large cast of interlocking major and minor characters moving and swaying together, their lives and destinies intertwined as if a great frieze of the Depression had somehow acquired life. Nancy Radford, Victoria's sister, and her penniless family, traveling back and forth across the drought-stricken deserts of the West looking for a place to earn their bread; Steve Carson, a farm radical from a family of farm radicals, torn between his attraction to the rising movement of striking auto workers in the city and his devotion to his pregnant wife on the farm; Lester Tolman, a vacillating but sympathetic radical intellectual who, though he cannot make a political commitment, is as vulnerable to political events as those who do; and many, many more, the reactionary as well as the revolutionary, the rich as well as the poor, individual and yet representative figures of their times and stations, and not only the living generations but the dead as well, lovingly recalled throughout the story because they are present in the memory of the living.

It is in the contrast between the commitment of the radical characters and the outcome of their actions that the meaning of the novel ultimately lies. The book is more than the sum of its characters. Despite their desire for a new social order, despite their need, the book as a whole does not believe with them that therefore change will come about. What people want and what happens to them are not necessarily the same. Neither in personal nor in political life does justice necessarily win. Despite the existence of the revolutionary movement, the destinies of individuals are as limited by external forces as they were in the periods of the earlier volumes of the trilogy, and radicals, although they believe otherwise, are not excepted. If the passion of the book is in its people, the dispassion is in its design: both in the forceful rhythmic alternation of scenes so that no one set of characters is ever allowed to represent the whole, and in the use of italicized inserts—a trademark of the trilogy from the beginning—which here carry the settings beyond the boundaries of the book in both space and time to indicate the ever-growing terrors, particularly in Europe, that the revolutionary movement must face. The principal action, including the story of Victoria and Jonathan, is set in the early 30s and is marked by its spirit of hope. The inserts are set in the later 30s and are marked by its spirit of doubt. The section of the book about Victoria's involvement in Cuba is preceded by an insert suggesting radical defeats in Italy and Germany. The climax of the text shows Steve Carson scaling a wall to join the strikers in an auto plant, but the climactic insert that precedes it is about the crushing of the popular armies in Spain. Throughout the novel two lines develop at once, the subjective and the objective, and at its conclusion they are, at best, at a standoff. This is hardly the didactic novel its "proletarian" reputation suggests. Granted that the wishes of the author, like the wishes of the characters, plainly cry out for change, the judgment of the author, unlike the judgment of the characters, is another matter. As beautiful as it frequently is, its lyricism can be misleading. Within its radical framework there is an authorial detachment for which Josephine Herbst has never been recognized. If *Pity Is Not Enough* was the capitalist "thesis," and *The Executioner Waits* was the anti-capitalist "antithesis," *Rope of Gold* ought to have been the revolutionary "synthesis," but history was failing to cooperate. The dialectics of the trilogy suggested victory but the actuality of experience suggested otherwise and Herbst shaped her fiction to history rather than the other way around.

While *Rope of Gold* follows both the history of the period and Josephine Herbst's personal history very closely, however, it is by no means literally autobiographical. As much the novelist as the reporter, she distorted time and geography, changed vital details, and altered or omitted certain crucial experiences of both her own and others that in autobiography would be highly peculiar to overlook. In *The Executioner Waits*, for example, Rosamund Wendel, like Helen Herbst, decides to have an abortion and she does die, but unlike Helen she does not die having the abortion. Helen's real-life husband, a newspaper editor named Andrew Bernhard, found the portrait of himself as Jerry Stauffer in *The Executioner Waits* and *Rope of Gold* to be impersonal, over-politicized, and flat. Although there are many such departures from life in *Rope of Gold*, none is more fundamental than the character of Victoria Wendel. Victoria is interesting, independent, and idiosyncratic, to be sure, but she is less interesting, independent, and idiosyncratic than Josephine Herbst. To take only the most obvious difference, Victoria is not actually a writer. For most of the novel she is in fact something of a homebody, a woman forlorn and crippled by the loss of her still-born child—something that never happened to Josephine Herbst—grieving because, while her husband is otherwise occupied, she is forced to spend so many hours alone. Where the real Josie, a writer of considerable reputation, went to Cuba alone on assignment for a leading radical magazine, the *New Masses*, Victoria, an unknown, goes as an assistant to another reporter, a man, and her persuading the Cubans to let her undertake the journey to the mountains is somewhat inexplicable. The portrayal of the marriage is also altered. The story of the relationship of Victoria Wendel and Jonathan Chance is so powerfully written that one recent critic has described it as a "shattering psycho-sexual conflict,"[22] as was the marriage of Josephine Herbst and John Herrmann—but it was not the psycho-sexual conflict described in the book. The precipitating factor in the break up of the marriage of Josephine Herbst and John Herrmann was her relationship with Marion Greenwood, which lasted for about a year.

To be sure, there are highly autobiographical features. The story of Nancy Radford is based on the Depression experiences of Josie's oldest sister, Frances Wells. The relationship of Victoria and Lester Tolman is based on a journey Josie made to the midwest in 1934 with another reporter during which they had, in fact, quarrelled over rights to their notes, and Tolman himself is based at least in part on Josie's friend, the writer Nathan Asch, with whom she had recently collaborated on a play about Spain. The shadowy refugee, Kurt Becher, who stands very roughly for Marion Greenwood, is based on the German Communist writer Gustav Regler, whom Josie had met in Spain. Many of the intimate details, like almost all of the historical details, are also real. Nonetheless, to the extent that life can be said to have a "plot," the plot of Victoria's life and the plot of Josie's are not the same. Victoria not only is less impressive a figure than Josephine Herbst in a worldly sense, privately she is considerably more innocent. "Something had happened to Jonathan, she did not know what,"[23] thinks Victoria, bewildered, on the bus from Miami at the end of her mission to Cuba. The real Josie knew.

Why the author of the trilogy made one or another particular departure from fact is a valid, and indeed fascinating, subject from a psychological viewpoint, but strictly as a literary matter it is a much less important question. The trilogy is an epic, not a confession; her intention was historical, not self-exploratory; and there is no way in which any alterations or omissions she did make undermined the sweep of the whole. The central demand of the trilogy was to link the story of "poor Joe" Trexler with the story of Victoria Wendel, the story of the period after the Civil War with the story of the period that followed World War I, and this she did. If the constraints of form, the limitations of the period, and her own personal inhibitions made her create a heroine less unlike the conventional women of her time than the author herself was, that is not very surprising. What is more surprising, in fact, than the modifications of personal experience in the trilogy is how far in the direction of emotional truth she was able to go. The story of Rosamund-Helen might be altered in detail, but it was there in spirit. The story of the marriage might be softened, but it was told. Trimmed as they are from the real Josie and Helen, in their radicalism, their zest for experience, and their determination to define lives for themselves at least to some degree independent of men, Victoria and Rosamund are among the earliest representations of modern women in fiction. Between Victoria and Rosamund in the trilogy and Molly and Anna in Doris Lessing's *The Golden Notebook,* written three decades later, there is a definite affinity of spirit and there are relatively few other such spirits in between. If readers of *Rope of Gold* and the other volumes of the trilogy must be cautious in drawing autobiographical inferences from the material, they should also appreciate how much is there.

IV

Apart from the people who read it at the time, few people have ever had the opportunity to read *Rope of Gold* for themselves. Like the other volumes of the trilogy, it was published and sold in quantities under 2,000 in a decade in which its potential audience had little money and its promotional budget was small. The majority of readers undoubtedly got the book from libraries and when those copies disintegrated they were simply never rebound. Nor was it only the physical products that disintegrated: it was also the moment in time. Both because of Josie's own radicalism and because of the subject of the book, the reception of *Rope of Gold* was so entwined with the collapse of the radical movement that it is impossible to wrest them apart. Appearing at the very moment when differences within the left over the nature of Communism were solidified forever by the Nazi-Soviet Pact, the reviews it elicited were not so much literary as they were polemical, extensions of the reviewer's politics rather than examinations of the author's book. To some extent this was true of reviews of the earlier novels also, but in the case of *Rope of Gold* it was extreme.

With the generalized radicalism of the earlier years of the decade on the defensive, if you were still sympathetic to "the movement" you liked the novel; if not, you did not; it was more or less as simple as that.

> "Rope of Gold" will delight those readers who share the author's political and economic beliefs. Other writers will not find the book dull, but they may wonder whether such modern proletarian fiction is any more effective as a medium of propaganda than was the sentimentalism of Dickens in "Hard Times" or the plain unvarnished accounts of oppression in Garland's "Main Traveled Roads,"

said the reviewer for the *Saturday Review of Literature*[24]—and he was probably righter than he knew.

Non-literary factors not only affected the immediate reception of *Rope of Gold*, they also affected the trilogy's long-run reputation. As intellectual anti-Stalinism merged with popular anti-Communism particularly during the Cold War, the trilogy was stigmatized as "proletarian literature," its criticism of the capitalist system an embarrassment, if not a threat. The only exception to the rule of unmentionability that affected the trilogy for many years was a brief sympathetic discussion by Walter Rideout in *The Radical Novel in the United States*, published in 1956. Another non-literary factor was the sex, not necessarily of the author of the trilogy, but of its central characters. The story of the masculine domination of American letters is by now too familiar to require retelling here, yet nothing is more remarkable in considering the trilogy's history than the extent to which the original reviewers simply failed to notice that one of the principal subjects of all three volumes was women. Steve Carson, the workers' movement, and politics in general were most often cited as the principal focus of *Rope of Gold*, not Victoria and Jonathan, and when Victoria was mentioned, she was misunderstood. Who among female readers of this edition, for example, would agree with the complaint of Philip Rahv in *Partisan Review* that Victoria's relationship to Jonathan is "poorly motivated"?[25] The absence of interest in women carried with it an absence of interest in family, and since, from the grandmother of *Pity Is Not Enough* to the mother of *The Executioner Waits* to the daughter of *Rope of Gold* it is the female line being followed, the trilogy's distinctive documentation of the history of an American family was never really discovered. What's more, it was a self-perpetuating cycle. Misrepresentation of the subject of the trilogy initially led to its misrepresentation later, even by editors who admired the books. There are two major anthologies of Depression literature,

The American Writer and The Great Depression, edited by Harvey Swados, and *Years of Protest,* edited by Jack Salzman with Barry Wallenstein, and while the trilogy is excerpted in both of them, in neither does any material dealing with any of the heroines, or even with any of the Trexler-Wendel family, appear. Considering that the family is at the heart of the novels, it is certainly a striking omission.

Imagine, for a moment, that you are Josephine Herbst. For ten years you have devoted yourself to a grand reconstruction of American history at least as ambitious as the comparable trilogies of your friends John Dos Passos and James T. Farrell, yet unlike those works, which gradually attain the hallowed status of classics, yours is never mentioned. You do not brood, but continue. Time passes, life changes, and even when your maturing sensibilities take you well beyond your youthful capacities into another realm of prose and another literary world, even those friends who admire your new work will not read the old for fear they might not like it and be distressed. Never intimidated by the lack of a place for the trilogy as much as disappointed by it, Josie maintained her own opinion of her achievement as marked, and indeed limited, by the time that it belonged to, but nonetheless valid and strong. "May a conscience be time-clocked and serve one decade and not another?"[26] she asked in an essay written during the 1950s. Her own was constant. If she could learn from the grave of this Feminist Press series, which fuses her natural interest in women with her radical ideas, there is no doubt that she would be pleased.

Elinor Langer
Portland, Oregon

Notes

1. For a complete biography, see *Josephine Herbst,* by Elinor Langer (Boston: Atlantic, Little-Brown, 1984), in which portions of this essay first appeared.

2. Josephine Herbst, *Pity Is Not Enough* (New York: Harcourt, Brace, 1933), p. 1.

3. Herbst, biographical sketch in *Twentieth Century Authors: A Biographical Dictionary of Modern Literature,* ed. by Stanley J. Kunitz and Howard Haycraft (New York: H. W. Wilson, 1942), p. 641.

4. Herbst to her parents, 1913, Beinecke Library, Yale University.

5. Herbst to her mother, 1913, Beinecke Library.

6. Herbst to Helen Herbst, 1913, Beinecke Library.

7. Sinclair Lewis, "Is America a Paradise for Women?" *Pictorial Review*, June 1929, p. 54.

8. Isidor Schneider's "The Fetish of Simplicity" appeared in *The Nation*, 18 February 1931; Josie's response, "Counterblast," in the same journal, 11 March 1931.

9. E.g., *The Atlanta Journal*, 9 June 1929.

10. Herbst, *Pity Is Not Enough*, p. 95.

11. Bruce Catton, Huntington, West Virginia *Advertiser*, 25 June 1933 and elsewhere.

12. Horace Gregory, *Books*, 28 May 1933.

13. Katherine Anne Porter to Herbst, 24 May 1933, Beinecke Library.

14. Gregory, *Books*, 28 October 1934.

15. William Carlos Williams to Herbst, Thanksgiving, 1934, Beinecke Library.

16. Herbst, "Josephine Herbst tells why she was fired from the COI," *PM*, 17 June 1942.

17. "The Starched Blue Sky of Spain," *The Noble Savage*, 1, 1960; "A Year of Disgrace," *The Noble Savage*, 3, 1961; "Yesterday's Road," *New American Review*, 3, 1968.

18. Herbst, *Rope of Gold*, p. 243.

19. Ibid., p. 264.

20. Ibid., p. 286.

21. Ibid., p. 229.

22. Walter Rideout, "Forgotten Images of the Thirties: Josephine Herbst," *The Literary Review*, Fall 1983, p. 32.

23. Herbst, *Rope of Gold*, p. 405.

24. R. A. Cordell, *Saturday Review of Literature*, 4 March 1939.

25. Philip Rahv, "A Variety of Fiction," *Partisan Review*, Spring 1939, p. 111.

26. Herbst, "The Ruins of Memory," *The Nation*, 14 April 1956, p. 303.

The Feminist Press offers alternatives in education and in literature. Founded in 1970, this non-profit, tax-exempt educational and publishing organization works to eliminate sexual stereotypes in books and schools and to provide literature with a broad vision of human potential. The publishing program includes reprints of important works by women, feminist biographies of women, and nonsexist children's books. Curricular materials, bibliographies, directories, and a quarterly journal provide information and support for students and teachers of women's studies. In-service projects help to transform teaching methods and curricula. Through publications and projects, The Feminist Press contributes to the rediscovery of the history of women and the emergence of a more humane society.